LIFE IN THE SHADOWS

THE NETWALK SEQUENCE BOOK ONE

JOYCE REYNOLDS-WARD

1 / LEAVE HIM — OR ELSE

JANUARY 2041

LEAVE HIM — OR ELSE

Someone's here.

Even before the overhead motion-cued light flicked on, Diana Andrews registered the presence sitting calmly in the darkness, whoever it was breathing lightly and steadily.

Hacked the security sensors—trouble!

She dropped her ski bag and whirled toward the corner where the person was, shaking the highly illegal zapper made by her boyfriend Will Landreth out of her wrist holster, sighting down the barrel toward —her mother.

Sarah Stephens stared steadily back at Diana, legs crossed and hands relaxed on the arms of the old wooden captain's chair Diana had borrowed from her father.

The other option.

Diana softened, sighed and dropped her hands, flicking the zapper back into its case.

I don't know which is worse, Mother or a kidnapper.

"I do hope I didn't see what I thought I saw," her mother said dryly.

Diana swallowed hard and picked up her ski bag. Sarah Stephens could make trouble for Will if she pushed it. Best to distract her and not fight.

"What are you doing here?" Diana ran her finger down the bag's seam and started dragging out her wet equipment. It had been a thoroughly mucky day on the slopes, temperatures barely above freezing, fog and mist and gloppy sticky snow that grabbed skis and snowboards.

But glorious nonetheless, because days like this were when she could meet Will with little risk.

"You've been out late, for conditions like they are today." Sarah steepled her fingers and touched her index fingers to her lips.

"I'm an adult." Diana grabbed a towel. As she dried her skis, she laid them on the sawhorses that served her as a waxing station in the condo. "I'll be at work on time tomorrow. That should be all that matters."

"You expose yourself needlessly." Still no emotion in her mother's voice.

"I had company. I wasn't alone. I had Security—Brenda, and she brought others—and friends. Zoë Wright. Zoë had her own Security."

Sadly, she hadn't much time alone with Will. But given the recent visibility of Stephens Reclamation in the news, bringing Security along not only gave Diana protection from anti-Third Force guerillas seeking to find leverage to blackmail her mother, but provided cover for her time with Will.

"And William Landreth. I warned you about him." Now the tiniest bit of anger crept into her mother's voice, a sharp tone matched by a scowl and furrowed brows.

Diana bit her lip to keep from lashing out in response. Anger was the easy way, but it just created more issues with her mother in the long run.

She continued unpacking her gear while she thought about what to say next, stuffing her boots on their dryer and hanging her parka. Then she slipped out of her soaked ski pants, conscious of her mother's angry glare following her every movement.

How did she find out?

Brenda Garcia and Tony Hernandez were *her* personal employees, not her mother's. Still, good as they were, good as Zoë's Security was, her mother had access to better tech.

Will had warned her this could happen.

When it does, admit it, he had suggested. *Don't risk an incident. We'll figure something out.*

"I saw Will," she said, keeping her voice low so that the anger choking her own throat wouldn't betray her emotions. "I'm an adult. He's not a competitor."

"Like *hell* Landreth Technologies isn't a competitor!" her mother snapped, grabbing the chair arms and sitting stiffly upright. "Your precious wastrel may just be a trust-fund snowboarder, but damn it, if you think Parker Landreth isn't going to pump his son about what he learns from you, you're an idiot!"

"Will doesn't talk to his father about us, just like I don't talk about Landreth Technologies to you," Diana said flatly.

She pulled off her sweater and sat in another captain's chair across the room from her mother, forcing herself to relax every inch of her lanky frame in the hard chair. Her base layers gave her little cushioning, but at least she was somewhat warm.

"Jesus, Diana, *Jesus!*" her mother spat, shooting out of her chair to pace the room.

Diana forced herself to breath slowly and steadily.

She reacted first.

Now if she could only keep cool in the face of her mother's anger, she'd win this round.

Silence mounted as her mother strode back and forth, back and forth. Diana watched sharply as Sarah worked to calm herself.

What's got herself worked up so badly this time? Sure, my relationship with Will interferes with her plans to marry me off to one of her allies. But this anger suggests more than that. What the hell happened?

Still, she stayed silent. Let her mother be the first one to talk.

At last Sarah dropped back in the captain's chair. She mirrored Diana's pose, leaning back in the chair, resting her hands lightly on the arms, legs stretched out in front of her. Her artificially white hair hadn't moved a strand during that quick flash of anger and Diana stifled a shudder as the brief wrinkles from Sarah's scowl unnaturally smoothed themselves out.

What kind of nanos is she playing with now?

"Parker Landreth issued me an ultimatum," Sarah said, voice

almost mechanical. *"Get your damn daughter the hell away from my son, or I'll own Stephens Reclamation."* Her intonation was almost a letter-perfect copy of Parker Landreth's snarl.

"There's no grounds for him to be able to do that," Diana pointed out mildly, mind racing even as she worked to keep her own voice calm. "Will's an adult."

"He has a position with Landreth Technologies, and he still has access to his trust fund."

"So? We're adults. And that trust fund is tied to Will's mother, not his father."

"Parker's fingered some tech he says you've been using, and he wants it back. With penalty compensation."

"That tech is Will's own creation, free and clear. I can document it."

"I don't want that tech mixed up with ours!" Sarah sat up, then visibly forced herself to relax.

"It's *not* mixed up with ours. It's linked to my own project which has *nothing to do with Stephens Reclamation!"* Diana sat up.

"Everything you are doing is tied to my company!" Sarah growled.

Diana took a deep breath. "Not this." *I so did not want to talk about this yet.* "This is a personal project that Will and I are developing. I don't do anything on it at work and I've kept documentation, electronic and visual, to confirm."

"In other words, you're stealing time and resources from me."

"I've been very careful about when and where I do things. Look at the evidence. I'll gladly show my logs to you."

"That's still sucking off time and energy that would be better spent on Stephens work." Sarah pointed a finger at Diana. "Since you seem to have all of this time available to work on *side projects* with William Landreth, then obviously you haven't been busy enough. Pack your things. I'm sending you to Vietnam."

"But my biobot project—"

"What's more important—your biobot project or William Landreth?"

Diana inhaled, shuddering. She didn't look away from her mother.

Vietnam. One of Stephens Reclamation's most difficult projects, not just in the work but the political dances required to keep it going.

Exile.

But it wouldn't be forever. Just long enough to reimburse her mother for the investment in schooling, the bills that had been carefully handed over with the unspoken demand that *you will pay these off before you go out on your own.* Two more years, until she was twenty-six and gained control of her trust fund. Two more years until full independence.

And besides, if Diana could make Vietnam succeed, then that would make her work stronger in the future. It held possibilities, where if she chose to betray her feelings for Will—there would be no turning back from that choice. Sarah wouldn't let her change, even in two years. There would always be something obstructing a relationship with Will.

A dry chuckle. "I thought so. Sooner or later, you'll learn that every man betrays you, Diana." Sarah tapped her fingers on the chair arms. "I had hoped you were ready to move into corporate management. That little idea of yours is promising. But I can't guarantee that you'll keep it free from William Landreth, so—" She shrugged. "Might as well have you doing something useful, like fieldwork."

"Then I guess I had better start packing. When do I leave?" Diana pushed herself up.

"You aren't going to argue further?" Her mother's brows furrowed.

"Why? What good will arguing do? You've clearly made up your mind."

A second positive to choosing Vietnam without argument was that her mother wouldn't dare send Diana's brother Peter along to bother her. *Peter* was too precious to risk in Vietnam for very long. If Diana stayed in North America and followed her mother's plan for her, if she pretended to renounce Will—then Peter's constant presence would be guaranteed.

She'd have a better opportunity to sneak out and see Will than if she lied and stayed.

"So be it." Her mother slapped her hands against the chair and rose. "You leave tomorrow."

"Understood."

Sarah marched to the door, then turned. "And don't get any ideas about creeping out to see Landreth tonight. Peter's on watch."

"All right."

Hopefully her mother didn't know about the comm Will had given Diana just today.

"No Landreth tech goes with you," Sarah continued.

"Understood." She would have to activate the comm's self-destruct. But she just needed to make one last call to Will.

They glared at each other.

Sarah shook her head. "Stubborn, just like your father."

Then she was gone.

Diana exhaled. She looked around the condo. What to pack, what to bundle for storage—she groaned and collapsed back into her chair.

Vietnam, damn it.

Will's comm buzzed. Diana picked it up, fingers trembling.

"We've been discovered," Will said.

"I know. Mom is sending me to Vietnam, tomorrow."

"The Petroleum Autonomous Zone for me." Will's voice was flat. "I'll learn about the contract when I get there. Oh girl of mine. We screwed up."

"We'll be able to see each other on visits. I was told to leave any Landreth tech behind."

"I'll figure out a way to contact you. We'll see each other again. Landreth Technologies has a Vietnam office. One way or another, we'll stay in touch."

"One way or another," Diana repeated. "But it's only two more years, Will. Only two years."

"Two very long years. But then—we'll be together. Stay safe, my love. I love you."

"I love you," she said back to him.

"Gotta go." He disconnected.

Diana sighed. She went into the kitchen, pushed the self-destruct button, and dropped the comm into the sink. Once it was destroyed, she exhaled and looked around.

Time to pack.

JULY, 2041

DAHLIA

DIANA TOOK BACK SKIMMER CONTROL FROM THE AUTOPILOT AS IT WOUND through the old pear orchards on the northeastern flanks of Mt. Hood, near the Columbia River. Rain clouds thinned into wisps, allowing the morning light to cast a glow on the brown grass of the ridges to the east. A faint anticipatory tingle made her shiver as she slowed, watching for the old white farmhouse that was part of the winery / farmstand where Will waited for her.

There.

She landed the skimmer near the bed of blooming lavender.

No other skimmers in the lot. Diana swallowed back her disappointment and climbed out. Will must be running late, which was unusual. Something must have come up.

A nagging worry pulled at her. Both her mother and Will's father would do anything possible to prevent them from having time together. Diana had barely ducked an assignment this morning, pleading time for her own rest and recovery. She only had three days left before she had to return to her long-term remediation assignment in Vietnam.

Will had a similar schedule, before he drifted off to his mysterious work in the Petroleum Autonomous Zone, for his father's company. But if something had come up to interfere with their meeting, Will would have let her know.

Wouldn't he?

Maybe she'd make Will look for her amongst the flowers, instead of her looking for him amongst the trees. As Diana walked through the beds of dahlias, pausing to admire a bright red one, for some reason she thought of her mother.

Not today!

Diana wasn't going to let thoughts of Sarah Stephens ruin *this* day. Not when she'd struggled so hard to set this meeting up with Will, not when she'd had to duck Peter's snoopy inquiries. Her brother was far more interested in her daily routines than Diana thought was healthy. Peter was becoming their mother's tough guy, the bad cop to Sarah's good cop when it came to business.

Unfortunately, he also seemed to feel that applied to keeping track of his little sister's personal life.

A nearby knoll caught her eye and Diana paused, studying it. A small, scraggly orchard topped the rocky hill, the tree leaves a surprising piece of green against dry grass.

How is it getting water?

Deep springs? Drip irrigation?

Diana resisted the temptation to whip out her comm glasses and look up the local water tables, check on the geology and cultivation history of that particular little orchard patch. Something about that grove didn't seem quite right, not quite in place.

No. Not working today. Time to have some fun.

Diana went deeper into the flower garden, meandering toward the orchard. Perhaps Will had parked elsewhere, and was back in the grove. He did that sometimes when they met here, and he was particularly fond of trees.

A ray of sunlight glinted on the knoll and she glanced at it again. Something about that golden play of light up there bothered her. Once again, she resisted the temptation to pull her glasses out of her pocket and study it. Thin wisps of cloud skittered overhead and cast the rocky hillside into shadow again, only to move on. Renewed sunlight cast the knoll into a malevolent brightness, making Diana shiver.

Silly. It's just a knoll, nothing more.

Or was it? Something wasn't quite right about that orchard, a particular symmetry and pattern that suggested it covered up monitoring equipment. Diana frowned, stopping to study it further. It was just far enough away that she couldn't be sure of it, but the tree branch angles didn't appear to be natural.

That's what caught my eye. It looks like a drone or communications monitoring site. High security, whichever it is.

Diana resolutely continued to resist the temptation to use her glasses for their magnifying properties, much less run a lookup to see what it was.

It's not my job. Not my business.

She was here to meet her forbidden lover, not try to figure out why a high-security site might be staged on that unobtrusive little knoll.

It's probably nothing. Why would anyone be monitoring this area?

Just being paranoid.

In any case, Will always carried blockers to interfere with electronic monitoring. Sometimes she thought his precautions were excessive, applying his experience in the twisted political world of Landreth Technologies to all of his life, above and beyond what was necessary.

Granted, she did find his precautions endearing when applied to her, especially when Will insisted that she carry a full blocking protocol. It made Peter complain that he couldn't find her when she activated it, which was a point in its favor, but still—excessive.

She was just a simple, low-level remediator. A grunt in the employ of Stephens Reclamation, still learning the ins and outs of big-project environmental remediation. Except for who her mother was, she wasn't anyone important—and she was sufficiently protected for Stephens Reclamation's purposes, sometimes more than she wanted. Stephens Rec wasn't as deeply involved in the political world as Landreth Tech was, and she didn't feel the need to block monitoring to the degree that Will did.

A skimmer whispered into the lot and she glanced back. Not Will's skimmer. Something about that skimmer looked familiar, even though it lacked a logo. Diana hurried into the trees, not wanting to be seen, Will's cautions and paranoia coupled with her notice of the knoll making her wary.

She had already taken steps to be careful. Renting her skimmer instead of using the Stephens skimmer assigned to her so that her mother couldn't accuse her of using company resources for personal business. Especially *this* personal business.

Bad blood existed between her mother Sarah and Will's father Parker Landreth, and, as was typical for her, Diana's mother hadn't gone into any details as to why it needed to spill over into the next generation.

"Psst. Di." Will's voice spun Diana around. He swung down from a fork in one of the trees and pulled her close, kissing her hard.

"I didn't see your skimmer—"

"Parked it at the store and hiked through the orchards. I had a knock-down, drag-out argument with my father about you this morning. Someone knows about this meeting—" Will's sudden tightening warned her.

"Easy enough to figure out that you two were meeting, and not hard at all to figure out where," Sarah Stephens said dryly, from behind Diana. "You two aren't as subtle as you think you are."

Will dropped his arms.

"Mom, I'm on vacation!" Diana turned around to face her mother, taking Will's hand. She shut her mouth hard on further objections as she saw Parker Landreth standing next to Sarah, a distasteful expression, as if he smelled something foul, twisting his mouth.

Will's hand tightened firmly on hers.

"This has to stop." Parker's scowl deepened. "William. You know how I feel about you fraternizing with *this woman*."

"Excuse me," Diana began heatedly. "But we're adults, of legal age, and able to make our own choices about relationships!"

"Except when they potentially violate non-compete agreements," her mother said, still in that dry, hard tone she used when she switched modes with Peter and turned into Bad Cop. The harshness of Sarah's voice scratched like sandpaper across Diana's nerves. Her only consolation was that Parker Landreth visibly winced when Sarah spoke.

"Since when does Stephens Reclamation have a non-compete that applies to Landreth Technologies, much less personal relationships?" Diana challenged her mother.

Will squeezed her hand in warning. His breath went shorter, quicker, as if he were preparing for a physical battle.

"That's not something you need to know." Sarah frowned at Diana.

"In any case, *I* believe that this is a violation of William's non-compete!" Parker Landreth snapped. "You endanger William's performance when he's on site by staying in touch with him. As it is, you've created more security problems for him when he goes back to the PAZ."

"Stephens Reclamation is under interdiction by the PAZ," her mother added, still in that hard, dry tone. "And Landreth Tech is not viewed well by some of our associates. This is a poor choice, Diana. Personally and professionally. There are appropriate channels for announcing and vetting relationships like this, and neither one of you have attempted to do it right!"

Diana sighed.

I can't argue with that reasoning, at least right now. And if this is a threat to Will—

She glanced at him, trying to ask the question without saying anything. He raised his brows, not moving his head, glancing quickly toward the knoll and back. She bobbed her head slightly, hoping her mother and Parker Landreth read it as a nervous twitch.

If I left Stephens and Will left Landreth, we wouldn't have this problem.

It wasn't a new thought. But the time wasn't right yet. Neither Diana nor Will had the funding nor the credentials to strike out on their own, at least for another year and a half.

I have to finish Vietnam with a big accomplishment. Will has to finish—whatever it is he does in the PAZ—with a success.

The tension winding her up spilled out as she faced the reality. Diana gave Will a sad smile.

"I guess I'd better get going, then," she said quietly. "I'm going on east, to visit my father," she added for her mother's benefit. "If we could say goodbye?"

Parker Landreth scowled even more, but Sarah spoke before he did. "Of course," she said, her voice softening from her previous dry, hard tone. "Give your father my best wishes, please, Diana."

"I will—and thank you."

Parker Landreth snorted. "William, I'll expect to see you in Corporate offices in an hour. We have plans to review." He stomped toward the anonymous skimmer parked in the lot.

The three of them watched Parker Landreth march toward the skimmer. They remained silent until his skimmer lifted and turned west, heading for the most direct route back to Portland.

Will slipped his hand from Diana's and slid it around her waist. "Thank you," he said quietly to Sarah. "I'd just as soon not have my father drag me off like a whipped puppy in front of Diana. But don't think this is the end of my seeing your daughter. At some point we'll be able to meet openly."

Sarah raised a brow at him. "We'll deal with that when the time comes. You'd best manage your father more effectively, William," she said, a shadow of the dry hard tone creeping back in. "He's a potential danger to my company, and I don't continence that one damned bit. Nor do I appreciate the threats he issues to me because of this relationship."

"I agree," Will said. "But I'll keep that aspect away from your daughter."

"See that you do," Sarah said. "Your personal systems are more compromised than you think. Until you fix that, my daughter is off limits. You're a danger to her, a danger to my company. I won't tolerate that."

"I'll make sure of it."

"You'd better." Sarah glanced at the sky. "Better get going if you're headed for the ranch, Diana. We have that meeting with your Vietnam suppliers this evening."

"I'll be back in time," Diana said.

"Good. Later, kids." Sarah smiled as another skimmer appeared. "Ah. There's Francis, back from his winery rounds. We'll see what he's found." She turned and walked away.

Three days. Three days and then I'm back in Vietnam.

"Will, what are we going to do?"

"There's not a lot of choices for today," Will said, sighing.

"There's a tracking station on that knoll." Diana started them walking. Will's hand remained on her waist as they walked.

"I overlooked that. Stupid of me. It's not Landreth, it's another company, but I bet if I look there's a sharing agreement with LT. Gonna have to find a new site to meet."

"And here I was thinking this was a nice, safe, romantic spot."

"It is. Just not—for us."

And there it was. Diana wondered just what place they could meet where neither parent could find them. Ski areas weren't safe. A country tourist farm wasn't safe. Where could they go?

Just another year and a half. Remember that.

She leaned into Will as they walked through the dahlias.

"Wait," Will said suddenly. He broke off the blood red dahlia she'd noticed before, and pushed it into Diana's hand. "My promise. *I will see you before you leave.*"

She glanced down at the mostly opened flower, the center still tightly closed. A promise for the future?

They stopped at her skimmer, and Will closed her fingers over the dahlia.

"I will see you before you leave for Vietnam," he repeated, then kissed her, at first delicately, then with more force. "I love you."

"I love you too," she whispered back.

I'll see you before you leave.

Diana glared at the knoll, now shimmering malignly in the late summer sun.

Not here, for certain.

She set the skimmer's autopilot for her father's ranch, a good three hours away by skimmer if the winds were right. She hadn't planned this trip, but after this sequence of events, it seemed good.

It wasn't until she was safely away that she looked down at the bright red dahlia she'd crushed tightly in her fingers. The center still had to open up.

An omen for the future?

"I'll hold you to that promise, Will Landreth," she whispered.

One way or another, they'd make it work.

They would get together, in spite of their parents.

DECEMBER, 2042—MARCH 2043

SHADOWS RISE

As Diana stepped out of the plane and onto the jetway, she let out the breath she had been holding from the moment the first-class flight attendant assigned to her had given the all clear to leave her seat.

Diana's Security head, Brenda Garcia, stood next to a nervous airline gate agent with a floater chair, waiting for the next VIP passenger. Brenda wore her full working Security blacks, including body armor and helmet with visor up, rifle slung across her chest with muzzle pointed down. Her full lips almost disappeared as she pressed them together tightly, watching, alert, ready to move, projecting a silent menace.

Brenda's face softened momentarily as she spotted Diana, then tightened back up as she stepped forward.

Good. Brenda's here.

Diana wanted to sag in relief, but now wasn't the moment to do it. Things were bad enough in Vietnam, but the news embargo the Chinese had thrown up after their takeover of the Vietnamese government six months ago meant she hadn't been getting much news or information from home. She tried to catch up during her layoff at the Narita airport, but too much had happened in the past six months.

God, the e-mails alone.

At least business-related e-mails had been going through. She suspected her mother had something to do with that.

But nothing, absolutely *nothing*, from Will, and he'd promised to stay in touch. Then again, Will was under similar restrictions, at his work in the PAZ, the Petroleum Autonomous Zone in what had been part of several Middle Eastern nations. But he should be coming onto a furlough soon, just like Diana was.

Then Brenda's warning text had popped up, just before Diana had taken her seat for the last leg of her flight home.

Full Security. Be prepared. Shadows are coming.

Shadows are coming.

The Stephens Reclamation universal code phrase for imminent unrest and close personal danger, that couldn't be discussed in any situation other than tightly secured cones of silence.

Damn it, what's Mom or Peter done to tick someone off now?

Diana smiled at Brenda, hoping to get some sort of clue about what was going on. She had hoped to catch up with news on the flight, but there had been data access problems which had shut down all but canned entertainment newslinks.

As if I wanted to see the latest vid star scandals — that's news I could get in Vietnam!

Brenda acknowledged Diana with a half-smile, then nodded to the gate agent standing nervously next to her. She glided to Diana's side.

"Give us time to clear the jetway first," she said, looking meaningfully at both the gate agent and Diana's personal flight attendant. "Once Corporate Security gives you the all-clear, we're good. Thanks for your help."

She didn't make a move to take the roller bag from Diana, but Diana didn't expect that from Brenda, not with the level of Security implied in that brief message. Brenda needed her hands free.

That was all right. It was just enough to know that she was back home, even for a few short weeks.

Diana took in another damp, cool breath, savoring the sweet familiar scent. Back home. Back in the Pacific Northwest, and away from Da Nang. Away from confinements, from structure, from the potential Chinese contract takeovers simmering throughout her work sites. Back to Security she knew and trusted.

Even if something was wrong and the shadows were coming.

Whatever it was, it probably didn't affect Diana. Her mother and brother were the ones doing the dangerous political work that made them targets. Except for her position as the daughter of Sarah Stephens, the President of Stephens Reclamation, she shouldn't need to worry about Chinese agents Stateside. Diana was still learning her trade as a bioremediator, still a lower-level bot manager and developer, a subordinate member of the reclamation team.

Except for that one small thing I'm carrying. Which isn't so small. And the fact that as Sarah Stephens's daughter, I ended up being put in a position of deciding some aspects of our policies after the takeover. And the recommendations I'm going to make to Mom about what we do with these contracts. But that will end up furthering Chinese goals, anyway, in the long run. They won't want me, they'll want Mom.

"Paul and Katrina are collecting your bags," Brenda murmured softly, her eyes darting about watchfully even as they walked up the jetway by themselves. "Once we meet up with Security, hand your bag over to Maggie. I want your hands free, ready to run, once we're in the open. Damn it, I wanted you in your armor!"

"I didn't think I needed my armor. That's usually Mom and Peter."

"Shadows are coming. You need to armor up every time you hear that," Brenda growled. "Get into that habit!"

"I do, in Vietnam. Besides, I was already in line to board when I got the message. The armor's in my checked luggage."

Brenda snorted. "You should *never* check your armor."

"I had my hands full with repair equipment to carry on," Diana countered. *And the stuff for Mom that it covers up.* "Brenda, it's a plane. What's going to happen there?"

"Lots." Brenda shook her head. "Di, you should have taken the time. Seriously."

"Sounds like a mess. Who triggered the Security alert this time? Mom? Peter? I've not been getting much news because of our Da Nang lockdowns."

Brenda stopped abruptly, swinging to face Diana, her tight worried face softening briefly. "No one told you? You didn't come across the news in Narita?"

"I've been locked down and cut off for six months, Brenda. I was escorted from my plane to a private lounge, and from the lounge to the plane in Japan, and the data feeds on the damn plane weren't working. No news exposure, and I've been trying to fight through archived company e-mail the Chinese wouldn't let through. It's a really touchy situation in Vietnam right now. I'm not about to push any data access limits, unless they're company-related."

Brenda sighed deeply. "Damn it. My job to tell you, then. Girl-friend, it's not them this time. It's you."

"*What?*" Despite her control, Diana's voice cracked louder than she wanted.

"It's your connection to Will," Brenda continued, her voice tight and hard. "I'll brief you when I can. Be prepared. Your mother and Peter are at the gate. They'll tell you some of it." She pivoted sharply and marched off. Diana hurried to match Brenda's strides, questions bubbling in her head that she didn't dare ask.

Yet.

They emerged from the jetway and passed another nervous gate representative. The waiting area was clear, with ten members of Stephens Security staged to cordon it off from curious passengers. Diana's mother Sarah and her brother Peter waited at the counter, her mother dressed in a white, high-collared jacket and slacks that Diana recognized as her version of Brenda's Security body armor; Peter wearing a nondescript dark gray suit that as far as Diana could tell lacked any Security protection.

Not that I'm up on the latest in male Security styling. So I need armor but not Peter? That's unusual.

"Good to see you," her mother murmured as Security closed in around them. Sarah moved to Diana's left and Peter fell in next to their mother.

"Got your bag," Maggie said, easing the grip from Diana's fingers.

Brenda stepped up next to Diana's right side. "Let's go," she said. "Longer we're here, longer we're exposed. Damn it, Diana, I wish you'd worn your armor." She tapped her earpiece as they strode out. "Bags retrieved. Let's go direct to skimmer," she directed the others.

The fast-marching pace was a relief after the hours spent flying.

Be glad when we finally get intercontinental shuttles running. Speed transit time up.

Diana kept quiet as they strode through the airport. No one would tell her anything important in a public setting.

What the hell happened to Will, and why has he put me in this sort of danger?

She couldn't think of any solid reason why ties to her lover Will Landreth could bring things to this pass. Granted, he worked for his father's defense company, Landreth Technologies, just as she did for her mother's bioremediation company. Her mother had opposed their relationship, along with Will's father.

But this? Actual danger? We're not even engaged, just—lovers. Occasional lovers. No serious commitment because—we just can't. Yet. Not with the non-competes. Not until we can both go independent.

Something must have gone wrong for Will in the PAZ. But what was it, and why did it affect her?

Their flying wedge of Security attracted some attention. To be expected. What she didn't expect were the startled looks of recognition as other passengers moved away from their Security.

How would anyone recognize me?

Clearly the information lockdown in Da Nang had worked against her.

"That's *her*!" someone shouted. "That's the Butcher's girlfriend!"

What?

Diana turned toward her mother. "What the—" A cup of something hot and wet smacked into her face, barely missing her eyes. Other trash—crumpled paper, other drinks—pelted their group. Two of their Security broke off to dive into the growing crowd, joined by five uniformed Airport Security that burst through unmarked doors to join them. Diana wiped her face, grateful that whatever had hit her seemed to be coffee and nothing worse.

"*Get moving!*" Sarah snapped to Diana as Brenda moved in close and grabbed Diana's arm with her right hand, her left pushing Diana's head and shoulders down lower as she pushed Diana along. Her mother's hand replaced Brenda's on Diana's shoulder, almost doubling her over as they broke into a jog trot.

"Over here!" an authoritative voice yelled. Diana had just a moment to spot the uniforms of more Airport Security before they were hustled through a doorway.

Sarah's hand slid off of Diana's shoulders. She brushed at the dampness on Diana's face. "Looks like coffee—black."

"Thanks," Diana managed to say back to her mother, straightening up, surprised at how she quivered slightly.

Buck up. Mom won't appreciate any show of weakness, not here, not now.

"*Now* will you listen to me?" Brenda snapped at the bulky red-headed man who seemed to be in charge of Airport Security. "She should have gone straight from the gate to secured passageways! I *told* you that!"

"She didn't appear as a high priority on our records!" the redhead growled back.

"Well, I don't know what freaking planet you're on, but Sarah Stephens sure should have shown up as a high enough priority on your records to get confidential treatment!" Brenda shook her head. "Listen, you'd better get us some coverage at the skimmer. The word's gotten out that Diana has arrived. The Freedom Army will be searching for anything that even vaguely looks like it's from Stephens Reclamation!"

"I think you'll find that's happening right now," the redhead said stiffly.

Brenda put her right hand up to her earpiece. "Approved." She looked over at Diana and Sarah. "Airport Security's just made contact with our skimmer and its Security. They're moving to a secured location on the apron next to this wing's jetways. We'll meet them there." She glanced over to the redhead. "Thanks. I appreciate it."

"I ordered that protection when we had to intervene."

"Where do we go?"

"This way," the redhead said, leading them through another set of doors and down a metal stairwell. They marched past surprised-looking baggage handlers and out another door to a fenced, screened area on the apron near their gate. The redhead raised his hand, and they waited while the black and gold Stephens skimmer glided silently toward them.

"Thank you," Brenda said to the redhead as the skimmer's door opened. "But next time, *anyone* tied to Stephens needs to have top confidential treatment."

The man shrugged. "I'll try. But higher-ups? I only was able to get this for you because that looked like a riot starting. My boss will have my hide if I'm seen to be giving you folks special treatment. I'm sorry. At least I was able to have my people on alert—that's the best I could do."

"You send me your boss's name," Sarah said softly, her tone no less threatening for its softness. "I'll have some discussions."

"I'd just as soon not, Ms. Stephens." The redhead's voice remained steady even though he winced. "Politics. There's—sympathizers connected to the Freedom Army in our higher levels." He glanced at Diana. "That's why I couldn't get you approval for anything more than I initially authorized."

"Then if you have any problems, come see me. We can always use good folks in Stephens Reclamation."

"I'll—keep that in mind, Ms. Stephens."

"Good. Let's get going," her mother said.

Just what the hell is happening?

"I'll give you the full story when we're alone," Brenda breathed into Diana's ear as they walked toward the skimmer. "Take what your mother and Peter says with a grain of salt. It's—not exactly accurate. I've had a bellyful of their comments so far. You and I know Will better than that."

Diana nodded.

Dear God, this is sounding worse and worse. What the hell has Will done?

Mild-mannered Will being called the Butcher? Freedom Army involvement?

Will, just what the hell is going on?

She wished she had something, *any* information from him to give her an idea. But she hadn't talked to Will since their last secret reunion six long months ago, when they had been able to sneak into Bangkok.

Diana bent double to crawl into the skimmer and picked out the seat with the most leg room, wanting to stretch out her long legs in the cramped seating. Peter grimaced as he sat next to her, even more cramped than she was. Their mother perched on the narrowest seat facing theirs, placing her much shorter legs between Peter and Diana's. As the door closed, the magenta light over the door that indicated an active cone of silence lit up.

"So just what the hell was that all about?" Diana asked, masking her wince at the sharpness of her tone. Absolutely the wrong way to start off with her mother and brother.

Predictably, her mother bristled.

"You *would* have given William Landreth a picture and a love letter when you two last met," Sarah snapped. "That's how they know you two are involved. Your face is plastered all over the tabloid news vids today."

How on earth did anyone get that—Will swore that would be safe!

"They called him the Butcher. Why?"

Peter laughed bitterly. "Because, little sister, your dearest darling lover is in jail in the PAZ. For torturing *American* agents."

"*What?* That's not Will—"

No, no, no, that's not Will, he wouldn't do that.

"He confessed," her mother said starkly, bitterly. "And he may have contributed to a major national security breach. God knows, somehow he's also managed to get the Freedom Army pissed off at him." Sarah paused, shaking her head. "One point in his favor," she said sardonically. "Anyone who can piss those people off as thoroughly as William did has to have something going in his favor."

"That's because Albert Lakely's part of the Freedom Army," Peter said. "They've spread his pictures over every possible media outlet."

"That—can't be," Diana whispered, her stomach churning. "That just can't be. That's not Will."

"I can't believe you don't know anything about this," Peter said, his tone only slightly improved. "What do you know about Landreth's activities?" He leaned toward her, glaring. "Damn it, Diana, what the hell have you gotten us into?"

"This is the first I've heard about this whole situation. I've been dealing with the Chinese lockdown in Da Nang!" Diana snapped. "Look, I've not had the time to try to hack through news. I've been *working*, damn it, on a tough project that requires sixteen-to-twenty-hour days, all right?"

Sarah sighed and sank back in her seat. "Peter. Leave her alone. Diana, we don't know a lot about what has happened." She sat up again. "What we do know is that *something* happened in the PAZ that involved Landreth Technologies and William. William's been implicated in torture of American agents and—possibly worse. And someone—whether it's Parker Landreth scapegoating William and his connections, or the Freedom Army, or even our own government—has been spreading your image in the last twelve hours as William's secret love interest. And hinting that Stephens Reclamation is also involved in whatever the hell happened in the PAZ." Her mother made a face. "I'm surprised you didn't catch a hint in Japan on your layover."

Oh God. Bringing the company into it.

That had to be a move by Parker Landreth, a jab at both Diana and her mother. Company involvement in a personal relationship that was turning out to be a scandal—that would be enough to thoroughly enrage Sarah.

I'm surprised she's so calm about it now!

"Like I said to Brenda, I got escorted from plane to lounge to plane," Diana said, fighting to keep her voice quiet and unruffled. "And I don't think you understand how tight the screen has been in Vietnam."

Sarah sighed. "And *that* is an entirely different situation that I need to know about ASAP, especially with this bullshit about you and William hitting the news. I'm already getting flak from our Chinese representatives, damn it. Things were already touchy before this."

"I didn't intend for any publicity to happen," Diana said.

"But they did. Relationships are messy, girl, and the sooner you figure that crap out, the better for all of us."

"It could easily be the result of a blowup between Will and his father. I don't trust Parker Landreth."

"*Good.* That shows one piece of common sense on your part. Wish it had happened sooner."

Diana bit back the retort she wanted to make.

Before she could say any more, her mother continued. "In any case, it's a good thing you're out of there. The lockdown's been happening on both sides. Your reports are the only reliable data I'm trusting at the moment. Diana, what do you think the Chinese want? Do they want us to continue, or do they want to take our projects over?"

Diana drew a ragged breath.

Refocus.

The Chinese demands were, after all, the primary reason why she had come home, above and beyond her announced vacation time—and why her armor was packed in her checked luggage. And talking about Vietnam was a welcome distraction from the worries buzzing in her brain about Will and just how the hell this situation had happened.

"My perception is that they want to absorb our work. Quan gave me his report about his interactions with the authorities. He's been winding things down. Here."

Diana reached for her bag and opened it, rummaging through what appeared to be typical biobot operating mechanicals in various states of repair, until she found the one bot that held her special programming work from the past month. Carefully, she lifted it out of the bag, depressing several buttons. The biobot popped open the secret cache and Diana extracted the fingernail-sized datachip it had protected.

Sarah extended her hand, and Diana dropped the chip into her palm.

"That should be everything," Diana murmured. "Quan and I had our teams collating all the data that we could possibly cram into that chip before I left."

Sarah tucked the chip carefully into a sleeve pocket. "Good. This may be all we can get out of there now. Quick impression. Should we fight to preserve these resources or are they compromised? Should we renew those contracts or not?"

"No, we shouldn't renew," Diana said. "Supply issues have been escalating. I've—not wanted to know what Quan was doing to get our supplies for the past month."

Her mother nodded. "Good. You shouldn't be in on that aspect of project management, not at your level of experience. Quan's sneaky and good. That's why I put him in charge of the Vietnam reclamation work."

"Yeah." Diana took a deep breath. "I haven't been able to check our pricing until I got to Narita, in fact when I wasn't doing e-mail, I was checking pricing. We can't supply the biobots at the price rate that our Chinese competitors can. Especially Mei-lein. Better to wrap up what we've done, and clear as much proprietary data out of the site as possible. I suspected that was the case, but I couldn't get access to competitor pricing info until I was at Narita. That—took priority over other information."

Her mother nodded. "Understood. What about our people on the ground there?"

"Quan has sent most of our people out on leave, at least the non-Vietnamese," Diana said. "Officially, it's holidays. Unofficially, he's getting everyone out."

"What's he doing?" Peter asked, straightening up.

Sarah snorted. "If he's smart, he's figuring out how to land a position with the Chinese to continue the projects." She slipped the chip back out of her sleeve pocket. "I'm going to read this report. Diana, I don't recommend you go to your condo. I've readied your suite at home."

Diana frowned at that but didn't argue further. Given the situation with Will, the Freedom Army, and everything else going on, it was probably the smartest thing to do.

And it gives her the chance to keep track of me.

Nonetheless, Diana had confidence in Brenda's ability to circumvent her mother's monitoring devices.

One way or another I'll find out more about Will. And what he did.

DIANA SHIFTED HER WEIGHT FROM FOOT TO FOOT AS SHE STOOD NEXT TO the large living room window of her small suite in the Stephens compound, arms crossed, hands clenched into fists that she nestled in her elbows. The compound's location near the top of the southwest Portland hills gave her a panoramic view of the lights of the city. She didn't speak, not yet, still waiting for Brenda to secure the area. Then a faint buzz vibrated through her body, followed by the blurring of the lights below.

Cone of silence active. Safe to talk now.

Diana turned to face Brenda, dropping her arms to her side and forcing her hands to open and hang loosely. "So. Just what the hell happened with Will?"

Torture. Will. That was the one line he swore he'd never cross. What happened?

Brenda sighed. "I don't know everything, Di." She gestured to the couch. "Might as well sit down. It's a long story."

"I've been sitting. For hours. I'd sooner stand."

Brenda nodded and dropped onto the couch. "Then I hope you won't mind if I sit. It's been a long day, and we had to scramble fast when this news hit."

"You mean the news about me and Will?" Diana paced four strides, coming up short at the breakfast bar that separated the kitchen from the living room.

"Yes. The story has the appearance of being launched by timed bots, possibly triggered by your airline ticket booking in an open link." Brenda grimaced. "I should have thought of that, but I didn't. I would have, if you had told me that you had given anything personal, electronic or hard copy, to Will."

"He was supposed to destroy it if he were compromised." Five strides back in the other direction, coming up against the fireplace hearth. Sharp turn. Face Brenda. Ice clenching in her gut. "I have a similar letter with picture from Will. Should I destroy my copy?"

"*Now.* Di, it's that bad. Destroy your copies and I'll brief you."

Diana sighed. As she walked over to the coffee table, she reached up under her shirt for the security pouch she kept affixed to her abdomen at all times. Gently, she pried it loose, wincing at the stickiness.

Lot easier to remove it when showering.

She knelt next to the coffee table and shook out the items inside the pouch, deftly keeping a couple of chips from sliding off of the table.

"That's not our design," Brenda commented. "It looks like a Landreth product."

"It is." Diana brushed through the papers, sorting them from her backup chips. "Will gave it to me." Diana sighed as she picked up Will's picture from the small slips of paper that had been in the pouch. She piled a much-worn, folded paper on top of it. "That's what I have from Will."

Brenda held out her hand. "You can't have that stuff on you, Di. Are those the only things from Will?"

Diana balked. "If I go back to Vietnam, I'll need this pouch. Quan wanted me to keep important notes on paper as well as chip backups. This is the most secure chip pouch I know about."

"Quan knew you had something like this on you?"

Diana shook her head. "It's SOP for our group there to keep separate backups from our official records, both chip and paper notes, at least for the most important data. Quan didn't worry how we kept it secure, he just wanted us to have secure records stashed and easy to grab. I didn't trust my quarters. I told Will about it—that's why he gave me the pouch."

Brenda reached for Will's letter but Diana blocked her hand. "You can look at anything else in the pile. Not that."

"Your letter to him went public. I might need to know what he wrote to you, in case it goes public."

"They shouldn't have gotten their hands on his pouch."

Brenda sighed in exasperation. "Di, he was betrayed by someone within Landreth. *Nothing* connected to him is safe for you right now, including your possession of this pouch!"

"I'll take care of these items, then. I can guarantee that no one but myself has seen them." Diana picked up the letter and picture.

She stood, grabbing the fire lighter from its cup on the coffee table, and carried it and the paper over to the fireplace. She opened the glass doors and the chimney's damper, then delicately set the folded paper on fire, dropping it in the middle of the clean bricks inside the hearth. She hesitated for a moment before burning Will's picture, staring at his image.

It was one she'd taken of him when they'd been skiing and snowboarding, on a stormy, moody day that was miserably wet. The day that resulted in her being sent to Vietnam and him to the Petroleum Autonomous Zone.

He grinned a rare big smirk in this picture, his long, straight, pale blond hair spiked with icicles jutting in every direction under his black helmet. Diana blinked back tears, remembering the wretched, marvelous day that she'd taken this pic. Then Will had snapped one of her—that had been the one he'd had with him. At least she still had the electronic version—that is, unless Brenda had already scrubbed it from her files in a security scan. Which she probably had already done.

God, Will. What happened? Why?

Diana swallowed hard and touched a corner of the picture to the last remnants of the flames that had consumed the letter.

When all that was left were ashes, Diana stirred them up. "I want a fire tonight," she said, reaching for the firestarter log waiting by the hearth. She brushed the ashes further inside and slowly lit the log on top of them. When the log was burning brightly, she added two more chunks of wood—real stuff this time—to keep it going. Then she stood up.

"Both letters were written by hand," she told Brenda. "If Will's letter was confiscated, then it was taken from him unwillingly, before he could destroy it. I'm sure of that. There should not be any more copies, especially anything electronic. Will was adamant about keeping our letters handwritten. The pictures—"

"I've taken care of your pix."

Diana sighed. "I thought so." Her voice cracked on the last word.

"I'm sorry, Di. God knows, I'm sorry. I know those pix meant a lot to you, but right now—look, you can't count on this pouch being safe, if Will's was taken from him unwillingly. I'll find something else for you to use if you have to go back to Vietnam. It won't be as good as this one, but I do have a few tricks up my sleeve."

Brenda hesitated, then delicately reached out and flipped through the remaining papers on the coffee table—a roster of private contacts for Stephens personnel in Vietnam, a copy of Diana's passport, small bills in several currencies for emergency funds, and other notes about the Da Nang operation that Diana had wanted to keep safe. She riffled the data chips separate from the papers, sorting them into their own pile, pushing the money off to another edge. Then she methodically unfolded each paper, glancing quickly.

Diana blinked back tears of fatigue and frustration.

Rest. Soon.

She started for the couch, then veered off toward the liquor cabinet hanging over the breakfast bar. Hard to say what was in here, but she could count on her mother to at least keep her own preferred choices stocked in Diana's cabinet.

She found a bottle of single malt Scotch—a Macallan, one of her mother's favorite brands—and poured herself a generous straight shot. Then she slowly walked across the room and dropped into a chair facing Brenda and the couch, suddenly very weary. Diana sipped on the Scotch. Brenda pushed the pile of paper toward her.

"Sorry. I needed to check."

"I know," Diana said automatically. "None of those items have left my hand until now. I've been very careful about that with both chip and paper." She took a bigger swallow of the Scotch and breathed deeply before continuing. "Tell me what you know about Will's situation."

"I don't know for certain," Brenda said, frowning, staring at her hands before looking back up. "I know what the evidence seems to suggest. I think Will was set up for this by—someone within Landreth Technologies."

A chill ran across Diana's skin. "His father? Or someone else?"

Brenda grimaced. "It could be either. Here's what we do know. The PAZ authorities arrested Will sometime in the last four months. I'm not positive about the timeline because the first I knew of it was when the PAZ authorities held a quick trial which was very public. A show trial. But I know they had held him for some time because of the shape he was in and—other sources. I've been working some deep connections, very quietly. We're not entirely sure of the time between arrest and trial. Based on what we can access of Will's communication records, it was something between three to six weeks. I know that some of his comm channels are heavily shielded, especially internal LT comms. He's dropped out of sight from all but LT comms before. According to my source."

"LT or government?"

"Military," Brenda said sharply. "Old friends from my Marine days. Can't say more. It's—semi-approved backchannel for other things."

Other things. God, what are Mom or Peter getting their fingers in now?

"And neither Mom nor Peter listened to that data?"

Brenda grimaced. "They had their own briefing. But—I have problems with those sources. Can't say anything, to protect my own source. I suspect their source has more credibility with Peter than your mother."

"Then was the trial taped?" Diana held herself tight.

Three to six weeks between arrest and trial. God, what did they do to him?

Will had spoken once about having to intervene in a situation in the PAZ, where he'd had to get a Landreth employee away from the PAZ authorities fast, just before he'd gone on leave himself. He'd whispered sketchy details, his blue eyes shadowed and haunted.

Oh God, I can just imagine what they might have done to him.

She'd not wanted to know more then. What little Will had told her had been enough.

Brenda pulled out her tablet and tapped something up. "No recordings, but pictures. Stills. My guess is that they didn't want Will's statements getting out."

She slid the tablet over for Diana to see.

Diana winced at the first picture of Will slumped at a table, his slight form weighted down with shackles around his neck, wrists and ankles locked to a belly chain. Deep, dark circles lined his eyes, sunk deep into his haggard face. She wasn't sure but she thought she saw the shadow of a bruise on one cheek.

It's bad.

She flipped through the series of shots, noticing how he hunched his right shoulder protectively, curling over himself slightly instead of sitting up straight. He held his left wrist with one hand in most of the shots. The one shot where he didn't, the left hand curved inward claw-like. She inhaled sharply at that sight, biting her lip.

Will worried about me getting hurt in Vietnam. He should have worried more about himself.

She could even now hear his light, laughing tone as he dismissed her concerns about his job in the PAZ. She was in more danger than he was, or so he'd insisted.

"What were the charges? Peter said he'd been accused of torturing American agents. That doesn't make sense for the PAZ to try him— were there other charges?"

"That's the reason given for our government not objecting to the trial of one of our citizens," Brenda said sardonically. "From what Zoë Wright and I have been able to figure out, the only alleged American agent involved was Albert Lakely, and he was far from a reliable asset."

Zoë. God, why didn't I think of her resources?

Her high school classmate was now a Justice Department attorney.

I'd have thought of it soon enough. Not like I've known about Will's situation all that long!

She took a big swallow of her Scotch. "What are the other charges?"

"Espionage," Brenda said grimly.

"As if! Good God, from what he's said to me, he was *supposed* to be reporting back, maybe not directly to our government, but if anyone doesn't think LT isn't giving the government edited versions of the information they gather, they're fools. What did he do, get in the middle of somebody's personal feud?"

"That's—possible. He did *something*. The question lies as to what exactly it was, just how willing he was to do it, and to what degree he was misled by circumstances. His claim at the trial was that internal Landreth Technology information showed that Lakely was a double agent working for subversive elements within the PAZ, seeking to overthrow their governments. That he stepped in to stop it because he discovered local LT employees torturing Lakely."

"What did the PAZ authorities claim Will did? Jeez, if he was catching dissidents for them, I'd think they'd give him an award, not jail him."

"That's the problem. *They* claim that Lakely was investigating those subversives for our government and theirs."

"But wouldn't Will have evidence?"

"He claims it was destroyed. But that's not the only charge. They charged him with the use of netspiders. Unauthorized use of technology on a human subject."

"Oh God." Diana fumblingly set her Scotch down and buried her head in her hands. "Netspiders? They're claiming he used *netspiders*?"

She shivered at the thought of the nanotech spidery devices, her skin crawling. Officially, the use of netspiders during interrogation was banned—but she knew, both from Vietnam and from what little Zoë Wright had said from her own experiences, that netspiders were tools secretly used both by governments and by corporate entities like Landreth Tech to extract information from unwilling subjects.

And LT is one of the prime developers of that tech. Entirely credible. Oh God.

But netspiders weren't the only tech that could be used. The Stephens biobots had certain—capabilities she had encountered, to her own painful discovery.

"So they have definitive evidence." Diana sat up and took a bigger gulp out of her Scotch.

"Not exactly. Those netspiders appear to have disappeared. The evidence comes from Lakely's condition at Will's arrest."

"That's convenient."

"Isn't it? But there's another piece that raises my suspicions about what has been reported," Brenda said harshly. "Will was apparently drunk out of his mind when he did it."

"*What?* Will doesn't drink. Brenda, this is sounding weirder and weirder."

"That's why I don't buy the official story that Peter and apparently your mother have accepted. Neither does Zoë. But that affects the charges, because it adds alcohol use and possession to the list. Will claimed he was drugged, but—" Brenda shrugged. "Again. No evidence."

"This whole thing is sounding creepier to me. What's LT saying about it? Why haven't they bailed Will out and brought him home?"

"Will had no support from Landreth Technologies during his trial. No legal support at all."

Dear sweet Mother of God. Parker Landreth threatened Will with consequences if he wouldn't leave me alone. This is what he meant. Oh dear Lord.

"So his father cut him loose," Diana groaned.

Brenda nodded. "Parker Landreth very publicly denounced Will. Your mother claims he had to do it to protect the company."

"Crap. You and I know better. Will himself told me his father would cut him loose at the first sign of trouble—and—"

Diana couldn't sit any longer, a mixture of anger, fear and dread pulsing through her gut. She began to pace. Three strides to the hearth. Five to the breakfast bar. Five back to the hearth.

"Why would he do it now?" she continued. "To get rid of Will? Why not just plain fire him, if he wanted to get Will out of the company?" *Because he wanted to punish Will for choosing me. God, they must have had one hell of a fight at some point.* "Me. They fought over me, and Will refused to give him what he wanted. That's what it had to be. His father threatened him in front of my mother and me if he wouldn't leave me alone." She stopped in front of the couch, staring at Brenda. "What was the verdict?"

"Death was the verdict sought, but it was changed to life in a PAZ prison, based on the theory that he was delusional and out of his mind at the time."

Diana's knees wobbled but she forced herself to straighten up. "Do we know if he's still alive?"

Maybe there was some hope. Quan had connections. Zoë had connections. Her mother's friend Francis Stewart might be willing to help her rescue Will—if she could persuade her mother to unbend in her animosity toward Will. Doable, if she could get Sarah away from Peter.

His father denounced Will, that should be enough to convince her that he's not a tool of Landreth Technologies. She'll remember that threat. If Will appeared to be drunk, he had to be drugged. He had to be set up. That's the only thing that fits the facts and what I know of Will, and his father hates me enough to do it.

"He was alive as of a few hours ago. They let their pet reporter talk to him."

"I want to see that story."

Brenda grabbed her tablet and pulled the story up. Diana skimmed it, noticing how even more hollow-cheeked and frail Will looked in the one picture than he had in the ones from his trial.

Not that there was much to report.

Will had said only one thing to the reporter.

"Shadows approach," Diana whispered, looking down at Brenda.

Brenda nodded, acknowledging. "When I read that, I knew for certain that Will was trying to send a message. I just don't know what it was. I hoped that you would have had a chance to see the story sooner and tell me."

"I didn't see this, thanks to technology screw ups. Or, dear God, I've have come out of that plane roaring for blood and action."

Diana looked back down at the pad, pressing her lips together tightly as she reread the brief, sarcastic account.

The reporter had taken Will's sole statement as a sign of delusion, a confirmation of the circumstances that had mitigated his death sentence.

Diana knew better. He'd been double-crossed, and was trying to get that message out. To *her*.

Oh God, he's trusting me to get him out of there.

"Something else is going on," she breathed. "Shadows approach. We set that up as a code phrase. In case one of our parents—" she swallowed hard. "In case one of our parents decided to sacrifice one of us. Will's idea."

"I thought it was something like that," Brenda said grimly. "Close enough to our own codes."

"I need to talk to my mother. Now." Diana drew in a deep, careful breath, and expelled it slowly. She dug her comm glasses out of her pocket, and tapped them into life, hoping that the glitches she had encountered on the plane were just an artifact of the plane's tech.

No such luck. Diana sighed and dropped her glasses on the coffee table. "These are dead."

"The cone doesn't help." Brenda rose. "I'll bring your mother here."

"Without Peter, if you can."

"I suspect Francis will be here and want to tag along."

"Francis is good. Just don't bring Peter."

Francis Stewart could sway her mother away from Peter's point of view. Francis's No Limits Enterprises could possibly help extract Will from the PAZ. He'd probably welcome the opportunity to thumb his nose at Parker Landreth, since both designed and sold security electronics.

"I'll see what I can do," Brenda said.

As Brenda left the room, Diana picked up her Scotch and went to the window, staring out through the cone of silence's blur to make out what she could of the city lights.

Shadows approach.

God, Will, I hope we're not too late.

"So you're telling me that William's interview is part of a rescue code?" Gray in her mother's eyes dominated the blue as Sarah glared at Diana across the breakfast bar, the tablet with the story about Will on the counter between them.

Diana met her mother's glower without flinching. "Will thought it was a good idea. We set this up when you sent me to Vietnam."

Her mother's brows shot up. "That long ago."

So she doesn't know everything about me and Will!

"Yes." Diana broke away from Sarah's gaze to sip off of her own refilled glass. "Yes," she repeated. "He was worried about the Chinese incursions into Vietnam. He—didn't like what I told him about our own recovery procedures."

Let's not go into the other contingencies our code system was set up to cover.

"Smart man," Francis Stewart muttered from his position in the overstuffed chair behind Diana. "Sarah, I've been telling you for years that you need to develop tighter Security for your staff. Especially if you're going to send bioremediators into politically disputed areas."

Sarah's eyebrows deepened into a sharper V as her frown tightened. "I assume you have more information than just this code to justify your defense of William! Next thing, I suppose you'll want me to lead a rescue effort!"

"That—um, was the idea," Diana said slowly. "Especially since Parker Landreth is thumbing his nose at you with this situation with me and Will."

Her mother's eyebrows shot up. "Oh? *Really?* Explain your reasoning."

"Remember last summer? When you and Parker Landreth interrupted one of the dates Will and I had set up?"

"Yes-s-s," her mother said slowly, straightening up, eyeing Diana thoughtfully. "That threat? Parker blusters like that a lot, Diana. I've learned not to get too excited about the noises he makes."

"What if he wasn't blustering in this case?" Diana took a deep breath. "Mother, from what little Will shares with me about how his father does things outside of North America—I believe it's entirely possible that Parker Landreth could have set Will up."

Sarah sighed. "Rumors. Nothing's ever been proven about Landreth Tech and dark ops. And William's his own son! Why would Parker do this to him?"

Diana met her mother's hard eyes directly. "They don't get along." She swallowed hard. "Mom, Parker Landreth doesn't tolerate disobedience very well. The things Will's told me about—"

"Kids tell stories. Even adult kids." Her mother winced.

"I've seen the scars. Mom, I believe Will. He's been abused. If it wasn't for the financials, he'd be gone from LT. I know that. But he owes his father and he can't be free from that until—he has six months until he comes into his mother's trust."

Sarah shook her head. "You could say the same about you and me."

"No. Not as bad. You hold a tight rein on me with the trust. But not like Parker Landreth. I could leave Stephens if I found another employer. I'm not under contract with legal binders. Will—can't leave LT. Not yet."

God, if Will knew I was telling my mother this--but she needs to know just how urgent this is!

"William's treatment by his father doesn't prove unapproved dark ops on the company's part. They're a defense company! I'm certain there's a certain amount of sanctioning of their actions from our government. That there's more to it than that is a hugely troubling assertion."

"Mom. Will's been documenting what he can find of the shady work LT does. Some of that work is sanctioned by our government, true, but—LT goes beyond that. Landreth Tech only does it in places they can't get caught. Like the PAZ. If anyone would know about LT black ops, it's Will. If Will came across something wrong in the PAZ, and he challenged his father—Will was angry enough to confront him the last time we spoke." Diana took a deep breath. "Mom. If something went down between Will and his father, and Will didn't destroy that letter I gave him—then I'm sure his father would be willing to take a slap at you by making the relationship between me and Will look bad."

Her mother shook her head. "Hatred of you, Diana? God, even if you throw in Landreth's hatred of me as well, that doesn't explain what happened with Will."

"It does if Will was preparing to blow the whistle on LT unsavory practices. Mom, they exist. Will's one who would know."

"Then Parker Landreth would be stupid to alienate William."

"Who says that Parker Landreth is rational? Besides, he's open about Will being a disappointment to him. He didn't support Will at his trial. Does that sound like a rational parent who has his son's best interests in mind?"

Francis thumped his feet down hard behind Diana as he stood. "Girl's got a point, Sarah. I've had my own doubts about Landreth. The obvious estrangement between Parker Landreth and Will Landreth is an open subject in the defense community, was even before the news broke about Will's arrest. No one's had the nerve to test how far Parker would go by bidding for Will's services. Yet." He circled the breakfast bar to stand beside Sarah, bypassing the Scotch bottle between Sarah and Diana for the bottle of red wine. He filled his glass, then grabbed the Scotch and topped off Sarah and Diana's glasses. "There's a lot about this story that hasn't smelled right to me."

"I also don't buy the PAZ claims that he was drunk," Diana said. "Will drinks a glass of wine every now and then."

"Good man." Francis grinned.

"But not enough to get drunk. He's always been the sober one, the one who watches out for us. Will's not a drinker. I've *never* seen him drunk, Mom. Never."

"We don't always see the dark side of the men we get involved with," her mother said, an odd note in her voice. "Just because he doesn't drink when he's with you—"

"Fits the profile I've heard about Will Landreth." Francis leaned on his elbows at the end of the bar, equidistant from both Sarah and Diana. "There's been some buzz, Sarah-girl. I've been interested in bidding for Will's services myself. I just haven't had the incentive to cross Parker Landreth yet."

Her mother sighed deeply and turned sideways to Diana, resting her hip in the L formed by the intersection of the breakfast bar and the kitchen counter so that she was looking at Francis rather than Diana.

"I know, Francis. But the ambiguity of these possibilities, and going against Defense on this one without sounder evidence than we have is a riskier step than I want to take. Especially with Peter so adamant on the subject of William's guilt."

"And just how many buddies does Peter have in LT, much less those shady connections to the Freedom Army you won't talk about?"

Diana raised a brow at that revelation.

What kind of game is Peter playing?

Her mother's eyes darted briefly toward Diana before returning to Francis, her scowl deepening.

"This isn't the place to talk about that subject, Francis."

"Sooner or later, you'll have to deal with it, Sarah!"

"This isn't the time or the place to talk about that." Her mother's voice quavered just the slightest bit but firmed up. "Peter has his reasons, and he doesn't answer to me for those activities. Yet. Brent's legacy to him means he has that forty percent share in the company."

While I have nothing beyond the trust fund Mother created for me, to match Peter's inheritance from Brent.

Not that Diana regretted it. She never liked their cousin Brent Stephens, and he always had more use for Peter than her. In any case, as soon as she could, she planned to break free from Stephens Reclamation and her mother's control. Peter was welcome to Stephens Rec. *She* had other plans.

"Your cousin was a poisonous twit, Sarah, and if you don't take control of your son soon, he'll turn out just like Brent."

"Peter's stronger than that." Her mother jerked her chin up tightly. "And his—tendencies—have uses."

"It'll bite you in the butt someday."

"I accept that possibility. But until I find a means, Peter has enough resources that I can't always control what he does." Her mother shook her head. "This is a distraction. Let's get back to the main issue. I'll admit I have questions about what I've seen and heard about Parker Landreth and his company's scruples."

Diana took a deep breath. "I need to speak with Zoë Wright for more details. Brenda has been getting information through her, enough to suggest a conflict between Defense and Justice on this issue."

"Interesting."

"It's only hearsay from Brenda, but it sounds like Zoë has doubts about Will's situation as well." God, she wished Brenda was in here now to back her up on what Zoë had said! But with both Francis and her mother present—no, better not to have Brenda present. Both Francis and Sarah would talk more freely without her around.

Her mother nodded. "Interesting," she repeated, setting her drink down. She clasped her hands together, leaning her chin on the V between index fingers and thumbs. She stared off into the distance, chewing her lower lip thoughtfully.

Diana kept silent, letting her mother work it through for herself.

At last Sarah dropped her hands. She held them out in front of her. "This is what we know for certain." She hooked her left thumb around the little finger of her right hand. "One. Parker Landreth threatened William with consequences—unspecified—if he continued to see you, Diana." She gave Diana a sideways look. "Did he?"

Diana swallowed hard. "Yes."

Her mother threw her hands up. "You *have* to learn things the hard way!" She rolled her eyes, then shook her head. "Okay." She hooked her left index finger around her right ring finger. "Two. *Something* happened in the PAZ. What, who, how—those aren't as important as the fact that something happened involving William." She raised her brows at Francis. "Right?"

"Right, Sarah my girl," Francis said, raising his glass to her.

"Three." Sarah hooked her left index finger around her right middle finger. "Landreth made no effort to help his son. No legal support, no working through government channels." She glanced sideways at Diana again. "You know damn good and well I'd not do that to you, no matter how estranged we are." Her voice hardened. "You don't do that to family. Now once I got my hands on you myself, you might wish I had left you there—"

Diana swallowed hard. "You wouldn't abandon me."

Peter would abandon me. Not you.

"Stupid move on Landreth's part," Sarah mused, tapping her lips with her index fingers. "I'd have bought a lot of the story—*did* buy a lot of the story—except for that piece. I kept wondering. I wouldn't leave William to his own devices. He knows too many damaging things about the company operations. Things I wouldn't want outsiders to know." Her face hardened. "There's just one thing. William *did* use netspiders, Diana."

"Inadvertently or on purpose?"

Her mother slammed her right hand on the counter. "There's no difference!"

"I disagree." Diana kept her tone flat.

"How would you know?"

"Have you ever had one of our prototype biobots turn on you? They're capable of creating similar effects."

Sarah snorted. "Since when have you had to deal with that?"

"Starting three months ago, we've been having problems with the newest prototypes unpredictably turning on a handler to try to run conversions instead of working on—" Diana broke off. "My God. Mom. That's the missing piece. The timing—those netspiders are similar—if there's been a glitch—"

"What?" Her mother leaned forward. "What's the missing piece?"

"Three months ago, we started having problems with biobot prototypes going rogue and trying to harm their handlers. It's new behavior, and unpredictable as hell. I'll bet that's what happened. Lakely was fiddling with prototypes and they blew up on him. Landreth designs and uses netspiders for reconnaissance purposes. Will's—careful not to talk in detail, but—what we do share tells me a lot. The inner workings of Landreth netspiders are very similar to the biobots that we use for deep site sampling and transformations or conversions, enough that we use their chips." She frowned at Sarah. "Against my recommendation, based on what Will told me."

"It's been cost-effective. But if this is true—"

"I'll bet it is. Something went off in a *lot* of proprietary items that have those Landreth chips. I've—been hearing rumors from other bioremediators about problems, specifically with prototypes using those chips. I'll bet Will discovered Lakely fiddling with the wrong thing, and it got him in trouble."

"Now that's an interesting idea," her mother said, straightening up and frowning. "Very interesting. What did the diagnostics on our biobots show?"

"We never did figure out that program glitch, other than the sole Landreth chip we have in it. Mom. We have to grow our own chips. That's why."

"Not the topic," her mother said harshly. "Later. What did you do?"

"We sidelined those prototypes to use different biobots and it slowed the work down. It's been driving Quan nuts—let me show you the specs. We didn't dare send these files over the limited open networks. Quan and I locked them down hard. Let me get them."

Diana whirled away from the breakfast bar, hurrying into the bedroom to grab her tablet from her carryon bag. After tracing through the security protocols and disarming the codes that would wipe the data from her tablet, saving it to yet another back door, she scrolled through her diagnostic spec documents as Sarah looked over her shoulder.

"*There,*" her mother said suddenly, delicately tapping one document with a forefinger, frowning. "That one, right?"

"The very one."

"I thought so. Francis, you look too."

"If I had only known about Will's situation when this started happening." Diana began to scan through the specs of that erratic bot's behavior, breaking it down to a code level. "Quan and I kept trying and trying to find the glitch—"

"It's hidden," her mother said, her voice suddenly tired. "Let me see." She flicked through the stats. "There's a Landreth part on that bot." Her voice hardened. "That model's just on your projects, Diana. Sabotage or equipment failure?"

"Let me see this more closely," Francis mused, pulling the tablet his direction.

"Francis—" Sarah cautioned.

"With your permission. I recognize this part. We've had problems with similar bots and those Landreth chips. There's a back door needed to pull its teeth if it goes rogue, but it's easy enough to hide command codes unless you know what to look for."

"Limited access. I *would* like to keep your access to *some* of my proprietary code limited, Francis!"

"Don't I always follow limits?" Francis asked archly.

"Not always. But this time, go ahead."

"I feel stupid," Diana said. "I should have thought of outside parts. I knew we had LT parts. I just didn't think of them being a problem."

Francis looked up from the tablet. "With all due respect, girl, you don't do enough defense work to recognize this." He slid the tablet over to Sarah. "It's getting an outside interrupt message to sneak in rogue code. It's not a Landreth hack. Someone else found this vulnerability. Who the hell was it?"

"Find who set the codes for Lakely and I'll bet we find who's been messing with ours," Sarah snapped.

Francis hissed in a deep breath. "Ours were Freedom Army hacks. Diana. How many of these bots were you using?"

"Three. They were prototypes. But one turned on Lien. Scrambled up her arm like a netspider, left similar marks on her skin." Diana shivered. "Disarming that one was tough. It turned on me." She pulled up her sleeve, showed Francis and Sarah the fading scars from the bot's attack.

"This adds a whole new dimension to this situation," her mother said, her voice harder than ever. "God. What that could have done to you—okay, Diana. Your William is giving you a rescue code. I sure as hell want to find out what he knows about these parts and how they're coded. I concede that you may be right about William being set up by someone, if not his father. I can see Landreth being blackmailed if this hack is from a third party like the Freedom Army, which could explain why he didn't help William. I'm going to have a little—*discussion*—with your brother. Not that it helps with this situation. What do we do next?"

"Diplomatic channels? Maybe we can negotiate through our connections."

"If there's something hinky about LT parts that William's discovered, that's a fast way to see your lover dead, no matter who set him up," Francis said. "As long as he's in the PAZ he's vulnerable. But we need what he knows."

"I don't know. Work through Zoë?"

"He's sentenced to life and Francis is right," Sarah said grimly. "It's very likely that any sort of diplomatic movement will mean a quick, secret death for William if what we're theorizing is close to the actual situation. We'll have to run an extraction, and I don't have the security staff capable of yanking someone from a PAZ prison. I doubt Landreth will lend us a hand, and in any case, they're probably under supervision. As are we."

Francis grinned at them. "Ladies, that is where No Limits Enterprises can be of service." He toasted them with his glass. "I have a *lot* of interest in figuring out just what is going on here. Diana, your boyfriend may have just done me a couple of favors. At the very least it's worth my time to set this straight. My guess is that we'll find just about every Landreth part in a non-Landreth bot is compromised. I'll have my crew itemize the Landreth chips we have in our bots. Whether this originates from Landreth or the Freedom Army, we've got a problem."

"Should have isolated Landreth chips from the beginning," Sarah growled.

"My dear, you'd have been the first to object to the cost."

"I know."

Francis was going to help Will. He really was going to help Will. Diana exhaled slowly, ignoring her mother and Francis as they muttered plans at each other, jet lag finally catching up with her. She picked up her drink and sagged onto the couch, at long last letting herself stretch out.

"Diana," Francis suddenly called. He dropped into the chair across from her. "Are there responses to Will's rescue code?"

"Yes."

"Input them." He thrust his tablet toward her.

Diana grabbed it and, resting the tablet on her knees, began to type phrases.

Shadows Fall. That meant no help possible, under surveillance and unable to move.

Shadows Lift. Wait for further information.

Shadows Unfold. Rescue forthcoming.

She handed the tablet back to Francis. "Can I come along?"

"Diana—" her mother started.

Francis shook his head. "You haven't the training to go with the team. You'd just slow them down."

"Will's not necessarily going to trust you, even with the response codes. You'll need me there at some point," Diana pointed out.

Francis studied her. "You sure you up to this?"

"I had to deal with a bot gone rogue in Vietnam. I helped Quan with security issues." Diana kept her voice level. "I'm not asking to go on the actual mission. I know that's above my skill set. I just want to be in the first safe spot you're taking him to." She met Francis's eyes directly.

"I can't support the risk," her mother said. "Diana, please—"

"I want to be there. I'll bring Brenda, that is, if you'll release her, Mom."

"You'll take direction?" Francis asked.

Diana nodded.

He looked up at Sarah. "I think it's a good idea."

"*Fools.*" Sarah threw her hands up. "All right. I know I can't stop you, and it's safer if Brenda is with you. But I plan to be there as well. And Diana—don't think this means I approve of this relationship. Right now, it has value to me. But I don't approve. Not with William's ties to Landreth Technologies."

"The important thing is getting him out of there," Diana said.

"Agreed." Francis stood. "Let's clear out of here and let Diana get some rest while she can. Diana, I'll call you when it's time to go. I'll message you a kit list."

"Thank you," Diana said.

Francis and her mother left. Diana didn't lie back down but tucked her knees under her chin, balancing the drink in her right hand, staring into the fading fire.

Shadows unfold.

Hang on, Will. We're coming. Hang on.

SHADOWS FADE

CLOSE, BUT NOT CLOSE ENOUGH TO WHERE WILL IS.

Diana slumped back in her seat in the darkness of her mother's private skimmer parked on the edge of a landing strip in God-knows-where-on-some-Mediterranean-island, careful not to disturb her headset.

Three days.

It had taken three nerve-wracking days to put Will's rescue plan together. Diana played her part, including a dramatic, tearful vid interview where she managed to slip the phrase *shadows unfold* into several of her angsty comments. The media ate it up.

STEPHENS HEIRESS MOURNS FOR TORTURER LOVER LOCKED UP IN THE PAZ.

God, her mother had just *loved* the inaccuracies in *that* story. Diana had to agree with her, though she had chosen to avoid breakfast yesterday so she wouldn't have to listen to Sarah's acerbic commentary about the twists and turns the story was taking on its own. The important thing was that the story was sensationalistic enough to go viral, which meant it was more likely to leak into the PAZ.

Would Will be able to see the story and pick up the code phrase?

Depends on what they're doing to him, Francis had answered when she'd asked. *They wanted him to talk about you. Odds are he'll see anything you say to the press. You're leverage they have over him.*

That's the problem of romantic connections, her mother had answered wryly, raising a brow at Francis.

But now the rescue was happening. Francis's team had been dropped in the mountains near the isolated prison which had been Will's last reported location. Diana wore one of Francis's headsets with limited voice communication capabilities, monitoring Francis and his comm team, waiting until they got Will. Then she just had to keep talking to Will to keep him calm while they brought him to her.

Be prepared, Francis had privately warned her. *We have no idea what they've done to him or what they've medicated him with. This could get ugly.*

Diana had some idea of Will's potential condition. At her request, Brenda had pulled strings to get Diana every bit of information available on PAZ treatment of prisoners like Will.

Netspiders. Drugs. God knows what else.

Dear sweet mother of God, she hoped Will was in his right mind and hadn't broken. He was tough, but what would this do to him?

Meanwhile, Diana waited. Listened to the terse, brief transmissions between Francis's team and the comm team. At some point they'd get approval to meet the extraction team. Then Francis would flip the switch which would let Diana be heard as well as letting her listen. But until then she had to wait.

Waiting. Mother of God, she hated waiting. If she were alone, she'd say a few rosary decades. Will had gotten her into the practice to mark time when waiting. But not around her mother. Her father—yes. Sarah—no.

Breathe. Yoga breathing. That works.

Her mother remained calm on the other side of the skimmer, focusing on her tablet as she flicked through reports. Diana envied Sarah her calmness. All she could do right now was wait and listen. She couldn't focus on her own tablet. All she could think about was Will, hanging on in the face of God-knows-what agony, hoping for rescue.

Movement. Her mother put the tablet down steadily, precisely, locking it into secured position. The slow, careful motion alerted Diana.

"What's up?"

"Arms ready, Diana. Incoming—and they aren't friendly."

The automatic security belts clamped down solidly across her body. Diana took her blaster out of its secure containment, heart pounding in her ears as she slid it into the scabbard locked into the arm of her seat. With incoming, evasive maneuvers would likely follow. She didn't want to hold onto that blaster when it happened.

"Any idea who they are?"

Sarah shook her head. "They refuse to ID themselves. We'll try to outrun them, but they fit the profile of Landreth skimmers. Not the PAZ."

Maybe they're coming to help—

Diana dismissed that notion quickly. Not if they wouldn't ID themselves.

Francis spat out a series of code phrases Diana didn't know. Her comm suddenly went dead silent. Then their skimmer shot straight up, pulling some Gs and pushing Diana down hard in her seat. It banked hard and tight, then accelerated, faster than typical for most skimmers.

Of course. Mom would have the highest performance skimmer she could get her fingers on, then mod it up.

An impact knocked them sideways. The skimmer rolled. Red lights flashed in the passenger cabin as a warning buzzer screamed. Clamps snaked across Diana's forehead, thighs and arms as the skimmer rolled again. Diana made herself breathe. In. Out. In. Out. She forced herself to relax against her restraints, remaining loose in case of further impact. Tense muscles would make things worse.

The skimmer stabilized, plunging down hard. The buzzer stopped blaring and the lights held steady.

What the—? Did Landreth just shoot at us? What kind of shape are we in?

The skimmer leveled and rocketed off faster than before. Diana's restraints eased slightly but did not release.

"Decoy. Us. Lower altitude. May evade," her mother snapped out tightly against the pressure pushing hard on them. "Other. Team. Priority."

"Got. It." Diana forced out. "Sorry."

"Bastard," Sarah growled. "Not. You. Parker. Shouldn't. Be. Necessary."

"Yeah."

Anything else she could say was interrupted by a sharp jerk sideways. The buzzer screeched incessantly. The red lights throbbed. The skimmer veered in the other direction, then up, down—Diana lost track of the movement. She focused on her breathing.

Calm. Calm. Stay calm.

She suspected that when they finally stopped, quick action would be required.

The wail of a two-note siren broke into the buzzer's roar.

"Decelerate! Do NOT evade further!" her mother snarled. "Crap, crap, *crap!*"

"What?" The pressure on Diana's body eased as they slowed.

"Fucking Landreth's locked a come-along on us and we can't break it. We have to stop. Francis is going on to meet the team. We're cut loose."

Diana's gut tightened.

What if we get Will free only to have to trade him to his father for our freedom?

The extra restraints released, retreating back into her seat. She flexed her arms and wrists.

"So are we giving up?" That didn't sound like her mother, but God only knew what Sarah Stephens would do in this situation. Her mother had capitalized on a reputation for unpredictability for years.

"Fuck, no!" Sarah released her blaster. "This is why I had Peter hold in reserve."

Peter knows? Crap, he's betrayed us!

"Mom, he probably told Landreth!"

"Why the hell do you think we're in *my* skimmer?" Her mother bared her teeth in a predatory grin. "Only way to keep you safe. Peter won't dare harm you."

"But if Peter wants to go after you—"

"I've got more than a few poison pills secreted in the inheritance structures to keep either one of you from getting that bright idea!" Sarah blew hard, shaking her head as the Gs eased off. "Peter knows that. I've made sure he's known all along, daughter mine. No. I have my reasons, including smoking out the other Landreth moles in Stephens Rec. We have at least two possible spies. If they haven't left yet, they'll be easy to track down once we're done with this."

The skimmer slowed even move, hovering mid-air, then lowering to land.

"So what's our next move?" Diana tapped on her headset. She was still getting dead air. She growled and pulled it off.

"Don't take that headset off," Sarah said, standing as their restraints released. "You'll still need that once the team gets Will. You're just not patched in until you're needed. Francis works that way. Now. Blaster. Do not disarm. Follow my lead, *exactly*."

As Diana readjusted her headset and stood, the cockpit door opened. Brenda slithered through the narrow opening. She surveyed Sarah and Diana quickly.

"Good. Armored?"

"Damn straight," Sarah said. "Both of us. Helmets?"

"Absolutely," Brenda said. "Here."

She opened an underseat compartment and pulled out two helmets. Brenda handed the one with the green fir tree logo of Stephens Reclamation edged in gold to Sarah, and the one with the silver-edged tree to Diana.

As Diana eased the helmet on carefully over her headset, pulling her neck armor up to link into the helmet, Brenda kept extracting other helmets. The rest of their personal Security cadre slipped into the main cabin and put them on. Brenda dove into the weapons cabinet, distributing the heavier, longer blaster rifles and flamethrowers.

She checked Diana's helmet, then Sarah's, while the other Security staff safeguarded each other's linkages. Tony, Brenda's Second, checked Brenda's helmet when she had finished with Diana and Sarah.

Sarah held her blaster in both hands as she took her place mid-cabin. She gestured Diana forward with her right shoulder. "Here. Next to me. Keeps us together and out of the way."

"I remember from drills," Diana murmured. Standing next to her mother like this was startling. Sarah barely came up to Diana's shoulder in height, but she projected herself as taller. "Phalanx formation?"

That earned her a quick grin. "Yes. You remember the movement?"

"I've been reviewing it in the field. Quan's been having me teach it to our staff for self-defense."

"Good girl."

"Ready?" Brenda asked.

"Whenever." Sarah clucked to her comm and her tone changed. "Landreth. What the hell do you want?"

Static crackled and then Diana heard through her headset. "I want you out of that skimmer. Now."

Was that a quaver she heard in Parker Landreth's voice? Diana and Sarah exchanged glances, Sarah breaking into a fangy, feral, sideways grin.

"You heard the man," she said, the flippant tone of her voice sending chills down Diana's spine. Flippant voice with the fangy grin from her mother was bad, very bad. "Let's show him that this can of sardines carries sharks."

Sardines?

Diana briefly puzzled over that reference before remembering. A small, oily fish. Once eaten by humans, now captive-bred for cultivation to rerelease into oceans as feeder stock to help recovering food fish populations.

"Offensive phalanx," Brenda snapped. As one, their Security staff cocked their weapons. Diana cocked her blaster, taking a deep breath, pleased to see her hand held it steady with no trembling.

This shouldn't be as scary as the firefight around our compound when the Chinese first moved in. But it's worse.

"Diana," her mother said quietly. "If your William wants to get into my good graces, he'll figure out just how the hell I can break free of his father's damn come-alongs!"

"If anyone can do it, Will can." *If he's in any shape to do it after this.* "I'll talk to him about it."

"Make it happen."

"Full open," Brenda ordered.

The skimmer door split, parting to each side, wider than Diana had seen it open before. The ramp lowered and the first row of Security marched out, lowering their weapons forward. As they reached the ground, they fanned out slightly, leveling their weapons at the Landreth Technology Security waiting for them. The second row filled in the holes in their line.

"Can you see Landreth?" her mother hissed to Diana. "Can't see over our people. Damn being short!"

Diana craned her neck, looking for Parker Landreth. The Landreth forces were armored, like theirs. She scanned helmets looking for insignia—ah. A lanky figure like Will's, with gold-edged insignia stood behind his own wall of Security, directly front of them.

"Front of us," she whispered back. "Aligned with me."

"*Good.*" Sarah signed something Diana couldn't see to the Security at her left. The wall of Security parted in front of them, and Sarah stepped in front of Diana. Diana moved sideways and followed a half step behind her mother. They strode three steps forward. Sarah held her blaster with both hands, muzzle pointed down. Diana kept her own muzzle pointed up, next to her right shoulder.

What the hell—Mom, this is nuts.

"You wanted us out," Sarah said. "Here we are, Landreth. You gonna have the guts to face us directly?"

"Disarm them," Parker Landreth ordered.

Sarah raised her blaster as Landreth Security pushed forward. Stephens Security swarmed into place around Sarah and Diana, leaving clear Sarah and Diana's line of fire toward Parker Landreth. Sarah aimed her blaster directly at where Parker's voice had come from.

"No." Sarah's tone brooked no argument.

Diana angled her blaster at Parker. "Move and I'll shoot." Her voice came out as firm and steady as her mother's, no wavering despite the tightness in her gut.

Parker's eyes darted toward her. "Chip off the old block," he sneered. "You got a mind of your own, little bitch?"

"Be glad my mother's here," Diana said levelly, throttling back the rage flooding through her. "Otherwise I might decide to go off script."

Sarah laughed one short, sharp, humorless chuckle. "I'd be careful playing those games with my daughter, Parker. Diana's a better shooter than Peter; you should try hunting with her instead of him. Might actually find something to shoot. In case you've forgotten, she's very much her father's daughter. Ranch girls aren't sissies." Her voice sharpened. "We're here. We're out. What do you want?"

"You're springing my son from the PAZ prison. I want him."

"*No*," Diana said, before her mother could speak. "You had your chance to help him. We're not going through all this work just to give him to you."

"What my daughter said," her mother added.

"He needs to debrief. He carries Executive classification Corporate secrets."

Sarah snorted. "If you were truly worried about that level of disclosure, he wouldn't be in a PAZ prison right now!"

"He knew the risks. He was supposed to have died rather than disclose. He had the pill if the sentence didn't go through." Parker Landreth's voice went cold. "He chickened out."

Her mother straightened up. "I suggest you tell your staff to stand down." Her voice matched Parker's for chill.

Parker Landreth stared at her for a moment. "Or what?"

"Or I'll shoot," Peter's voice came from above and behind Diana, to her right.

The click of more weapons being armed resonated all around them.

How the—stealthsuits. That's right. Peter's been researching stealthsuits with Francis.

The question as to how and why Landreth Security hadn't detected the stealthsuits could be answered later.

"Stand down," Parker ordered.

As the Landreth Security lowered their weapons, Diana eased her blaster down, still holding herself tight in case she needed to react. Now she could feel the winter chill in the evening breeze.

Still not that far from the ocean.

She didn't let herself shiver.

Figures in gray and black armor with the Stephens fir tree on their helmets closed around them.

"Get out of here," Sarah said, her voice cold and quiet. "Take your people. Peter, track him. I don't care where Parker Landreth goes, as long as it's not where we are."

"You're making a mistake, Sarah Stephens!"

"Maybe I am," her mother said icily, menace dripping from every word. "And maybe you should have made a greater effort to extract your son yourself. *I don't leave my people behind.* Especially if one of them is my own flesh and blood."

"You'll see me in court!"

"I look forward to every minute of it," Sarah hissed.

Parker glanced at Diana. "Have fun with my boy," he said mockingly. "With whatever's left of him, that is. Enjoy your mother's Christmas present!"

Diana bristled but her mother spoke before she could. "If you think I'm just doing this for my daughter, you're a bigger fool than I thought, Parker Landreth. I'm still not thrilled by her connection with your son. But—I see value in the information he has to share."

"Good luck with that," Parker snarled.

Peter stepped to his side. "Let's get you out of here."

Diana remained tense as Peter and his much larger staff herded Parker Landreth and the Landreth Security forces back to their skimmers. Now, the tunnel vision that had locked her down eased off and she could see where they were. The half-moon hung low in the clear cold sky as the last rays of sunset played across the courtyard of the wrecked building where they had landed, outlining the stark silhouettes of scraggly date palms around the compound.

We're in the PAZ itself.

"Is this a safe location?" she quietly asked her mother.

Sarah shook her head. "We don't dare take off again until we have Francis and his fleet back with us. Peter was shadowing the Landreth skimmers and provided some defense. But even he can't counteract those damn come-alongs of Landreth's!"

Diana looked around them. "Should we expect PAZ incoming?"

"I hope not. Francis paid enough in bribes to shut this sector down for the night."

"What's Francis getting out of all this?" Even as she asked Diana realized. "The chips can't be enough—wait. A link to that stealthsuit tech and Landreth?"

"That's one possibility." Her mother looked around, spotted the remnants of a stone wall, and moved toward it. "I'm sitting down. You might as well, too. Better to wait this way. Brenda, can we safely start a small fire?"

"I wouldn't advise it," Brenda said tersely.

Sarah sighed and sat on the wall. "Sit. Conserve your energy."

Diana sat near her mother, silent, waiting, watching the half-moon slowly descend along with the light at the western rim of the sky. The winter shadows stretched long, darkness wrapping around them. Diana watched as the stars became brighter in the dark. She studied the constellations, comparing the configurations to what they would be this time of year at her father's ranch.

She'd lost track of time when her headset suddenly crackled back to life.

"Coming in," Francis said sharply. "Diana. Talk."

"Will? Will, talk to me?"

"*Diana*," Will groaned. "Isth you?"

He doesn't lisp.

"It's me. Yes. Will. It's me."

"Diana." Another groan. "Diana." Fainter than before.

"Will. Keep talking. Francis, how far out?"

"Fifteen minutes. Diana, he can't say much. You keep talking."

"Will. God. Hang on." *What's safe? Vietnam. Little stuff from Vietnam. Talk about your daily routines.* "Grunt at me once in a while, 'kay?"

Will moaned. "Isth try."

"I'm back from Nam. The sunsets are gorgeous. But I hate the damn humidity." She kept babbling on about trivial stuff involving everyday life in Vietnam, quickly censoring any references to Quan, Stephens Rec, anything other than her daily patterns.

It was one of the longest fifteen-minute periods of her life.

But at last, the No Limits Enterprises skimmer touched down in the courtyard, others like it whispering softly as they hovered above them.

"We can't linger," Francis said as the door to his skimmer popped open. "Sarah. Diana. Get on board. We'll drone your skimmer."

"Damn it, Francis, I can't afford to trash—"

"You can't afford to keep it now. It's laden with Landreth tracker viruses."

Her mother sighed.

Diana needed no further invitation to hurry aboard. Francis grabbed her quickly. "Be advised. He's in tough shape. Bigger than I can handle on this skimmer. We're headed for the medical center at my European headquarters."

"Thanks," Diana whispered as Francis released her. She knelt by the small—far too small—white-wrapped figure on the cabin's floor. "Will?"

Her stomach turned. Bruises covered what she could see of his face and his jaw sagged at an angle, a cloth holding it. Slings held both arms in place, and she was grateful that a blanket covered his legs.

"Oh God, Will," she murmured, barely touching the back of his left hand with her index finger.

His eyes flickered open. Will tried to smile at her and winced.

"Will, don't speak. I'm here."

She continued the steady patter she'd been babbling as the skimmer took off. Will kept his eyes fixed on her, occasionally groaning.

It seemed like forever before they landed at Francis's European headquarters. She stayed with Will as the medical staff worked over him, continuing to talk softly. At some point they escorted her out.

She remained on vigil until he was safely ensconced in a hospital bed.

Only then did Diana let herself relax. And even at that, she still sat in a chair next to Will's bed.

Sooner or later, they'd have to pay a price for this help.

But for now, she was simply grateful that Francis and her mother had listened and helped.

We'll pay the price later.

Whatever that would turn out to be.

However, being separate isn't going to be a part of it, she vowed.

No matter what, she'd hold to that piece.

"WILL?" DIANA LET HERSELF INTO THE CORNER CONDO SHE AND WILL shared on the third floor of an old Southeast Portland industrial building.

No answer.

I'd think he would be back from the hearings in D.C. by now.

For the past two months, while she'd been away surveying a new Stephens Rec account in Brazil that was outsourced to the new company she and Will had formed six months ago, Will had been closeted with a hush-hush investigative panel about the recent government coup in the PAZ.

Diana had no idea what he was telling them. He just seemed very weary whenever she could find a hotspot in the Amazon to call, looking more worn and frailer each time. But he promised to be here when she arrived.

I'm late. He should be here.

Then again, the weather had been rough enough to interfere with all air travel. Skimmers could be crankier than airplanes, and Francis had promised Diana he wouldn't let Will fly public. Not after that last assassination attempt, allegedly by PAZ sympathizers.

I'd have thought he'd have messaged me by now.

She came further into the open kitchen and living area to put her things down on the kitchen table, frowning as she saw that Will's things were here. His small suitcase leaned against the back of the couch that separated kitchen from living space. His tablet lay on the couch.

Did he go out for a moment?

A chill tightened her gut. Will was skittish about going out on his own these days. She looked around the living area. No more signs of his presence.

Did he have a relapse and go to bed when he got back from DC?

Will's recovery after escaping the PAZ hadn't been as quick or as easy as she would have liked. He still coughed a lot, and his strength was still about two-thirds of what it had been before.

As if to confirm her suspicions, she heard a rustle in their bedroom.

"Will?" Diana pushed the door open. Despite everything, worry clenched at her gut. He was subject to varying mood swings and sometimes she feared she'd come home to find him hanging—*no. He promised!*

But she still worried because of the depression that seized him at odd moments.

She silently let out the breath she'd been holding as Will startled up from the armchair where he had been staring out at the late afternoon sun, obscured by the fog that had only partially broken up and had contributed to the delay of her own arrival. He looked ten years older than the thirty-two he had just turned, face drawn and haggard.

"Di. Sorry. I didn't hear." His voice trailed away and he sank back into the chair.

Diana sat on the chair arm and stroked Will's forehead, frowning. He was slightly clammy and warm to the touch. Will closed his eyes and leaned against her hand.

"You doing okay?"

He shook his head. "Not sleeping. I keep seeing those netspiders —" he stopped, dropping his head into his hands. "I can't tell you, Di. It's about Lakely. It touches on—locked areas."

Diana rose and gently rubbed his neck and shoulders. Even now Will still ached from the aftermath of the daily beatings in the PAZ prison.

He was supposed to die rather than disclose, she remembered Parker

Landreth's cold, bitter voice. From what little she could piece together, it was surprising that Will had managed to survive until they rescued him. Telling, too, was the news her mother had mentioned when they had met in the security lounge at the Las Vegas airport to talk about the new Amazon contract.

Rumor has it that Landreth has been banned from future defense contracts. You watch your step with William. He's a marked man, thanks to his testimony.

God, what did that mean? Her mother had shrugged when Diana had asked if Will had anything to do with his father's losing the contracts.

"I'm back now," she murmured into his ear. "I'm back and I'll keep those nightmares at bay."

His right hand snaked back and took hers, pressing it tightly without words.

"Is it the testimony about your father's company?" she asked softly. "My mother said something—"

Will turned quickly, more quickly than she expected. "What has she heard?" His hand clamped down harder on Diana's.

"Just that rumors say that Landreth Technology is banned from future defense contracts, and that you're a marked man, thanks to your testimony." Diana decided to leave out the bit about *watch your step.*

Will's grip eased. He heaved a heavy sigh and went limp again, pulling his hand away from hers as he leaned against the chair's back, staring not at Diana but at the ceiling away from her head.

"She's speculating in dangerous areas," he said faintly. "But understandable. Di, don't go there. Seriously."

"How dangerous is it?"

"Enough."

"Enough to activate even more of a Security presence than we have now?" She had fought to gain what little privacy they possessed. Their infant company definitely needed a Security arm independent of Stephens Reclamation.

Next lump sum payment, Diana promised herself.

"I've been drawing up a budget for increased Security levels," Will said tiredly. He closed his eyes. "It helps me sleep on the bad nights.

We need to amp up our Security program. I have a whole program laid out for Do It Right."

Do It Right. An in-joke of a name, born of the painful hours Will had already spent recovering. As in, *if we ever get a chance to strike out on our own, we're going to do it right.*

Do It Right. Born of a surprise cash gift from her father and almost all of Will's maternal inheritance. Part bioremediation company, part tech company for Will to design the security devices he had dreamed of making while working for his father. To distract Will in the early days of his recovery, she had handed him everything she knew about the malfunctioning Vietnamese biobots, showing him her own scars and describing how the bots had gone rogue.

Those aren't that different from my father's devices in design, just applied to different uses, Will had said. Then had puzzled out a modified biobot her mother hadn't wanted.

Doesn't fit my needs. But it looks useful. Why don't you take that out on your own? Sarah had said. No direct funding, but—Diana's workload had shifted to give her time to work on that particular prototype. It wasn't targeted precisely enough for the radioactives her mother had wanted it to detect, but it worked quite nicely on toxic sludge remediation. And other messes, as Diana kept discovering.

The Little Bot That Could, she and Will had dubbed it.

And it was starting to land them contracts that weren't Stephens Rec subcontracts.

"You're worried about your father."

Will nodded, still keeping his eyes closed. "We'll always need to worry about him."

"Will, is there anything you *can* tell me about what happened?"

"Just that—" Will hesitated. He swallowed hard. "I went along with his program for too damned long. I didn't realize how deep he dragged me into his world. It's—it's going to be a few years before I'm completely clear." He opened his eyes, now looking directly at Diana.

Diana slid around to sit on the footstool. "What does this mean for us?"

Will sat up, leaning his forearms on his knees. "The Third Force wants me on call at least part-time. There are some issues they're still working through."

"So are you under contract to them?"

"In a manner of speaking." He sighed and studied his hands. "Like I said, the trade-off is my availability for consultation. Unquestioned, at any time they want."

"And if not?"

"Secret trial." He grimaced. "Actually, just the sentencing. I've been tried."

"Will—"

"Couldn't share. Not over interceptable coms. Bottom line, I cooperate, or—prison."

"For how long?"

"At least five years."

"And if they ask you to cross a line—"

Will buried his head in his hands. "I was pretty firm on that one. No more. Thanks to Zoë, I've been able to negotiate a reasonable conscience clause. But. We need more security. Tighter, faster, with more tools. We need a more secure base of operations than this loft."

"I can't promise you the funds to pull that off for at least a year."

"I know." He took Diana's hands. "Most of all, I've just been thinking. I've been watching the shadows and remembering. The light here —I remember watching the shadows march across my cell, just before Francis and the team grabbed me. I thought they were coming to finally kill me."

Her hands tightened on his and she looked down, swallowing hard. She couldn't find words.

"Di." Will's voice was softer, lighter. "Watch the shadows with me? Please?"

"It will help?"

He nodded and scooted over in the big chair. She carefully slid in beside him. Will draped his left arm tightly around her and leaned into Diana. She snuggled in tight.

Together, they watched the sunlight fade.

4 / SHADOW HARVEST

MARCH, 2044

A RANCH DESTROYED

THE LAND IS IN WORSE SHAPE THAN JAN AND DAD SAID IT WAS.

Diana frowned as she used her right hand on the Western saddle's cantle to balance herself as she looked behind. Her dark bay mare Kokanee danced sideways. Diana clutched the cantle tighter as she studied the barren landscape around them.

"Quit," she growled at Kokanee. She turned forward and gently raised her left hand to take up contact with the curb bit. The mare shook her head, clacking the roller on her bit, and moved back into place on the trail behind the old copper-colored Appaloosa gelding that Diana's father Dan rode.

Diana kept a slightly stronger touch on the romal reins to remind Kokanee that her rider was paying attention.

I should have brought some soil analysis tools. Maybe a bot or two.

When her father and stepmother had said there were problems with the land, Diana hadn't thought it would be *this* bad. After all, when they rode through the small stringers of Ponderosa pine that crossed over the top of the ridge, she could almost pretend that nothing had happened; that the stark empty landscape with patches of snow was just typical winter in the North End. What she saw on brief visits around the house didn't suggest there was a major problem.

Until they rode into the open meadows between the stringers of trees. Diana *should* see dead, dry grasses with the faint fuzziness of early spring green growth around the roots.

Instead, nothing but stark, muddy ground mixed with frost-heaved ice crystals met her eyes. Barren clumps of sod marking where bunchgrass had once grown. No birds in the trees. No tracks on the ground.

Nothing.

But soil quality wasn't the only problem that brought Diana to the ranch. She had received an urgent message from her stepmother Jan a week ago, just before leaving Do It Right's latest tough project in the Amazon for her quarterly home visit.

Your father really wants to see you. His health has taken a turn for the worse, and I'm not sure he can handle a trip to Portland. He doesn't talk about how he feels but I can see it. Besides, you need to see the ranch. It's gone to pieces and we can't explain why. If you can get away....

Gone to pieces didn't begin to describe what Diana saw around her. And as for her father's health, he still wasn't talking. Diana narrowed her eyes to better study him as he guided Charlie down the short, narrow drop to the next stringer of trees and the final small bench of land at the point of the ridge, before it dropped steeply into the narrow canyons leading to the river.

Dan sank in on himself as he rode, instead of sitting straight, like she remembered. Oh, he still handled snorty old Charlie with a deft, light touch, flowing effortlessly with the gelding's movements. But he swayed in the strong gusts of the March winds roaring up from the canyons below. Once, he grabbed the saddle horn for stability.

Dad never used to grab the horn. Never.

Charlie's behavior was different, too. He delicately picked his way among the rocks and uneven ground, pausing when her father swayed in the wind. One ear remained flicked back toward her father, as if Charlie, too, was studying him. Instead of using a slight slope as an excuse to break into a short jog, Charlie minced down the hill, placing each hoof with care.

This was behavior she expected from a beginner's steady packer than from a rancher's working mount. Charlie hadn't even pulled his usual half-hearted crowhopping at the beginning of the ride. He ducked his head once, her father popped the reins, and Charlie lined out steady.

Not the way she was used to seeing Charlie act. Or her father, who had once enjoyed Charlie's pretense of being a bucker.

Dan stopped Charlie at the end of the point, looking into the depths of the canyon. He yanked on the brim of his weather-beaten silver-belly Stetson to anchor it more firmly against the wind and scowled, rubbing his grizzled chin.

"Now do you see why I had to get rid of the stock?" he said.

Diana stifled a groan as she dismounted, aching muscles already protesting. She pulled her coat snug against the winter wind and knelt to check the barren ground, clucking softly to switch on the enhanced sensors in her glove as she riffled her fingers in the dust.

Not that she needed to look closely to know that there was a problem. Diana had spent enough time doing nanobot-driven biological remediation—granted, in jungle environments instead of this mountainous high desert—that she had been mentally cataloging all the things wrong with the Andrews Ranch during what had once been a lovely scenic ride. It had been what—two, three years since she last rode on the ranch with her dad? Things hadn't been that bad then.

What went wrong?

"No grasses. Not even thistles." Diana rocked back on her heels. She looked up at her father. "Dad, you're a better range manager than this. What the hell's going on?"

Her glove sensors relayed the quick soil analysis to her eyeglass comm overlays. Diana frowned, brows rising quizzically.

Radiation count high, and more. What's that other stuff in the mix?

Dan snorted. "Global warming. They say."

Diana shook her head. "Dad, even with climate change, this looks more like it's smack in the middle of the desert than the northeastern Oregon mountains. Something else is wrong." She waggled her fingers. "Especially with the data my sensors are showing." She waved at the barren slopes, the withered, dying trees. "Shouldn't look like this!"

"We had overspray from the national forest several years ago. Some secret combination treatments to knock down competitive brush growth on the Ponderosa pine seed orchard over there—" he pointed across the canyon toward another dry, sterile slope. "They claimed the heat dome and drought afterward did the killing, not the overspray. But I have my doubts."

"Were you compensated?"

Diana pinched soil samples to take back to Will and slid them into glove pockets designed to carry them, then stood and grabbed her canteen off of the saddle to rinse her gloves.

"Whoa, Koko," she said as Kokanee startled sideways. Behavior she'd expect even from old Charlie in this wind.

Why isn't Charlie acting up?

"And why are they worried about brush growth in this climate?" she continued. "This isn't the Cascades, for God's sake!"

Dan shrugged. "I'm still waiting on the claim."

"Those things shouldn't take that long." Diana shook her head. "Especially with Mother as powerful as she is—"

"I'm *not* begging my ex-wife for help!" Dan snapped, loudly and firmly enough to startle old Charlie into raising his head and taking two steps back. "Quit!"

He popped the reins and Charlie stopped, head higher than ever, ears back. Her father growled and Charlie froze. Then Dan lowered his hand, softened the reins, and Charlie blew out softly, lowering his head.

Oddly, this behavior reassured Diana.

About time Charlie started acting like himself.

"Dad, what's going on?"

Her father rested his hand on the saddle horn and sighed. "Di, I'm not the only one waiting for a claim. These things take time. The overspray happened before the Third Force takeover. The system is swamped."

"If you go through channels." Diana picked up her reins and eased her left foot into the stirrup. She mounted, biting her lip to stop the groan as her tight leg muscles protested. "It's not a lost cause. Look, I'll give you a break on the rehab work."

"Di, if the circumstances were different, I'd like nothing better than to hire your company to rehab the place. You and Will would make this ranch a showplace. If Jeremy had survived—I'd be more interested in doing something like that. Rita's just too young, and Jan has enough to deal with managing the mess that is her own family affairs. I can't ask her to take on more than she's got already." He shrugged, a helpless expression flitting across his face before it went blank again. "Who else would want to manage the ranch?"

Diana drank from her canteen, swallowing the brackish, warm water in an attempt to loosen the sudden tightness in her throat. Jeremy. Her younger half-brother, killed during the unrest during the Third Force uprising that had overthrown the old United States. He had been well on his way to taking over the ranch when he had been in the wrong place at the wrong time.

"Dad, this place is worth the cost of a rehab job."

"I don't have the seed money to hire you. Jan's tapped out thanks to her brother's stupid behavior during the Uprising." He didn't have to add *that got Jeremy killed as well.* Diana was thinking it and her father's expression suggested that he was as well.

"I could front the basics," Diana said, shoving aside the guilty thought that this year's trust fund payment was already doubly, if not triply, allocated. She and Will had few resources of their own to spare. Every penny they could scratch together went toward growing DIR.

Will would understand if I chose to spend the money on this. I think.

"Can you outbid the Third Force?" Her father straightened in his saddle and picked up his reins.

"I'd have to see their offer."

The Third Force hasn't targeted the North End for relocation, have they?

Third Force relocation projects moving into the area should have alerted her mother. Sarah and her friends Anne and Francis were leaders in the Third Force Congress. Diana would *think* that one of them would advocate for her father.

Or did Mom offer, and anger Dad in the process?

Always a possibility with her divorced parents.

"Honey, don't saddle yourself with this place. You're doing good work, important work. That's worth more than this ranch."

"Dad, if you want to stay here, we can figure something out."

Could DIR fundraise a campaign to fix the ranch?

Except—they didn't have the resources even to do that. Expanding DIR was Will's current fundraising and networking priority. Diana didn't have the time, either. The South American bioremediation contracts that had given Do It Right its start required her full attention. Saving the ranch might provide a platform for expanding DIR into North America, but at the moment they didn't have the people or the funding to spare.

"Have you talked to Peter?" Her older half-brother had better ties into their mother's Stephens money than she did. Maybe he'd do something.

Dan stiffened at the mention of his stepson. "I doubt Peter would lift one damned finger to help me! Besides," his voice dropped and she could barely hear him. "I can't keep up with the place, Di."

"Hire help. I can pay them for you."

Could be a DIR training internship. They'd learn a lot from Dad.

"The cancer's come back. I don't have that much time left. I need to provide for Jan and Rita. You have Will and the Stephens money, but Jan just has the ranch to support herself and Rita—and possible liabilities with her family. Maybe if Jeremy had lived, there would be more options."

"Dad, let me and Will help you."

Dan shook his head. "The Third Force is getting active in the North End. Depopulation."

"There are ways to work with that. Have you talked to Mother about it?" Dread clutched at Diana's gut.

"As if that would do any good." Dan spun Charlie around.

Crap. This is Mom's idea.

"Dad—"

"Honey, I know what it takes to get this place in order. Maybe if you talk to your mother, see if she'll hire you to do the rehab work in the name of the Third Force—"

"I'll try," Diana said reluctantly.

Another part of this year's inheritance dance.

Besides, her mother would be more likely to give the job to Peter and Stephens Reclamation. Keep the money within *her* side of the family and not give any to Diana, who had sided with her father.

Another year, until I get the rest of my funds.

But she didn't have another year.

Do I even have two weeks before I go back to the Amazon? As stiff as Dad's holding himself in the saddle….

She hadn't thought much about the ranch property until now. It was just *there*, just like Dad would always be *there*.

Don't want it to disappear into some Third Force oligarch's holdings like a lot of the other relocation projects seem to do. I have to do something. I'm just not sure what—yet.

"Dad. If I find funding, will you consider a different offer?"

"You find a way to help Jan and Rita, I'll think about it. But don't you go sacrificing your company for this ranch! You finally got free from your mother. I don't want to see you losing what you've gained."

"I wouldn't."

"See that you don't." He faced forward and clucked, squeezing his legs against Charlie's sides. The old gelding took off in a singlefoot gait. Diana urged Kokanee after Charlie. She had to extend Koko's trot to keep up, and the path didn't allow her to ride by him and talk.

It gave her time to think.

INHERITANCE DANCE

"What's that?" Diana winced at a particularly loud scream in the streets outside her inner Southeast Portland loft as she dressed to meet her mother that evening. She pulled black pleather pants over legs still aching from today's ride.

"A streetie, most likely." Will shook his head as he stared into a computer screen, midway through running compatibility tests between his big desktop and one of the new 3-D hologlobes. He tapped on the screen, then leaned back, carelessly brushing long blond bangs out of his eyes.

"Should we call the police?"

"Police won't come for a streetie fight. Anyone else has the call buttons. I don't go out without mine." He stood up and stretched. "I've used it in a couple of situations when I got involved, before we hired our own Security. The cops told me that the only reason they came was because I hit my button. But they wouldn't help the streeties." He pressed his lips together in a thin line.

"Honey, you aren't LT Security anymore."

Damn it, Will, I don't need you to get killed over a streetie dispute!

"I'm still trained." Will scowled at Diana as he dropped back into his chair. "That's more than what most of these kids have. A lot of them have been relocated by the Third Force."

Diana bit her lip, counting to ten before she spoke. "You can't save everyone, Will, " she said in a low voice, unwilling to voice the rest of what she wanted to say, the shadow that still hung over them.

Trying to save who you thought was an innocent got you into trouble in the PAZ.

Will flinched, as if she had spoken her thought. "Di. I know. I just —" he shook his head and dropped it into his hands. A shudder rippled through his body.

Diana winced in turn. She rested her hand lightly on his shoulder. "Sorry. Didn't mean to trigger memories."

Will exhaled heavily and sat up, rubbing his face. Diana let her hand fall to her side.

"I have to face them. Even though those kids—" the shiver flowed through his body again, "—even though it's just like that damn PAZ all over again!"

Diana placed both hands more firmly on his shoulders. "Will. I—" She couldn't find words for her desire to make things better for her husband.

I have to get him out of here.

But where could he go? That was the problem. Diana considered the options yet again.

Will couldn't go to Brazil with her. He was under sanctions because he knew too much about the inner operations of Landreth Technologies, his father's defense and security technology company. Both political and corporate entities would pay to get that knowledge for less-than-savory purposes.

At least here, the Third Force could provide a modicum of protection. It was in their best interest to keep Will Landreth safe, as a foil to his father Parker.

She had once wanted to send Will to stay at her father's ranch, especially after Jeremy's death. But it had been vetoed as a residential location, both by the Third Force and by Will's initial rehab needs. And that circled back to other concerns.

We need an HQ close to the urban area to make the Third Force happy, but far enough away for Will to relax, damn it. But I don't know how to make it happen—yet.

Will sighed and pried Diana's hands off of his shoulders, squeezing them gently, interrupting her fretting about their situation.

"Di. I know you want to help. It's just hard. The Third Force relocation centers aren't doing squat for the people they're pushing into the city. I want to help them. Even when it's futile."

The thought she'd been trying to avoid crystallized into being.

This could be Rita's fate.

Her bold little sister, capable of riding any horse that came her way, surviving on the streets?

Diana bit her lip.

Not enough time to talk this out with Will. Has to wait until after I meet with my mother.

"I worry about you," she said instead.

"I can take care of myself, Di. Besides my Security, I've got some informal support from my snowboarder friends in Sellwood. You're the one I worry about."

What could she say to that? Diana hugged Will, then pulled on her white silk shirt.

Will followed her into the bathroom. He leaned against the doorframe and watched while she put on her face paint in lieu of sunscreen, applying the white/black domino look she preferred back when they had gone clubbing or during her occasional performances with Will's old band.

She switched to business talk. Not enough time, never enough time.

"This Grady I've hired. I think with a bit of seasoning I could work him into a division head position in Rio Bravo, so I could start developing work leads up here, within a year. Then we wouldn't be apart so much. Only seeing each other once a quarter is making me crazy."

"It would be tempting," Will admitted, grinning. "I've been building some leads. But—"

"—We're not quite at the point where we can finance that operation." Diana finished his sentence. "I want to move our operations base out of the urban core, too."

"I keep following the depopulation regs. We still don't have the funds to fund a relocation waiver, even closer in." Will crossed his arms. "We're approaching that number, but we're not there yet."

"We need to have several big contracts or some steady medium-to-smaller customers to qualify for a five-year startup deferral. It's worth thinking about."

Wonder if we could pull down enough contracts to finance that property near the highway up on the Mountain. That would be a perfect Do It Right base—close enough to Portland for major transportation, out of the city but not too rural to be completely depopulated, rural enough to get a waiver for resettlement because we provide jobs. But we don't have those numbers. Yet. Worth me taking some extra time on this trip to search out contract leads?

Could be a cheaper relocation fee than if we set up in the city. That could be a solution for Will.

But I can't see Dad settling down there. What am I going to do about Dad?

"What about your dad?"

Diana startled, unaware that she'd spoken the last thought aloud. "It's ugly, Will. The cancer's back. And the property is trashed. Dad says it's due to overspray from the old national forest seed orchard. My quick scan results were puzzling. I'd like you to look at that data while I'm meeting with Mom. If you have time while you're running those compatibility tests. Getting those globes up is probably more important than whatever this is."

"Almost done. Don't need to babysit them. Come on, Di. When were you going to tell me about your dad and the ranch?"

Diana smiled quickly at him before turning back to the mirror. "After I came back from dinner."

"I have the time now." Will uncrossed his arms. "Tell me what you know."

"Thank you, love." Diana took a deep breath, forcing herself to relax. "It's not much. I gathered soil samples and took a quick scan. Dad has an offer from the Third Force, but it's nowhere near what that place's potential value could be. He'll consider another offer—maybe."

Will nodded. "I'll take a look at what you found. You said he had to get rid of the stock? Was that because of the conditions?"

Diana finished painting her face.

Still have the touch.

The paint would protect her face against ultraviolet rays and was more elegant than plain sunscreen. She stepped back from the mirror and rinsed her hands. She frowned.

Maybe a few sparkles. Been a while since I've really dressed up!

She spent all of her time working in Brazil, and since Will had returned from the PAZ, it wasn't feasible for them to go out except for official occasions.

"All but saddle horses for the family, but I don't know if he sold the stock because of the land conditions or if he just couldn't keep up with the care." She shook her head. "I wish he hadn't done that. I didn't have time to ask about the broodmare and young horse bands. I'd have taken some young stock, found a place to let them grow up."

"Would you really be able to do something with them?" Will asked softly. "Do you have the time to take on another project?"

"Probably not. But I know several folks who would pasture them for me until I found the funds to manage the herd more intensely. Dad spent a lot of years building his bloodlines, and I want to see his breeding program preserved. I need to find a place to park Kokanee, preferably where Jan and Rita could do something with her. She's a product of his breeding program and all I'd need was someone reliable to take care of her. I just—" She threw up her hands. "Dad is so damned worried about providing for Jan and Rita without interfering with my life that he would sooner dump everything rather than let us help."

"That's rough."

"I was fantasizing about that land on the Mountain we keep talking about. We might not have to pay so high a relocation fee. Might even get a break because it's not a depopulating priority, and we would employ local workers. It would be a good North American base. That wouldn't solve the issue of Dad. I don't think he'd thrive in that dense a forest. However, it could solve the problem of where to keep the young stock and broodmare band."

"Hmm." Will turned and leaned his back against the doorframe, scratching his chin thoughtfully as he stared straight ahead. "Di, that could work. We're close to being able to fund something like this. But we need a big contract to make it happen."

"The ranch," she said. "If we could get startup financing, the initial recovery work would be showy enough that we could land more contracts and get funding for the later work. It would give us time to build up our systems here."

"It all depends on what condition the land is in. What's your assessment?"

"The ranch is recoverable. But the soil is down to bare dirt in places. My sensors picked up other stuff besides the spray. Radiation levels are puzzling. And it wasn't just Dad's ranch. I noticed similar patterns around the area."

"I'll check it while you're meeting with your mother."

Another sore spot. Sarah still disapproved of Will Landreth. Diana's occasional meetings with her mother happened without Will present—*probably a good thing*. Diana wasn't always certain she could keep him from snapping at her mother on days when his pain flared. And while Sarah tried to be understanding, her mother's version of "understanding" was not always Diana's when it came to Will.

More shadows.

The entrance lock access chimed.

Peter already?

"You anticipating anyone dropping by? Heaven forbid that my brother would be early, much less on time."

"No." Will palmed one of his needle guns and stepped out of her way, following Diana to the security panel. "Go ahead."

"Diana Landreth," she said, pushing the remote entry com button.

"Me," her brother Peter said into the com, brushing aside his sunveil so she could see his face in the small remote entry screen.

Diana punched in the entrance codes. "Will, it's Peter—"

"Got it." He tucked the gun into his sleeve holster and went to the door.

Diana went back to the bathroom and put the finishing touches on her makeup while Will let Peter in.

"Landreth." Peter's curt tone irked her.

"Stephens." Will responded with matching abruptness.

Silence. Diana hurried out of the bathroom. Peter stood near the door, his long white-blond hair carefully pulled back into a ponytail. He'd gone conservative for his attire, black suit and white shirt, black narrow-brimmed sunhat with matching sunveil that he held in black-gloved hands.

Peter groaned as she pulled on her thigh-high black boots with the white solar-charged insets.

"Di, damn it, why are you dressing like this? We're going to Greenways and you know how Mother feels about your band look. Especially *there*."

Diana shrugged. "I prefer this look."

She stood, shaking each leg to start the light cycle running up and down the outside seam of her boots. Maybe she should have chosen a less-confrontational ensemble, but in her experience, conciliatory measures only showed weakness to her mother. Sarah Stephens respected a good foe—and Diana had developed maternal confrontation to an art these days.

Besides, they were on the same side when it came to bioremediation, even though they were competitors. Sarah and Diana shared the same professional priorities, including their dedication to remediating toxic sites.

Personal and family issues were a different story.

"You *could* use a sunveil."

Diana snorted. "As if that's enough protection." She rummaged in her jewelry box for the four little skull earrings, focusing on keeping her hands steady as she slipped them into their designated piercings.

"*I* think it works," Peter snapped.

Jesus, Mary and Joseph, is he on the prod.

"Peter, what's going on? You're sure snappish tonight."

"Mother *could* use a little less drama from you," Peter muttered.

Despite herself, Diana laughed. "She's the queen of drama herself!"

"And what's got you all wound up?"

"Bad news about Dad and the ranch."

"Third Force relocations? He can buy his way out."

"Peter, he doesn't have money for a waiver, and the cancer's back."

"Then he should take the first offer." Peter shrugged. "That's what those offers are for."

"That's not enough for them to survive on. What the hell else is there to understand, Peter? He's sick. He's the stepfather who raised you when your own father wouldn't! "

Peter's face paled. "So this is what your clothing thing is all about."

"What? You and Mother didn't think I was going to find out? That I wasn't going to get pissed off about it? Peter, that ranch has been in the family for three generations! It's going to kill Dad even faster to leave it—and what about Jan and Rita? That Third Force offer isn't going to help them!"

"*Your* family heritage, not mine," Peter snapped.

"It was part of *your* family heritage for more than a few years growing up!"

"And I'm glad to be clear of it!" Peter shook his head. "To be honest, you're just as glad to be as free of that place as I am. Otherwise, you'd have stayed."

"I'm *not* going to see that ranch just disappear into some playboy's pocket because of Dad's cancer. One way or another, I'm going to find a way for it to stay in the family, even if it means I have to cut a deal with the devil himself to save the ranch."

"I wouldn't do that if I were you," Peter said.

"Well, anything is possible." Diana pulled on her soft black leather jacket, checked the sleeves and pockets for the security tools Will had recently implanted into the fabric, made certain of the small knives and pocket derringer in sleeves and boot top, and picked up her clutch. "Let's go. Get this over with."

She bent to kiss Will. Before she could pull away, he gently hugged her.

"I have an idea about the ranch," he whispered. "Do what you have to, but don't piss your mother off too much or burn any bridges. Talk when you get back."

"Thank you," she murmured. "I'll do my best."

She straightened up and nodded at Peter. "Lead on, brother mine."

Peter's mouth quirked in a quick smile and his eyes briefly brightened. "You haven't said that to me in years." His voice was softer than it had been.

"Sometimes it's a good idea to revisit old habits."

Peter nodded but didn't say any more. He deftly swiped the sunveil out of the way before settling the sunhat firmly on his head, then settled the dark veil that obscured his face. Diana picked up her own gloves and hat and put them on.

"Good luck," Will called after her.

"Thank you." She followed Peter down the stairs.

A FISH DINNER IN GREENWAYS

DIANA PICKED AT HER PEN-RAISED SALMON, THE BLAND FLAVOR AND HER knowledge about commercial fish contamination joining with nerves to spoil her appetite. The salmon was the least objectionable item on Greenways's menu from a food safety point of view, and the radiation levels were Stephens-certified clean. Her mother's company was the top of the line for radiation certs, so Stephens was the only cert Diana trusted for radiation.

But there were other problematic possible contaminants in the salmon, and the companies that did those certs weren't ones she trusted as much as she did Stephens.

Diana gave up on the salmon and sipped on her wine, avoiding her mother's probing glance. Old logging pictures covered the walls of the dark-paneled private dining room, some of them from operations run by Stephens Reclamation's predecessor, Stephens Timber. Greenways was located in what once had been the Stephens Timber executive suites, and this room had probably been the office for both Diana's grandfather and great-grandfather.

"You aren't eating much." Her mother ignored her own barely-touched plate with the same salmon. "Are you sure you're not sick?"

Diana shrugged. "Being sick is a fact of life in the Amazon basin, but no, I'm not sick. I'm just not used to eating a lot anymore."

Sarah Stephens put down her fork. She seemed smaller and

younger than usual in Greenways's big, high-backed armchairs. "You're working too hard." She frowned. "I can tell you've lost weight. You eating enough?"

And who would have I have learned how to work too hard and not eat much from?

"You're looking better than ever," Diana said as a diversion, sipping more wine.

"Another procedure." Her mother picked up her own wine.

Peter grimaced and took another bite of his steak. "You women and your *procedures*." Unlike Sarah and Diana, he had only juice to drink.

Wonder what's in that powder he keeps stirring into his juice? He's a fine one to talk.

"No surgery." Sarah sipped daintily at her wine. "Nano-directed cell regeneration. A new trial. Only rewires the cells to tighten up the skin enough to drop twenty years, but I'll take that."

Nanos?

"You sure they're safe? That's a fairly new beauty tech." Diana had started to research the use of nanos as part of biobot control programming. Safety factors led her to discard them.

Sarah shrugged. "They're not as invasive as those filed nano networks you tried to use for directing robots before leaving Stephens. They have less autonomy, therefore less likely to go rogue. And I have good access to medical support."

"It's still not ideal yet," Diana cautioned. "We've noticed psychological effects on our early adopters."

"Duly noted," Sarah said dryly. "I'm not too worried about it."

Silence fell around the table again. Peter picked at his steak while both Sarah and Diana studied their wineglasses. Diana bit back the temptation to speak first, focusing on the deep reds in her wine.

At last Sarah took a sip, then set her wineglass down. "Let's get to business," she said brusquely, dropping her tablet on the table. She traced a couple of symbols lightly on the screen, then flicked her fingers.

Relieved, Diana pulled out her tablet. The screen lit up as her mother's authorization code landed in the banking file. She traced in her matching authorization, and the figures popped up as the money transferred to Diana's personal account.

She studied the figures, frowning.

Not enough!

Not if she wanted to help her father. Maybe adequate for seed money to begin the North American expansion.

But still insufficient for everything I wanted to do this year.

A large chunk of contract money was also supposed to be included in that trust fund amount, but Diana didn't see a line item for that contract.

New bookkeeping system?

She could hope that a second payment was forthcoming.

"Is there a problem?" Sarah asked.

"I—well, I'd expected more. Especially for that subcontract from Stephens Rec. I thought that was a different line item to be added to this payment. Is it being made separately?"

The overtime on that contract alone would provide startup funding for the ranch rehabilitation.

"I *intended* to have that payment ready tonight, just as the contract said. But—slow pay to me from the Third Force," Sarah grimaced. "Sorry. I'll transfer those funds to your corporate account as soon as I get paid. You'll get it soon, I just can't confirm how quickly. Might be another year. I'll double the contract's late payment interest rate. The Third Force is having tax collection issues, and I can't make it up to you out of Stephens funds just yet. We've had some big long-term project launches in the last quarter."

"There's no way you could advance a partial payment?"

Oh, she understood what was going on, all right. No surprise that the Third Force was having problems collecting taxes.

How much of the relocation waiver funds are being siphoned off into private accounts? Along with tax payments.

"Not tonight, I'm afraid." Her mother's tone was polite but firm. Still, it held a tiny note of hesitation that hinted more negotiation might find a solution.

"I'd settle for quarterly payments." Was that a smirk on Peter's face? Diana resolutely refused to be distracted by her brother.

"I'd have to check." Still that faint hesitant tone.

Damn it. She wants me to beg. No. I won't beg.

And then Diana thought of little Rita practicing the barrels on her ancient pony in the old arena back at the ranch.

For Rita's sake…I might have to beg.

"I'd appreciate it if you could get back to me tomorrow." Diana deliberately let her voice waver on the word "tomorrow."

Sarah arched one brow. "Still, it's more than last year. Do you need a business loan against what I owe you? Your collateral's good for that." Her mother's mouth quirked in one corner and she looked down, but not quickly enough to hide the predatory sharpening of her gaze.

She took the bait.

Now for more delicate maneuvering.

Diana shook her head. "That amount's enough for business purposes."

"If you need a personal loan…" Sarah let the sentence hang.

"I'd—prefer not." Diana took a deep breath. "It's not for me. The Third Force has made Dad a relocation offer."

That earned her both brows shooting up.

Don't tell me you're surprised, Mother!

"Considering the condition of the ranch—" Sarah began.

Why am I not surprised she knows the ranch is in bad shape, but won't help Dad?

"Dad has nothing to do with the shape that ranch is in right now. Will's examining a soil sample I brought back. Someone sprayed toxic stuff on that property. If that spray's what I think it was, it'll take a lot of work to overcome its effects. Somebody *wanted* that ranch to fail."

"Because of his connections to me. And he hasn't the money to reconstruct it," Sarah's voice was surprisingly tight and brittle. "I know the situation, Diana!"

"He's dying." Diana fought to keep her voice emotionless. "Did you know *that*?"

Her mother's eyes briefly widened. "I didn't know."

"Cancer. Months, if not weeks. Or days. He's pretty frail."

"The Third Force proposition will give them something."

"Not enough to support Jan and Rita for long. He's given up. That's not Dad's usual behavior." Diana choked and swallowed hard. She took a long drink of wine, savoring the sweet cherry notes amongst the sharp dry tang. She blinked. Swallowed again, and coughed. "Rita's just eight." Her throat tightened again. "I've looked into the health care costs. If he'd told me sooner…."

"I can't fix this," her mother said. "Even if I'd known about the cancer, I can't."

"*Can't*, or *won't?*"

Sarah drew a deep hissing breath through her teeth. "Both!" she snapped. "That ranch is a silly albatross of an anachronism hanging around his neck! He had so much more potential—" Her mother stopped, biting her lower lip. Carefully, precisely, she took a tiny sip of her wine. Another sip. A third. "That's neither here nor there," she continued in a lower, calmer voice. "Issues you don't need to know about. More to the point, Di, my business financials are overcommitted right now. That's the *can't* piece. I might be able to squeeze out a quarter payment. That's the most I can do, and it'll take more than a day to pull it together."

"And the *won't?*" Diana's voice cracked.

"Helping your father makes him—and Jan and Rita—a target for certain interests to use against me." Sarah's tone was flat. "Helping him through you makes both you and them a target, more than you are already. And—well," her voice sharpened. "Quite frankly, the risk isn't worth the effort."

"I see," Diana said. "Well. Parker Landreth still owes Will royalties on devices Landreth Technologies continues to use. He's been wanting Will to sign over rights for stupidly low prices. My lawyers have advised us to avoid going after him unless we really think it's worth the expense. Now, maybe it's worth the hassle to try to collect."

The quick dismayed look on her mother's face was priceless. Then it faded, and Sarah laughed one short, sharp chuckle. "I could find a way to help you with *that* project. I'm sure Anne and Francis would kick in as well. Did I tell you Parker called me after your engagement to demand that I get my predatory bitch of a daughter away from his son?"

"After we pulled Will out of the PAZ. I'm not surprised," Diana said, keeping her voice neutral. "Though I can't say you've necessarily been much better about him."

"At least *I* didn't demand that Parker drag William away from you. I did thank him for the compliment. Told him that of course you were a predatory bitch, you were my daughter."

"Thank you." Diana drank the rest of her wine. Her mother had blunted the edge of her anger with that last comment about Parker. "Nonetheless, I think that in the worst case I'll be pursuing that option."

"That *would* be a worst case. I'd advise you to find other means."

Diana bit her lip to keep from commenting further. Sarah was just going to dance around the issue. A typical evasion pattern that her mother used when she didn't want to commit to something.

This is going nowhere. I have other things to do.

She stood up. "I've had enough to eat. Thank you for the money and the meal."

"Damn it, Diana!" Peter put down his fork. "I'm not done yet!"

"Nothing says you have to leave with me," Diana told him. "I'm perfectly capable of summoning my own cab and Security."

She put on her comm glasses and blinked up the code for the cab company. A matching alert went to her Security. Neither her brother nor her mother spoke as Diana brusquely ordered the cab.

She plucked the glasses off and tucked them into a jacket pocket. "I'll be seeing you at the Corporate Conclave." She bowed politely to her brother, then to her mother.

Peter scowled but nodded back, picking up his fork to continue eating. Her mother stared down at her plate, not meeting Diana's eyes.

She's pissed because I won't stay and argue with her about Parker Landreth and the ranch. Too bad.

Diana started to walk away. One step. Two steps. Three steps. If she played this right, though, her mother wouldn't let her go without some last zinger, some last offer.

Pushing it, pushing it—

"Diana." Sarah's voice was soft but firm. "One thing before you leave."

Diana stopped sharply. She pivoted to face her mother, but didn't come closer.

"Mother, I really don't have a lot of time to fool around with bantering, much as I know you love to play that way. I have to get back to work. I had a ton of research and budgeting to do to prepare for Conclave even before I knew about Dad and the ranch. Figuring out what to do with that situation just adds one more item to a very long list of things that need to get done before I return to Rio Bravo. One way or another, I need to find a solution for Dad, Jan and Rita."

"I understand," Sarah said wearily. "Believe me, I understand more than you think I. Listen. You need to go back up to the County."

Diana raised her brows at the traditional use of *the County* to refer to Ogden County. Not the typical reference from Sarah.

"I can't say more, at least not directly," Sarah continued. "But I can tell you that there may be other options besides the Third Force offer."

"Dad doesn't know about them."

"He wouldn't. And I am not welcome in those particular option discussions. Nonetheless, they exist. Would be best if you nosed them out quickly. I don't know something for certain, but if Relocation Affairs is involved, the faster you tie up an alternative deal, the better. If I were you, I'd go to the County tonight. I can get Anne to deflect for the next forty-eight hours, but—" she waggled her hand. "—I can't guarantee very much easing of RA's schedule."

"Noted." Diana softened her voice. "Thank you."

"I'm not *doing* anything except talking to your godmother," her mother said, looking away and picking up her fork. "Just making suggestions. Better go catch your cab before it attracts attention from the streeties."

"Thank you," Diana repeated. She hurried out of Greenways.

CONVERSATIONS ONE

"That's interesting," Will said as Diana repeated the key points of the meeting with her mother. "What's she up to now?"

"I don't know." Diana checked the mirror to make certain she'd cleaned off the last of her makeup, then splashed her face with cold water. "I think she's right. But I don't know just who I'd find up in the County to bankroll Dad."

"There are possibilities," Will said carefully. "At least there are options other than going to my father. I mean—*really*, Di? My father? I don't want to deal with that son-of-a-bitch, even to collect those damn royalties. Let sleeping dogs lie."

"He owes you. He owes my mother and Francis for getting you out of the PAZ."

"He left me to die." Will's voice turned cold. "As far as I'm concerned, even though I'm entitled to those damn royalties, I'd just as soon not even waste the time of day waking up that possibility for misery. Not an option, Diana. *Period*."

"It did get Mom off of her butt."

"Conservation allotments already exist up there. Working with a conservation group would be ideal. Jan and Rita could stay as tenants, possibly even working tenants depending upon the group. I've been trying to see if there's any interest."

"Can we trust your contacts not to blab this around?"

"Yeah. At least the folks I talked to. Family and friend associations from my school days." Will shook his head. "The Stephens connection —even as tenuous as it is for your father—makes their interest problematic. Besides, the people I talked to thought this sort of reclamation project is too ambitious for where we are right now."

"What do *you* think?"

"*We can do it.*" Will leaned forward, tapping the side of his right hand against his left palm to emphasize each word. "With the right amount of support and funding, we can do it." He sat back up. "However. Those groups won't provide it."

"I keep going back and forth about the feasibility," Diana said in a low voice. "It would be a big project."

"It would be a *huge* project." Will stopped tapping his hands and clasped them behind his head. "It's bigger than what most conservation groups would bankroll these days, without building a resort. There are other, less-damaged sites they could restore with fewer restrictions and more potential payback. However, if the tribe files Intent to Acquire on the land under the new laws, that stops the Third Force RA process while they're investigating that acquisition."

"Tell me more." Diana pulled up a chair. "I didn't think the tribe would take a serious look at the place, considering the condition it's in, as well as Dad's ties to my mother. Otherwise, I'd think they would have talked to him by now."

"There's a lot going on in Ogden County. They may not have gotten to the Andrews Ranch yet. Another possibility is that they're waiting to pick it up after the Third Force takes the property. However, that puts the tribe at risk of being outbid by a more affluent bidder. So—" Will shrugged. "I've been looking at angles to encourage the tribe to stop the RA process."

"What have you come up with?"

"We offer a significant discount on rehab services from DIR as part of our proposal," Will said. "I've created a DIR rehab proposal for turning the ranch into a destination recreation and wildlife resort. There are at least two similar projects in other North American tribal areas. If you can locate your father's broodmare herd, then that adds an authentic feel to the exclusivity of the ranch. Not many other high-end places can offer that sort of attraction, and there is a market for it."

"I didn't hear who bought the mares. Could be out of the area, but I'm hoping that maybe the tribe picked up the mares. If they did, that could sweeten the deal," Diana mused. "Heritage ranch and all that, with original stock."

"I added a training center as an additional project in my proposal. DIR supervises tribal rehab, and uses a facility on the ranch to train tribal rehabbers on DIR biobots. Once we've stabilized the ranch, there'll be continuing projects elsewhere. Create a partnership with the purpose of developing and training rehabilitators through DIR internships. Then that could give us a hiring pool of DIR-trained kids for future work. Both proposals have elements that let Jan and Rita stay on the land."

"An internship program like we've been developing in Rio Bravo?"

"Yes. It's time to do it here. Hmm. We could set up another central training program at a place like the Mountain property, once we get the startup funding pulled together. Begin with the ranch. A small project while we build a larger facility and team at the Mountain."

"The more I think about this idea the more I like it."

"Then you'd better dial up a skimmer and get your butt moving up to the County. Your mother's right, the faster the better. I'll flash you the final proposal." He dropped his hands, spun his chair around, and began typing. "I've sent you a list of potential contacts. I'll make a reservation at a Corporate residence for you—I'm assuming you don't want to bother your family just yet?"

"I'd rather not have Dad looking over my shoulder while I'm negotiating."

"Then I'll deal with reservations and dial the skimmer."

"Thanks." She kissed Will before going to pack.

DISCOVERIES

OLD HABITS REASSERTED THEMSELVES WHEN SHE WAS BACK IN THE COUNTY.
Diana was out of bed before sunrise, just like she used to do on the
ranch. Will had booked her into a small Corporate residence on Ogden
Lake. Diana remembered it as the home of an older couple that had
once been involved with County artistic politics, sponsoring sculptors
and painters. Some of their commissions decorated the house,
including bronzes of bucking horses, elk, and ducks. It was odd to
have the big single-level house to herself, the only other presence that
of on-site Security, feeling almost as if she were a little girl trespassing
in places she shouldn't be.

Diana shook herself.

Get over it.

But shadows of old childhood memories kept reasserting themselves. She picked up her coffee and ventured into the enclosed sun
porch overlooking the partially iced-over lake. Light snow had fallen
last night, and was now melting in the morning sun.

She considered the report she had skimmed last night while
drinking her coffee. Will targeted tribal acquisitions similar to her
father's ranch. Most tribal purchases had happened at auction, after
the Third Force's Relocation Affairs had paid off the former owners,
at well below the market price. As the North End ranchers failed to
pay their taxes, more claims had been filed. The tribe had purchased a

few, very few, ranches from the owners instead of from the Third Force.

A very interesting acquisition pattern.

She sighed and picked up her tablet. Time to see if anyone had followed up on Will's discreet inquiries.

Her third message was the one she had been hoping to see.

Get a horse from the stable at the head of the lake. You know what trail to start with. JayR.

Joaquin. Diana half-smiled.

Of course, the tribal contact would be her old high school buddy Joaquin Ridge. She hurried back to her room to change into riding gear.

A HORSE WAS ALREADY TACKED AND WAITING FOR HER AT THE STABLE. Her high school best friend and former neighbor, Terry Martin, grinned at Diana and pointed to the saddled black and white Appaloosa standing hipshot at the hitching rail, his bridle hanging from the saddle horn.

"That one's for you."

"Thanks, Ter." Diana hesitated. "Everything going fine with your family?"

Terry's mouth tightened slightly. "Mom passed last spring. Lung cancer. And—my father's sick as well. My sister's had breast cancer surgery. It's in remission, but she won't go near the ranch."

"Terry, I am so sorry. I didn't know. Too damn busy in the Amazon to keep track of people."

That's why the Martin ranch was one of the tribal purchases.

Terry shrugged, her face softening. "The People are taking care of us. They bought the folks' place and gave me the job here."

Maybe there's hope for this solution.

"My dad has leukemia. I'm worried about Jan and Rita." A chill shivered down Diana's spine. What if the ranch's problems weren't just from the spray? What *was* that radiation trace?

Cancer cluster? Downwinder effects?

Northstar.

Both the Andrews Ranch and the Martin Ranch were right smack in the middle of the downwind patterns that could carry radiation from the old nuclear reservation in the desert at Northstar. Diana had not considered that implication before. Supposedly any Northstar airborne radioactive releases had been monitored and announced. She had scanned those notices last night on the way here, following a longshot hunch. There hadn't been any notice of recent accidental toxic releases.

Except. Dear Mother of God. Northstar was supposed to be undergoing intensive remediation. The company doing it had outbid her mother's company.

A mistake, in Diana's professional opinion. Stephens Reclamation was the best in North America at radiological reclamation, much more effective than the secretive former defense contractor, Argos.

Did Argos accidentally release something and not announce it? Dirty, dirty, dirty, but they've done it before and always been able to buy off the Feds. Third Force probably isn't any less bribable. That might be an additional explanation for the ranch's condition—oh ho. That also explains Mom's evasiveness about helping Dad. Why she won't intervene directly. Reclamation politics. Why wouldn't Mom have said something outright? Because Argos might be involved. And Argos management culture is such that they would definitely try to act against her through Dad. She has to lay low. But me—I see your plan now, Mom!

Terry frowned. "Your dad's ranch looks worse than our place."

"He says it's overspray from the old Fed program, but now I wonder." Diana kept her voice low.

Terry looked around cautiously. "You're right to be concerned. We never had the support to follow up, but with all the weird sicknesses over the past few years, there's been more than a few of us with questions. What do you think? You're the pro."

"I don't have enough information yet, but what I've been seeing is suspicious."

Okay, Mom. You can't openly help Dad. But I can, because Do It Right isn't a competitor with Argos in radiological rehabilitation like Stephens is. God. Why couldn't you have gotten me involved sooner?

Then again, how fast had this situation been developing? Her mother had burned too many bridges in the County during her divorce from Dan Andrews over thirty years ago. Ogden County was the only place that Sarah's usually adept political skills seemed to falter. She might not have known how serious the situation was here until last night. If Sarah suspected Argos was up to something, it would have been wiser to wait for Diana's return. Alerting her before she came back from Brazil would have attracted unwanted attention.

God, Mom, what a gamble.

It wasn't an encouraging thought.

Relief flashed across Terry's face. "I didn't think we were imagining it. But we were told not to spread rumors because things are politically touchy."

"I'm getting that same vibe loud and clear, Terry."

"Our negotiations were really quiet until we went to the Tribal Council. Never was clear on why. I hope you can get it figured out, Diana, this is really worrying."

"I'm doing my best."

"Good." Terry nodded toward the horse. "There's a locked old-style GPS in the pommel saddlebag. You probably don't need it for the first part but it's there. Seems very cloak and dagger to me, but hey. Our deal operated like this, too. The People really want to keep some acquisitions quiet. One reason Jay wanted me to set you up this morn-ing. I already know the dance. Follow the GPS and—well—good luck."

"Thanks. Where's the bill?"

Terry shook her head. "No bill. It's—covered."

"Terry—"

"It's covered," Terry said firmly. "Just—do what is needed."

"Thanks, Terry," Diana said, feeling inadequate. "If you ever need anything…"

"I'll keep you in mind. You'd better get going." Terry headed out of the stable office, heading for the horse. "Griffin here is steady-footed on snow and ice, but even so, you'll need to tie him and snowshoe part of the way."

Diana nodded, noting the snowshoes tied to the horse's saddle. "He'll be okay?"

"Feedbag in the saddlebag on this side." Terry slapped the bag. Griffin switched his tail but didn't startle. "He'll be happy."

"Got it."

Diana checked the cinches and investigated the saddlebags, including the long bag on the gelding's right side that held the snowshoes. She looped the lead rope over the saddle horn, then slipped the bridle on over the halter. She adjusted the reins, mounted, grunting at the stiffness tugging at her thighs from the ride just—yesterday? Seemed like longer.

"What happens when I run out of satellite links?" Connectivity could be an issue in the mountains.

"Rest of the route is dictated," Terry said. "That's why the old-style GPS instead of using your comm glasses."

Diana hung the GPS around her neck. She clicked it on. "Everything's voice-activated?"

"Yes."

"Then I guess I'm off. Thanks, Terry."

"Good luck." Terry stepped back as Diana spun Griffin around and pointed him toward the mountain trails.

The GPS confirmed her trail choice. As soon as they passed the low head hydro plant on the creek and started climbing, Diana relaxed in the saddle, occasionally checking the GPS to confirm her memory of this trail. It switched back and forth as it wound up the mountainside, and before long the occasional snowbanks in the shade became first a skiff of icy snow, then deepened.

But there was still a trampled path through the snow for the sure-footed Appaloosa to find his way, until they reached a wide spot with a fallen tree, where the GPS directed Diana to leave Griffin. A bay gelding was tied to the downed tree with a nosebag on. He raised his head high, pricking his ears toward Diana and Griffin.

Diana dismounted, slipped off the bridle and hung it on the saddle horn, then took Griffin over to the icy mountain stream to drink before tying him further down the fallen tree, out of reach of the other gelding. Griffin forgot all about the other horse as soon as she secured the nosebag on his head.

Diana strapped on her snowshoes and checked the GPS. Now it was a list of instructions.

Hike .45 miles up the trail to the lodgepole widowmaker.

"As if there aren't already enough widowmakers in these trees," Diana grumbled. Nonetheless she set the GPS to warn her at .44 miles and trudged uphill. Surprisingly, the lodgepole widowmaker stood out, leaning against a dead white fir on the other side of the trail.

Turn right to go downhill. Follow the tracks.

Diana eyed the tracks. It looked like Joaquin had simply chosen to go bushwhacking.

How far downhill do I go?

She looked at the GPS again.

When the tracks disappear, take off your snowshoes and walk upstream.

"Damn it, I really didn't want to go wading," Diana muttered.

Still, she plunged on, grateful she wore waterproof boots. When Joaquin's tracks ended at a creek, she pulled off her snowshoes and began wading up the unfrozen portion of the rivulet. She knew what he was doing now. Joaquin had always enjoyed playing cloak and dagger scenarios, and after talking to Terry—well, if Argos and Northstar were at issue, she could understand why he wanted to keep things quiet.

When the rivulet faded to sheer ice, she stopped and looked around. Nothing.

Diana waited. She breathed deeply, savoring the cold, pine-scented air, dry, crisp, and icy.

A branch snapped behind and to her left. Diana turned her head to catch the faint movement, then faced buckskin-and-moccasin-clad Joaquin, squatting on top of a downed log and grinning at her. He resembled pictures she'd seen of old-time trappers from the nineteenth century, although his long black hair was neatly plaited into two braids, topped by a black fur hat that looked more Cossack than Native American. Smile wrinkles marked the weathered skin on his brown face.

"Joaquin. It's been a while."

"It's good to see you, too, Di." He stepped off of the log while Diana scrambled out of the creek.

"Did we need this much secrecy?" she asked.

"Given what we're talking about—yes. And we'll need to be

discreet on our way back." Joaquin led her to a tent. "Welcome to my woods office."

"It's comfortable." She sank gratefully into one of the two camp chairs. The tent was warm, a heating brick glowing steadily near her chair. Diana stripped off her gloves and unzipped her coat. "How's your folks?"

"Doing well," Joaquin said as he brewed tea over another heating brick. "Happily retired and living on the river. Dad's teaching kids how to fish while Mom is the Basket Queen."

Diana chuckled. "She's always made gorgeous baskets. Someday I hope to have enough extra cash to buy a couple. What about your sister?"

"Nita's getting a degree in bioremediation."

"Have her contact my husband Will in Portland. We have openings from time to time, and she might be able to finance her studies by doing contract work for us."

"That would be a good thing. Nita's been hoping that she could find something in a company like Do It Right instead of Stephens or Argos."

"We can always find a place for friends as we expand," Diana said. "And you?"

"Busy. Lots of tribal business." Joaquin handed Diana a cup. "Lots of negotiating. I'm the chief land acquisitions negotiator for the tribe."

Diana wrapped her hands around the cup, warming up before beginning more serious talk.

"Weather's quite a contrast from the Amazon." She sipped the slightly astringent herbal blend, tempered by a hint of spearmint.

"I imagine so." Joaquin settled in his chair and stretched out his legs, sipping his own tea. "How's your family?"

"Will can't leave the country yet. Part of his parole for the PAZ and —other things." Diana stared into her cup, deciding not to talk about Will's PTSD. "I'd like to change that so we could be together more, but," she shrugged. "The Amazon is where my core business is right now. A long-term commitment. But it's near the point where I can put someone else in charge most of the time. While I can expand my business overseas, I'd like to develop some further options."

"So you'd like to find something in North America."

"Something with potentially the same scope."

Joaquin nodded. "Your father's ranch."

Here we go.

"It's a possibility. But I need more funding than is available to me," Diana sighed. "And I understand that there's some political concerns."

Joaquin chuckled. "You could say that. Terry talk to you?"

"She said her family got help from the tribe." Diana looked down into her cup, then looked back up. "Joaquin. What the hell is really going on here?"

"Long version or short version?"

"Whichever version tells me what I need to do to save the ranch."

Joaquin laughed. "Straight to the point as always, Di!"

"Jay!" At last, she felt comfortable using his nickname. "What am I getting into?"

"Tell me what you already know, so I'm not wasting our time."

Diana drained her teacup. Joaquin poured more for her. She studied him, noticing the additional tension lines around his eyes and the gray strands in his dark hair, the leathery skin pulled down tight against his high cheekbones that made him look older than he was.

Not been an easy time here. He's my age but he looks older.

The transition from the old US to the Third Force coalition had not been easy on people or organizations.

"I know something got done to Dad's ranch, possibly others around it. Dad's dying of cancer. Terry's family is fighting cancer. I suspect if I look around at nearby ranches that I'll see that the alleged overspray struck in other places. I've only skimmed Will's preliminary report so I can't give you details, but my quick scans suggested radiation levels weren't right, and there were other elements that suggested more than overspray happened."

Joaquin nodded. "I'd be interested in seeing Will's report."

"I have it and can send it to you when we're done here. Keep in mind that it's just a prelim," she cautioned. "We need to take more samples to have a comprehensive result. I'm hoping to do that today."

As well as break the news to Dad about what I'm doing.

"Good. I'll be eager to see what your scans show, and cross-check the data we've been collecting. I can tell you, from what little we've been able to do in that specific area, that your father's ranch is the worst hit."

"Can you give me your data as well?"

"Certainly."

"Thanks." Diana stared into her cup, gathering her thoughts further. "Dad's gotten a low-ball offer from the Third Force. He's already sold all the livestock, including, damn it, the broodmares and young horses. If I want to rebuild his bloodlines, Kokanee is the only product of his breeding program that I have left."

Joaquin shook his head. "The stock is not a problem. I've been keeping track of where most of the herd went—the tribe has an interest and they went to friends. They can be recovered." He raised a brow at Diana. "After all, if the People work with the Andrews Ranch, we'll want the distinctive bloodlines your father created, for both horses and cattle."

You stinker. You've been thinking about this for a while, haven't you?

"Yes," he said, as if she had spoken her thought out loud. "We've been looking at the North End ranches for some time. Given your father's breeding programs, we have—shall we say—an interest in what becomes of his ranch."

"This wouldn't be happening if—well—circumstances. Money. That's the big issue. Dad needs money that he doesn't have. He won't talk to my mother, and what resources I have are limited." Diana shook her head. "I have to attend Corporate Conclave, and then I'm back in the Amazon. I don't know if I'll be able to pull everything together in this short a timeframe, but I can get things started. Will can manage it from there."

"Parents." Joaquin grimaced.

"Yeah." Diana leaned back in her chair, savoring the warmth creeping through her body. "Both of mine. Mother could have stepped in to help but she can't and won't because—well, now I have to wonder to what degree Argos is involved in what happened at Dad's ranch and the neighboring ranches. I know for certain she suspects that Argos is a factor."

"That all you know about what's going on with Stephens and Argos?" Joaquin's eyes narrowed.

Diana shook her head. "Mother doesn't keep me in her confidences. If the People and Will come up with data that points to illegal substance releases by Argos and file against Argos in the name of my father and the other ranchers affected, then I'm certain she'd provide indirect support. All in the name of sniping that Northstar contract away from Argos for Stephens Rec, of course."

"Of course."

"Joaquin, I'm not running a stalking horse for my mother."

"Did I say you were?"

"The needed rehab to keep the ranch viable and provide an income for Jan and Rita once Dad's passed on will be expensive. Will and I can't raise the funds ourselves on this short a timeline. Conservation groups aren't interested because of Dad's connections to Mom, and they can't develop it into a resort property like the tribe can because of Third Force regulations. Which leaves—" She met Joaquin's eyes directly. "The tribe. The People. We've checked your acquisition patterns. You're looking for places like my dad's ranch."

"Can Do It Right do the recovery project at a price we can afford? I've made inquiries. It's difficult to get data about your company, unless you're in the reclamation industry."

"It's a stretch to start with," Diana admitted. "But the challenge is a logical next step in our business plan. I hadn't planned for an opportunity to come up this soon. A year from now, maybe."

"Opportunities seldom happen as planned."

"True. We're willing to cut a deal. Use the ranch to build a rehabilitator training program. At the end, we'd hire the best workers for other projects, leaving us with a full training program up and running. That's what Will and I are doing in the Amazon. It means jobs and retraining options for local residents, and helps us build a pool of rehab staff to expand operations in North America."

Joaquin nodded. He leaned back in his chair, intertwining his fingers together and resting his chin on his folded hands, staring at the heating brick. "Your proposal is with you?"

Diana took a deep breath. "Yes. I have a formal site plan with different alternatives."

Thank God Will kept our templates up to date so he could knock it off last night while I was traveling. This is a bigger proposal than we've done in the past.

"We will need to update it with more data as I gather it," she added.

Joaquin pulled one of the new hologlobes out of his pocket. "Will it open in this?"

"Will makes his work easily transferable."

"Good. Flip it over."

Diana pulled out her comm glasses, and flashed their Preliminary Proposal for the Andrews Ranch Remediation and Development to Joaquin's globe. He traced through it, nodding to himself, then flicked it out, shutting the globe.

Diana raised a brow at Joaquin. "What's the process going to be?"

"I've sent it to the Tribal Council though my special connection. They'll look at your proposal this morning," Joaquin sighed. "Di, I don't have the authority to accept this contract on my own. The best I could do is to get you a slot today on the Consideration Calendar—did that when I got your message, expecting this—and a promise of quick response. We're running tight on funds ourselves. This might be doable, but I don't make the final call. I just negotiate."

"Thank you."

"We will get back to you quickly, to give you time to search out other options if necessary. We can say yes or no today, hash out the details over time if we accept. I just can't guarantee anything until we see your data on the contamination."

"I need *some* assurance, Jay. Other options will to take longer than Dad has."

"What happens when your father dies?"

"Unless he's changed his will, it all goes to Jan. At that point she'd have to sell. She and Dad had to split out finances a few years back, thanks to her family situation."

"He could leave it to you."

"I don't have the money to support it yet. Not on my own. If I could get some backing, from the tribe or someone else, then that's a different proposition. But without funding, there's no way I could dedicate the time this project would need. We need to get this settled before he dies."

Joaquin nodded. "Understood. Well, then, Will's report would be a good addition to your proposal."

"At the very least, can we get the Council to file Intent?"

"*That* I can and will promise. With the sending of this data, the process for filing Intent has been started. Putting this proposal on the Council's Consideration Calendar freezes the RA option."

"Thank you."

"Dealing with this problem is not going to be easy, Di. If Argos learns what you're trying to do—they'll counter-propose to Relocation Affairs, and the Third Force could swing their way. It's touchy. If we have data suggesting malfeasance on the part of Argos and their fronts, then we're protected, but we need that good, strong, data. Even *I* know that your mother is reluctant to take Argos on."

"But between Anne Whitman and the resources of the People, I'd think she'd be a strong candidate to challenge Argos—"

Joaquin shook his head. "The Council won't work with your mother directly. Never with her. Long story and I don't have the authorization to share it. But you, that's different. Put on your glasses." He flashed her a file. "Send this to your Will when you are back within data range, highest security. Don't do it here. Too easily traced."

"I can do that. So what's in the file?"

"Data we've gathered on Argos. If you can add to it and confirm that data, then that gives us more support to pick up the option on your father's ranch and award Do It Right the rehab contract."

"I will keep this safe." She blinked up Will's report and sent it to him. "Here's Will's report on the soil samples and the data I gathered off of Dad's ranch yesterday. If you can send us the report on Tracy's folks' ranch, he can add to it."

"We'll send that. Thanks. The data I've given you—not to be shared with your mother in that form," Joaquin cautioned. "Run it through filters first to eliminate all non-DIR links before you give it to her."

"Why?"

"Your mother can use it to best effect through her connections, but she is—possibly compromised through other connections. We will work with you. Not with her. We trust your security. This information was gathered from resources that she and others best not know about."

Internal sources. A chill ran down Diana's back. *Possibly illegal. Mom and Stephens are signatory to a lot of alliances that DIR and I aren't. And then there's her connection with Francis. God. Am I just a conduit for information here?*

She couldn't, *wouldn't,* explore that line of thought further. There was caution and then there was stark raving paranoia.

Except when it comes to Mom, Anne, and Francis. They're laws unto themselves.

"I'll protect that data."

"See that you do."

Diana swallowed hard. "Before I look at this data, I need to know. Is possessing it likely to cause a problem for Will? I don't want to be in the Amazon and find out that he's been taken into custody for violating industrial espionage agreements."

I won't put him through anything that even smells like the PAZ situation.

Joaquin sat back and raised one brow. "It shouldn't be an issue. But if it is, I'm betting that your mother wants this information enough that she will protect you, and through you, us. We will defend your husband should any problems arise."

"Will the tribe offer him—us—a refuge if that becomes necessary?"

Joaquin raised a brow. "Give me a moment." He traced writing inside the hologlobe, then waited, studying the globe. It flashed once. He looked back up. "If refuge is needed, it will be extended to both of you. The risk is worth it to all of us."

"That's a big gamble."

But precisely calculated, if it's good enough.

Coming from Joaquin, the odds *would* be carefully calculated. He might be a gambler, but as she remembered from past poker games, Joaquin usually won when he committed to a bet.

Joaquin smiled. "I'm sure it's a risk you'll be willing to take."

She drained her tea. "So we have an agreement. Intent will be filed today?"

"Intent will have been filed by the time you return to the stable."

"Why are the People working with me? Why not directly with my mother? Stephens Reclamation carries much more weight than Do It Right. What did my mother do?"

"Trusting Stephens Reclamation and your mother is—" Joaquin waggled a hand back and forth. "—an uncertain proposition. As I mentioned before, the door is closed to working with your mother. I have people to protect. You would be sufficiently careful to protect them from Argos's wrath. Your mother—she might choose to protect, she might not."

The ranch doesn't mean much to Mom, while that's a hold over me. This deal gives the ranch to the tribe. But—Dad and Jan and Rita. If the ranch goes to the Third Force, God knows what they'd do with the land. I know the People will preserve it.

Diana finished her cup and set it down carefully. "I had best be going. Even with the People filing Intent and stopping the Third Force acquisition timeline, I have many other things to do, including fundraising for this project." She stood and stretched.

They shook hands. "Someone from the Council will contact you today. I think you might find that possibilities for additional support funding will already be waiting."

Diana snorted. "Jay, have you been waiting for something like this to come up so you could drag me into tribal politics?" She let herself smile.

Joaquin laughed. "Di, even without our past history, you come well-recommended by our friends in the Amazon. With you in charge of this rehabilitation, I am certain that justice will be done. This situation provides a catalyst for many things to happen. I look forward to the prospect of many years of successful collaboration between the People and Do It Right. And if this collaboration means that Do It Right becomes a force for bioremediation in North America as a result —then I am even more pleased."

"As am I."

If I have to be indebted to anyone for saving the ranch, I'd much rather it be the People.

CONVERSATIONS TWO

THE NOTICE OF INTENT POPPED UP ON DIANA'S COMM GLASSES WHEN SHE switched it on. Diana skimmed it, then smiled.

On our way now.

She set the skimmer on automatic return to the Corporate residence and went to work. She edited and encrypted Joaquin's file, then sent it to Will. Finally, she checked her calendar to see if any of the other appointments she requested had come through.

Two denials, with regrets.

A third, the least likely possibility, came through. It listed no time for a meeting, so she would have to contact them to set it up. Diana frowned at that one. The Coalition for Environmental Responsibility had been the long shot on Will's list because of its corporate ties and past investment history.

Still, the Coalition was quirky, and they could legitimately be unhappy about what had happened at Northstar. Worth talking to them, even if their confirmation lacked a firm time, and no mention of who would be meeting with her. She sent back the confirmation notice, adding a request for a specific time. At least she could listen to what they had to say.

As Diana took over the controls for a direct landing, she saw someone standing by the skimmer pad, squinting toward her rented skimmer. For one quick moment she thought it was Will—same slight, sparse build coupled with long blond hair. Then she noticed the Landreth Technologies logo on the other skimmer parked on the pad, and her gut tightened.

What the hell?

It had to be Will's father, Parker.

What is he doing here?

Diana felt for the defensive weapons Will had built into her sleeves.

Had Argos had gotten wind of her interest in the ranch? Parker Landreth had done work for them in the past.

Damn, damn, damn. Parker is bad news.

Diana took a deep breath before switching off the skimmer, gathering herself up, and crawling out. Parker scowled at her as she straightened up taller than him and slipped on her comm glasses. His lips pressed together tightly, just like Will did when he was angry about something.

How the hell do you greet your estranged father-in-law? Especially when he looks angry enough to kill you—and has the tools to do it?

She stood in front of Parker, meeting him glare for glare.

You treat him like he'll sting you when you least expect it.

"Parker." She kept her voice neutral. "A surprise to see you here."

"I'm not exactly delighted, myself."

Diana slung her bag over her shoulder, taking that moment to grab another deep breath. "So do I owe the pleasure of your company to— my mo—*brother*," she changed quickly, "or someone else?"

Her mother wouldn't sic Parker Landreth on Diana over the Andrews Ranch. That would be something Peter would do. Peter worked regularly with Landreth Technologies on defense weaponry. Her mother—dislike couldn't begin to describe Sarah's attitude toward Parker. The only mutual agreement between Parker and Sarah was their initial objection to her marrying Will.

"You contacted the Coalition for Environmental Responsibility to discuss a conservation estate," he growled. "I'm your contact."

What. The. Hell?

Will wouldn't have set up a solo meeting with the Coalition if he thought his father was involved. Diana glanced about. No sign of Landreth Technologies Security.

"Let me check with Residence Security to ensure the conference space is secure." She tapped her alert code into her wrist sensor, acutely aware that Parker's eyes followed her fingers.

Damn. He's even more alert to possible sensors than Will.

"I came without Security," Parker said.

Her glasses confirmed it when she blinked the inquiry. "I'm surprised."

Parker smiled, but it didn't touch his lizard-like eyes. "Let's just say that I saw an opportunity to get to know my son's wife a bit better."

Diana tagged another code to alert Residence Security. "I'm flattered. It's been long enough since Will and I got married. I'd have thought curiosity would have sparked your interest in me sooner."

Parker offered his left arm to Diana. "Then it's even more important that we talk."

The courtly gesture took her by surprise. *Was* he being courtly? No. She'd have to give him her right arm. With her wrist sensors. *Not* a good idea.

Diana let her bag slide off of her left shoulder. "Darn bag." She caught it with her right hand and swung it over her right shoulder. "Sorry." She offered Parker her left arm, the one without sensors. "My bag's more stable on this side."

A brief scowl tightened Parker's lips before his face went expressionless. Without comment, he delicately twined his right arm with her left, bringing his left hand over hers to keep Diana from feeling for his sensors.

Diana stifled the absolutely inappropriate giggle.

God, Parker's everything Will said he was.

But she couldn't keep the corners of her mouth from turning up.

"Something amuses you?"

Was that irritation in his voice? Almost too easy to provoke him.

Careful. He's not Mom. He won't have her tolerances for smartass mouth.

"Just the delicate dance there." She glanced sideways with faked demureness.

"My son taught you well."

Was that a hint of admiration?

"Don't assume I learned everything I know from Will," she said.

They reached the house. To Diana's surprise, Brenda, her personal head of Security, opened the door.

She's not supposed to be here until Conclave.

It didn't matter. Brenda was present, and a welcome sight with Parker Landreth clinging to her arm.

"Brenda, could you please escort Mr. Landreth to the conference room?" Diana deftly untangled herself from Parker. "Please give me a moment to freshen up," she said to Parker.

"I came here without Security," he growled, glaring at Brenda. "That implies a level of trust."

"I understand." Diana exchanged a glance with Brenda. "Please make Mr. Landreth comfortable, then return to stations, Brenda."

Brenda nodded twice curtly, acknowledging the phrase *stations,* their code for *remain out of sight but be ready to move.* "We just arrived," she said. "Fresh coffee made, brought the beans with us from Brazil."

Fresh coffee. Code phrase for *urgent summons. Brought the beans* identified Will as the one issuing the call. Cold prickles danced down Diana's spine.

Something set Will off. But why didn't he say anything last night?

"Fresh coffee from Brazil?" Parker's voice was noticeably much more cheerful. "I definitely can't pass that up."

"Right this way," Brenda said, guiding him toward the kitchen.

Diana hurried into her bedroom and grabbed her tablet.

A message from Will came up. *Forgot to tell you last night. Too much happening, slipped my mind. Sent for Brenda and Tony. Should be there by midmorning. Something about this ranch situation doesn't feel right.*

Diana snorted. "I'll say," she said out loud. A second, urgent message flashed on the tablet, from Will.

What's going on? MESSAGE ME.

Had she sent him her schedule this morning? She'd been in such a hurry to meet Joaquin that she couldn't remember if she had done that or not. And she hadn't sent an explanation with Joaquin's file.

Met with old friend Joaquin who's the tribal contact, she typed. *He's the source of the file I just sent. Brenda and Tony are here. So is your father, claiming to be the rep for the Coalition for Environmental Responsibility. What the hell?!*

She slid out of her riding clothes, dropping them into a secure bag for Brenda to screen later. Hopefully any bugs Parker had planted on her were just on clothing.

Brenda can scan the quarters while we're talking.

She would be careful until Brenda could scan her personally. Diana popped into the shower for a quick cleanup, then pulled on the formal suit she had brought for meetings like this. After dressing and scowling at her lanky form in the mirror, she picked up her tablet again.

Dad's had many interests over the years but this is new to me, Will had texted back. *Confirms my suspicions about CER, but I'm not certain of all the linkages. Damn glad I got Brenda and Tony there. You be careful. I'm on my way.*

"Now what the hell does *that* mean?" Diana whispered, staring at her tablet.

Whose game am I playing?

Her head spun with the possible combinations. Nonetheless, she needed to find out if she had half a chance to convince her father-in-law—or those he worked for.

She dropped by the kitchen to check in with Brenda.

"Got *him* settled in the sun porch conference room," Brenda said as she scanned Diana's arms. "We'll pull out of the house, like he wants." She plucked a minuscule dot off of Diana's left wrist. She flicked it into a secured pouch, then scanned again, nodding to herself. "Clear now. You secured the clothes you were wearing?"

"Absolutely." Diana picked up the waiting cup of coffee.

"Good. I'll scan the clothes and your bedroom, then pull out. Tony will be ready, in case you hit your hot button before I'm done." Brenda tsked and shook her head at Diana. "Didn't Will ever tell you not to let his father touch you?"

Diana grimaced, remembering how her mother had needed to ditch a skimmer that Parker had immobilized, and Francis arguing with Sarah about the need to leave it. "I remember Mom's skimmer. But I've never been in a position to worry before now, and—well—I couldn't think about anything other than keeping him away from my sensors. I had to play bag games."

"I saw that. Good move. I'm surprised he only got you with one. Old man's slipping. Or else he gave up when he couldn't bug your sensors. Got your tablet set to record?"

"I have. Does he have one?"

"Yes."

"Then it's mutual. Any further suggestions?"

"Just—be careful. He probably wants the sun porch so he can tight-beam to his Security." Brenda scowled. "Didn't have time to set up our blockers. I'll try to get them active while we're outside."

"No. Leave it."

Brenda raised her eyebrows.

"Let's not give him any excuse to create a situation or claim we've manufactured a recording. And if his recording differs from mine...."

"Good move."

"Okay. Here I go, into the lion's den. Wish me luck."

"Just remember that lionesses are the better hunters. Luck."

Diana headed for the sun porch. Her father-in-law stood at the window, staring out at the lake.

"I didn't know you had an interest in the County." Diana set down her tablet and her coffee on the table behind Parker, triggering her tablet's recording function.

He turned, still scowling. "The Coalition has had interests here for many years, since long before you were born."

"Oh." She gestured to a chair on the other side of the table. "Please sit down."

Why did I not know this?

Diana frowned at a shadow skittering across the lawn. She should know about any ties the Coalition had to the County. She'd grown up here. There was one possible explanation. If the Coalition had been here that long, it meant that it had deeply buried ties to old and reclusive County families that were on the outs with the Andrews clan.

Powerful families—none of them environmentally oriented. God. Could this have been an astroturfing group from the '00s?

"I've—not heard of the CER in the County before," she said carefully.

"You wouldn't have."

"I guess you learn new things every day."

Parker snorted. "That's not what I'd expect Sarah Stephens's daughter to say."

He set down his coffee and flopped into a chair, hands resting gracefully on its arms, giving her the same keen-eyed stare Will would when he considered one of her difficult new project assignments. Unlike Will, his lips twisted in a slight sneer.

Oddly, that reassured her. This particular type of scrutiny was something Diana had grown to live with over the years.

So you're Sarah Stephens's daughter. Are you as tough as she is?

Familiar ground.

"I'm also Dan Andrews's daughter." Diana matched Parker's glare. "I'm here as an Andrews. The Third Force has sent my father a relocation offer. I want to keep my family in their home."

"You mean Do It Right has nothing to do with this little proposal Will sent the CER?" Parker asked mockingly, raising his brows as he leaned forward to grab his coffee. "Sure didn't look that way from what I read."

Diana sipped her coffee, counting to herself. *Two. Four. Six. Eight. Ten.* She didn't look away from Parker, waiting.

At last he chuckled. "You don't stampede much, do you girl? Starting to see just what it is my son likes in you."

Diana balanced the cup in her fingertips, giving Parker a small smile. "In some respects, I'm also Sarah Stephens's daughter."

Parker nodded. "True. But the question still stands. Do It Right is written all over that proposal."

"You think I'd hand over rehabbing my father's ranch to my mother's company? You don't know me very well if you think that's the case."

"Do you even know who and what's involved in that ranch's condemnation?"

Argos. He knows that the Northstar contamination is a factor. But why use the word "condemnation?" Did he just tip his hand or was that a slip of the tongue—and do I acknowledge or ignore it?

Acknowledge. Let's see what I can get him to admit.

"That's an interesting word, *condemnation*." Diana carefully kept her tone neutral. "Especially since, to my knowledge, that word hasn't been used in any discussions the Third Force has had with my father."

"Come on, Diana!" Parker scowled at her, his face and neck reddening. "Will couldn't have prepared that report without knowing that Northstar is the source of that ranch's contamination! Those levels are damned near condemnation ranges."

"But they're *not* at condemnation ranges." Diana stretched her legs out in front of her, taking full advantage of her greater height to dominate space. "I find your use of the word interesting. As if you have access to data I don't have."

"Hah!" Parker snorted. "Don't tell me you haven't gotten an earful from your mother about Argos and its problems with Northstar. I know you had dinner with her last night. She's preparing a filing contesting that contract for failure to perform."

"You think the Northstar issues are going to get resolved in Stephens's favor anytime soon?" Diana forced a laugh. "You have more confidence in the Third Force's legal processes than I do. Even if the surveys come back the way I think they will." *Like they already have.* "Meanwhile, I have a father, a stepmother, and a young sister who need to be provided for. That's my interest."

"And getting your company a toehold in the North American rehabilitation market."

"There is that," Diana conceded. "But I'd be a fool not to use this opportunity."

"I would expect nothing less from a daughter of Sarah Stephens."

"Or of Dan Andrews. My father made money at ranching until his land was contaminated and he got sick. Running a ranch successfully, without outside investment, has been a lot harder to do these days."

"Oh, I'm not arguing that." Parker held his hand up. "Trust me, I've heard of your father's reputation. That mare line of Mocha's has a few individuals I wouldn't mind picking up for my own stock operation."

Diana raised a brow at Parker. "You raise stock?"

"I—invest in a few nice cutting horses for my own ranch. In Southpeak, Montana. In fact, were you thinking about selling that Kokanee mare of yours?"

"Kokanee isn't for sale!" Diana snapped.

A sick feeling came over her. Southpeak. That area was an Argos stronghold. The major shareholders in Argos had showplace ranches in Southpeak, and her father's horses had always outshone theirs in reined cowhorse competition. Hell, she'd shown—and won—against Southpeak horses.

"Too bad." Parker swallowed some coffee. Then he sat up. "Here's the deal. The rehab plan looks good. We would normally advance you a grant to provide for the initial setup but for one factor."

"Which is?"

"The parts of the proposal that include Do It Right as the primary contractor are unacceptable. Too much of this rehabilitation project depends on a skill set managing radiological elements that Do It Right lacks."

Despite herself, a sharp, bitter laugh broke free from Diana's throat. "You would advise that this contract work be done by Stephens Reclamation?"

That's it. The CER is definitely not an option.

"Not at all," Parker said, grinning toothily at Diana. "There are other companies."

He must mean Troy Environmental.

"Do you seriously think an Argos subsidiary would get approval to clean up their own messes?"

Parker shrugged. "Troy would be more acceptable than Stephens Rec. Who would you have subbed to, anyway, if not Stephens?"

"Will has the connections," Diana said carefully.

"William?" Parker snorted. "My son's ambitions overreach his abilities. You haven't discovered that yet about him, young lady?" His smile turned pitying. "Best you think carefully about any risky proposition my son devises."

"Thank you, but I think I'll go with my own experience with the value of *my husband's* business advice," Diana said, fingers tightening on her coffee cup as anger surged through her. *After all Parker's done to his son, he dares talk like that about Will?* "So that's the bottom line? A grant to fund start-up rehabilitation only, on the condition that Do It Right withdraws from participation in the rehab work."

"That's right." Parker's grin reminded her of a shark zeroing in on his prey.

Diana took a deep breath. She set down her coffee and stood up.

"I suppose this means there's no real need to discuss this possibility any further."

Parker Landreth rose, and again, in a gesture that reminded her of Will, bowed in her direction. "Indeed, that's exactly the situation. Are you interested in this offer?" The predatory grin tugged at his lips.

"I don't believe I will be." Diana shrugged, pretending a casualness she didn't really feel. "If it wasn't my father's ranch, perhaps I'd feel differently. But if it wasn't my father's ranch, I wouldn't be here."

"True." Parker inclined his head. "Nonetheless. You might want to think this over. You may find that other possible assistance is not as likely as it seems."

"Very possible," Diana said. "But I'm firm on my stance."

"I suggest you consider it further," Parker said. "And keep one thing in mind. Argos may not want to have Stephens find out what's in their scrubber mix. Getting support for your proposal might be harder than you think. You might not want to trade on your mother's name or help her against Argos."

"You're threatening me?"

"Take it any way you like, Diana. Like I said, don't be too hasty to reject this proposal." His voice sharpened. "Twelve hours and this offer expires. And you'd better be damned sure of what you're getting into. Tell my son this can be a Lakely situation if it goes the wrong way."

"A Lakely situation?" Diana repeated, not quite believing what she heard.

He dares bring up Lakely!

Albert Lakely had been the LT operative who had betrayed Will in the PAZ. Will had found other LT agents torturing Lakely using netspiders—or so he had thought at the time. Will had intervened, but it had been a trap set by Lakely and unknown others meant to eliminate Will. While Will and Diana suspected Lakely had put together the conspiracy on Parker's orders, they never had found a tangible connection.

More shadows.

"A Lakely situation. And girl, it matters not one bit to me that you call yourself a Landreth or an Andrews. You'll never be a Landreth or an Andrews to me. You're a Stephens, as much as if it were your mother herself standing in front of me. You understand what I'm saying?"

"Loud and clear," Diana said bitterly. "Nice talking to you, *father-in-law.*"

The angry stare he shot in her direction before marching out of the room was worth that final jab. Diana went back inside the kitchen and watched as he stomped over to his skimmer, Brenda and Tony following a precise three steps behind once he was clear of the house. Landreth climbed into his skimmer. It took off, exploding off the landing pad as if the pad were contaminated. Before the skimmer disappeared over the ridge, another one with Landreth markings popped up from behind the fold of a hill to follow it.

"Well, *that* certainly wasn't the best outcome," Diana said to the empty room.

But she had to admit it was educational.

SHADOWS OF THE PAST

PALPABLE TENSION VIBRATED THROUGH THE KITCHEN AS WILL LEANED ON the center island, listening to the recording of Diana and Parker's meeting. It had been the first thing he wanted to do upon his arrival.

Brenda stood near the door, studying her own tablet as they listened.

"He had the nerve to call this a Lakely situation?" Will exploded as the recording ended. "Damn it, I *knew* something felt hinky! I am so glad I called Brenda and Tony back and beat feet to get here. First thing I'm going to do is rescan everything in this house. *Everything.*"

"I had Brenda and Tony already do it. Twice," Diana said.

Will wheeled around, throwing his arms wide. "Diana! We're talking about my father!"

Diana gestured toward Brenda. "Brenda. Show Will the scans."

Brenda wordlessly handed the tablet to Will, a habit established from the early days after his rescue. Then, they had needed to scan their surroundings several times a day to relieve his anxiety.

He flipped through screens, frowning. "All right." He exhaled slowly, looking up and handing the tablet back to Brenda. "You incorporated my new trial frequencies."

"It *was* your father, after all," Brenda said.

"Yes." Will pressed his lips together firmly and paced around the kitchen island, his hands clenching and unclenching. "And I don't completely trust those scans. I think this location is compromised."

"We can use cones of silence and scramblers. We're already doing that," Diana said.

"That may not be enough," Will said, reversing direction, shaking his head, looking more frantic than ever, his fists trembling, his breath coming in short sharp gasps.

Oh no. Diana recognized the pattern she thought had finally faded. *The shadows still have their grip on him.*

Brenda met Diana's eyes, raising her brows in a familiar question. Diana nodded, gesturing toward the door. Diana waited until Brenda left, then stepped into Will's path, blocking him with her hands on his shoulders. He halted, startled, quivering under her palms.

"Will. Stop," she said, voice quiet and soothing, not commanding. "It's okay." He hadn't had a panic attack like this one in ages.

Dare I go back to Brazil if he's regressing?

The haunted face Will turned to her brought back ugly memories of the nightmarish days after his rescue from the PAZ.

"It's never going to be okay," he whispered. "Never. Oh God, Diana, when you said he'd been here—"

"Breathe, Will. Breathe."

"If he'd harmed you in any way—"

"But he didn't. And Brenda and Tony were here."

"God, Diana, if I'd known he was a part of it, I'd have never contacted the CER. I wouldn't risk you like this. God!" Will shuddered.

He squinched his eyes shut and drew a deep, trembling breath. Then he pulled her close, hugging her hard. They clasped each other tightly until Will's breathing slowed and his grip eased on her. He pulled back, fingers lingering on her arms before sliding to her hands.

A short panic attack. Good.

But it was still worrisome.

"I—I guess I'm not as over things as I thought I was," he said, his voice quiet. "I think I am, and then something like this happens. The shadows come back. Any threat to you brings back memories of the PAZ. I don't know why. Things go white."

"You don't need to explain." Her voice matched his tone. "I've not wanted to impose on my father, but maybe we should relocate to the ranch."

"We need to get him more Security support. Fast."

"We can set up a station there."

And that will distract you from this trigger.

"I think that would be the best thing to do."

"Let's get staff moving. I want to collect more samples. You brought bots?"

A faint grin briefly flitted across Will's lips. "All sorts of bots."

"I need to send some data to my mother. It'll be okay for me to do that?"

"Use scramblers."

"Doing so now."

Diana pulled her tablet over. She sent Brenda an all clear, and then began to type a message to her mother.

"What do you think he meant by that line about Argos?" she asked Will as she worked. "Offering to buy Kokanee and disclosing his Southpeak ranch just means that he's connected to them. Will, that area's been an Argos stronghold ever since I was a kid. I rode in competition against their horses. If your father has a ranch up there, then he's definitely tied to Argos."

"This is all new to me. He wasn't into ranches or horses when I was younger, and Argos wasn't that big a connection." Will pushed his bangs aside. "You're right. Either he's working with Argos, or he's going to include them in the ranch rehab."

"That makes me more nervous than ever."

"I hate to say this, but—" he hesitated. "You may want to call in Stephens Rec and your mother as backup."

"I just hate to do that," she said. "Besides daring him to come after us, the tribe won't like it, and without the tribe—"

"I know." Will slumped onto the island. "One other possibility. I've been talking with a couple of Japanese rehab companies that have radiological experience. They might end up outsourcing some work to Stephens—"

Diana closed her eyes and reopened them. "That sort of indirect connection would end up being more acceptable than Argos or

Stephens to the tribe. If we can get this proposal accepted. Now I'm worried."

"We've got reasons to be concerned about fallout from my father's interest. I—yeah. Let's do it. Hint to your mother that we may approach her indirectly about participation in this project."

"I need to review and tweak this proposal before I send it to her."

"I'll get the move going." Will squeezed her hand and kissed her before leaving the room.

Diana sighed. Will having panic attacks again wasn't a good thing. Then again, she'd been running her own quiet scans to check Security ever since Parker Landreth had left.

Relocating will help both of us. Will's not the only one haunted by shadows.

She considered calling her mother instead of just sending the file, and rejected that idea. She wanted more information first.

Besides, Diana felt reasonably certain she'd be hearing from Sarah soon enough. Odds were high her mother knew about Parker Landreth showing up with a proposal by now.

I'll give it an hour, but I bet I won't need to call her.

It took exactly thirty-two minutes and twenty-four seconds for her mother to call, just after they climbed into the skimmer. Will raised a brow as the connection chimed. He fired up the skimmer and sent them off the pad, almost as abruptly as his father.

Mother, she mouthed to him.

Will nodded curtly, lips tightening into a thin line.

"So," Sarah said. "Parker Landreth got involved."

"How did you know?"

"Ever since you married his son, Parker never passes up a chance to slam you when he can. I received a message five minutes ago telling me to get you out of the County." Her mother laughed sharply. "He should know better than that."

"He certainly should," Diana agreed.

Thank you, Parker.

If anything could push her mother into helping with the ranch, her father-in-law's demands would do it.

"Want to hear what he said?" she asked.

"I was hoping you recorded that conversation! Given the way he was spluttering when he talked to me, I knew it had to be *good*. You must have nailed him hard at some point."

Diana half-grinned. "I always record these discussions, except for ours, per our agreement. Glad to hear I made an impression—here you go." Diana started the recording yet again. "We're on our way to the ranch," she added. "Will's flying. He's heard it. I'm keeping it for your ears only, so he doesn't get distracted."

"Thanks," Will whispered.

"Good idea." Her mother went silent as she listened to the recording, then chuckled at Diana's final comment. "That's my girl. You got him right where it counts. Good job." She fell silent for a moment. "So he's after Dan's Mocha bloodlines amongst other things," she mused. "Kokanee's—her daughter? Granddaughter?"

"Granddaughter, top and bottom lines. Mom, he owns a Southpeak ranch. I haven't heard of anyone up there who doesn't have a connection somehow to Argos."

"Put me on," Will muttered, knuckles clenching white on the skimmer's yoke.

"Mom, Will wants to say something."

"You know something about this, William?"

"It's news to me that he has an interest in horses, much less ranches."

Sarah snorted. "It wouldn't be the first time some jumped up moneybags blows a wad on a ranch and thinks he's a horseman. I can just hear your father on that subject, Diana. Parker Landreth wanting that mare? Way out of his league. I knew Mocha's dam. She was a king-hell bitch on wheels for anyone but your father, and she damn near killed *him* when he was starting her. Took him a while to win her over. Your mare's a double Mocha. Extra sensitive. I doubt Parker could handle a horse like her. Damn sure he's a heavy-handed rider. On second thought, don't tell your father about Parker's interest in

Kokanee. Likely to give him a heart attack. You hear anything about what happened to your father's breeding stock?"

"I've been assured that they're in decent hands."

"Good. But that's a distraction and not the major stake. My guess is that Parker is angling to grab your dad's ranch once the Force condemns it. Then his Argos buddies can work their magic to turn the ranch productive again, but not like it should be. Do It Right is the company to do that."

"I absolutely don't want the ranch falling into Parker's hands," Diana said.

So Mom's on board with DIR doing the primary contracting. Nice to know.

"Definitely. He'll cover up for Argos. I'll sic Anne onto Parker. Keep him busy and out of your hair for a while."

"So to what degree is my father-in-law carrying water for Argos? I always wondered about the Coalition's connections."

Sarah snorted. "Your guess is as good as mine. I know there's been past ties, but Parker's never felt the need to share his concerns with me."

"Except when the two of you kept trying to break us up."

"Can you blame me?"

"Now? I may understand the reasoning but I don't approve of it." Diana took a deep breath. "That's not relevant to what we're doing today. Mother, what do you know of Argos's activities at Northstar? Especially in light of his claim that you're preparing to file a failure to perform action against them."

"Nowhere near enough. And I'd sure as hell like to know where he got *that* little notion about the filing. I've had limited discussions with Legal, but until now, I haven't had enough data to justify a filing."

"He seemed convinced you were doing it."

"And sometimes he has an overactive imagination."

"More likely you have a leak, Sarah," Will said. "My father doesn't say things like that idly. You can assume he knew Diana was recording."

"William, I'm pretty damned sure my crew is safe, but I'll run another check. It's probably a lucky guess."

"He has an insider in your organization," Will said more firmly. "My father wouldn't say something like that, with Diana openly recording, without having some definite proof on his side. You better check your lawyers."

"I have my suspicions. But I'm not the only one who's noticed the problems with Northstar. He could make those conclusions without having an insider."

"So what do you know?" Diana asked.

"I have—some links that suggests there's a problem. More than that, I can't say. My guess is that Argos got in over their heads. Not surprising, considering they've not worked a project as big as Northstar before."

"How *did* they beat you out of that contract?" Will asked. "It seemed to be a sure thing for Stephens."

"Argos' friends in high places outmaneuvered my friends in high places, William. Doesn't matter now. Anne's star is on the upswing, and that plus any disclosures that come out about their mishandling of Northstar will make a difference. Diana. I saw that the RA claim has been put on hold. You convinced the tribe to consider the prospect of investing in your father's ranch?"

"Yes. It's not a done deal, and we may need to scramble to find the funding. And Mom—it's not just Dad's ranch that's affected. My source says other places are suffering similar impacts. I spoke to a former neighbor."

"Who?"

"The Martins. Terry Martin. They've lost family members to cancer."

"Damn. The Martins are good people. I remember them—" Sarah's voice broke. "Same as what your father has?"

"Tracy only talked about her mother and sister."

"Elaine Martin—is she all right?" Sarah asked.

"She died last spring. Lung cancer."

"She was a good woman. She tried to help me—" Sarah's voice broke again and she took a deep breath. "If you see Terry again, please pass on my regrets to the family." She sighed. "Expanded locations with more effects could change how we can manage this situation. Does your data include information on these other sites?"

"Yes. Though the source indicated that Dad's place was the worst hit."

"I was afraid that his ranch would get the worst of it," Sarah said slowly. "I was very much afraid of that. Diana. If other ranches are involved and have similar issues, this could be a game changer. I need to see all that data, and I'd like you to find out what happened to the other Martins." Her voice hardened. "I'm sorry to hear about Elaine. The Martins were good people. They didn't deserve this."

"No. But Terry said the tribe has been taking care of them."

"Then I don't think you'll have many problems getting the tribe to help with your father's ranch."

"Politics could be an issue," Will said cautiously.

"That's why we need more data on these other ranches. Any chance we could work out a trade for information?"

"I thought you wanted to keep the connections between us under wraps."

"I'm not liking the type of activity I'm seeing from Parker," Sarah said.

"Does that mean funding from Stephens for this project?"

"Not for your father's ranch," Sarah said firmly. "Not if you get the tribe to pick it up. But if this is big enough, Anne might be able to get directly involved."

"That brings in the politicians," Will said.

"Which needs to happen for me to get what I want," her mother said. "*I want Argos out of Northstar.* What you've told me about the ranch and the Martins confirms it. Either Argos is stupid and incompetent, or else they're malicious, and I think it's a combination of both. They're fucking with people I've cared about, and *something* has gone wrong with Northstar." Sarah paused, and her voice went quieter as she continued speaking. "I'd heard things. I knew it was bad. But until you told me what was going on with your father's ranch, Diana, I didn't realize it was this bad. I also don't like that disclosure of long-term Coalition involvement in the County. That doesn't match what I remember."

"It doesn't match my memories either. But what can we do?"

"I still can't do anything directly. Bad blood between me and the tribe, something stupid I did years ago that can't be remedied. Fallout from the divorce with your father. But—Anne can. Get me enough data to get her legitimately involved. Anne can work a deal with the Third Force relocation bureaucrats to get them off of your father's back. But I need that data about other sites. Deal?"

"As soon we get more data, we'll send it on," Diana said slowly.

"That's all I need."

"Should I talk to Anne? I usually have a devil of a time getting access."

"She'll contact you."

"Sure of that?"

"Yes. Let her contact you. I need to go, Diana. Good hunting. You've confirmed a few of my suspicions, not just about what's happened with your father's ranch but with the CER and Argos. I owe you something for that. And." Sarah's voice sharpened. "I'm dropping a warning note to Parker. Anything happens and Stephens Rec comes in hard and fast. He wants to get personal and play hardball, he can try. I have more diverse resources than he does—and Anne will back me up, along with Francis. If he wants to take on No Limits Enterprises as well as Stephens Rec, plus the Third Force—well, baby, let's play ball. Hold on. Let me check one last thing."

Diana tapped her fingers on the seat armrest as she waited. The com chirped in her ear, switching the conversation back to her and her mother only, cutting Will out.

What does she want to say that she doesn't want Will to hear?

"There!" Sarah crowed. "Came through faster than I thought. You'll find the quarter payment in your Corporate account. Had to move some line items around."

"Thanks. I appreciate this, Mom."

80,000 credits. That money freed some funds to use toward the ranch. Not enough, but a start.

"And Diana?"

"Yes?"

For some reason, her mother seemed to be floundering for words.

"Um-okay." Confidence replaced the momentary hesitation. "Check your personal account."

Diana pulled that one up on her tablet screen. 20,000 credits.

"Mom—I—uh—thanks." It was her turn to fumble with words.

"*Nail* that motherfucking son-of-a-bitch. Take him out of the game. Your William wounded him when he testified against Landreth Technologies, but William didn't go far enough. Finish the job. There's more at stake than you can be told right now—things I don't have the right to share."

"We'll do it right," Diana said, her voice tight and hard, mouth dry.

Her mother snorted. "That *is* your company's name, isn't it? Good luck." The connection went silent.

"So?" Will asked.

"Mom scraped up 80,000 from Corporate accounts for our quarterly payment."

"That'll help."

"There's more," Diana said slowly. "20,000 in my personal account."

"Personal?"

"She wants to take out your father. Bad. But she says there's more at stake than I can be told right now, that she can't share."

"Oh crap," Will said. "Since when did *she* get involved in those discussions? I thought she was walled out of them!"

"Then you know what she's talking about?"

Will shook his head. "Not for certain. But I have a very good idea and," he sighed, "it's something I can't talk about either. Military. National security. Things I was sworn not to disclose upon pain of— well, you know what the rules are."

Chills ran down Diana's spine. "Is it Argos or Northstar?"

"That, and more," Will said grimly, flinching. "My minder chip won't let me say anything more than that. Not without—you know."

She did know. Memories of the chip-induced muteness coupled with sharp zaps that Will had endured when trying to tell her what had happened in the PAZ made Diana shudder.

The skimmer vibrated slightly as Will switched come-along repulsers to a higher level, slowing the skimmer's speed as a result.

"Di, turn off your com. Emergency only," he ordered. "We're running on full stealth from now on when we're flying, until this ranch situation gets resolved. I'm messaging Brenda to do the same thing with the Security skimmers."

Diana reached up to her glass and tapped her com off, a detached dead sensation spreading out from her gut as she did it.

Welcome to the big game, Diana.

SHADOWS OF THE PRESENT

HER MOTHER'S NORTHSTAR DATA HAD FINISHED DOWNLOADING BEFORE Diana switched off the link. She breathed a silent thanks to Sarah for being so prompt with the information, and skimmed through the file.

The data sent her eyebrows straight up. Northstar was a weapons reserve where nuclear, chemical, and biological weapons were assembled and stored. While the weapons had been decommissioned years ago, contamination from the manufacturing and decommissioning processes left a festering mess, both liquid and dry.

Diana had *hoped* that the Northstar site management and remediation would have improved under the Third Force.

If this report was reliable, it hadn't.

Diana looked up from her tablet. "Northstar is a worse mess than ever."

"Not surprised," Will said.

He had throttled the skimmer back after they went into stealth mode, threading through the linked canyon drainages rather than following the ridge lines like Diana usually did on her way to the ranch.

It was a good thing that Brenda and Tony knew their destination, otherwise they would likely be swearing at Will for taking this longer, more difficult route through the canyons.

"I'd hoped for better," she said.

"Not going to happen with Argos," Will said. "You know that already. Tell me what you see."

"I want to run a globe. Will that distract you?"

"Put up a shield."

Diana activated the shielded view of her portable hologlobe before she brought up the 3D model of the Stephens radiological data. She fingered through the data, pulling aside subfiles for deeper examination when she had more time. Detecting a trend, she traced through the connections to a deeper level.

"New particulate contaminants," she reported. "Compounds I need to research when I can safely run a lookup. They look like Argos proprietary bioscrubbers gone bad. Similar molecular pattern up to Chain 18, and then it goes completely off pattern. At that point, it's not a scrubber; it has the potential to let the toxins being scrubbed re-chain in their old toxic forms, or worse. I've not seen this profile before."

"Tag it for me."

"Done." Diana chewed her lip, studying the profile. "They're lighter than standard, so they carry farther. Bigger cluster on the North End ranches." She pressed her lips together even more tightly, biting back anger.

If I didn't know better, I'd say it was targeted. But the design is not complex enough to be able to target like this. Can't design it like that. Yet. Unless this is an Argos breakthrough. Could that be what they're working on?

"Do you think it's deliberate?" Will's cold tone matched Diana's mood.

Diana blew her breath out slowly. "Given the circumstances, I just don't know. It's a complex process, and it's conceivable that in trying to defang that Northstar mess, the bioscrubbers got away from Argos." She shook her head. "Argos should have been modifying and monitoring their bioscrubber air releases so that they're neutral by the time the particulate leaves the grounds. That particular nano can be turned off if it goes rogue, and they didn't do it. That's a stupid mistake with a scrubber process. It's Radiological Bioremediation 101. I learned how to do it on my first job with Stephens."

"Then a deliberate mistake?"

Diana pondered the possibility. "It—could also be incompetence.

But that would open Argos up to filings from Stephens and other companies. It's the kind of screwup that gets contracts yanked. I'm surprised that Mom and other radiological rehab companies aren't all over this."

"The other companies are probably like your mother and building a case for a petition to re-award that contract. Unless my father's gotten to them. Or it could be sabotage by someone else entirely."

Diana tapped her fingers on the seat's armrest. "Sabotage? I hope not. That opens more problematic boxes. It's not stupidity. You just don't let a discharge like this happen by accident, and not report it. It's something even a beginner should know how to modify. How long did Argos expect to hide this? It doesn't make sense."

"Making sense may not be the issue." Will stared straight ahead, his knuckles tightening on the skimmer's guidance yoke. "Let's say that Argos and its allies want to start something. What's the motive? Aimed at your father?"

"If so, then there's a lot of collateral damage. That nano hit all the North End ranches. Sooner or later someone is going to—someone *is* noticing. My mother, thanks to us. Argos has to have a plan. I can't believe they'd so stupid as to think people—*my mother*, for one, and Joaquin and the tribe for another—wouldn't notice."

"You could argue a level of casual racism for them to dismiss the tribe."

"But me? My mother? Come on, she's got too many connections for them to dismiss us. Do they really think she'd walk away from this, especially if I get involved? I just can't believe Argos is stupid enough not to have a plan."

"They want to start something and they don't care, because what they seek to gain is worth the gamble. Or they're being used by someone. Like my father. Argos may care about collateral damage, but my father won't. Still, if he has that much of an influence over Argos—no. That doesn't make sense." Will frowned. "There has to be another explanation. He can't have that much influence over Argos."

"I don't know, Will. Do you?"

He shook his head as he aimed the skimmer lower into the canyon.

Diana leaned forward to examine the canyon walls as they

threaded through the narrow chasm. According to the map on view in her tablet, they hadn't yet crossed the boundary of the ranch yet. This was Third Force repossessed land, and it didn't look as bad as the ranch did. She spotted dried grasses on the creek bottoms under the tall pines and some bushes still had dried leaves clinging here and there.

"Where are you going up to the ranch?" she asked.

"Crystal Creek drainage," he said.

"Good." That would give her an opportunity to look at a creek bottom on her father's ranch. "We can eyeball any changes between Third Force land and Dad's."

"We're going slow enough to release a data bot."

"Do you have one ready?"

"I programmed several for on-the-fly launch on my way up from Portland, just to be prepared for this sort of contingency." Will's gaze darted sideways, briefly, one brow raised.

"Let's do it. Do I have to get up?"

Will shook his head. "Loaded in an outside compartment. You tell me when and where to launch. I loaded three."

"Oh God, William Parker Landreth, I love you to death. That will be *perfect*. Saves us time." Diana blew Will a kiss.

A grin flitted across Will's face, and his hands relaxed slightly on the yoke. "I thought it was best to be prepared for any contingency."

"And I love you for it. Now I can focus on other things." Diana checked her map. "Can I program launch coordinates?"

"Protocol 9-47," Will answered.

"Got it." Diana pulled up the protocol and quickly inserted the autolaunch settings into the three bots' programming. All that was left was the pilot's confirmation of release settings. "Back to you."

Will nodded, scanning his displays. He clucked a setting into place. "Autolaunches confirmed."

The bright blue blossom for RELEASE GO flashed in triplicate across her tablet. Diana reduced the program, satisfaction filling her.

Now we're getting things done.

"Back to the topic. " Will's hands clenched the skimmer's yoke as he stared straight ahead. "Why is your father a target? I have a hard time believing that my father has the ability to influence Argos to this degree."

"Targeting Dad's ranch specifically would require a closer discharge location than from Northstar."

"Too crude for Argos." Will chewed on the left half of his lower lip. "So targeting your father is likely a secondary factor. What's the primary factor? Politics?"

"That doesn't make sense. I'd expect more Third Force involvement, especially since the tribe's being aggressive about picking up the ranches at condemnation auction—hmm."

They rounded a rocky point, and Diana felt a subtle shift in weight.

"Bot two off," Will said. "Right on time. Here we are in Crystal Creek." He angled the skimmer up the narrow canyon. The skimmer quivered again. "There goes bot three."

"God, it's bare." Diana shook her head as she looked at the slope. "And look at that! All those dead leaves and brush. Deeper than it should be." She swallowed hard. "I wonder what the decomposer counts look like?" she mused, possible explanations spinning through her thoughts.

"We're here." Will changed back into landing approach mode as the ranch buildings came into sight. Diana spotted Rita racing her sorrel pony Spooky across the pasture, riding with only a halter and lead rope.

"I'm sending a request to Stephens to see if they have any access to mineral data, now that we're here."

Diana switched on her glasses comm, then quickly drafted a short message to one of her contacts inside Stephens Rec. She sent it off as Will settled the skimmer, then packed away her tablet and picked up her bags. Will opened the door as hoofbeats announced Rita's arrival.

"Will! Diana!" Rita called as she slid off of Spooky, quickly unbuckling the halter and setting the pony free. Then she crawled through the fence rails to bounce eagerly next to the skimmer. "Mom said you were coming!"

"Just a moment." Diana smiled, infected by her younger sister's contagious excitement. Rita charged into Diana, seizing her in a fiercer hug than usual, trembling. Diana realized her little sister was fighting back tears.

"Ree-ree, what's wrong?" Rita wasn't a crier.

Rita snuffled and buried her face deeper into Diana's belly, moaning something into her torso.

"I can't hear you, Ree." Dread gripped Diana as she eased Rita's stranglehold on her waist. She dropped to one knee so that she looked upward into her little sister's face, twisted as it was with the effort *not to cry*.

The Andrews's don't cry.

It had been part of her own indoctrination growing up.

"Is it Dad?"

Rita nodded violently. "He's really sick today."

"It's okay, Ree." Diana pulled Rita to her. "You can cry about this. I—I want to cry, too." They leaned into each other, trembling with partially contained tears. She heard Will directing Brenda and the rest of Security around them and was grateful for his quiet support. Rita's reaction brought the fact home even more than ever.

Their father was dying.

She had to save their home, so Rita could charge around on Spooky.

If it's even still safe for her here—I'll make *it safe for Rita.*

At last Rita's tears eased. She sniffled as she tried to rub away the dampness with a grubby hand.

"Let me do that." Diana used her thumb to brush away the tears.

"This might work better." Will tucked a tissue into her hand.

"Thanks." She flashed him a quick smile before wiping Rita's eyes. "We're still tough Andrewses," she told Rita. "We can cry but still be tough. 'Kay?"

Rita nodded. Diana rocked back on her heels and stood up. They walked toward the house. Diana noted the three other parked skimmers. One bore a Stephens Rec insignia. The other two were Do It Right security. She raised her eyebrows at Will and jerked her head toward the Stephens skimmer.

"Called in some resources," Will said. "Red Morley and his crew.

They borrowed equipment from Stephens—it got offered, I accepted. Your mother wanted more support here. You okay with that?"

"You bet." Diana relaxed at this news. Red and his family were part of an extended clan of Southeast Portland skateboarders and snowboarders that served as backup Security for both Do It Right and Stephens. The Morleys helped Will develop repulsers that were now proprietary tech from Do It Right and Francis Stewart's No Limits Enterprises. The Morley clan also kept busy doing Security contract work for Do It Right, Stephens, and No Limits. Depending on what the family had done lately, they might show up with tech from any of the companies—though Do It Right had first call for their services.

Diana's glasses chirped for an incoming call. Joaquin. She blinked the line open, stopping in place, her arm still around Rita's shoulders.

"Have you seen the news?" Joaquin demanded.

"No. I've been in transit to the ranch, with my comm shut off for security's sake."

"You need to see this." Joaquin tossed her a link. Diana tapped it open. Preston Myers, current CEO and President of the Coalition for Environmental Responsibility came on screen, fumbling his tablet with shaky hands, not looking up at the camera. His long white hair twisted around in flyaway bits. The neatly buttoned flannel shirt he usually wore was half-buttoned and seemed rumpled.

Almost looks like they dragged him out of bed!

Diana resisted the temptation to wonder *with whom.*

Myers cleared his throat and lay the tablet flat on his desk. He focused on it, glancing up occasionally at the camera.

"The Coalition for Environmental Responsibility has the sad duty to inform the holders of Grant 2537 that we must cease all current funding, due to a violation of our sponsors' interests in patterns of land acquisition. We will not seek any return of monies already distributed but as of 13:00 today, all Grant 2537 monies are frozen."

The clip stopped. Diana pressed her lips tightly together, blood pounding hard in her ears. "I'm assuming Grant 2537 means CER contributions to the tribe."

"Land acquisition funding, to be exact," Joaquin growled.

"I need to share this with Will. He's here."

Joaquin nodded approval.

"Will."

Will turned away from Red and Brenda. "What?"

Diana broadened the link to Will's glasses so that he could join the conversation. "Check this out. The grant in question funds tribal land acquisition."

Will froze, tight, watching. "Damn it! My father's doing. Joaquin, I'm sorry. Diana's told you about my father's involvement in this mess?"

"I hadn't, yet. Joaquin, I know what triggered this. Parker Landreth met with me this morning, representing the CER. He made me an offer he thinks I can't refuse, and gave me twelve hours to accept. That was this morning. He's double-crossing me!"

"Not necessarily," Will said. "It's a means of putting pressure on you, Diana. Joaquin, were there any side messages?"

"Nothing," Joaquin said grimly.

Diana's message link pinged with a screened message warning.

"I just received something," she said.

"Don't open it without me checking it," Will said.

Diana extended the link. Will poked at it. Nothing happened.

"Is it good?" she asked.

Will scowled. "You have to open it yourself—I could break it open but not a good thing. That's locked LT tech. On the other hand, it's safe. No nasties that I can pick up. Be careful."

Her mouth suddenly dry, Diana cautiously opened the message, sharing it with Will and Joaquin.

You've seen the link. You can still change that situation. Seven hours. PL.

"Dear sweet mother—" Diana broke off as she suddenly remembered Rita next to her, quivering under her hand. "Rita. Why don't you go to the house and let Mom and Dad know we'll be in soon?"

"It's going to be okay?" Rita asked, her voice quavering.

"As okay as I can make it. Scoot!"

"So this—" Joaquin began.

Diana shook her head. "Wait." She held up her hand where Joaquin could see it. "Let Rita get in the house first." When Rita went inside,

Diana dropped her hand. "Jay, this is blackmail, plain and simple. Is the tribe going to stand for it?"

"I hope not," Joaquin said. "But you definitely need to make your case at the Council. You're on for an evening meeting—seven pm."

"We'll be there," Diana said firmly.

"Good." Joaquin winked out.

Diana turned to Will. "Let's go inside."

The screen door slammed and Jan and Rita walked toward Diana and Will, Rita clinging to her mother. Ginger, Rita's red heeler, trailed along behind Jan and Rita, a worried expression in her golden-green eyes. Her ruff rose slightly as she sighted strangers. Rita placed her left hand on Ginger's head.

"Looks like they want to talk outside." Will took Diana's arm. His arm briefly reminded her of his father's touch, and she shivered.

More shadows.

Will started to pull free, but Diana shook her head.

"Your father took my arm almost like you just did," she said. "I want to get rid of that memory. Override it with the feel of your hand."

Will growled softly. "God, Di, when were you going to tell me about *that*?"

"Haven't had time," Diana said. "I'm sorry."

"Sorry, myself. I'm just touchy."

Jan looked more strained and tired than she had the day before. Diana dropped Will's arm and hugged Jan.

"Your father's pretty tired," Jan said as she pulled back from the hug.

"Is he worse?" Diana asked.

"I think he's just tired." Jan wearily smiled down at Rita. "Yesterday was the longest he's been up for a week or so." She looked back up at Diana. "No criticism, Di. He was the happiest he'd been in a while after that ride. He just—he had to rest."

"I hate to impose on you with all this chaos."

Jan shook her head. "No. It's all right. He wants to talk to you. Alone. About the CER." She glanced at Will. "Will, can you walk me through your Security setup?"

"Now's as good a time as any. I'll introduce you to Red Morley—I want to leave him here after we go back to PDX."

"Jan, Dad's in the bedroom?" Diana asked.

Jan shook her head. "Once Dan heard you were on your way, he went to his office. Get him to stay down, if you can? Hopefully he hasn't decided to migrate from the daybed to the desk."

"I'll try. No guarantees."

Jan rolled her eyes. "He might be more inclined to listen to you than to me."

"Maybe, but I wouldn't count on it."

"Like father, like daughters," Jan murmured. "So. Will. Just what are we dealing with here?"

Jan and Will headed for the barn, Rita tagging along. Diana walked slowly toward the old white ranch house. Toby, her father's old red heeler, lifted his head as she climbed the steps, tail thumping slowly. Diana knelt by Toby. He hadn't followed them on yesterday's ride.

That, too, was a change, and not one she liked. She rubbed Toby's head. "Good boy," she crooned. "Did you want to go inside?"

Toby lurched to his feet and stood with his nose pressed to the door, stub tail waving. Diana opened the door slowly. Familiar scents of leather, breakfast, dogs, wood polish and incense triggered old memories of life at the ranch when she was Rita's age. Toby hobbled across the room to her father's office under the big staircase, his toenails rattling on the varnished, mahogany-stained floor.

"Who's there?" her father called querulously.

"Me," Diana answered.

Damn, his voice sounds weak.

She pushed the door to her father's office open carefully.

Dan Andrews reclined on the daybed, a threadbare plaid Pendleton blanket across his legs, papers on his lap. A bag of clear liquid was strapped to his arm, attached to an implant inside his elbow. Diana pulled the old leather executive chair away from the wall and dropped into it. Toby stood next to the daybed, tail wagging slowly as he looked up at Dan.

"You know you can't make it up here," Dan said to the dog.

Toby whined and sat. He raised one paw, eyeing Dan.

"If you want him up there, I can help him," Diana said.

"Spoiled dog." But despite the disapproving look Dan gave the dog, his voice was fond.

Toby's tail thumped on the floor and he scooted as close to the daybed as he could. He rested his muzzle on the mattress.

Her father patted Toby's head. "Help him up, please, Di. He has his own version of what I have. Poor fella."

Diana gathered the old dog carefully in her arms and placed him near her father's feet, only now noticing how thin Toby was. He wriggled between Dan's knees, nuzzled the papers on her father's lap, then settled with his head on Dan's knees, gazing steadily at his human.

"Dad, is it even safe for the three of you to be here?"

"From what we were told—yes." He glared at Diana, his expression daring her to argue the point. "I had the house and barn areas scanned, several times. Couple of times the tribe offered, once the CER. These twenty acres are okay. Scarce on grass because I pulled everything back here before I sold it. The big pastures are what's affected. The ridges. The canyons."

What you need for grazing and a viable ranch operation.

Diana drew her breath in sharply.

The CER did a scan?

"Di, I'm aware that we've probably been lied to about this situation." He scowled, shifting his weight. Toby whimpered. "Sorry, fella. I can't see that we really had a choice but to accept the offer of a free scan from those people. I couldn't afford it and—I didn't want things to get too bad before I did something. I've been paying for Rita and Jan to get regular checks. They're clean."

"Northstar's the potential source," Diana said. "There are political implications."

Dan raised his palms off the bed, shrugging. "Was it any different when you grew up here? Or me, for that matter?"

Diana sucked on her lower lip, considering how she wanted to tell him. "My preliminary examinations show that the contamination contains Argos proprietary scrubbers from Northstar. What I can't figure out is how they got here. Wind currents don't quite explain everything. Dad, when did you talk to the CER?"

"Two years ago, when things started to get bad, before the tribe bought the Martin place. I was told that the CER had made an offer to the Martins as well."

"An offer?" Diana's voice screeched out of control. "Dad—"

"I turned them down outright, but I accepted their offer of a property scan. Here's the paperwork." He thrust a sheaf of papers toward her.

Diana took the papers. Her father patted Toby's head and murmured to him. She skimmed through the pages, worry clenching her gut even tighter as she noted where the offer deviated from standard contract language. Parker Landreth wasn't one of the names referenced, but several phrases caught her eye, all referring to the dismissal of complaints the seller might file against corporate entities due to hazard exposures.

"What the hell! Dad—"

Her father chuckled but there was no mirth in it. "You found that ticking time bomb pretty damn fast."

Diana shook her head. "How did they expect to make this enforceable?"

"I don't know. They allegedly offered the same proposal to the Martins. Difference was, Elaine Martin was dying and I hadn't been diagnosed yet. I thought Mike was going to kill those people, way he ranted about it." He patted Toby's head before he lay back. "Shortly after that, he sold to the tribe. But Di, look at that price."

She'd skipped over that detail, as engrossed as she'd been in the contract wording. Diana flipped through pages until she found the actual offer.

Twice what this place is worth!

"Why didn't you tell me about this?"

"I had other things on my mind. And their scan showed we were in good shape."

"Why were the scans happening?" Diana asked.

"Cancer cluster concerns. I'm one of the later cases, Di."

Diana dropped her head into her hands. "God, Dad, I wish you'd told me about this offer sooner. There's some—big implications tied to what's happening now." She lifted her head. "Why does the CER want these properties, especially if their scans show it's clear?" *If those scans were even legitimate.* "Who did the scans? Stephens?"

"You think I'd let your mother's company anywhere near this place? No. Troy Environmental."

"That's Argos's in-house rehab group, Dad."

"Do you think this is the first time I've been given an unsolicited offer on the ranch? That was the only one I had since Argos took over Northstar, but—" he shrugged. "I thought it was just some wannabe wanting to own a nice ranch."

"And now you've got a RA condemnation offer."

The front door opened and Toby raised his head. He barked twice before Dan growled at him to stop.

Will's light, firm steps echoed across the floor. "Diana, where are you?" The urgent tone in his voice made her gut cinch in even more.

"In here," she called back.

Toby half-rose as Will slowly pushed the office door open.

"It's okay, big fella," Will said to Toby.

"Will," Diana said quickly, before he could speak. "The CER made Dad a ridiculous offer before he was diagnosed, two years ago. Twice the property value, but with a clause restricting Dad from suing for damages due to hazard exposures."

Will snorted. "Sounds like something my father would think up. We have a problem, Di. Something's jamming our screens."

"What? I didn't notice any problems yesterday."

"It started up about fifteen minutes ago. And there's more." Will swallowed hard. "Contamination levels are rising sharply, and have been for the past twelve hours. This doesn't fit the profile of a Northstar release." He looked sick. "It looks like—"

Toby twitched, whimpering as his body convulsed. Then he collapsed on his side, panting, whining softly. Wetness spread on the blanket underneath him. Diana quickly scooped up Toby and the blanket, sliding him onto the floor.

"Get Jan in here," she ordered Will.

Her father pushed himself up as Will left. "Diana, I can help."

"Stay there. Dad, does he do this regularly?"

"This is the first time for him," Dan said. "Toby, old boy—" His voice broke.

Toby whined. His body tightened. His head lifted a half-inch from the floor, then fell back.

"It's okay," Diana breathed, rubbing Toby's shoulder. "Steady, Toby, steady."

Then another convulsion wracked Toby's body. When it was finished, he lay still, eyes glazing, whimpering painfully. A third convulsion wrenched through him.

"Dad, what is this?"

"He's dying," her father said, a bitter note in his voice. "This is what happened to Genie." He reached for Toby's head. "Good boy, Toby, good boy."

The door banged, followed by Jan's quick steps. She burst into the room, vet kit in hand.

"Toby too," Jan said. "Dan, what do you want me to do?"

"Don't let him suffer," Dan said harshly.

Jan nodded. She opened her box and brought out a syringe and vial. Diana took her father's free hand as he continued to stroke Toby's head. Will crowded in, Rita next to him.

Silence dominated the room as Jan injected Toby. He stopped breathing and his body went loose even before she finished the injection. Diana looked up, into Rita's wide, frightened eyes. Will rubbed her back in a steady circle, soothing her just like he did Diana. Will's expression was even more worried.

"Christ," Will muttered. "This too."

"If the contamination is starting to spike, are we all getting exposed from a Northstar release?" Diana said. "I need my tablet to calculate the exposures."

Will shook his head. "Coupled with the screen jams, no way. This is too local for a Northstar release. My other scans would have picked up a surge in overall contamination on our way here if the rates have been rising this much area-wide. No. This is a local target." His voice sharpened, grew angrier. "This is the work of a war machine. My father's work."

"War machine? What the hell are you talking about?" Jan asked.

Will took a deep breath. "The kind of thing my father makes for a living. The kind of equipment I used to work on. If I can find the damn thing…."

"What do they look like?" Jan asked.

Will pushed himself up. "I'll get our tablets." He looked pleadingly at Diana.

"I'll tell them what a war machine is," she said, her throat tight.

"Not here," Jan said. "Let's meet in the living room. More comfortable."

And we won't be in the room that Toby died in.

Jan gathered Toby's body in her arms. "Let's give it a few minutes. I want to bury Toby."

Dan sighed. "I want to help."

"No!" Diana and Jan spoke together.

"Perhaps one of our Security staff could do it?" Will suggested.

Jan hesitated.

"I'll show them where if you just tell me," Diana said. "Maybe Rita could supervise." She desperately wanted her little sister away from this discussion. "Then, when we're done talking and he's buried, we can go to the grave."

Relief flowed across Jan's face. "I think that's the best idea of all."

"I'll take Toby," Diana offered. "Why don't you get Dad settled in the living room?"

Jan nodded. Diana stood up and gently took Toby's body from Jan's arms. Jan delicately tucked the blanket around Toby.

"Have them bury him in this, please, Di."

Diana nodded. "I will."

She followed Will out.

"I'll send Red over," Will said. Diana stood by the steps. Rita meandered toward Diana. Ginger trailed Rita and flopped at her feet.

"Dad wants him under the lilacs," Rita said.

"You can show Red just the right place."

"Don't want to bury Toby," Rita muttered.

"Neither do I, honey," Diana said.

Red came over to them, carrying a shovel in his left hand. He glanced at Diana and offered his right hand to Rita for her to shake. "My name is Red. You're Rita?"

"Yes." Rita shook Red's hand, gazing up at him solemnly. "Are you the man who's going to bury my father's dog Toby?"

"Yes," he said. "And you are going to tell me where to bury him, right?"

She nodded. Diana could see wetness forming in the corners of her eyes. "Toby was a good dog."

"I'll bet he was." He looked over at Ginger. "Any relation to that dog?"

"Her father," Rita choked.

"Okay honey." His voice softened even more. "We'll do right by him. Can you carry my shovel?"

She nodded. Red took Toby's body from Diana's arms. "A good old dog. Okay, Rita, show me where we need to go."

Diana's eyes blurred a little as Rita led Red away. Then Will nudged her arm. She numbly took her tablet from Will and let him steer her back toward the house.

Jan and Dan waited on the big couch. Her father glared sharply at them.

"All right. What the *hell* did the two of you mean about Parker Landreth and his war machines?"

"Didn't you tell them earlier when you set up the relocation?" Diana asked Will.

"Not everything," Will said. "Just that there had been some threats because of your attempts to save the ranch, and that we needed a safer base."

She scowled at Will.

"Look, his end of the line wasn't secured!" Will snapped, before she could say anything. "I'm not going to mention details like that over a partially open line!"

"You're right. But still—" She dropped into a nearby chair. "Dad, the person who represented the CER's offer this morning was Will's father. Parker Landreth."

"*That* son-of-a-bitch," her father growled. "What the hell is *he* doing with them? Didn't care too much about who was aligned with the CER in the past, but if I'd known Landreth was an associate of theirs, I'd have done more than give them a polite no when they tried to buy the ranch. What does he want?"

"Kokanee. The Mocha bloodlines. At least that's what he's claiming right now."

"That damn mother—" Dan shook his head, face flushing.

"I don't think that's the real reason." *And you called Dad's reaction right on the nose, Mom!* "Parker talked about Troy Environmental doing the recovery—that was a condition of the CER funding offer to me. Will and I think it's an Argos coverup."

Dan sagged against Jan. "If I'd seriously known that either of those entities had been involved, I wouldn't have given the CER the time of day. I hope you didn't."

"Why do you think Will wanted us out here instead of the Corporate residence? I told Parker Landreth no. Thus starting all of this stuff —except if that release has been going on for twelve hours, then it began before we talked. What the heck is going on, Dad? Parker claimed the CER has had an influence here for years. Neither Mom nor I know about it. Do you?"

"Your mother wouldn't have known. All of your mother's political involvements were elsewhere, not local. She promised me that, after the fiasco in Neahcom. The local CER committee wasn't active when she was here."

"Dad, is this something I should have known about? An old feud or something?"

"Nah, not likely." Her father sighed. "The original membership of the CER here was meant to counter any significant environmental activism. One reason why I warned your mother off of *any* political action. And then, at the end, she blew it."

"Does the CER have reasons beyond the current situation to target you beyond your connection with Sarah?" Will asked sharply, looking up from his tablet. "Because the patterns I'm seeing from both the jammers and the increase in contamination levels match that of a war machine. Diana, I wonder if this is a Northstar issue after all."

"If it's not Northstar, then it's personal," Diana said. "But that doesn't match the other details. The contamination release patterns we've seen. The other ranchers. It could be two separate contaminations."

"That makes even more sense. Northstar with a war machine added to the mix." Will placed a hologlobe generator cube on the coffee table in front of Jan and Dan. "Here's what a war machine looks like." He activated the hologlobe.

Diana shuddered as the oval shape of one of the Landreth Technologies war machines formed inside the globe. Will reached inside and tapped on the machine. It opened, revealing varied small devices. Diana's heart raced as she recognized the sharp, elegant lines of a netspider configuration amongst other items. As she looked closer, she saw even more netspider pieces in the machine.

"The LT 9572," Will said, a sardonic, angry tone to his voice. "LT's smallest and finest instrument of destruction. Capable of dispersing sedatives, poisons, toxins, infectious agents in this configuration, including radioactives and things I probably don't know about any more. Limited range. Additional comblock abilities available for a price. Most commonly used in the Petroleum Autonomous Zone. I played with these darlings daily when I was in the PAZ. Capable of carrying up to twenty netspiders."

"Are you detecting a LT 9572?" Diana asked.

"When I left LT, the process of countering detection by the type of tools I now have available to me was just getting started." Will rose, beginning to pace. "I get echoes that suggest yes, one is in the area. But." He stopped sharply, spinning to stare at the device in the globe, his face tightening into an even grimmer visage. "Our data bots also use similar frequencies, because of the work I've done with them."

"I've seen something like that before." Jan leaned closer to the hologlobe, studying the war machine. "Over by the Martin place."

"I've never seen anything like that," Dan said.

The door opened, admitting Rita, Red, and Ginger.

"I saw a shiny thing like that." Rita plopped down on the floor next to the coffee table. "Spooky shied, and Ginger wouldn't go near it. But Toby ran at it. He barked. There was a really bright light. Then he whined and ran away."

Shocked silence filled the room. Will and Diana stared at each other.

Diana finally found her voice. "When and where did you see it, Ree?"

Rita shot a cautious glance at her mother.

"It's all right," Jan said. "We need to know, Ree."

Rita frowned, looking unconvinced.

"Was that the day that you thought you'd lost Toby?" Dan asked. "Last week?"

Rita nodded. "He whined, and took off running. Faster than I'd ever seen him. Ginger stayed with me. But she and Spooky are okay! Daddy, they're okay! I didn't think—I didn't see it before!"

"Honey, come here," Dan said. He patted the couch next to him. "Tell us what happened. It's okay. No one's blaming you for anything."

Rita slowly went to Dan.

"Tell us what happened, Ree." Diana did her best to keep the dull dead fear in her gut from coloring her voice.

"Wanted to get pretty pictures for Daddy to make him happy because he's so sick," Rita said. "I saw elk on Mud Point."

"The Martin place?" Diana asked.

"Uh-huh. Tribal land now. I thought I saw baby elk. So I rode a long, long way around. And when I got there, I saw—that." Rita pointed at the war machine's image.

"Did you get a picture of it?" Diana asked.

Rita nodded.

"Can you show us?"

"I'll go get it." Rita hopped off of the couch and ran up the stairs. Diana met Will's eyes again.

"If there's a Landreth war machine on tribal land, things may not be what they seem," Will said.

Rita returned. She handed a chip to Will. He popped it in his tablet's reader, and handed it to Rita.

"Can you show me the picture?" he asked Rita.

Rita nodded slowly. She ran her finger along the tablet, then stopped. "That one."

Will looked at the picture. He blanched. Then he carefully took the tablet from Rita, tapping on it.

A second image popped up, identified as a Landreth war machine.

Except for the fact that Rita's picture showed Toby barking at the machine that was lying on its side, they could be the same thing.

"So that answers *that* question," Will said. He straightened up. "We have to disarm and retrieve it."

"How?" Diana asked.

A wry expression flitted across Will's face.

"Used to be my job in the PAZ, every day. Diana, we have some hard questions for your friend Joaquin, as well as for the CER and my father." He drew a deep, ragged breath. "And I have to report this to the Third Force. Needless to say, that war machine isn't supposed to be used domestically."

"Does it have to be you?"

"Yes." Will's tone brooked no argument. "I won't take the risk of it going rogue on us. Di, this is what my father meant by a Lakely situation. Even the Third Force won't know how to disarm that war machine without triggering it."

"You're sure?"

"I'll need your help. You and Red are the most skilled bot wranglers on site. My father knows about this. That's—" his voice quavered but he quickly corrected it. "That's the version that—went rogue on me. With Lakely. My father is aware that I know how to disarm it. It's a message to us."

Diana shivered. "What do we do?"

Will's face hardened. "We disarm it, and hope to hell there's no traps."

"How soon?"

"We leave in five minutes," Will said.

"So is this the cause of all of our problems?" her father asked.

"Not all of them. I'll know more when I get my hands on it." Will looked at his tablet. "Rita, do I have your permission to save this to my files? I need it."

Rita nodded.

"Can I delete this picture from your chip? This is—" his voice faltered again. "This is not the sort of picture you should have on anything of yours. It's not safe."

"Am I in trouble?" Rita whimpered.

"No, honey. You are very much not in trouble." He swallowed hard, his face tightening even more before he met her eyes again. "But it is a very dangerous thing. Spooky and Ginger were right to be afraid of it. If you ever, *ever* see anything like this again, *do not go near it.* Okay?"

Rita nodded again. "What do I do?" Her voice was very small.

"If you *ever* see one of these things again when you're out riding, use this to take a picture." He brought a small camera pen out of his pocket and handed it to her. "You were lucky. That thing could have killed you just for taking a picture of it. Use this."

Rita studied the pen, then looked up at Will. "I push this button?" she asked.

"Point this end and push the button," Will said. "It will automatically send the picture to me. Ride as hard as you can to get away from it, and *call me.* When you get to the house. And don't leave the house. Okay?"

"O-kay," Rita said.

"What do you do?" Will asked.

"Take its picture with this pen," Rita whispered, her eyes fixed hard on Will's face. "Ride hard to get away. Call you."

"When you get to the house," Will prompted. "That's important."

"When I get to the house. But do I have to stay in the house?"

"Yes," Will said, his voice dropping. "Until I tell you it is safe."

Will saved the file to his tablet and handed Rita's chip back to her.

"I'll put this back." Rita ran up the stairs to her room.

Will sank back on his haunches, shaking his head, his body trembling. "Dear sweet Mother of God. I saw kids killed by those machines for doing less than that in the PAZ. Oh my God. Harvesting all my shadows right now."

Diana knelt by him. "You okay?"

"My father is going to pay for this," he said through tightly gritted teeth. "I don't care *what* my parole says. *He will pay.*"

"Don't do something stupid, son," Dan said. "We'll not let Rita out alone any more. I thought she was safe enough with the dogs."

Will heaved a heavy sigh and rose. "Luckily it was a slow trigger, Dan. Your poor dog probably got the full force of its defensive response. Saved Rita. Di, I need to spend time with our Security training them on safe response for these—these monsters." His voice grew firmer. "But I *will* break my parole and design the remote killers that pen can trigger if I have to. I'm not supposed to play with that tech any more but damn it, *she's your little sister, Di!*"

"Don't do something you'll regret," Diana said, even though the taste of the words were bitter in her mouth.

"I'll try not to." Will turned to leave. "I'm getting our equipment ready. I *hoped* I'd never have to use it again." He headed toward the door, feet falling in a steady but reluctantly-paced tread.

"I'll be right out." Diana turned to her father. "I'm messaging Anne Whitman. This has to be reported to the Third Force."

"Looks like Will left his tablet," Dan said. "Might want to send a picture." His eyes met Diana's. "Maybe it's time to forget the old grudges. Tell *her* to bring help."

Diana nodded, understanding that *her* was not Anne. As far as she knew, her father had always gotten along with Anne.

She picked up Will's tablet. The picture of Toby barking at the Landreth war machine came up. Taking the tablet over to a chair, she pulled up her mail account and, after some thought, addressed her message to Anne, copied to her mother and Francis.

I don't know how much Mother has told you about the situation at Dad's ranch. Whatever she has, it's escalated. Diana took a deep breath before she continued typing. *My little sister took the attached picture. You know what it is. It is on tribal property next to the ranch. The dog in the picture is dead. Rita appears to be all right so far.*

Combined with Parker Landreth's appearance as the CER rep this morning, I think this points to a situation bigger than we can handle without political help. Will and I are going out to defuse the device. I think the Third Force needs to know about this aspect of the situation.

"Di!" Will hollered, sticking his head inside. "Let's get moving!"

"Right there!" Diana quickly sent the message. "You left your tablet in here. I'll bring it."

"No," Will said. "It needs—it should stay here. Just in case."

"I sent the picture to Anne," Diana said. "We may need political help. This is bigger than I want to take on by myself."

Will nodded. "Let's hope it doesn't come to that. Come on!"

Diana hugged her father.

"Good luck," he said.

"Thanks, Dad." Diana hurried to the door, pausing to hug Jan before she headed out to join Will. "Stay safe," she whispered to her stepmother.

"We will," Jan assured her.

Diana strode across the porch and down the steps.

God, I hope I made the right call back there.

But copying her mother and Francis on the message to Anne was the right thing to do, wasn't it? After all, the situation was serious enough to have her father hint that Sarah be kept in the information loop.

That *should* make it right.

Shouldn't it?

WAR MACHINE

Will landed the skimmer near the device coordinates from Rita's
picture.

"Still have about a fifteen-minute walk," he muttered as he put the
skimmer in secure sleep. "Close as we can get, with all these downed
and half-broken trees. Let's hope to hell we don't have to do a remote
skimmer call."

"What we need is a set of power suits," Red said.

Will snorted. "Like that's going to happen. Those are LT proprietary." He stood up. "Red. The box?"

Red brought out a black box from under his seat. The red and
orange sun and flames of Landreth Technologies glowed on the top,
the flames seeming to flicker malevolently.

Will stared at the box. "I've not touched one of these since—since
Lakely. This could be a trap. Most likely *is* a trap, in more ways than
one. If my father even *suspected* that I'd stashed away one of these
devices against a future need...." His voice trailed off.

"Should I be the one to use it?" Diana asked.

"You don't know how it works." Will flipped back his bangs. "It's
personalized to me only." His hands clenched into fists, then released.
"But I need you to be my backup. That was—Lakely's job. When I
thought he was being tortured, that the 9572 had gone rogue on him—
no. A fake. He twisted my unit so that he was the controller, not me."

She didn't know what to say to that—and they still had work to do. "Should we program it outside?" she asked. "There's more room."

Will shook his head. "Less possibility of the device or its controller picking us up before I get our shielding tuned. Let's get suited. Then we put—this on. After that, helmets. We need weapons, each one of us. The 9572 will have a nearby controller, and if we've been detected…." his voice trailed away again. "We may have to fight our way out, and if that's the case, I'll kill the machine. But I'd much rather disarm it. Suits first."

Red put the box down. Diana checked her armor suit, tapping the links at ankles, knees, hips and elbows to make it fully functional. She wore a suit like this out in the field, only her field suits didn't have this much armor. Yet.

That may change after this.

She straightened, waiting for Will. Red poked at her, checking her links, and she checked his. Then she faced Will. He stared at her with a thousand-yard gaze, his eyes leaden and shadowed like snowfall at dusk. His fear writhed like a snake between them, cold and gray and dark like his eyes.

"Are you going to be all right?"

"I have to be. These nets—this is the only neural device that scares the crap out of me. It always has. It's a difficult son-of-a-bitch. The 9572 has netspiders as a defense. And after Lakely—" He shuddered. "I need you to keep me centered. Sane. It will amplify my speed. My reactions. Make sure I don't do—the wrong thing."

"I will."

"Then let's get it done." He knelt in front of the box and traced a password around the blazing sun with the barest touch of his index finger. Orange lines edged in red sprang up behind his fingertip. The box's lid slowly separated, revealing two silver and copper wire hairnets, intricately webbed, resembling elegant artwork. Next to the hairnets lay a simple copper disk.

Will picked up the disk. "Red. You first."

"What do I do?"

"Nothing right now." Will ran a finger over the disk. It glowed coppery-red. "I'm placing this behind your right ear." He attached the disk to Red's skin.

Red winced. "Ow!"

Will frowned and removed the disk. His fingers tapped on it, moderating the glow. "Sorry. That was a stronger setting than we need. Try again."

Red nodded. This time, he didn't flinch when Will attached it. The disk glowed orange instead of copper.

"Di. That's the color you want to see on the disk when we use it. Anything other than orange means it's compromised. Don't always need to use it, but since we're not tuned to this device…Red's our backup. Usually, we just need two controllers."

Will picked up the hairnet which had more copper than silver in the finely woven mesh, dangling it from his fingertips as if he didn't want to touch it. He held it out to Diana. "You need to put this on. I'll adjust it once you've done that."

She hesitated before taking the net from Will's fingertips. "How delicate is that weave?"

"It's tougher than it looks," Will said. "Better if I have less contact before you put it on. The connections…leave traces. You want it personalized to you."

Diana's fingertips tingled as she shook it open. "Is it already live?"

"If you're feeling a vibration, that's normal. It's still in sleep mode, but sleep mode for LT devices isn't the same as for ours. Faster response."

"Will I trigger it?"

"No. Won't activate without my net."

Diana slid the fine weave over her head. Will pressed the metal to her skin at forehead and temples. He tucked each side behind her ears and traced the edge to her skin behind each ear, left first, then right. Then he tugged the back of the net over the ends of her short hair and touched the edge along the nape of Diana's neck, just as he had done behind her ears.

Her whole head tingled. "This feels funny. It's not like our cap controllers."

Will went back to the box, not speaking. He slowly picked up the remaining net. His hands trembled as he slowly fitted it over his head and repeated the process he had just done with Diana's net, only more quickly.

"Controller live," he said.

Complex visual projections sprang up around her in the skimmer cockpit. Numbers scrolled past, codes she didn't understand attaching themselves to what she recognized as crucial skimmer operating and defensive systems.

Attack codes, she realized. *Identifying vulnerabilities.*

"Friendly." Will said, slowly turning in place.

The codes faded.

"Reset." Will growled a set of codes. Green, yellow and red dots appeared.

"Stealth," Will said. The buttons grayed out, but Diana could still identify the basic colors. "Okay. Put on your helmets. We're ready to go."

Red handed helmets to Will and Diana before putting his on.

"Will, what are those buttons?" Diana slid her helmet on. She pulled up her suit collar to seal it to the helmet's bottom. Red checked both her seals and Will's seals.

"Green—go, yellow—pause, red—stop. Correlates to which hand is being used." Will checked Red's helmet seals. "I've set your systems for beginner use. You see a warning, say side and color. Don't mess with yellow. So left, red or right, red. Got it?"

"I hope so," Diana said.

"It's not that different from cap systems once you get the feel of it. Just—the goal programming," Will said, voice dead and cold. "Let's go."

The skimmer door glided open.

It was weird to walk in the woods behind Will in full armor. He whispered codes that echoed hollowly in her helmet cam. An overlay map with a green target sprang up on her helmet screen. As they walked Diana saw their three tracks—Will as blue, herself as green, Red in blue-edged red—move toward the target.

Forest sounds and movements sounded different from her usual armor experience. No birdsong. Unfamiliar data readouts spun past her visual field as she looked around. It made her dizzy.

"Will," she said softly. "I'm getting a lot of readouts that I don't understand, and I'm afraid I'll develop vertigo. Is there a translate command?"

"Activate translate backup," Will answered. His voice softened. "Sorry, Di. Not thinking."

"Thanks."

AVIAN popped up on her visual field as she looked off to the side. Diana experimented with a soft cluck series to locate the bird, the type of cue she'd use if it were a Do It Right device. Her vision telescoped quickly to zoom in on a tiny brown creeper clinging to the trunk of a Ponderosa pine. Diana reeled to a halt as the zoom disoriented her. She kissed softly and the overlay resumed normal focus.

"Diana!" Will growled, turning toward her, irritation roughening his voice.

"Control check," she answered. "Zoom is fast. I need to slow my cues."

"This is *not* the time to play with controls!" Underneath that cold, dead voice she heard a faint fearful note.

"Understood." She kept her own worry out of her voice, but just barely.

"There's a human controller somewhere near here," Will continued. "Don't fuck around. Assume hostile. No games!"

The fear in his voice was stronger than before. Diana's heart throbbed in her ears, so loud she almost thought Will and Red could hear it. Will afraid like this? The only time she'd heard his voice show this much alarm was in the first months after he'd been rescued from the PAZ. She knew what that meant.

Will was terrified.

Terrified Will was not good. Terrified Will defaulted to the paranoid, defensive tool that Landreth Technologies had created in him.

Parker Landreth had meant his surviving son to be his personal enforcer, had trained him from early childhood for that purpose.

God. I want to help him but I can't. Not right now.

Diana's mouth went dry. She let the IDs for mammals—*RODENT, UNGULATE*—slip by without trying to focus in on them.

The target pulsed larger and larger in her overlay.

Then Will stopped, raising his right hand. They waited. Then he waved them forward, standing still. He tapped something on his left wrist.

VISUAL CONTACT, scrolled across her overlay. *LOCATE CONTROLLER?*

Diana looked at her own sleeve to see if she had anything to type back a response. Will shook his head as she looked back up at him. He tapped his wrist again.

KEYBOARD FOR ME ONLY.

She looked back at him and nodded to show she understood.

LOCATE CONTROLLER? flashed in brighter colors across her overlays.

Diana swallowed, trying to bring up enough saliva to moisten her mouth so she could ask how.

Red tapped on her shoulder and pointed toward a small grove of head-high Ponderosa saplings to her right, on the downslope of the canyon wall.

"You take that sector," he whispered, the comm off. "You see a human, you whistle. Comm will carry it. Drop down about fifty feet, stop and scan every four steps, 180. I go the other direction, do 180. Will goes straight ahead. He deals with the device. You keep the device on your left side, circle round in front of it, come up that way. Owl hoot means start, crow caw means stop. Hold line set at ten feet from the device, preferably out of line of sight. Thought Will had the plan ready to share but...." he let his voice trail off.

Diana completed his thought. *That thing's got Will rattled.*

Why? It was only a machine. But, given Will's reaction, she would think the damn thing was evil personified.

This isn't getting the job done, Diana! Get to work!

She gave Red a thumbs up and turned to face her assigned direction, still trying to get enough moisture in her mouth to form a credible whistle.

Owl hoot in her ear. She moved forward four steps, stopped, scanned.

AVIAN, RODENT, RODENT.

Four more steps.

AVIAN, AVIAN. A gray jay scolded her from a nearby tree.

She brushed through the Ponderosa saplings, feeling silly and scared at first because she couldn't see very far in the small grove, but relaxing a little as she realized the Landreth net showed her all heat signatures within a twenty-foot range.

Below the narrow string of saplings, the slope opened up. She saw only rocks, low brush, and a few grasses under the tall pines. By the time she'd gone close to fifty feet, she was certain that Will was wrong and that this device lacked a controller.

Diana repeated her progress across the slope, feeling stupid as she stopped and scanned every four steps. Surely, she'd see someone if they were there? Will was at the hold line by now, according to her overlays.

So wouldn't that controller have revealed themselves by now?

She was parallel with the target. Time to turn and walk uphill. Diana winced at the thought. She couldn't see Will and the device here; they were on a tiny meadow at the point of the ridge and she would have to detour around a cliff face to get to her hold line. It would take some serious scrambling to climb the sidehill next to the cliff.

Get it over with, Diana!

As she spun uphill, a buzzer sounded in her ears.

HUMAN. FRIEND OR FOE?

God, she didn't know this cue!

The heat signature was by a rock. She couldn't *see* the person. Diana tried to whistle, but only soft air passed through her lips. She licked them and tried again. A very faint note leaked out. She crouched low, lower than she already had to do to scramble up the steep, rocky slope.

Where the hell is Red?

Surely, she hadn't gotten through this brush faster than he had?

She tried a single, soft cluck to zoom in on the rock, even as she heard a faint whistle in response. The rock suddenly popped out in stark detail. No rock, but a cleverly designed shelter of some sort. And the human using it was focused uphill, most likely on Will—

Then, faster than she could have anticipated, the human gathered itself up and launched toward Diana.

Repulsers!

She scrambled and slid backward, but not fast enough as the man tackled her. They rolled downhill. Dirt and shards of rocks cascaded with them, clattering over the cliff edge. Dry dirt clods rolled under her feet like marbles, making her footing even more treacherous.

Diana wrestled with her captor, yelling inarticulately as she tried to break free from his grasp. They slid to a stop at the cliff's edge. The jagged points of a knee-high rocky outcrop kept them from pitching over the brink and dropping at least ten feet to another slick slope.

She kicked and yelled as the man pinioned her wrists, trying to restrain her. Diana slammed his armored hands futilely against the rocks to try to shake them free.

Will yanked the man off of her.

"You son-of-a-bitch!" Will bellowed.

The other man attacked Will, who kneed the other man in the gut, going for deep body blows rather than wasting his time on the other man's helmeted head. The other man went down and Will followed him, knees on the other man's torso, grabbing the man's helmet and slamming it hard against the rocks, growling and cursing.

Diana froze, unable to move, staring.

He's going to kill that man because he attacked me.

"Will! Stop! Will! Enough!" Red yelled. "Diana, help! Get Will off of him! I'll take care of the controller!"

Red's voice shocked her into action. Diana tried to wrestle Will off of the man. Despite her greater height and strength, it took every ounce of determination she could summon up to wrench Will away from the other man and push him uphill, away from the controller.

Will fought her blindly. It wasn't until she had him almost all the way to the controller's hideout that he finally stopped struggling and sagged against her, hyperventilating.

Her heart pounded. A low, malevolent, hum rumbled over the comm.

Will stared at the man. "Lakely, you motherfucking goddamn son-of-a-bitch," he gulped, his voice somewhere between tears and anger. "You motherfucking son-of-a-bitch!" He lunged forward to attack again, but Diana grabbed Will and spun him so that he faced away from Lakely.

Lakely. Albert Lakely. Oh God, this is him?

"Will." She had to get his attention off of Lakely, so they could defuse the machine. "Will. Will!"

The sinister hum grew stronger.

The controller chuckled. "Landreth, you sure made my job one hell of a lot easier by bringing your wife along."

The hum escalated into a whine. Yellow lights started flashing. Will startled.

"Oh my God. Diana! Come with me! *The damn thing's activating!*" He darted past her, scrabbling uphill fast.

Yellow changed into red on her overlays as Diana scrambled up the hill behind her husband.

The side of the device opened as she joined Will.

Long, slender, metallic claws with scythe-like talons extended from the opening. The first netspider grappled for a purchase to pull itself out.

Will muttered codes, but the netspider lurched onto the side of the device, raising itself high on its eight legs, preparing to leap.

Diana's skin tingled over old scars, memory of those sharp claws digging into her skin still vivid. Not from a netspider but from a Stephens soil sampler bot gone rogue in Vietnam, suddenly behaving like a Landreth netspider.

But the bot's sampler claws were nothing like the knife-like blades that formed the legs of the netspider. Blades wired to shock targeted nerve bundles. Capable of ripping humans and machines apart. And other uses.

"Stop, stop, STOP!" Will yelled. The netspider crouched. "Damn it, the thing *isn't listening to my overrides!*" He yanked off his armored gloves and grabbed the netspider with his bare hands as it launched itself at Diana. The netspider dug into his palms.

Will screamed.

Diana lunged to knock the netspider off of Will.

"No, stop, Di." His voice quivered with agony. He continued, through deep, painful-sounding gulps for air. "No. Bloodbond. Have. To. Bloodbond. My. Control. Overridden. *Shouldn't be!"*

Bloodbond? What the hell?!

Red lights flashed intermittently in her overlays. Two turned yellow, then three, then all were yellow, as Will writhed in the grip of the netspider. Diana reached for Will—*don't care what he says, they're hurting him*—but he shook his head.

"Others. Watch. Use vocals. To stop them."

She stared at the device as a pair of claws waved from the opening, grappling like the first one had. Two yellow lights flashed on the left side of her visual overlays.

"Left red!" she barked. It was similar to what she would have done to control a Do It Right or Stephens Rec rogue bot.

The claws stilled but did not retreat back into the device. The yellow lights stopped flashing.

"Good," Will groaned. "Secondary controls stable. Just...need...gain...primary—there!"

As all of her lights turned green, the netspider in Will's hands crumpled into a glittering ball. He flung it back into the opening. He brushed the other two claws back inside, his hands shaking.

Diana cried out as she saw his bloody palms. Will ignored her and placed his hands on the device, muttering code phrases as he left crimson smears of blood on the device's skin.

As Diana watched, the blood faded away.

Will growled. "Not enough." He fumbled for a knife in his pants and popped it open, slashing the prominent blood vessels across the back of his left hand.

"Will!"

He looked at her, grimacing as the blood spurted and he pressed the back of his hand against the device. "I need more blood to make the bond."

"No. Will, there's got to be a better way!"

"There is no other way, Diana." The desolate, empty look he gave her chilled Diana to the bone. "Not with the 9572. Damn it, this one was

supposed to be mine only!" Anger and anguish mixed in his voice. "But that bastard twisted her. She doesn't know me anymore. Yet. But she will. With enough blood, she will!"

"You're talking about a machine as if it's alive." Diana stared. Was it her imagination or had the device's skin bulged to form a mouth? Then the skin rippled and a metallic fang extruded, plunging into Will's hand, pinioning it so he couldn't move. Helpless, Diana stared at Will and the device. "Oh God, Will. *God.*"

"What did you think I meant when I said Landreth Technologies required a blood price?" Will groaned and sank to his knees beside the device, his pinioned hand awkwardly twisting his arm. "This is blood-bonding, Diana. This is interdicted LT tech." He whimpered and leaned his head on the device. "It wants me back. Body and soul. Oh God. Oh God."

"Will. No." Diana wobbled to kneel beside Will, taking his other hand.

"Help," Will moaned. "She's going to take me, Di!"

"*No she's not.*" Diana pulled her hand free from his and yanked off her gloves, grabbing Will's dropped knife and slashing her own hand.

Will grabbed at her bleeding hand, but she jerked it away. "Di, *no! Not like this!*"

"It's the fastest way, isn't it?" She slammed her bleeding hand down hard on the device's skin.

Another fang extruded and plunged into her hand.

Pain lanced into her and Diana shrieked.

But there was more than pain.

PAIN KILL DIE, flooded into her brain, a wash of primal emotions. Diana nearly yanked her hand free from the 9572's fang. Instead, she bit her lower lip and cinched her eyes shut, breathing hard to help herself focus and channel the pain away so that she could bear it. If Will could stand it, she could. She was doing this for Will.

For Will.

Images followed emotion, images of Lakely, his crazed eyes focusing on the machine as he tweaked the programming and netspiders swarmed out to crawl over bound subjects who twisted and fought as the netspiders dug their claws into their victims' skin. One of the victims was Will, as she'd seen him after Francis and his men had pulled him out of that PAZ prison. Diana's stomach cinched tight, sending a sour taste into her mouth. She swallowed hard to force it back down.

A soft, sinister chuckle in her ear, enough to make her jump and open her eyes. No one by her side, no one close except for Will staring at her, agony twisting his face.

Diana, please, his lips formed, but she couldn't hear him over the laughter that rose in volume, drowning out every other sound.

"Oh so *convenient* that Will brought you here," the laughing voice cackled. "We can have so much fun now!"

Albert Lakely, Diana realized, as Will's eyes widened.

Without thinking, she grabbed Will's free hand.

"*No,*" she said, thinking it hard as well as saying it. "He's *mine.*"

PAINPAINKILLDIEPAINKILLDIE swelled, bursting through her. Diana bit hard on her lower lip, hard enough to draw blood. It distracted her enough from the interior voice to separate her thoughts from those emotions as Lakely continued to cackle.

Was what she feeling coming from Lakely or from the 9572?

No matter. Her response had to be the same.

Both wanted to take Will from her. Both wanted Will for their own ends. Both wanted Will back as Parker Landreth's weapon.

That's not going to happen, boys.

"*Mine,*" she insisted. Her hand clenched down hard on Will's. "He's mine. Get out of our heads, Albert Lakely!"

Will's grasp tightened on hers. He pulled her hand close and leaned toward her. She followed his lead and he touched his forehead to hers.

"Ignore Lakely," he gasped. "Must. Control. 9572. That's—the driver. Cut him. Out. Of links. Then no mindspeech."

She nodded. "What? Do?"

"Contact helps me…center. Remember myself." He drew a long, painful-sounding breath. "I'll manipulate codes. Your hand on my shoulder. Keep contact with me."

Diana painfully eased her hand free of Will's, slowly sliding her fingertips up his arm until she could cup her hand around his shoulder joint. He nodded, reaching inside the LT 9572 with his free hand. The din rose to a shrieking mélange of sound and images flooding too fast for her to identify more than fleeting glimpses of Will, Lakely and Will, Will writhing in bonds as netspiders scuttled over him, unknown figures twisting and dying—

And then the images shifted, slowing. Lakely images faded, and the mad disorganized mix settled into a focused slideshow of targets.

pain. kill. die, whimpered through her brain. It repeated itself, fading with each repetition, until it was no more.

9572 compiled and ready for service. Command, flashed across her overlays.

Save memory to wlandreth@doitright. Will's green overlay flickered.

All memory? the 9572 queried.

All memory, Will confirmed.

Done.

New secondary. Diana Andrews Landreth. Confirm new bloodbond. dlandreth@doitright. Save memory.

New bloodbond for Diana Andrews Landreth confirmed. Memory saved.

Hard shutdown. Manual override protective systems. William Parker Landreth confirm. Will turned his head to Diana.

"Diana Andrews Landreth confirm," she said out loud.

Hard shutdown commencing in fifteen seconds. Fifteen. Fourteen. Thirteen. Twelve. Eleven. Ten.

At "ten," the fang withdrew from her hand. Diana started to move it, then noticed that Will kept his hand on the 9572's skin.

At five, the opening closed.

At zero, a click sounded. The 9572 vibrated slightly, and began to cool. Images, emotions, voice and that *presence* in her mind faded. Will shakily pulled his hand away from the 9572 and Diana followed suit, reeling slightly as she stood.

"We can transport it safely now," Will said, his voice quavering.

Diana nodded. She pulled the comealong net out of her pack.

Red shoved Albert Lakely up the slope toward them, Lakely's hands bound behind him. Lakely staggered and swerved uphill as he tried to keep his balance without the use of his arms. His helmet was off and blood trickled down from his temples and forehead. Red gingerly dangled a fine-meshed metallic net from a stick he'd scrounged up, a match to the net that Will wore.

"Pulled the net like you asked, Will. Wasn't pretty," he said.

"I told your goon that wasn't the best thing to do," Lakely sneered.

"Thank you," Will said. "That gave us the edge we needed, Red. Otherwise we'd still be fighting netspiders."

"I'm gonna get brainburn," Lakely whined. "Already getting the headache. You know better, Landreth. You can't yank a net like your stupid grunt did without wrecking connections."

Suddenly, explosively, Will leapt from beside the 9572 to Lakely's side. He slapped Lakely's face hard, leaving a bloody smear on it. Lakely staggered back a step, still sneering. Will grabbed the net from Red and ripped it apart.

Diana watched tensely, hands clenched, letting Red make the decision about stopping Will's actions.

When they were done with this ranch business, Will had a lot to explain. She didn't care if the data about this aspect of the Landreth war machines was interdicted. She wanted to know more about this technology, especially if it had the potential to re-emerge and interfere in their lives like this at some unknown point.

How much more interdicted rogue Landreth technology is unaccounted for, and how will it come back into our lives?

There was going to be a reckoning for Parker Landreth as well. He considered her to be nothing more than her mother's daughter?

Let him find out what *that* really meant.

Lakely stumbled and dropped to his knees next to Diana, grimacing as he fell. Will dropped the remnants of the net in front of Lakely and stood over him.

"I destroyed every damn connection you had to my 9572," he snarled. "With any luck, I've just made it so you can't connect to these damned devices ever again. Just like you tried to do to me." He grabbed the sparse hair on the back of Lakely's head, forcing Lakely to look up at Will. "You motherfucker, you damned near killed my sister-in-law. A little girl. Stupid irresponsible crap. Just like you did in the PAZ. How many more babies and little kids have you hurt and killed since then?"

"I—I—I—" Lakely gulped. His eyes darted back and forth between Will and Red, ignoring Diana.

Will slapped him. "I designed these damned devices, not you, not my father. I'm the one who can take them out. Thanks for giving me what I need to do just that."

Lakely spat at Will. "Might be a harder job than you think, *coward*."

Will slapped him a third time. "I'm not the one who picks on people weaker than me. About time you got a taste of your own medicine."

Lakely tried to twist up to his feet and Will pushed him over.

"Take these cuffs off of me and we'll see how far you get, Landreth!" Lakely snarled as he struggled back upright. "But you never did have the guts to finish the job, did you?"

Lakely's trying to goad Will into beating him. Why?

"Will—" she started to say.

"I may not be as strong as I once was but I can still beat the crap out of you!" Will ignored her. He slugged Lakely in the gut. Lakely doubled over.

"You're a chickenshit, Landreth. You don't dare cut me loose," he groaned. "I've seen your medical reports. I know you're still in rehab."

Will's face tightened in white-lipped fury.

"*Will*," Diana groaned. "This isn't solving anything."

Will kicked at Lakely. Lakely dodged the kick, rolling to his feet with a speed and agility that belied his earlier clumsiness. Lakely charged, head down, at Will and butted him in the stomach. Will staggered back a step. Red dove to grab Lakely, but not before Lakely kicked Will's bad knee. Will's knee flexed backward, more than it should have.

Will went down, choking back a scream. He rolled to his good side and shoved himself back up, dragging his right leg, fists clenched. He stumbled forward and fell again.

"God damn you, Lakely!" he gasped, balancing on his hands and his left knee, head down, right leg limp and extended. "God damn you!"

Now Diana could move. Four strides and she was by Will's side.

"That's enough. This isn't solving anything, and we don't have the time to spare for this." Much as she wanted to slap him silly in return for giving in to his anger, it wasn't the right time.

"It's foolish. Idiotic. Macho. But it makes me feel better."

"It may have made you feel better at the cost of more knee rehab."

Will gulped. "Yeah. You don't need to tell me that. Damn knee. But the pain brought me out of berserker mode. God, Di, the ease with which I can slide back into that, especially with the link to the 9572...." His voice trailed off as he threw his right arm over her shoulders and braced himself against her left side.

"Ready?" She shifted to a squatting position, balancing herself precariously on the steeply angled slope.

"As ready as I'll ever be."

"One. Two. Three." She wrapped her left hand around Will's waist and straightened up slowly, bearing as much of his weight as she could. Will cried out once as they rose. He breathed hard as they stood there, wobbling slightly.

"Brace in the skimmer," he said. "I can't walk there on my own. Damn it. And we have to get Lakely and the 9572 to it."

"That's not all. We have to talk," Diana said.

"Oh yeah," Will said slowly. "This little incident changes everything."

"I can bring the skimmer closer," Red said.

Will nodded. "I didn't bring it nearer in the first place because I didn't want to trigger the 9572. It's okay now."

"I'll take Lakely with me," Red said.

"Watch out," Will cautioned. "He's a motherfucking weasel."

Red shoved Lakely ahead of him. "I'll watch. Back soon."

"You shouldn't stand while we're waiting," Diana said. "I'll help you sit, then get the comealong on the device. When Red gets back, we'll put the brace on your knee. That should help."

Will groaned as she helped him back down and popped his helmet off. She gave him a drink of water from the flask at her belt, then turned to the device. It only took a couple of minutes for her to attach the comealong net to the 9572. She tried to avoid touching the skin, but when she did, the metal seemed to arch into her touch, as if it were a cat seeking attention.

Diana shuddered. "Will, are you sure it's off?"

"It will react to your touch now, on or off. The only way to shut it down completely is to pull the brain, and I don't want to yank those circuits just yet. I have uses for them," Will said in a tired voice. "Like it or not, you're Landreth bloodbonded. You're my new second. When you're wearing a net, any Landreth device that I'm bloodbonded to will respond to you as well."

"Okay. What the hell is bloodbonding? I've—Will, this is technology I didn't think was possible. I—*have you been putting this into our own devices?*"

"It's a long story, Di."

Diana squatted next to him, lightly holding the tether for the 9572's comealong in her fingertips. "We have time now. Tell me." She fumbled with her own helmet and popped it off. "I'd damned well better know what I'm in for if I'm Landreth bloodbonded."

"It's—" Will rubbed his face, then slowly dropped his hand. "It was Dad's attempt to create secure controlled devices. Not as secure as he originally visualized, as you can see. Lakely hacked me. Goddamn it, *Lakely* hacked me!"

Diana didn't react to the outrage in Will's voice. "You're not invulnerable."

"Yeah. I learned that one in the PAZ."

"What does bloodbonding do?" Her knees ached from balancing on the slope, so she rocked forward to kneel next to Will.

"It speeds up recognition cues as well as provides a hard-to-hack secure control," Will said. "Command processing is linked to those neural nets. Crude auditory inputs, primitive compared to what I'm trying to do with our command bots. At least I'm bypassing the nets with our devices."

The net. Speaking about it made her suddenly aware of the pressure on her head from the contacts. Diana reached up to the Landreth net pressed against her temples. Eerie that she hadn't felt it until they'd started talking about it.

"I'd like to take this off."

"Don't. Not yet. Not until we're in the skimmer and you can box it. I guard those nets with my life, Di. An unguarded net is like handing over a blank credit chip to the bad guys, now that you're bloodbonded. You never, ever let someone get their hands on your nets. One of the LT systems vulnerabilities. Lakely got mine in the PAZ. Twisted it. This one—was my backup."

"If it's so insecure, why are you lugging that box around?"

"Without that box we'd be screwed now," Will said grimly. "It's what let me deal with this damned device safely in the first place. Especially with Lakely's override. That box is why we're not dead or in Lakely's control now."

"Will." She tried to keep her impatience out of her voice. "How much Landreth tech is in our own devices?"

Will groaned and flopped back onto the ground, throwing an arm over his eyes. "As much as I can safely import without fear of reprisals from my father or Military Affairs," he said in a quiet, choked voice. "Next-gen stuff, the stuff my father feared and didn't want. Chip-based controllers, not net-based. No military apps. No netspiders."

She thought of the soil sampler bots and shivered. "I'd disagree with that last. The soil samplers."

"Superficial similarities. Our designs are more elegant, but more importantly, they're not weaponized."

"Anything could be weaponized." As she spoke, she heard the whisper of the skimmer's approach.

Damn it, not enough time to talk about everything!

Will dropped his arm from his face and pushed himself back up. "I've left out key structures in the hardware." He stared at her, his face stark, flat, and empty. "Not just for fear of Military Affairs or of violating patents—though *I* hold the damn patents, not my father. If anyone wants to weaponize my designs for Do It Right, they have to add chip hardware. Di, I *know* how you feel about this crap. But the tech is what will put Do It Right over the top." He rubbed his face and groaned. "I'm just trying to exploit some useful pieces to give us an edge."

She didn't look away from Will as Red scrambled down the slope, the skimmer hovering near the 9572.

"I hope to hell you're right," she said finally, as Red stopped next to them. She handed him the tether to the 9572. "Can Red move the device, or should I?"

"Red can do it."

She took the knee brace from Red. "I'll take care of Will."

"Got it." As Red took up the comealong's slack, the 9572 lifted, tagging along behind him like a compliant puppy.

Diana carefully fitted the brace over Will's armor, then helped him up.

"One last question," she said quietly. "Does this bloodbonding mean I have access to all Landreth devices or just the 9572?"

Will's eyes met hers. "Like I told you. Every damned one that I have access to with my net, you now have access to with yours."

She didn't know whether it was dread or the thrill of power that shuddered through her. "How much control?"

"Individually? Not much. But together—" he hesitated. "My hands have been tied because I haven't had a reliable backup. I couldn't do some of the things Military Affairs wanted me to."

"Such as?"

A feral, predatory grin briefly touched Will's lips. "Together, we could take out every damn interdicted device my father thinks he controls."

She stared back at him. Will nodded.

"Do you want to do it?" she whispered.

The fierce joy that lit his face was her answer.

"The ranch first," she said. "But after that—"

"Yes," Will said. "After that."

This time she recognized the shudder as the thrill of power.

You're going to pay, Parker Landreth. You're going to pay.

SHADOW HARVEST

Now we harvest the shadows.

Diana bandaged Will's hands and wrapped her own as Red piloted the skimmer back to the ranch.

Thankfully, Red put Lakely's helmet back on with faceplate down when he locked the prisoner in the back of the skimmer. He'd also switched off Lakely's com. She didn't want to see or hear the man right now.

Her Landreth net stirred into action as they arrived at the ranch. Overlays popped up on her glasses to identify the presence of other skimmers. Diana gave silent thanks for the skimmer identification aspect of the Landreth net.

Will needs to give Do It Right this capacity.

At least she knew who they were facing.

Anne Whitman. Francis Stewart. And—her mother.

All three had brought Security, with the numbers and weaponry from No Limits Enterprises and Stephens Reclamation dominating over Anne's Third Force escort. But Anne's escort bore military IDs.

Not good for Will.

A sudden *ping!* identified yet another party en route. Tribal ID. Joaquin?

Will stirred. "Quite the greeting party, isn't it? I thought you had only messaged Anne. Did she get Francis and your mother involved?"

Diana swallowed hard. "I messaged them as well. Dad's suggestion. Might be an overreach, but he doesn't idly suggest that I include my mother in anything. Is there a problem with that?"

"No, it's a good thing. Look at that ID on Anne's escort. Military. They're here to take me back into custody."

Diana's arms tightened around Will. "I figured that might be the case. They'll have to go through me first."

"You won't have much to say about it. But Francis and Sarah being here helps. They might have to take you—*will* have to take you as well, since you're Landreth bloodbonded."

"My mother will argue with them."

"Damned good thing for me that you're my Second now. Big consolation is that we're bringing in Lakely. The Third Force has been looking for him for the past year. I'm surprised my father hasn't shown up yet. Given the linkages I picked up off of Lakely, he's going to be the answer to a lot of the Military Affairs questions about Landreth Technologies, better than I was."

"Then why have they been hammering on you so hard?"

"Because I hold the patents to a lot of Landreth tech," Will sighed. "Not on my own, not all of them. But enough for Military Affairs to keep me under wraps."

A new blip showed up on her screen, coming in fast without identifiers. "Will, what's that?"

A dry, sardonic cackle from Will. "Right on cue, there's my father. I wondered if he was monitoring coms and the 9572. There's my answer."

"To what? Will, how do you know it's him?"

"Because *my* readout shows a very subtle tracker I slipped into his signals. He thought he dealt with it, but he's wrong. He thinks he's anonymous now," his voice turned sharper, harder. "But my tech's better than he realizes."

The skimmer settled. Red turned toward Will and Diana. "The military wants me to hand Will over right away. What do you want to do?"

"Shove Lakely out the door and give it a minute," Diana said. "Will. How do I activate external coms on this net? I need to talk to Mom and Francis."

Red cocked an eyebrow at her. "Shove him out the door?"

"Escort him out. He's a distraction, but one they'll want to see. Will, should Red bring out the 9572?"

"No. That's what we do. Activated and under our control." Will rolled to his hands and good knee as Red eased past him to get Lakely. "They won't touch us with a live war machine under our direction."

"Jesus, Will, are we setting ourselves up for a suicide mission? I want to talk to Mom and Francis before it gets that desperate."

"*I'm not going back into custody.*" Will's voice was low, but his voice quavered and she could hear the desperation in it. He stared at her, and Diana realized he was still terrified, even more than before.

"Then get me linked to Mom and Francis, *now.*"

Will nodded. "We have to activate the 9572 to do it."

Of course. Diana drew a deep breath. "Let's make it happen."

"The military will know and react. Things could get ugly. I just want you to know that."

"If we time it to your father's arrival?"

"We need to have it active before he gets here." Will's voice cracked. "Otherwise he'll try to grab me—no, *us*, now that you're bloodbonded—before the military gets us and the 9572."

Red and Lakely could serve as a distraction—and as messengers.

"Red?" she said.

Red steered Lakely past them to the door. "Yes."

"Talk to my mother, Francis, and Anne. Promptly. They need to hold the military back. We're activating the 9572 because Parker Landreth is coming in fast. We believe Parker Landreth wants to take me, Will, and the 9572. We have to activate it for our own safety."

Red nodded. "It may take a moment."

"Tell them I'm Landreth bloodbonded. The military will have to take me along with Will. Same for Parker, and—I won't let anyone take Will without me. You make sure my mother hears that."

"Got it."

The skimmer door opened and Red left, pushing Lakely ahead of him.

Will stared at Diana, his expression bleak. "It's not too late for you to avoid this nightmare." His voice wavered. "I—I wouldn't blame you if you did. You still have a future. Your mother would protect you."

"It was too late when we got married. God damn it, Will, *we* have a future. We have Do It Right. Maybe kids someday. I'm not leaving you alone to face—whatever. We're in the right here. Either your father or Lakely put that war machine here. We didn't have a choice but to use your skills to defuse it. If that's a violation of your interdiction, then those motherfuckers need to not be planning on using you for their purposes."

A faint smile crossed Will's lips as his hand tightened on hers. "Damn it, Diana, I love you. I don't want to see you go through this, but damn it, I'm glad you're staying."

"I love you too. And *we're* going to face this—together."

Her tablet chimed with a message. Without looking away from Will, Diana fished the tablet out of the skimmer's safety latch with her free hand. She held it where they could read it.

The message was from her mother.

You and William get your butts out of that skimmer with that war machine ready and active ASAP. Landreth's incoming makes for a good distraction, and Francis's team is ready to fight. I couldn't keep the military away. Landreth reported William as acting in violation of his parole. Suspicious but they had to respond. Anne was able to defer the assignment to her military Security.

Will raised his brows. "Never thought until now that I'd be grateful for your mother's tendency to carve her own path."

Diana let herself grin. "Her help comes with a price. She wants the tech, Will. So does Francis."

"Right now, her price looks pretty damn good." He exhaled slowly. "So it begins. Let's wake up the baby. Time to begin your lessons in Landreth War Machine Ops 101." Will levered himself up and gimped back to the internal storage compartment which *just happened* to be the right size to hold the 9572.

Never thought I'd be doing this.

Diana hurried to help Will guide the 9572 out of the compartment.

He tapped on the side, and a faint hum sounded from the sleek machine. And then she became aware of that *presence.*

I wonder what a non-military version of this level of communication would feel like?

Will coughed, and she refocused. "Not enough time to teach you the startup routine, this time. But watch carefully in case you need to do this without me present."

"I'll record it."

"Good idea. Tell the net to send it to dlandreth@doitright when we're done. Then wipe from your overlays. That way if someone takes you into custody, they won't have that data." Will traced an intricate pattern onto the 9572's skin. He paused in places. Each point he hesitated at lit first with blue, then green as he moved on. As Will continued tracing the pattern, little red dots sprang up before his finger. The sequence seemed to be random, as Will would bypass some dots, then double back.

More overlays popped up as Will finished. Diana created her backup, and saw COMM 1 INT in green and COMM 2 EXT in red.

"We have comm now," Will said.

"COMM 2 is what I need to talk to Mom and Francis?"

"Yes. Activate by saying its name, then ID the channel when you see which one they're using. You can activate up to three channels."

Mom, Francis and maybe Anne will be on the same one.

"COM 2 EXT activate," she said. A list of channels appeared. As she hoped, the SR1 and NLE1 identifiers for Francis and her mother were on the same link, NOCLA. Familiar patterns.

"Link NOCLA," she said.

"Goddamn it, Francis, we've got to be patient," her mother said. Sarah's voice sharpened and a wary note came into it. "I have no fucking idea—Diana. Is that 9572-2 link you?"

A flood of relief washed over Diana. "Yes. We're active now. Is it safe to come out yet?"

Before her mother could answer, 9572-1 and 9572-MAIN lit up as links to their line.

"Warning," a mechanical voice droned, 9572-MAIN flashing to identify it as the speaker. "Incoming skimmer arming up."

"We need to shield!" Will snapped. "Dad's coming in shooting. Di, we've *got* to get out of this skimmer, *now!* Francis, Sarah, get shields up fast!"

The 9572 glided forward, Will resting his hand on it as it flew through the cabin. Diana scurried to catch up.

"My hand too?" she asked Will as the skimmer door opened.

"Yes!"

The skin erupted and a claw closed around her wrist as she slammed her hand down on the 9572's skin. She didn't have time to yell before the 9572 shot forward, yanking her off of her feet.

"Grab it!" Will bellowed. "Clamps!"

She struggled to wrap herself around the 9572 like she saw Will doing, gasping as it sped out of the skimmer. Clamps cranked down around her arms and the one leg she was able to snake around the 9572 but her other leg whipped free as the war machine dodged a shot. Diana managed to wrestle her leg awkwardly onto the 9572. As it made contact, more clamps wrapped around the leg. She was grateful for the support as the war machine rocketed straight up. The machine wobbled as her body strained against the fastenings.

"Flatten yourself!" Will yelled. "You're throwing the balance off!"

"I'm trying!" she screeched.

Diana managed to brush her midriff against the 9572. Yet another clamp wrapped around her torso and snugged it close to the war machine. The irregular flight steadied, and the machine arched into a tight parabola. Diana struggled for breath against the gravitational pull as a blast whipped past them.

From Parker Landreth's skimmer.

Will growled something she couldn't hear. The 9572 trembled under them.

Something detonated over Parker Landreth's skimmer.

"Will! You didn't!" she screamed.

"Disable only!"

She lost sight of Parker's skimmer as the 9572 snaked around.

Breathe in. Breathe out.

Diana fought to keep her breathing steady against the pull of gravity, and wondered just how often Will had done something like this in the PAZ.

I'm glad I didn't know about this before now!

Their flight slowed. Diana's breath caught as they angled straight up and down. Fins extruded, pushing her left leg aside. She was momentarily grateful that they didn't appear to be landing upside down. Or was Will oriented in a different direction? She realized now that she didn't know if that was the case. She couldn't see him.

"Dan Andrews, what the hell are you doing?" her mother yelled, a note of panic in her voice, like she'd not heard from Sarah in years. "Jesus Christ, will you get your butt back in that house!"

Why is Dad getting involved?

Then they were down. Clamps released. Diana rolled as she landed, looking around wildly for Will as gunfire and blaster fire exploded around them, sending up puffs of dust. Will somersaulted from his upside-down position on the 9572, drawing a blaster shot even as a deflector sprang up between him and an incoming blast—*from Parker Landreth*, she realized, sick to her stomach. Diana scrambled to her feet, watching Landreth throw away that blaster and flip a second one live. For a moment the shooting stopped. Diana swore that she saw Lakely's fallen, bleeding body.

And then several weapons sounded simultaneously, one rifle, several blasters. Blood exploded out of Parker Landreth's head. He fell backward.

Diana froze. She looked at the house. Her father stood on the ranch house's porch, trembling, lowering his old deer rifle, the stock broken, his face gone fish-belly white with the effort. His chest glowed with a direct blaster hit.

Who else shot?

She followed her father's gaze, to where her mother had leapt on her skimmer. Sarah stood in a similar position as Dan, keeping her blaster trained on Parker Landreth's prostrate body, even as she looked grimly back at Dan.

Dan dropped his rifle and sagged to his knees, tumbling down the porch steps. Diana bolted for him, Will hobbling behind her. Jan beat them, struggling to lift him. Diana grabbed her father, helping Jan, and was shocked at how featherlight he felt.

Someone shoved Diana aside. She rolled back to her feet, then hesitated as she realized that someone was her mother. Sarah and Jan both steadied Dan on his knees as he coughed, blood trickling from his mouth.

"Daniel Andrews, you're a damned fool," her mother growled, and Diana was surprised to hear the affection in her voice. "We had this under control!"

Her father gasped for breath, deep, rasping gulps for air. "Dying anyway."

"Now we have a fucking mess."

"What else new?" Dan coughed again, sagging hard against Sarah and Jan's arms. "Not first time."

"You didn't have to do this," Jan said. "God, Dan!"

"*My* ranch. *My* daughter. *Mine* to do."

"I had this!" Sarah insisted.

Dan drew a deep, shuddering breath. "You did it for Peter. I did for Diana."

"We *both* did it for Diana."

Dan smiled, but the smile faded into a grimace. "Yeah." He sagged in their arms, eyelids drooping.

"Dan! Dan!" Jan shook him.

Sarah dropped her arms and stepped back. She looked at Diana and gently squeezed her arm, then moved away. Diana reached for Dan.

Dad. Oh Dad.

"Is he—" she breathed to Jan. "Medic! NOW!"

Jan nodded, tears flooding.

"Oh my God. I—I—God, Dad!"

"Don't," Jan gulped. She wiped the tears from her eyes with the back of her hand. "He went out like he would have wanted. He didn't die in bed. He was terrified of that."

The medics shoved them aside. Jan shook her head as she stood.

"But Rita—you—the ranch—God, Jan, we've got to save him!"

"He didn't want extraordinary measures. No extraordinary measures!" Jan repeated to the medics.

"Do what you can," Diana said. "Just—"

"You get the ranch." Jan's voice faltered. "He rewrote his will."

"That doesn't matter. Save him!"

Sarah's hand tightened on her shoulder. "Diana. He's—" Her familiar pressure persuaded Diana to move away. Diana barely felt her mother's grasp as she stared at her father and the medics working over him. They brought out the defibrillator, set it up, then stopped, studying the readout from their diagnostic scanner.

The lead medic looked up at Diana and shook his head. "Blaster damage direct to the heart. He's gone."

"No," Diana moaned. "No." She brought her clenched hands to her mouth.

"William. You take her," Sarah said. Her words seemed to come from very far away as she gave Diana another strong hug. Will's hands replaced her mother's, steadying her, keeping her erect.

"There's nothing we can do," he growled in her ear. "Hon, straight blaster shot to the heart without shielding. Strong enough to cause bleeding. I'm surprised he stayed alive long enough to say anything."

She turned into Will's shoulder, choking back tears. Now was not the time to cry. Too much, damn it, too much. She had things to do, but —*oh God, Dad*. Will rubbed her back.

"Maintain," he breathed. "Maintain. Someone got Lakely, too. Wouldn't be surprised if it wasn't your mother. Maybe my father, but unlikely."

"Jesus, Will, what are we going to do? Mom—Dad—oh crap, what are we going to do? What does your father's death do?"

"Your father's death in these circumstances freezes the RA takeover plans," Will said. "Lakely's death introduces something new into the mix." He straightened. "Unless I'm more seriously out of the loop than I thought, Parker made Lakely his heir when he disowned me. With both of them gone, there's no one left to take over Landreth Technologies. Except me." His body tightened. "Correction. I *am* the one left. Takeover codes flowing to me now."

The medics gently covered her father's body. Diana followed as Jan directed them inside. Rita opened the door as they carried him up the steps, her face frozen with shock as she stared at the sheet covering their father's body. She reached for Jan, but Jan didn't see her, brushing by her daughter.

Rita's face crumpled.

"Rita," Diana called. She knelt as Rita hurled herself in her direction, almost knocking Diana onto her rear and down the steps. Rita buried her head in Diana's shoulder, sobbing. Diana leaned her head against Rita and let herself cry, too. It hadn't been okay to cry when it was Will or her mother holding her, but it seemed all right to cry with Rita.

"Hon." She looked up at Will through a blur of tears as he spoke. "I'll deal with this other business. Let me talk to Francis and Anne and get things unsnarled. You and Sarah need to be clear of it. Deal with family."

"Thank you," she gulped. Then she focused on Rita, her own sobs dying as Rita's continued. She murmured wordless comforting noises, as much for herself as for Rita.

"Diana." Her mother stroked Diana's forehead, pausing to cup the back of Rita's head for a moment. "We'd better go inside." Her voice sounded tight and strained, as if she wanted to cry along with them. "William has the situation under control here, as much as it can be at the moment. *God.* Your father...." She swallowed hard and Diana could swear that she saw wetness at the corners of her mother's eyes. "Every damn time I come back here, something horrible happens." Sarah rubbed her eyes.

Diana nodded. "Ree, let's go inside." She wondered what Sarah meant by that last comment, but didn't have the strength to ask.

Rita gulped. She burrowed deeper into Diana's chest. Diana took a deep breath, then staggered up, hoisting Rita onto her hip. Sarah steadied her, one hand on Diana's shoulder, the other on Rita's back.

"You both look like your father," she said quietly.

Why did she say that? Diana blinked to clear her eyes. *Gone. Dad's gone.*

Sarah guided her through the door. Thankfully, Jan had the medics put Dan's body in the office so he—his body—it—wasn't there.

She sank onto the edge of the couch, where he'd been last—*no. Don't go there.* Rita whimpered in Diana's arms, clutching her firmly. Her mother collapsed on the couch next to them, looking older than Diana had ever seen her appear before.

Sarah kept glancing around, studying different parts of the room.

"I—I never lived here with Dan." Sarah finally met Diana's gaze. "It was his parents' place. Pete and Rita's place. I—we—named Peter after Dan's father. Even though Dan wasn't Peter's father. They must have named your sister after her grandmother." She drew a ragged breath. "We lived in the bunkhouse. You and Peter spent your first years there. I don't know where you lived after I left."

"I don't remember the bunkhouse," Diana said, fighting back her own confusion. Her mother *never* talked about her days on the ranch. "I lived here. Grandma lived with us after Grandpa died, I don't remember Grandpa. Just Grandma and Jan and then Jeremy."

"You wouldn't remember living in the bunkhouse. You were too young." Sarah looked around the room again. "A lot happened. I'm glad you don't remember."

Why?

Jan left the office, followed by the medics.

"Sheriff's on the way. Joaquin's already here; he's covering things for the tribe." She dropped onto the loveseat perpendicular to the couch and buried her head in her hands, shaking with silent sobs.

Sarah and Diana exchanged glances. Then Sarah rose, an awkward and uncomfortable expression on her face, and sat on the edge of the loveseat next to Jan.

"Easy." Sarah's voice shook slightly. She stiffly rested her right arm across Jan's shoulders. "Maybe you should sit next to Diana and Rita. There's—comfort in that."

"I'm fine." Jan's fingers muffled her voice.

The anxious stare Sarah gave Diana would have been funny, if Diana hadn't been feeling so drained and empty.

"Mama?" Rita whimpered, stirring in Diana's lap.

"Oh, honey," Jan gulped. She dropped her hands from her face and sat up. "Come here."

Rita slid off of Diana's lap and went to Jan. Sarah gingerly dropped her arm from around Jan's shoulders and returned to Diana's side, twining her fingers in a tight ball. The steady click of an old clock was the only sound other than Jan and Rita's sobbing.

Then footfalls on the porch, ponderous, measured footfalls. The door opened and Will hobbled in, using a stick for a cane. He dropped into the rocker that faced the couches, resting his elbows on his thighs, staring at his clasped hands. The stick clattered at his feet.

"This is what our different Security teams have been able to figure out so far," he said, not looking up. "Parker attempted a transmission to the 9572 as he came in. When it didn't respond, his skimmer's weapons went to an autoresponse with preprogrammed targets."

"Targets," Diana repeated. "That means—"

Will gave her a sideways glance, pale brows furrowed hard, before staring back down at his hands. "You. Me. Sarah."

The door opened again. Francis strode across the room as two Security slammed the door closed and went into her father's office. "Sheriff's here as well as the tribal representative."

"I should probably go—" Diana started to rise.

"No." Will raised his head. "Stay here, Di. Please. It's covered."

"I need to talk to Joaquin."

"He'll come in once he's done with the sheriff," Will said. "Look. We worked this out, Francis, Anne and I. They'll handle it. Anne is the point person. Our Security heads will support her."

Diana sank back down.

"How much have you told them?" Francis asked.

"I'd just barely had time to start. Then you came in." Will rose, unclasping his hands and glaring at Francis. His eyes narrowed and his lips tightened as his hands tightened into fists. Silence hung between the two men.

"Sorry," Francis said finally. His shoulders slumped a quarter-inch and his brows softened. He looked away from Will, over at Sarah. "Continue."

Will heaved a sigh. "We have three dead and seven injured. Preliminary examination indicates that Parker Landreth fired the primary shot that killed Albert Lakely, and Dan Andrews fired the primary shot that killed Parker Landreth. Security is now determining who shot Dan Andrews. From the angles, it was most likely Parker Landreth."

"That's—a very convenient way to phrase those findings, William," Sarah said.

Will glowered at Sarah. "You would have it any other way?"

"You know there's more to it than that."

"Are you sure the authorities are going to accept those findings?" Diana asked through the tightness in her throat. God, this would make things so much easier, in some respect, but for it to be *her father* who had killed Parker Landreth, and Landreth who had killed him....

This is a mess. A really big mess. And didn't Will originally say it was my mother who appeared to have killed Lakely? Why did he change that?

"That's why Anne is handling the discussions with the sheriff and Joaquin." Will brushed back the forelock falling over his face. "We've just the one last piece—"

The Security team came out of the office. One nodded at Will before they left the house.

"And that piece is settled," Will continued. "Parker Landreth shot Dan Andrews."

"Don't think I don't appreciate this. I really do." Sarah pushed herself up. "But I know better. Dan and I both shot Parker. And you know it, too, William Landreth. Ask your wife how I feel about owing undeserved favors."

"I'm not going to stop you from confessing if you feel the urge," Will snapped back at her. "Just remember. You're dealing with *me* as the head of Landreth Technologies right now." He drew a ragged breath.

"This is going to shoot the Conclave all to hell," Francis said. "With Landreth Technologies having a new man in charge, that leaves quite a power vacuum."

"It does, doesn't it?" Sarah raised a brow at Francis.

"And we've dealt with a problem," Francis's face settled into a tight line.

"Yeah." Sarah turned to look at Will and Diana. "What are your plans for this new turn of events?"

"I—um—" Diana looked up at Will. "What *are* you going to do?"

Will shook his head and sat next to Diana. "Military Affairs will want an audit of Landreth Technologies. We'll see what's left after that."

"I'm sure there'll be plenty," Sarah said. "Are you planning to continue in your father's footsteps?"

"I'm already under interdict. Even if I wanted to, I couldn't do much with the Landreth production lines that remain." His hand clamped down tightly on Diana's.

Sarah raised her chin, glaring at Will. "So you're selling it off randomly? I think the Conclave as well as Military Affairs will have something to say about that."

"Mother," Diana said. "Give him some time!"

"Until I know what I have first, I'm not making any major decisions on what I keep and what I dispose of." Will's hand cinched down even harder on Diana's. "My main priority is now, and always will be, Do It Right. My wife and I have built this company. I am not going to say more than that. Understand?" His fingers tapped a signal into Diana's palm, tight, tense, pressing harder than they would normally.

Get me space. Fast.

She nodded, then pulled her hand free from Will's, standing up slowly.

"This is no time to be talking about these affairs." Diana measured each word carefully. "We have people to bury. Other things to manage and negotiate. What becomes of Landreth Technologies can wait, at least until I know how the fate of this ranch comes out." She stared down Francis and Sarah. "Meanwhile, even though Anne is handling the situation, I'd better find out if I still need to attend that Tribal Council meeting tonight. And I'd like to have some fresh air."

She turned and walked toward the door, Will at her side. She took his arm to support him as they went out. He quivered as he leaned on her.

To her surprise, the sun still shone. Someone had whisked away Parker Landreth and Albert Lakely's bodies. The sheriff's skimmer lifted and turned away, followed by a couple of other skimmers that bore the ID of Anne's military escort. Readouts scrolled down her glass, a summary of the sheriff's findings which repeated the information Will had given them. Diana glanced sideways at Will.

He grimaced, then bobbed his head.

She pulled her shoulders back. They half-walked, half-hobbled toward Anne and Joaquin.

"We need you and Will to appear before Military Affairs next week," Anne said. "I've given my word as bond for your appearance." She sighed. "I'm not liking this reappearance of the 9572, and I don't like your arguments to keep control of it, Will. But I do understand the circumstances. Otherwise, both of you would be under arrest."

"We'll be there," Diana said, not looking at Anne but focusing on Joaquin. "Joaquin, how does this affect our meeting tonight?"

"It's your ranch now, from what I've been told," Joaquin said. "Do you still want to sell it?"

"I can't keep it as a working ranch. Nor do I have the time to develop it as a resort property." Diana spread her hands. "I have a stepmother and sister who need a place to live. I need an opportunity to prove that my company can do as excellent a job in bioremediating in this climate as we do in tropical settings."

Will cleared his throat. "There will be resources available from Landreth Technologies. Not enough to fund a resort property. But it will be enough to match tribal investment in a Do It Right training program. I can't guarantee fast money. But I can't think of a better way to reinvest Landreth Technologies resources than to create a Do It Right North America program."

Joaquin raised a brow. "Do you even *need* tribal money now?"

"Even if every penny we could spare from Landreth Technologies gets dumped into the ranch as a Do It Right training project, we still need resources and people," Will said. "It's slow money. I can borrow against my company. Consider it our guarantee. As Diana said, we can't do the property justice because we can't be here, and you can. If that's what she still wants to do, and what Jan said is correct about Diana inheriting it. Whatever the possibilities, consider Landreth Technologies a partner. Now."

"We can work out a partnership with the tribe," Diana said. "This is not the time to negotiate, however. Not—not while Dad's not even cold yet."

"Understandable. Get us the data on what Landreth can contribute, and we'll hammer out an agreement. Your father's death in these circumstances gives us a reason to extend the RA hold longer, and with Landreth resources—they aren't going to bother with moving very quickly on this property. We should have time," Joaquin said. "My regrets, Diana. Your father was a great man."

"Thank you," Diana said mechanically.

Joaquin left. Anne hugged Diana, then headed for the house. Diana took a deep breath and looked around.

Mine. For now.

So much had changed. And Will?

"So you're Mr. Landreth Technologies now," she said awkwardly.

"Only for as little a period of time as I can make it," he growled.

"Will. Are you sure you want to commit to this program, to the ranch?"

"Given my father's role in your father's death, I can't imagine a better use of those resources. I meant every word I said. I'm going to fold as much of LT as I can liquidate into Do It Right. Argos will back off once the word gets out that LT is a backer of DIR. This solves a lot of issues."

Diana almost asked Will if it really *had* been her parents responsible for the death of his father.

Then she decided that she really didn't want to know.

"We have a lot of work ahead," she said instead.

"Yeah," Will said. "A lot of work." He took her hand. "But between the ranch and what we'll end up with from LT, Do It Right will be a power to reckon with in the future, not just a spinoff of Stephens Rec. Like you wanted, right?"

"I just wish there had been a different way." She stared at the blood on the steps. Her father's blood. Shed by his father. Will had his own shadows that stalked his dreams and memories.

How long will these shadows haunt me?

"I don't know that there was a better approach. And I can imagine alternative scenarios which could have been even more ugly."

"Yeah." She shuddered. "But the cost..."

"We harvested quite a few shadows today. But we also created more." His hand tightened on hers. "You can't get away from the shadows. You just hope to settle a few along the way."

"Will, how do you stand it?"

"Day by day. That's all you can do. Take it day by day. Some days the shadows hardly exist. Others—" He drew a long, ragged breath. "Let's go inside, Di. We still have things to do. That's how you deal with the shadows. Some days you get lucky, and you get to harvest and settle some shadows. Other days, you just make more."

But the price you pay for harvesting shadows is a bitter one indeed.

Oh Dad.

It didn't matter that he had died protecting her in a manner that hearkened back to their pioneer cowboy roots. He was still dead. She sniffled and wiped her eyes. Then Diana pulled Will close, to help him hobble back to the house.

Damn, she hoped that Grady was going to work out for managing Rio Bravo. Back home was where she needed to be. Will's new role meant she needed to take a greater role in the management of domestic Do It Right.

It's what I wanted. Just not this way.

But she intended to seize the opportunities her father's sacrifice had offered by making the Andrews Ranch one of the best bioremediated sites in North America.

Once we can afford it, scholarships. Internships. Dan Andrews will not be forgotten.

The Andrews Ranch would continue as his legacy. That, she promised to herself, to Rita and Jan, and to her father's memory. She would make it happen.

I owe him nothing less than that.

5 / LUCIFER HAS FALLEN

SEPTEMBER, 2046

WHAT IS TRUTH?

"AND I SAW LUCIFER FALL FROM HEAVEN. HOW YOU HAVE FALLEN, OH Day Star, son of Dawn—"

Francis Stewart gestured wildly with his full goblet of pinot noir. It sloshed over his hand as his loosely-belted, burgundy-colored velour robe fell open to reveal the sparse mix of gray and black hair on his narrow chest.

"Damn it. Waste of good wine. Fix that." He gulped down about a quarter of the remaining wine in the goblet.

"Now *you're* quoting the Old Testament, and not doing it well either," Sarah Stephens groaned, rattling the ice in her Scotch as she sprawled in her chair, feeling the ache in her joints in spite of her anti-aging nanos. "You're getting tiresome and repetitive. Worse yet, you're starting to sound like those Freedom Army yahoos."

She played with slipping her feet out of her flats and flexing each foot before sliding them halfway back in. Left, right, right, left. The exercise was good for them, or so her doctors said. Did she believe that?

Not really. But she did it anyway.

"What do those verses from the Bible have to do with anything, anyway?" she continued.

"You should know." Stewart smirked at Sarah as he dropped into a heavy armchair next to his bed. "Wisdom can be found in the strangest places." He grabbed for the wine bottle on the round Mission-style oak side table and topped off his glass, his robe blending in with the heavy window drapes behind him.

Sarah snorted, eying the level in the wine bottle, and wondering if she even wanted to make the effort to stay.

Get no sense from him tonight. Today must have been one hell of a board meeting for No Limits Enterprises.

"If I wanted Bible quotes, I'd visit family in Neahcom. And I probably know *these things* better than you. The right quote is "How you are fallen from heaven, O Day Star, son of Dawn! How you are cut down to the ground, you who laid the nations low!" Isaiah 14:12. If you're going to talk apocalypse literature, *get it right*."

Damn. Too close to the name of her daughter's company. A sore subject right now. Diana was being protective and rightly so, with a difficult pregnancy. Still—damn it, she could *use* her daughter's help with the Disruptions. More particularly, Diana's husband William. But her son-in-law was *so damn touchy*. Almost like his father, and Diana hadn't seemed to modulate *those* behaviors. If anything, she encouraged William's paranoia.

He is going to turn into another Parker Landreth if we aren't careful. I wish Diana would listen to me about that.

Sarah brooded over her drink. William had seduced Diana into becoming bloodbonded to Landreth Technologies programming. She had turned around and gotten pregnant right after that.

What did that damn bloodbonding mean for her grandson, and the child Diana now carried—a daughter?

"Will you fucking pay attention, Sarah?" Francis threw a lanky leg over one chair arm and gulped down more wine. "I'm not talking about religion. Not one whit."

Francis was usually more observant of her moods. Normally, by now he'd be rubbing her shoulders and whispering sweet nothings as a prelude to seduction, not engaging in drunk rantings that could have come right out of a Freedom Army video.

What the hell is eating at him?

"You need to get your quotes correct." Sarah's voice sharpened. All right. If he wanted to play this game—well, she had grown up with it.

"Usually when I hear these rants, it's all about the End Times and Jesus coming back in fire. Just what the hell else could you be talking about?"

"What if the Biblical accounts described something real?" Francis arched his brow and drank.

Sarah focused on the ice cube bobbing in her drink. "Fine. What is going on? Is this a drinking game or something, Francis? Like I said, you're sounding like the Freedom Army. Cut it out. You're smarter than that." She sipped her Scotch.

"Come on, Sarah. What if the Freedom Army's right about some things?" Francis put his goblet down carefully, his words coming clearer and sharper. "You're usually good at considering extreme possibilities, and these Disruptions do have a Biblical element."

How can he say something so outrageous, yet sound so damn sober? He's sucked down damned near half a bottle of wine. Not his normal behavior.

"Define extreme possibilities." Was it really worth it to try to shake him out of this mood? "Francis, really. I've had too damn many people yelling at me today about this stupid Disruption bullshit. If that's what you're talking about—"

"That's *exactly* what I'm talking about. Aren't you worried about these Disruptions?"

"What the hell do you think? Random city attacks coming so fast that disruption of service messages provide our first warning of what happens. No identifiable source? You're damn right I'm worried. But I'm being rational about it." Sarah took another sip of her whisky. "Damn it, Francis, we don't have time to chase after End Times delusions. Whatever is causing these Disruptions could strike anywhere. You aren't going to find the answers in the Bible!"

Francis picked up his goblet. "These attacks aren't naturally caused."

"Of course not! Someone's behind them."

"What if it's something supernatural?"

"Ah hell, Francis, are you on *that* bandwagon? Did you join the crazies?" Anger flooded through Sarah. "I go back to Oregon for six months to take care of business and you turn fundie politico on me? Damn it, I expected *you* to be one of the fucking sane ones!" She tossed the rest of her Scotch back in one neat swallow and slammed her glass on the table. "I'll see you in the morning."

She made certain her shoes were solidly on her feet and headed for the door.

Francis leapt from his chair and grabbed her wrist. "Sarah, you need to listen to this, damn it. *Lucifer has fallen and we're all going to pay.*"

He wobbled slightly, the drink starting to take him.

Like it used to do to—no, she *wasn't* going to let herself think about her damn adoptive parents.

"You're drunk and listening to stupid paranoid conspiracy theorists." Sarah yanked her wrist free.

"Ah Sarah. Don't be like that. Sarah." Francis snatched at her wrist again, but this time she was quick enough to keep it from his grasp. "Listen. We're in big trouble."

"I know that *you* are in trouble if you're listening to those people. I don't need to hear it from a lover. I'll see you at breakfast."

"Sarah." This time Francis grabbed her shoulders. "You have to listen to me. Lucifer has fallen, *and it's not what you think it is.*"

Sarah wrenched away from Francis.

If he grabs me again, I'll deck him.

Maybe it was time to end this on-again, off-again relationship.

When did I let him think that he could just grab me like this?

The mistake she had made with Peter's father Jeff, all those years ago. Here she was again, repeating fucking history.

Well, at least she was post-menopausal. And she had made damn good and sure that the anti-aging nanos wouldn't revive her ability to reproduce. So she wouldn't be repeating *that* little misstep.

"You're drunk and delusional, Francis, and what you're saying doesn't match that quote. That's a quote about the doom of Nebuchadnezzar."

"Isn't it about Satan?"

Sarah sighed. "Francis, you're a novice at this game. I grew up with it. Look. We'll talk in the morning." She opened the door.

"Sarah. Please."

Despite herself she turned to look at Francis, damning herself for her weakness. "I'm *tired*, Francis, and we have a busy day tomorrow."

"Sarah." He stood tall, holding his hands wide and open, making a pitiable face. She almost turned back.

"In the morning, Francis," she said softly. "At breakfast. Usual place and time."

"Lucifer has fallen, Sarah," he whispered. *"Lucifer has fallen, and it's not what we think.* I hope you listen to me before it's too late."

"Go to bed, Francis. We'll talk in the morning."

"It'll be too late by then."

Something about the way he said it chilled her blood.

Just not enough for her to turn back when he'd had too much to drink.

Learned my lesson about that one years ago, with Jeff.

DISCERNMENT

"Didn't expect you to stay here tonight." Anne Whitman looked up from the tablet in her lap as Sarah let herself into the condo they were sharing while they attended the Third Force Congress. Anne was a government representative, Sarah a business representative.

"Francis may be sucking down the pinot, but he sure sounds like he's been drinking something stronger," Sarah grumbled as she headed for the bar. "Not worth staying, especially when he starts blathering."

She fumbled for the bottle of twenty-five-year-old Macallan and poured herself a tumbler almost to the brim. She debated about adding an ice cube, then decided to err on the side of caution and plunked one in.

When she turned, Anne whistled softly. "You're hitting it hard tonight."

Sarah snorted. "Nothing like Francis. He had a snootful before I got there."

"That's not been uncommon for him over the past few months." Anne raised a brow at Sarah. "What the hell happened? You all right? You look pissed. Usually, you put up with the crap he spews when he gets drunk. Not get pissed about it."

"I'll be fine. It's probably just a case of not being around him lately."

Sarah took a taste of the Macallan.

Not meant to be gulped, she reminded herself. No matter what her mood was.

"I've been thinking it's time to end that aspect of our relationship for good," she continued, trying out the sound of the idea.

It didn't hurt, but she didn't expect it to. Not with the shape their relationship had taken over the years. Off-again, on-again, in and out of each other's beds—but tonight's antics not only wearied Sarah, they angered her, more than she had expected.

Flashbacks to childhood, I suppose.

Anne's other eyebrow arched. "You *are* pissed at him."

"I feel like turning over a new leaf." Sarah kicked off her flats and sipped the Scotch cautiously, sucking it down to a safe, non-spilling level before she eased into the deep armchair across from Anne and put her feet up on the soft ottoman. "Anne, he was switching between drunk and sober literally between one word and another. It was —spooky."

And too much like my adoptive father.

Maybe that was what had set her off. Too much like the parts of Neahcom that she wanted to bury forever.

Anne put the tablet aside and sat up. "You're not the only one to notice that. Bolgorev pulled me aside this afternoon, between hearings, to ask me if Francis is always this disjointed."

"Yeah. I know." Sarah let herself ease down even more into the chair's softness. "I'm hearing it from the business side." She stared down into her drink, swirling the ice cube around. "But I've not seen it directly myself. Until tonight. Damn it, Anne, he started spouting Bible verses at me, before he went raving off on how Lucifer has fallen. *Lucifer has fallen.* That's what he said. Lucifer has fallen."

"That's worse than I had heard." Anne padded over to the bar. "I didn't figure Francis for a religious drunk. How obnoxious. What are you going to do?"

Sarah allowed herself a bigger swallow of whisky. "Tonight? Finish this drink and go to bed. Tomorrow? Review my options and start damage control." She flung her head against the chair's back, staring up at the bland white ceiling. "I did not need this. Not at the beginning of the session. It was already going to be bad enough. But with Francis going deep-off-the-end irrational on us? It's going to be a long six months."

"I was hoping you'd pull an intervention." Anne sat down, a glass of wine in her hand.

"There are times when someone's just too far gone."

"We need him—sane and reasonable—in the coalition, Sarah. We need the resources of No Limits Enterprises."

"I can pull some business votes to offset Francis. And maybe I can convince Diana and William to bring Do It Right into the coalition." She didn't sound convincing, even to herself.

"Locked down? Committed? Tomorrow?"

"I just got here today. I'm not a miracle worker. But I can get them."

Anne shook her head. "Not if Francis scares them off with his talk. I needed you here a week ago."

"I had other matters to handle." Sarah took another swallow of the Macallan.

Like dealing with the problems arising with Diana and William.

"I need you to fix Francis, at least long enough for us to get through the Coalition vote. Will you do that for me?"

Sarah glared at Anne. Her third swallow emptied the glass and she held it up. "Fill this, damn it."

Anne smiled. "Thank you, dearest." She rose and brought the bottle back, refilling the glass and leaving the bottle on a side table within Sarah's reach. "Welcome back to Washington. About freaking time that you got your butt out of Portland."

"With a reception like this I'm ready to head back," Sarah grumbled as she took the glass from Anne, staring into her drink. Getting Francis off of a kick like this was going to be a real pain.

Anne briefly cupped Sarah's cheek in her hand, then squeezed her shoulder. "Don't stay up drinking tonight, darling. I promise I won't spout Bible verses at you."

Sarah quickly smiled at Anne. "I appreciate the thought, dear. But you deserve better than being second-best for the night, and I'm afraid that right now I'm not fit company for anyone I really care about." Her smile faded and she sighed. "I'll finish this one, maybe half a glass more, then go to bed. The ghosts won't haunt me then."

"I wouldn't think of it as being about second-best for the night." Anne's fingertips traced up Sarah's neck and along her chin. "I know what the rules are."

Sarah closed her eyes, savoring the pleasant tingle of Anne's light touch for a moment. Then she reached up and gently took Anne's hand.

"No. Not tonight. I meant it when I said I'm not fit company, and besides—" she hesitated. "I need to think more on what Francis said if you're going have me run an intervention. Despite the sound of it, I don't think he was quoting the Bible after all. And if he's not—Anne, I need time to think."

"Understood. But the offer still stands."

"Thank you." Sarah carefully set her drink down on the glass side table.

"Get some rest," Anne murmured before kissing Sarah. She left.

Sarah stared at the bookcase behind Anne's chair for a few minutes, frowning.

Where have I read that phrase—not Biblical?

A niggling suspicion pulled at her. She pushed herself up to retrieve Anne's discarded tablet and ran a search, muttering as she excluded Bible commentaries and Satanic references.

At last, she found the reference that had been whispering around the edges of her memory.

A Canticle for Leibowitz.

Old science fiction. Sarah quirked her lips worriedly at the title, remembering its subject well, even though she hadn't read the book for years. Then she brought the book reference up quickly, skimming until she found the passage she remembered. Reread it several times, her frown growing with each reread. Then she put the tablet down and sipped on her drink, staring unfocused as worry snaked through her stomach.

Nukes? No, that was the prevalent issue of the 1960s, when this book was written. The Disruptions use dirty radionuclides, but not nuclear bombs.

So far.

But they could bring about the end of civilization as we know it if we don't get a handle on how and why they're happening.

Lucifer has fallen. What the hell does Francis mean by this? A weapon — but whose is it?

A further memory inserted itself into her thoughts. Francis had said "*Lucifer has fallen and we're all going to pay.*"

Whatever he knows, he's afraid of it.

Sarah finished her drink and, as she'd promised Anne, only partially refilled her glass.

Francis doesn't spook easily. If the Disruptions are caused by a weapon, and he knows enough to get smashed because he's afraid of it — then God, what the hell are we getting into?

Maybe she had left Francis too soon, triggered by the Biblical nature of his rants and her own dark childhood. Those memories didn't always grab her like this, but in retrospect she wasn't surprised by her sudden, knee-jerk anger. The mark of Neahcom still lingered under the sophisticated façade she had created when she left that Oregon coastal town for good.

Maybe she should have tried to pump Francis for more information. No, as drunk and defensive as he had been, he would have continued to be coy and evasive until he passed out.

Sarah considered Anne's offer and rejected the prospect for tonight.

Some demons were best confronted alone.

LUCIFER HAS FALLEN

Francis didn't appear for the usual breakfast appointment that they kept at Roses during Third Force sessions. Sarah wasn't unduly surprised when she entered the little breakfast café near their condo, and Francis wasn't there yet.

Disappointed, perhaps, but not surprised.

He was probably sleeping off his epic drunk and would appear in either a hearing or in her office at some point, laden with flowers and apologies.

On the other hand, he could come bouncing in late for breakfast. Nonetheless, given the state of her sleep last night, she could use quiet over the meal.

Sarah sipped on her jasmine tea and slowly poked at the granola and yogurt mixture in her bowl, taking her time, concentrating on the moment, deliberately *not* thinking about Lucifer, weapons, or Disruptions, damping down the news screen at her table to its lowest volume level.

She focused on the lavender-colored silk rose on her table. Lavender roses were safe. The only man in her life who had given her lavender roses was Dan Andrews, her daughter Diana's father.

This morning, she could feel regret for the choices she had made that led her away from Dan. He had been a good man. And his dying act had freed Diana and William from Parker Landreth.

But it wouldn't have worked for you to stay with him, the despair that accompanied the memories from those days reminded her.

Sarah sighed. Not even memories of Dan Andrews were safe this morning.

A blast of noise followed by flashing red text brought her attention back to the news screen mounted on the table.

Sarah scowled at the screen. As images of people collapsing in the street began to scroll across it, she tapped up the sound. Her comm glasses vibrated with the silenced emergency warning. She snatched them before they quivered off of the table.

"Another Disruption in Brisbane," the news announcer said.

Sarah winced and shut down the audio of people screaming. The visuals were bad enough. Her stomach roiled and she shut off the screen, waving for a server as she fumbled with her glasses to turn them on.

Urgent Council meeting. All Executive Council members report in fifteen minutes. Urgent Council meeting.

The message flashed in bright red until she tapped acknowledgement.

Her stomach clenched tight.

Oh God, are we next?

Sarah flipped the comm settings to full access as she settled the glasses on her face. She scanned the flashing links, looking for Francis's acknowledgement sigil. Nothing.

Her usual server Jenny came over, face pale and sick-looking. "You saw?"

"Yeah. Gotta go. Bill to my account?"

"Got it." Jenny shook her head. "My brother's there. In Brisbane."

"I'm sorry," was all Sarah could manage to say.

Her mind was wildly spinning.

Lucifer. Lucifer is whatever's causing these damn Disruptions. Francis knows something about what the hell it is. I am going to find Francis and pound that information out of his head if he won't tell me up front!

As she left Roses, she tapped up Francis's quick link on her glasses.

Nothing.

Where the hell are you, Francis? Or are you passed out and didn't answer the phone?

Her steps slowed as she reached the intersection where she had to choose whether she'd turn left for Francis's condo, or right for hers and Anne's. He had to come to this meeting as well. Maybe she could kick him out of bed.

Incoming call flashed on her glass. Anne.

"You saw?" Anne asked.

"Enough to make me glad I'd finished eating."

"What does Francis say?"

Sarah hesitated, unsure which direction to take. "He wasn't there, Anne, and he didn't answer the call. Yet."

"Christ. Sarah, we need to get to the Council. Pronto." There was a quaver in Anne's voice. "We need to find a way to hunt this thing down."

"This—*thing*?"

That news was enough for Sarah to make up her mind. She headed for their condo at her fastest walk, unwilling to run. Not in autumn humidity.

"They've identified a potential cause," Anne said. "There are pix. You should be able to see them on your glass."

"Haven't looked yet. Still walking. I'm at the condo. We'll go over together." Sarah palmed the door open and clicked off her glasses, pushing them up on her head. She darted past Anne and rushed to her office to pick up her tablet in its sleeve, quickly checking inside to make sure she had everything she needed.

Anne waited by the door. "I've looked at the pix. It's a machine of some sort."

"A war machine?"

Who the hell—not created by anyone I would know. I don't think. All those machines are accounted for. Parker Landreth is dead. Diana won't let William make any more of those machines—will she? Or has William Landreth gone over the edge, just like his father?

Sarah briefly closed her eyes, the memory of her son-in-law's sudden quick rages so similar to Parker Landreth's surfacing. One reason she had lingered in Portland—to be available for Diana in case that anger turned against her daughter. So far, William Landreth restrained himself around Diana and their son Andrew.

So far.

Like mother, like daughter. Our tastes in men—damn it.

"War machine is the closest description of what it could be," Anne said. "Doesn't look like anything I've seen before. Definitely nothing like the LT 9572 or any other Landreth machine."

Well, that was a relief. Maybe.

"What about Francis? Should we get him up and going?" Speaking of *bad choices in men*, she still had to deal with her own.

"God, Sarah, I don't think we have the time, and if he's in the shape you said he was in last night—"

They hurried back toward the street and into the waiting skimcab.

"He'll have to come when he can," Sarah decided. Nonetheless, she texted him a quick message.

Get your butt to the Council ASAP. Whatever bullshit you were talking about last night, park it. We have bigger issues to deal with.

Their skimcab took off, headed for the Council offices in what had once been the Pentagon. Sarah leaned back against the seat, only now allowing herself to study the images from Brisbane in her glasses.

But she could still hear Francis's voice echoing in her head as she watched the raw footage of a blurry machine floating above the areas where people collapsed.

Lucifer has fallen.

Just what the hell *was* this machine creating these Disruptions?

Who's capable of building such a thing?

Sarah did a mental inventory of the list of companies she knew that could produce such equipment. None of them had any such items currently in production—war machine manufacture was strictly regulated by the Third Force. And Diana's husband—Parker Landreth's brilliant, snowboarding, eerily competent son William, one of the people who could have put something like this together, had disbanded Landreth Technologies. Allegedly defanged them, and was in control of the last Landreth war machine. Was working in Diana's company, Do It Right, on bioremediation biobots.

Another possibility. William wasn't the only Landreth war machine designer. This *could* be a Landreth rogue—someone who had escaped to the Petroleum Autonomous Zone? No Disruptions had occurred there. Yet.

I need William's help to identify those possibilities. Need more data.

"Have you talked to Will and Diana yet?" Anne asked, echoing Sarah's thoughts.

"Diana's at the Andrews Ranch with their new baby, and William's supervising construction at their new facility on Mt. Hood. I want to find out more before I talk to them." Sarah tried pinging Francis again. "What the hell is he doing? I still can't reach Francis." Worry niggled at her. "I wonder what he meant by saying that it would be too late by the morning. What's his game? At the time I thought that maybe he was guilt-tripping me."

Anne grimaced. "I don't like the sounds of that. Even as drunk as you said he was, normally he would at least respond to the alert."

"That's what I was thinking." Sarah frowned, then clicked up the Third Force Security link.

Check on Francis Stewart's whereabouts, she texted. *Did not respond to my ping this am.*

The response was quicker than she expected. *All contact lost with Stewart. Security en route to his condo.*

"Shit!"

"What?" Anne looked up from her tablet.

"Security's lost contact with Francis. He *never* switches off his tracer." Sarah started drumming her fingertips on her armrest.

She pulled her tablet out of its sleeve, to bring up greater detail, and scanned the data flooding in from Brisbane, to distract herself from her growing worry.

After a few minutes, an incoming call flashed on her glasses. Her son Peter, affiliated with Third Force Security.

"Peter."

"Mother, did you stay with Francis last night?"

"No. I was there until—Anne, when did I get back to the condo?"

"Eleven o'clock," Anne said, still focused on her tablet.

"I left his condo around ten fifty-five last night, then. He was drunk, very drunk. He didn't show up at breakfast this morning."

"He's not in his condo. No signs of a struggle."

"When did his tracer shut off?"

"Mother, you know I can't—"

"When did his tracer shut off?" Sarah's voice cracked and she realized how deeply afraid she was. "Peter, he said some wild stuff last night, connected to the Disruptions. And he was drinking heavily and hard. When I said we'd talk in the morning, *he* said it would be too late."

"That—puts a somewhat different light on the situation," Peter said. "I'll get back to you about his tracer. It appears that at some time last night, his Third Force tracer was masked by a short-term clone that imitated ours. So we're not sure yet just *when* the switch happened."

"Oh God," Sarah said, a sudden suspicion rising. "Did you get a recording of our conversation?"

She hadn't considered No Limits Enterprises as a source for that Disruption machine. But Francis's company had the capability to build such things—*and his damned board had exactly the collection of people that could be capable of doing just this!*

"Wiped." The starkness of Peter's tone—so much like his father Jeff —told her that they were thinking alike. "It's not looking good for him."

"No. And I don't record when I'm with him alone because—well, that's personal. Crap, crap, crap."

"I'll be in touch. Send us anything you can."

"Memorializing what I remember of our conversation now."

"Good. Later."

Sarah pounded her fist on the armrest, startling Anne.

"Sarah, what's wrong?"

"It looks like Francis may be tied to this machine."

"What?"

Sarah repeated what Peter had told her.

Anne shook her head. "Puts a different aspect on last night, doesn't it?"

"It certainly does," Sarah said, typing what she could recall of their conversation. She was almost finished when a file bearing Francis's icon popped up on her glass.

"Something from Francis!" she told Anne. "A file."

"Better let me look, too," Anne advised. "You need to protect yourself."

Icy prickles crept up Sarah's arms at that idea, but Anne was completely right—at this point she needed to protect herself from whatever Francis had gotten himself into. She tapped up the skimcab's big viewscreen and sent the file to it.

A recording.

Francis appeared on the screen, fully dressed in casual wear, the burgundy robe hanging loosely over his clothing. The wine goblet from last night still sat on the table beside him, as did the wine bottle, level not much different from what it had been when she left. The recording time stamp suggested he'd recorded this clip fifteen minutes after she left him. But he had just sent it to her—manually, with location trackers blocked.

So he's all right. But he's avoiding detection.

"Sarah. I'm sorry, but I told you that this morning would be too late to talk." He stopped to take a sip from the goblet. "By the time you get this, I'll be out of North America. I would have told you, would have brought you along, but—" He shrugged. "You made a different choice."

"*Crap,*" Sarah breathed, not doubting his betrayal now.

"By now, you'll know that Lucifer has fallen again." Francis cracked a brief, wry, smile. "You'll also have figured out where I got that quote from. I know you. You went back to the condo and tracked down the reference."

Sarah caught the quick glance Anne gave her and nodded.

Francis coughed. "My—*associates*—in the Freedom Army think they have a lock on the machine causing the Disruptions. We're on our way now, to try to capture it. I've spent the last six months building a team in collaboration with them in order to make this happen."

A sick feeling oozed through Sarah's gut.

Oh no, this is not good. Something like this in the hands of those rebels is so not good.

"He's cooperating with the Freedom Army?" Anne breathed. "Oh. My. God. That explains a *lot.*"

"This means the end of our relationship, but my suspicion is that after last night, it's gone anyway." Again, Francis smiled wryly and took another drink. "Give my regards to the Third Force. Maybe they'll figure things out—but not if I can get my hands on the device first. Sorry, but you had the opportunity. Goodbye."

"*Damn* it and *damn* him!" Sarah snarled as the clip ended.

"*Would* you have gone with him?" Anne asked.

"If only to figure out a way to keep those fanatics from turning that machine to their own uses, you bet." Sarah shook her head. "Anne, there's something different. *He's not afraid.* The man I talked to last night was *afraid*. This was recorded fifteen minutes later. What the hell happened?"

Anne shrugged. "Maybe he was afraid of *you*."

"He had damned well better be afraid of me. If he'd even given me a hint, things might have gone differently."

Or did he give me one?

Sarah rubbed her eyes and stared at her notes from the night before, which had taken on even more urgency.

No. No, he didn't give me a hint. Not beyond "Lucifer has fallen."

"What are you going to do?"

"Send this clip to Peter, for one. He can pass it on to Security. Finish off my notes. Call Diana and William for help."

And hope to hell that the two of them are willing to join forces with us.

Francis, you're going to pay for this.

Even if it took the rest of her life to pull it off.

DECEMBER, 2046

A NEW HOME

"WILL, YOU'VE DONE WONDERS WITH THE PLACE!" DIANA SPUN TO TAKE IN the packing box-lined living room of the family suite at Do It Right's new mountain headquarters. "I—I—this wasn't at all what I expected. Not from the blueprints, not from the pictures. You've been holding out details on me." Their infant daughter Melanie whimpered and Diana jiggled her for a distraction. "Of course, I've been in a postpartum daze, so you could have told me details that I've already forgotten."

Will grinned and flushed slightly. "I've added a lot of finish work that wasn't in the plans, because I wanted to surprise you." His voice hardened and he stared out the window, his lips tightening as his face tensed. "Every time I had a chance to tell you, another Disruption happened."

"We can't help that." Diana shook her head, trying to forget all-too-vivid memories. The last Disruption had been in Rio de Janeiro, and a couple of plant-killing viral strains from that Disruption had spread as far as Rio Bravo, her company's South American headquarters. Rio Bravo staff managed to contain the strains, but the efforts had set back their Amazon bioremediation projects by at least six to ten months.

"No. We can't." Will's face relaxed and he looked tired instead of haunted. "So. Here it is, like you requested. Finally. A headquarters with a kid-friendly residence compound. Just like we've wanted." He paused as their three-year-old son Andrew yelped happily in the neighboring room, then went to the playroom's door. "Find something good, Drew? Nice. Let me show you a trick with that."

Diana heard the happy note in Drew's response to Will and heaved a relieved sigh. She worried about Drew. He had been an unhappy, cranky infant.

Then the first Disruption struck five weeks after his first birthday. She and Will had gotten sucked into the search for a cause for the intermittent and random chemical, biological, and explosive attacks on major urban areas around the world. Between the demand for Will's services to try to capture that device and counter it, plus their own concerns about safety, the past two years had been unsettled. Nor had Melanie's birth helped Drew's attitude.

Drew reminds me of Will's father.

Diana shivered. But weren't there men like that in her own family, after all? The Stephens timber barons had been powerful, manipulative men. As was her brother.

I just don't want Drew to be a throwback to them.

Melanie mewled with hunger and Diana went to the rocking chair next to the sliding door. She settled in the chair and put Melanie to her breast, humming a soft monotone.

Melanie was nearly done with the first side when Will returned from Drew's room. "Princess is eating again?"

"Just about every hour and a half. Still. I guess that's preemie life."

"You're getting enough sleep? Want some water?"

"Yes, please. It seems like I haven't had time to do anything but feed her." Diana winced at how petulant she sounded. A good thing that Will was in the kitchen. Maybe he wasn't hearing the whiny note in her voice quite as strongly. "Having everything right here that I need for work while managing the kids will be wonderful. Staying with Jan and Rita really helped, but—it wasn't good for Drew."

"I told you that our own defended, safe place would be your Christmas present this year. Works?" Will returned with her glass of water.

"Absolutely," Diana breathed. She drank the water in two swallows.

"When you're done, let's go look at our office."

Diana switched Melanie to the other breast. "It's hard to imagine that we're finally living in the same place." She leaned her head against the chair back. "Our first Christmas at home. Nothing complicated this year, except maybe Christmas dinner. How are those plans going?"

"Zoë Wright confirmed, with an unnamed escort, and of course Tony and Angela. Probably some of the Morleys, but that depends on a pending contract. I didn't talk to your brother, and I've not heard back from your mother to find out if she and her friends are coming. Have you heard from her or your brother?"

"I may have forgotten to send an invite to Peter, and Mom's been strange. Standoffish. She's not sending messages to Drew, and she used to dote on him." Diana frowned thoughtfully. "She could just be busy, though. I've not seen her and Francis in the news of late. That usually means she has a serious secret project going."

"Understood. I'll try again."

"No. I will. I should, anyway. Being lazy. I've just let you handle communications because Melanie's needs have been so overwhelming. I should get back into focus."

Melanie pulled away from the nipple, drowsing. Diana adjusted the burp cloth, but Will grabbed the cloth, tossed it on his shoulder, and gently took Melanie.

"My turn. I've not gotten enough time with her, and you need a break. You lazy? Good grief, between parenting a preemie and managing that Rio Bravo mess, I'm surprised you're still on your feet. Go see the office. I'll be right there."

Diana organized her clothing and pushed herself up from the rocking chair. She checked on Drew, in his playroom. He grinned up at her, pausing from piecing together a set of blocks that flashed colors when he made the correct connections.

"Mama see?" He held one up to her. "Daddy says they're right when they flash blue. I make *all* blocks flash blue. Not yet but soon."

"I bet you can do that really fast once you figure it out." Diana realized the pieces replicated basic Do It Right nanobot coding schematics.

Is Will starting programming training early with Drew? Well, he's bright enough. But is it too much?

Andrew sniffed. "I trying." Then he refocused on his blocks.

Diana kissed his forehead and ruffled his hair. She looked around the playroom and saw a double door.

Didn't notice that in the schematics.

She opened the door, to discover the office. Diana unlatched the top half so it would stay open in case Drew needed her, and closed the bottom behind her. On her side, she saw that the bottom half was covered by a nanofiber layer. Tapping it lightly, she discovered that it could change from opaque to transparent. She set it to transparent so that Drew could watch her. Then she locked the setting, straightened up, and looked around the room.

Crib in the far corner. Will's work space was on the other side of Drew's door. Paper, a couple of tablets, and two hologlobe cubes, one which had an active globe spinning above it with a 3-D nano chain, cluttered the desktop.

That meant the other desk, next to another double door, must be hers. Drew could see her at work from his door. A hologlobe generator cube sat on the desk, and was that a matching pattern on the middle of the floor? She knelt to check. Yes. Another globe generator, set to go life size.

Perfect for nanobot simulations. Good.

"You like it?" Will entered through a door from the living room and laid Melanie in the crib.

"I don't know how you found time to do this." Diana now noticed the bookcase next to her desk, full of her treasured hard copy books. A protective fabric cover similar to the nanofiber on Drew's door shimmered over it.

"Planning it helped me on the hard nights while you were either in the Amazon or at the ranch." Will led her to the other double door. He opened the top. "When Melanie's older, we'll put this room together for her."

"This is the best Christmas present ever." Diana hugged Will. "I—I can't give you anything like this."

"Having the three of you *here* is your present to me." He leaned his head into her shoulder.

"I didn't think we could afford this much remodeling work."

His grip tightened briefly. "Thank the final dispersal of Landreth Technologies for that. I got more out of that sale than we calculated, so —" he pulled back. "I used it to finish the headquarters and our residence. There's not much left of the old buildings. Too much asbestos and mold, so it was easier to rebuild than remodel."

"It's wonderful, Will."

"I wanted my family to be happy and secure." He smiled at her.

"Daddy!" Drew cried out in frustration. "I can't get this last one to work!"

"You'd better go help him." Diana dropped her arms. "I'll call my mother."

"She's not been answering me."

Diana shrugged. "I can try to get through to her."

"Good luck."

COMPLICATIONS

Sarah didn't answer, so Diana left a message.

Is this going to be one of those times when she makes me pester her before she answers?

Sometimes the games her mother wanted to play were so damn frustrating.

To Diana's surprise, her mother called back an hour later, during a diaper change.

"Will! That's Mom. Can you get it?" she called to Will.

"You can activate a globe from the changing table," Will answered. "Use your usual code, add globe 1 for the small globe and globe 2 for the large globe."

Diana frowned. "DL10ARG9. Globe 1." At least the changing table was in line with her globe. "Mom. Sorry but you've caught me in a baby moment."

She looked up from Melanie and froze. Her mother looked horrible.

Sarah coughed. "I know I look bad."

"Have you been sick?"

Or is it yet another nano that's gone bad?

Her mother collected nanobot beauty treatments like other people did livesim games. Sometimes those nanobots conflicted. Diana wracked her brain, trying to remember which nano could possibly cause Sarah's haggard, drawn expression and dark-circled eyes.

She looks years older than sixty-three.

"No. Just—busy."

Her mother didn't *sound* like herself. Diana finished diapering Melanie. She hurried to her desk so she could examine Sarah closer.

"What's wrong? Will's been trying to confirm whether you'll be here for Christmas. You know Drew's always happy to see you, and you'll want to meet Melanie."

Sarah shook her head. "I've seen William's calls, Diana. I—I just don't have the heart for it this year."

"Politics? I know those Disruptions have been a challenge."

Things *had* been difficult with the Third Force Governing Council during the last eighteen months. The Disruptions had grown more and more destabilizing as whatever caused them ravaged the globe. The attacks crossed known alliances and ideologies, with no predictable patterns. A metallic device or devices that resembled the war machines Will's father used to sell was the one thing all these attacks had in common, but they weren't Landreth Technology creations.

No credible connection had been established between the Disruptions and any person or group causing it. Like every other government, the Third Force was in pursuit of the machines and the creators. Given the nature of their work with remote and wireless robots, nanos and machines in complex and dangerous bioremediation projects worldwide, both Diana's Do It Right company and her mother's Stephens Reclamation had been active in trying to stop the Disruptions.

But Sarah's involvement went deeper.

She held a Governor's ranking in the Third Force Governing Council, along with her friends Anne Whitman and Francis Stewart. She had to have been busy.

"No." Sarah's voice seemed to choke up. "It's not that, Diana. Well, okay, the Disruptions are a factor. But not like you'd think."

"Then come. Everyone invited has high enough clearances to talk freely."

"Not a factor." Sarah started to reach for the off switch.

"Mom. Stop. Now. What's wrong? You know Francis and Anne will love to play with the kids."

Her mother's face crumpled momentarily, then tightened. "I'm sure Anne will be willing to come. Invite her. But I'm staying out."

"Mom! Come on. Do I have to beg? Look. We'll talk. Drew misses you."

"I haven't the heart," Sarah repeated.

I've never heard Mom talk like this before. She mentioned Anne—Francis. Oh God. Francis. What's happened to Francis?

"Mom, is there something wrong with Francis?"

Anger flashed across her mother's face. For the first time in this conversation, Diana caught a glimpse of her mother's usual demeanor.

"Francis disappeared just before the Brisbane Disruption," she snapped. "He may be connected to the tech behind them. And—" her voice cracked. "He's married."

"Married—"

Her mother switched off the connection.

"What's up?" Will leaned over the double door leading to Drew's playroom.

"That was Mom," Diana said slowly. "She's not coming. Will, she said Francis disappeared before the Brisbane Disruption. He may be connected to the tech behind them. And he's married."

Will swallowed hard. "That—changes things in a big way. *We need to know what's going on.* It could blow a lot of things out of the water security-wise, for us as well as other people."

"I'll talk to Anne." Her mother's other lover might know more.

PLANNING AN INTERVENTION

"She cut me out of the loop, too." Anne frowned. "But yes, I'd certainly love to join you for Christmas Eve dinner. Let me work on Sarah. I might be able to budge her."

Diana studied Anne's expression carefully. She looked nearly as tired as Sarah, appearing older than the sixty years she claimed. Was it the stress of trying to counter the Disruptions, or was it just the hologlobe's effect on features? Anne hadn't been as deep into beauty treatments as her mother.

"Do you know what happened with Francis?"

Anne bit her lip and looked down, then back up. "Diana, your mother is really touchy right now. What happened with Francis caught her in a very vulnerable place."

"I understand that. But Francis disappearing? Connected to the tech behind the Disruptions? Married? Why didn't Mom tell us?"

"Francis and No Limits have done a lot of favors for me and Diana over the years." Will's voice cracked as he slid his chair next to Diana's. "So if what's happened between Sarah and Francis has compromised us—I'm already redoing my security measures. But I'd sure like to get some idea of how big my parameters need to be. Why wasn't I told before now?"

"The short answer, Will, is that you'd better assume that everything

No Limits has touched is compromised, and everyone who's had any doings with him is in that position." Anne shook her head. "Sarah's not reacting in a way that I expect. And as for the details, the night before the Brisbane Disruption, Sarah was supposed to spend the night with Francis. She came back to our condo saying that he was drunk and talking wildly about *Lucifer has fallen.* The next morning, he didn't respond to the Council's all-call after Brisbane. Your brother told her Francis switched off his locator, using a clone to mask it, shortly after she left his condo the night before."

"Wow. But why didn't anyone tell us?"

"We should have been informed," Will added.

Anne brushed a strand of dark hair out of her eyes. "Because the Council hasn't wanted the news to get out. We've been trying to keep Francis's disappearance quiet for the past three months. We know he's alive. The Council has received messages—live and recorded. We haven't seen Francis himself, but analysis confirms his spoken messages are legit. No Limits Enterprises is operating as usual, under parameters Francis set up years ago for when he wanted to step back from daily operations. There have been no security breaches in Council affairs that we can directly tie to Francis."

"Still sounds like something we should have been told," Diana said.

"Your mother is the primary reason why. Sarah insists he could not have gone willingly. We've seen no evidence to the contrary, but Sarah is stubborn to the point of irrationality about that likelihood."

"And the marriage?"

"Unconfirmed except for some information Peter turned up during the initial search for Francis. Sarah also claims to have received private messages from Francis displaying her. She's some woman from the Freedom Army."

"What the—I didn't think Francis had any connections to the Freedom Army! Now Peter has—I'd believe him. What on earth would they have to do with his disappearance?" Diana laced her fingers.

"I've been following them," Will said, voice flat. "They're increasingly more involved with Disruption protests in North America. No connection to the Disruption tech, at least that I knew." Will scowled.

"Damn it, Anne, if the Freedom Army has compromised Francis, and he's tied to the tech behind the Disruptions, then this is a real mess. It's data I need to know for chasing down those Disruption devices."

Anne sighed. "I've been saying you needed to be in the loop, Will, but the Council's more compromised by Francis's disappearance than Do It Right is. It's frozen us up. Decision-making's been paralyzed. And Sarah's been no help."

"She could have had nanobot system conflicts on top of the emotional issues," Diana said. "I've been worried about that. Francis's disappearance could have triggered them, because a stress like that— for that matter, any stress she's been under could trigger them. The Disruptions. Everything."

"You're one of our experts on nanobot systems," Anne said. "But you know how far that subject goes with your mother."

"All too well." Diana sat back in her chair. "I suppose I should talk to Peter." She made a face.

"Your mother has been consulting with him more frequently than usual."

"An intervention over Christmas Eve dinner." Diana grimaced.

"It sounds like we may not have much of a choice," Will said.

"It's going to be one heck of a Christmas dinner," Diana said.

"Dear God, I'll bring a bottle of your mother's favorite Scotch," Anne said. "That might just lure her out."

"Two days before Christmas Eve is a bit late for an invite," Peter grumped from the hologlobe connection, scowling at Diana as she burped Melanie. It had taken her a couple of hours to reach her older brother.

"Yeah, well, between Disruptions and babies, I'm not as organized as usual. My bad. So I'm sorry. Forgive an absent-minded baby sister with a premature infant."

"Is Mother coming?"

"That's—the problem. So far, she's resisting. Peter, what the hell happened with her and Francis? I know he's gone, and that we're really not supposed to know. But Mom told me."

Peter shook his head. "It's a mess. Have you talked to Anne?"

"Yes. She gave me the details, then routed me to you."

"Our mother thinks he's been influenced somehow. I'm still trying to get to the root of it. She's being unusually irrational."

"Peter, there's another factor. Her nanobot routines need to be checked. Francis's disappearance on top of the Disruptions could be sufficient to create conflicts. If we can get her here, maybe we can get her to consent to testing—*private* testing—and adjust them if needed. We have the tech."

"You think nanobot routines are an issue?" Peter leaned back in his chair, tapping his fingers on his desk.

"I wouldn't rule it out. She mixes up her plastic surgeons too much for my liking, and none of them are as familiar with the hard limits of wetware nanosystems as we are here at Do It Right. I didn't like the way she looked when I talked to her today."

"It's worried me." Peter's face remained expressionless but his fingers kept tapping, harder than ever.

He really is worried.

At least it hadn't progressed to full-scale drumming with a pencil. That, from Peter, meant extreme concern.

"If we can get her here, and you support it along with Anne, we might get her to relax her paranoia and let us test—and treat."

Melanie belched loudly and whimpered. Peter jumped, then suddenly chuckled.

"That's the baby?"

"I'd hope I wouldn't be that crass in conversation," Diana retorted.

"Oh, I don't know." But a smile played around the corners of Peter's lips. "After a few drinks, I've heard some epic burps out of you."

"Not likely these days."

"No." Peter straightened up. "Okay. I'll get Mom to Christmas Eve at your new place, ready for testing. I think she'll listen to me, especially since I can tell her we've talked and that we both agree there's an issue."

"I'll let Anne know."

"Good. See you then." Peter switched off his connection.

Diana went to change Melanie.

Gonna be an intervention all right. Lovely. Just another delightful family Christmas.

ONE HELL OF A CHRISTMAS DINNER

The next forty-eight hours flew by, until it was almost time for people to arrive for the Christmas eve dinner.

Diana took a deep breath and surveyed the living room, brushing a wrinkle out of her green velvet skirt. She and Will had managed to put the public areas of their quarters into order and decorate, even with the complication of another Disruption virus flare in Rio Bravo.

Research had donated one of their quick-harvest biofilter conifer trees along with 3-D printed experimental bioscrubber decorations, for the Christmas tree. Will had taken time off from securing systems this morning to work with Drew and his building blocks to create flashing snowflakes, cabins, snowmen, and tree decorations that now twinkled from shelves, windows, and walls. Brenda had set up her Nativity set before she, Tony and Diana tackled the food preparation.

Drew whimpered from his playroom cot and Diana hurried to get him up. When he first woke up from a nap, he was her sweet boy and not cranky.

Diana treasured those all-too-rare brief moments with her son. They banished the dread that he might turn out to be like his Landreth grandfather.

Drew blinked sleepy blue eyes at her, his pale blond hair askew like his father's frequently was, and held his arms up to be lifted. Diana picked him up, holding him close for a couple of moments before he squirmed loose.

"Potty, Mama."

Afterwards she helped him dress. "You're a handsome young man, Drew." She tweaked the small clip-on bow tie, combed his hair into place, and stood him on the counter so he could see his full self in the mirror. "See?" She smiled at their reflection.

He eyed himself solemnly, then nodded. "Mama, Grandmama here for dinner?"

"I don't know, honey." Diana tightened her lips and helped him off the counter. "We've asked her. She has—a lot going on right now. But Auntie Anne is coming, and I think your uncle Peter will, too."

"Then Grandmama here," Andrew said firmly. The yearning expression on his face nearly broke her heart. How could she protect her son from the varying moods of his grandmother?

"I hope you're right."

Mother, if you let him down....

Melanie started whimpering. Andrew tightened, frowning.

"Let's get your sister up and dressed," she said. He pouted, dragging his feet as he followed her from the bathroom. "Come on, you can be a big brother and help me."

"I've got her," Will said, to Diana's relief.

The doorbell rang, playing the first line of "We Wish You a Merry Christmas."

"That's Zoë and her date Jerry," Brenda called from the kitchen.

Diana looked down at Andrew.

"All right. Dad is taking care of Melanie. It's not Brenda and Tony's job to answer the door once they've identified who's there. We need to greet our guests. You ready to be a host, Drew?"

His eyes widened and he nodded.

"Anne's with them," Brenda added, just before they reached the door.

Diana looked down at Andrew. "Down or up?"

He considered for a moment, then raised his hands. Diana boosted Drew to her hip and opened the door. Zoë, Jerry, and Anne swept in, juggling packages and bottles, their wraps having been left with front door Security. Andrew tolerated Zoë's kiss and Jerry's pat, but he hugged Anne and would have gone to her if her arms hadn't been full. He slid down from Diana's arms.

"Those for me?" he asked Anne, ignoring Zoë and Jerry.

"Some are," Anne said. She handed a tall box to Diana. "That's for adults," she said to Diana, then turned back to Drew, giving him a smaller box. "That one is for your father, but I have things for your mother and your sister as well as you. Why don't you help me put them under the tree?"

Diana popped the lid to identify her mother's favorite Scotch.

Zoë grinned. "Well, I guess we know who *he* likes. Girl, how are you doing? It's been too damn long." She gave her packages to Jerry and hugged Diana. Then she reclaimed three of the boxes from Jerry. "These go in the kitchen. The rest go under the tree."

Will and Melanie came out of the bedroom. Diana and Zoë went into the kitchen. Zoë eased two of her packages into the refrigerator, then put the third in a warming drawer. Brenda saluted them with her water glass from her seat in the small nook booth just big enough for four people, focusing on her tablet. She kept speaking into her mike. Diana quickly checked the oven and the dishes tucked into the warming drawers. Brenda tapped her comm glasses as Diana joined Zoë and Brenda in the booth.

"Morleys just got here. Red brought Maria and the kids."

"Cool," Diana said. "That just leaves Peter and my mother."

"So what's in the box?" Zoë asked.

"A little incentive for my mother to come. I hope." Diana pulled the Macallan out of the box. She eyed it, wondering if she dared break the seal, then decided against it.

"She's been awfully quiet lately. Got something big coming out of Stephens Reclamation, or is she just sucked up into fighting the Disruptions, like you and Will have been?"

Zoë slipped a flask out of her pocket and took a swig, then handed it to Diana. Diana looked hard at it for a moment, then shook her head and handed it back.

"Thanks, Zo, but tonight's not the night to get wound up. My metabolism is still all whack from pregnancy and nursing. One drink and I'll be flat on my rear."

And I need to be sober to juggle Mom, Peter, and the kids…if that all happens.

Zoë rolled her eyes. "And you don't think you need a little relaxant? I can feel your jitters clear across the room."

"Annd, there's your mother and Peter," Brenda announced. "Separately."

"Oh God." Diana took a deep breath, exhaling slowly. "It's showtime."

"What the heck? Di, what's going on? Some drama with your mother?"

"You could call it that."

Diana went to greet her mother. Zoë might have a high-level clearance from her Justice Department work, but she didn't need to know everything right this minute.

"Grandmama!" Drew galloped across the room.

Sarah didn't look nearly as haggard as she had two days ago. She knelt to hug Drew. Then Diana came closer and saw the lines in her mother's face.

"I'm glad to see you," Diana murmured.

Sarah rose and awkwardly gave Diana a quick hug, then seized her wrist. "Peter says you can check my nano levels," she said, pitching her voice low so that only they could hear.

"It's a short walk to the lab." Diana's tone matched her mother's. "When do you want to do it?"

Sarah leaned in closer. "As soon as possible. I think Francis may have done something to me, and you're the only one I trust."

"Why didn't you ask before now?" Diana struggled to keep her voice quiet.

"Grandmama, come on!" Drew pulled at Sarah's hand.

Sarah knelt again. She said something into Drew's ear. He pouted. She kept whispering, and at last he smiled and nodded. Then he scampered over to Anne, pulling at her hand until she turned from Will and Melanie. She knelt and he whispered something in her ear. Will looked at Diana and raised a brow. She jerked her head toward the door. Will's other brow shot up, and he nodded.

Anne got up and started to speak, but Will motioned toward Diana and Sarah. Anne and Will came over, Drew trailing until Anne pointed at a box, then at Zoë. Drew squealed and grabbed the box, then ran over to Zoë. Apparently early present-giving was happening, to keep Drew distracted.

"What's up?" Will asked, keeping his voice low as he bounced Melanie.

"Mom and I are going for a little walk," Diana said.

"With Anne," Sarah added firmly.

"It's what we discussed," Diana said.

"Need any help?" Will frowned. "I could ask Brenda to take the princess."

"No, we'll be all right," Diana said. "You stay here and manage the party. Brenda should be pulling out the roast soon. Why don't you let her know what's going on? Just keep wearing your glasses, and I'll comm you if I need help."

"Peter should be informed as well," Sarah said.

"Got it." Will drifted away, pausing to talk with Jed Morley, then Peter, before drifting toward the kitchen.

"I'm glad Will's got it, because I don't know what we're doing," Anne said.

"We're going for a walk," Sarah said. "Come on."

Diana led them out the front door and into the corridor that led to the main entrance.

"So what's going on?" Anne asked, once they had passed the first Security station.

"Diana's checking my nano levels," Sarah snapped. "Not the place to talk. Diana, do we have to get our coats again?"

"No." Diana stopped at the entrance to the next wing. She pressed her fingertips to the door lock, then added her palm. The door opened into another corridor. "The lab's down this way."

She led Sarah and Anne to Biolab 3, the current clean lab for nanobot screenings.

"Mom, sit over there." She gestured at a chair. "It'll take me a moment to set the tests up." *Good thing I put the programming in place this morning.* She grabbed one of the clean hazard suits and handed it to Anne. "You need to suit up."

Sarah groaned. "Diana, nanos in the blood don't spread that easily. Is this necessary?"

"It is for a clean sample. We're not protecting ourselves from you, we're protecting your sample from anything we might carry."

Diana didn't look at her mother as she helped Anne, suited up herself, and set up the blood draw. Sarah didn't respond but exhaled deeply, leaning back in the chair and staring up at the ceiling. Diana drew several vials of blood, then loaded the tests.

"Now we wait. Mom, what the hell is going on that you won't talk, even around high clearances?"

"I think Francis fed me something long-acting to keep me from thinking straight," Sarah said in a low voice. "Something that lets him control my mind."

Diana froze halfway through stuffing her suit into the decontam unit.

"What?" Anne stopped fumbling with her suit to stare at Sarah. "Sarah, that sounds crazy!"

"I *know* how it sounds. But I feel like I'm two people, and that's something that's happened since he left. It is most decidedly *not normal.*" Sarah slapped her hands against the chair arms as her voice rose. "I can feel the difference. It's real. I think there was something in Francis's drink as well, to affect the way he was thinking."

"Who on earth would do something like that?" Diana helped Anne get her suit off and disposed of it.

"The Freedom Army, who else?"

"What the—Sarah, come on. Really?" Anne frowned. "How would they get access in the first place?"

"Well, he certainly had access to *her* more than four months ago. His *wife.* She's Freedom Army," Sarah retorted. "They have a daughter."

"Oh, Mom." Diana kept one eye on the test run and another on her mother. "You're sure?"

Sarah pulled out her comm glasses. "Let me show you how I know. You have a secured globe? Something that can contain viruses?"

"Yes, but—"

"I'll only open this message there. I don't trust anything right now."

Diana checked the time. "Five minutes more processing before we get results and recommendations." Her glasses chimed and she fished them out of her skirt's hidden pocket. She recognized the code as Brenda's and put them on. "What's up?"

"Five-minute dinner countdown," Brenda said.

"Stall it. Situation here. Tests still running."

"Open info or closed?"

"Will and Peter only."

"Got it."

Diana switched off the com and set her glasses to privacy before she replaced them. "All right. That was our dinner call."

"This message won't take that long." Her mother's face went stony and unreadable. "Pull up your secured globe."

Diana carefully pulled the secured globe's power cube out of a locked drawer. She pulled the tab marking it as clean and secure, and activated it, then held her hand out to Sarah. Her mother gave her the glasses.

"Unlocked?"

"Unlocked and set to run on remote trigger." Sarah's voice was distant. "Diana, I'm not being silly. After the first time I saw this message, *something* interfered with the files I had in my active storage. My people detected a virus, but it took them a long time to disable it. It's a very nasty sleeper."

First time. Of how many? That's not her normal behavior. View once, done, and delete. Deeply ingrained pattern, so deep I'm surprised that Francis being a butt can change it. Dear God, she may be right about someone feeding her and Francis a nanobot that can affect cognition. But what, and how could it last for more than a few days?

Diana set the glasses within the field and activated the remote trigger. Francis's image came in, blurry and wavering, then steadied, though still fuzzy.

"Anti-tracker," Diana muttered. "Will needs to see that."

"William can play with these glasses all he wants," her mother said. "I won't use them again. Ever."

"Hello, Sarah." Francis's voice seemed artificially formal to Diana. "I'm sorry about the way things happened, but—" he shrugged. "You made your choice. As have I." He waved and a young woman carrying a child came forward. "Let me introduce you to my wife, Karen, and our daughter, Regina. We have an entertaining little setup in the Freedom Army, or so I've discovered." For a moment Diana thought she could hear a trace of the Francis she had known, that characteristic, devil-may-care lilt. "It seems that in the Freedom Army, we have wives to reproduce, and comfort women to play with."

"Bastard," Anne whispered.

Diana glanced at her mother. Sarah's face remained set hard, staring ahead and not at Francis's flickering shape in the globe.

How many times has she watched this?

The woman and child moved out of sight again.

"I've shown them so you know where I stand." Francis's voice hardened, returning to the formal tone. "If you think that I'll come to my senses and return to you and Anne, like you said in your last message, well. That door is closed. You chose the Third Force, and the Third Force has chosen a wrong path. They worship false gods." Behind him, a metallic shape glided forward. "All those who fight against the Disruptions are fools. They must bow to a superior wisdom."

Diana punched the pause button. She used the remote to isolate the metallic shape and expand it, her blood running cold.

The machine Will had identified as the cause of at least three Disruptions.

"Will *has* to see this." Her throat tightened and she found it hard to swallow. "How on earth did Francis get hold of a war machine? Much less one that looks like a Disruption machine?"

The chime sounded to let her know the results of her mother's tests.

"Let the rest of the message go," Sarah sighed. "It's just ranting about false ways and everything he was saying that last night while that *thing*—" she choked and buried her head in her hands.

"Mom." Diana rested a hand on her mother's shoulders, feeling inadequate. "Why couldn't you tell me this?"

"Because the message tripped every security alarm I have," her mother responded, her voice muffled through her fingers. "Because I've been getting anonymous threats since then that are keymarked to this message. Blackmail, warnings about what will happen if I don't cooperate. *God!*" she screamed. "*And then there's the voices!*" Her voice cut off abruptly, choking off a sob. She shuddered, then drew in a deep breath. "I know something's hacked my nanobot systems. That's what those voices are. It's the only rational cause. But I can't go to just anyone. I didn't dare trust any security lesser than your William, and every time I thought about trying to get in touch, the voices...." her voice trailed off.

Anne and Diana exchanged worried looks.

"I'm not crazy," Sarah whimpered. "But it keeps getting inside my head."

"Let's see what's here." Diana pulled up the results. "Holy crap," she murmured.

"What?" Sarah lifted her head. "What's in those results?"

"I'm calling Will first." Diana fished her glasses out and thumbed them back on.

"We have a situation with Mom, all right," she told Will. "I need you here to look at these results. Sending you code now."

"Be right there."

Diana tapped in the codes she saw, then slipped her glasses back in her pocket, hand shaking slightly.

"Diana." Her mother fixed her with a steady, stern glare. "*What's in those results?*"

"I need Will to see them first, before I get into any details, because I might be wrong." Diana swallowed hard. "But Mother, the next damn time you have something like this happen to you, don't wait around to get help!"

"There's a virus?"

"Significant conflicts between nanobot regimes. It's manipulating the wrong set of neurotransmitters."

"So I was right about Francis?" A hopeful note sounded in Sarah's voice.

"It's going to take more analysis than that quick and dirty five-minute scan to identify origins, Mom."

The door beeped a warning before Will entered, already gloved up. He pulled a hazard suit off of the stack with one hand as he stared at his tablet with the other. He shoved the tablet into the workstation clamp and pulled on his suit.

"Need to do a full decontam after this one, Di. You've kept every-thing isolated?"

"Just the samples, and that set of comm glasses that Mom says trig-gered all sorts of problems with her systems," Diana answered. "They have a message from Francis on it. He's gone way off the deep end."

"That should do. I'm more concerned about direct blood contact."

"Are we all right, or should we have remained suited up?" Anne asked.

Will pulled on his hood and finished adjusting his suit. "Diana, check me," he said, his voice muffled by the hood. "No, you two are okay," he continued. "Anne, you've probably been exposed already, so if you're not having a problem now, then you're all right. Diana, you used the usual protocol?"

"Yes."

"Then all's fine. Sarah, I assume your doctors have implanted a port for nano infusions?" He went back to the workstation and tapped on the tablet screen, nodding at what he saw.

"Yes." Sarah leaned back in the chair as Will went to one of the coun-ters and began to pull tools out. "Are you doing something with it?"

"To start with, I'm putting a filtering system on your port. Need to run a cleaning infusion for the next four hours, so you'll be chained to a pump. After that, we'll replace your port, then reload what we can of the nanos you're supposed to have in your system, at least as best as I can replicate them."

"Make sure there's no conflicts," Diana said.

"Of course. Can you stay overnight? That would be best. Give you time to rest while the systems reload."

"I hadn't planned on it," Sarah said reluctantly.

"We have guest quarters," Diana said. "Private. Comm systems. Room for Security."

"It's for the best." Anne rested a hand on Sarah's. Sarah grabbed it.

"William, what is wrong? Diana's being cagey about the results."

"That's because those are Landreth Technology codes and she knows just enough to be aware that they mean trouble," Will said, his focus on the tablet screen. "They shouldn't be active." He tapped the screen impatiently. "All right. There. Sarah, you have three things wrong, and one of them is well on its way to killing you. One. You have two beauty maintenance regimes working at the cellular level. Never should have happened that way, because there's a conflict in the deep codes between the two."

"I've never had problems, until four months ago."

"You were playing with fire. Nonetheless. Under normal circumstances they can cooperate, as long as there isn't excessive overload on your body systems, or you don't develop an inflammatory syndrome. Two. Something caused excessive inflammation, which made a mild conflict worse. So yes, you have nanobot system conflicts. But then there's the worst one. You have a slow-release toxin in your system which is straight out of one of my father's war machines. The damn thing shouldn't be in the wild. That's what is killing you. Are you hearing voices? Seeing things that shouldn't be there?"

"Yes."

"How long?"

"Since Brisbane and Francis's disappearance." Sarah's voice quavered slightly. "I think he may have fed something to me in a drink, that affected him as well as me."

"Could be but not likely," Will said. "Not how that third thing gets transmitted." He put a device on a tray along with several instruments as well as an infusion bag, and rolled the tray over to Sarah's chair. "I'm putting the filter on your port now, then hooking up the infusion. Ready?"

"Yes." Sarah bit her lip and closed her eyes.

Will leaned the chair back. He motioned Anne away and bent over Sarah. Diana watched, fascinated, as Will delicately peeled back the artificial skin over her mother's infusion port, then slid the filter over the port. He reattached the skin, the filter revealing itself by bulging slightly under the artificial skin, then inserted the connection to the infusion bag that sat on the tray. Finally, he clamped the bag to Sarah's left forearm and slid a support sleeve over the infusion bag.

"Should hold up even if Drew wants to hang on you," he said.

"I—I won't contaminate him?" Sarah asked.

Will glanced at the tablet screen. "Anything of danger in your system should have been inactivated five seconds ago. But inactivation isn't a cure. That's why the filter. The toxin is very dilute, but in four hours, you'll be free of it. It's a reliable tech. I've used it in the field for years."

Sarah coughed. "Thank you."

"Oh, we're not done yet," Will sighed. "It's going to be a long night. Might as well return to social life and get dinner. It'll keep us distracted. There'll be time to talk later, when I have results from more detailed testing." He started to pick up his equipment. "Go on ahead and get people settled in, Di. I'll be right there. Let me clear this and set my next level of testing."

Diana and Anne helped Sarah up. They were silent on their way back.

Once inside, Diana left Anne and Sarah to join Brenda in the kitchen.

"We're doing dinner now?" Brenda asked.

"Now," Diana said.

Thankfully Brenda didn't ask any questions as they quickly moved food from the kitchen to the dining room table, with places already set. Zoë and Maria Morley joined them in adding the final touches.

Just as they gathered around the table, Will slid into place at the head. Diana settled Drew at his right hand. She sat next to Drew, and her mother next to her, with Anne beside her. A flurry of serving food followed, and somehow during the course of the meal, Diana ended up with a glass of white wine.

Dinner and gift exchange passed in a blur. Soon enough, it was time for her to put the kids to bed, as Will escorted their guests out and went back to the lab with Sarah.

After both children were settled in bed and the monitors on, Diana went looking for answers. She glanced into the living room and didn't see anyone, so she continued to the kitchen.

Will, Sarah and Anne sat at the nook table, shot glasses filled with whisky in front of them. An empty glass was next to Will's. Diana slid in next to him.

Her mother pushed the bottle over. Diana shook her head.

"Go ahead and take a drink," Will said. "Your mother and I have been talking."

"About what?"

"After watching that message in full, I think Francis is the key to finding the Disruption device." Will's voice remained harsh. "Once we get a lock on him, we can catch the device."

Diana swallowed hard. She reached for the bottle with her free hand and poured herself a single finger's worth.

"Excuse me." Will gently pushed against Diana's shoulder. "I need to get out. It's time for me to set up stage two of the treatment protocol. I'll comm when it's time for Sarah to be there."

"Okay."

Silence fell over the three of them as Will left. Finally, Sarah reached for the bottle and poured herself a half-glass. She held her glass, contemplating the amber liquid.

"I haven't drunk Macallan since the night Francis left," she said, her voice husky and tight. "Francis appeared to be drunker than hell. He kept saying *Lucifer has fallen* and making bad Biblical allusions until I got sick of it and left. It wasn't until after he'd disappeared that I realized he was talking about the device."

"The Disruption Machine?"

Her mother nodded.

"None of these Disruptions make any sense," Anne said. "Who gains from them?"

"Oh, there are forces who'll gain." Sarah chuckled bitterly. "If Parker Landreth was still alive and running Landreth Technologies, he'd be making money hand over fist right now designing defensive systems. Just like those who swarmed in to replace him are doing."

"But this much? Are they trying to destroy the whole world as we know it? Who would do such a thing?" Diana asked in a low voice.

"Chaos exists." Sarah sipped her drink. "And no matter what, we need to stop this."

"And then what?"

"Depends on who's behind the attacks."

"What about Francis?"

Sarah shrugged. "Well, it appears he belongs to someone else." She scowled. "I won't be anyone's *comfort woman*. Damn it. Even knowingly. The fucker. Just the way he said it—" she shuddered.

"He used *both* of us," Anne said sharply.

"True. And I'm sorry I brought you into this mess, dear." Sarah reached for Anne's hand."

"I'm angry because he hurt you worse than me," Anne said.

"Mom. I'm sorry. He meant a lot to you."

"Thank you." Sarah tossed back the rest of her drink and poured herself another, albeit a smaller amount. "I'll survive."

"Just survive?"

"What? This isn't my first betrayal, Diana. Nor was it my worst." Sarah tossed back this drink and pushed her glass away. Her voice sounded very tired as she continued. "The way my mind has been clearing since your William started the scrubber process tells me a lot. I've lost four months to that damned thing, and it makes me angry that Francis—or someone else—did it. They'll pay."

Diana's comm glasses chimed. "I'm ready for your mother now," Will said.

"Will's ready." Diana slid out of the nook. "I'll walk with you."

Sarah nodded and slid out. She exhaled heavily, then straightened up. "Let's go. Time to get this over with. One hell of a Christmas celebration, isn't it?"

"Absolutely," Diana agreed. "One hell of a Christmas celebration. Let's hope that future ones run more smoothly."

Sarah snorted. "Good luck with that."

"It's worth a try," Diana said.

"May you have more luck with William than I ever did with any of my men," her mother said. Despite her words, she squeezed Diana's hand, then fumbled for Anne's. Then they headed for the lab.

One hell of a Christmas dinner. But at least she had Will for a partner, and not Francis.

7 / VALENTINE DISRUPTIONS

FEBRUARY, 2048

GETTING AWAY?

"Okay, so here's the list of Melanie's latest behavior triggers, and Drew's allergies. Mel needs her ADHD meds every twelve hours since she doesn't do well with the twenty-four-hour meds...." Diana's voice trailed off as her stepmother Jen grinned at her.

Her children, Andrew and Melanie, skittered past Diana and Jen, leaving the door wide open to the winter cold.

"Get the door!" Diana snapped, sighing. The kids knew better. But they seemed to forget every bit of their manners when they first arrived at the Ranch.

Melanie froze, and Andrew wheeled to slam the door shut. Before Andrew could catch up to her, Melanie bolted up the stairs to meet their teenaged aunt Rita. Five-year-old asthmatic Andrew struggled to get ahead of his athletic, hyperactive, three-year-old sister.

"Melly, no!" he whined, shoving her against the railing. "I go first!"

"No, *me!*"

Melanie hurled herself against Andrew, shoving him into the wall. She darted to the top of the stairs as Andrew struggled to regain his balance and fell, giggling as she reached Rita. Diana didn't hear what her half-sister said as she knelt and spoke softly, but Melanie pouted.

Andrew recovered and scrambled back up the stairs. He swung his right fist wildly at Melanie as he reached the top. Rita blocked him, set him on her other side, then scolded the kids in a low voice. Diana only heard the tone, not the words, but from Drew's scowl to match Mel's, Rita had dished out equal reprimands to both kids.

Diana sighed with relief.

Jen chuckled. "That kid's well on her way to becoming a kid whisperer as well as a horse trainer."

"She'll need it with these two," Diana said. "Smart *and* strong-willed. And Mel can hold her own with Drew even though she's two years younger, so neither of them are afraid to get physical."

"They wouldn't be your kids without being smart and strong-willed," Jen said. "Isn't that how you and Will got where you are?"

"True," Diana acknowledged. "Now, about those instructions."

"Di." Jen tapped her tablet before setting it down on the foyer table. "You sent me this list before your skimmer left the Mountain. So. Hello. Deep breath. Your children will survive two nights away from you. Good grief, the two of you fret. Will went through the same list with me, before he went out with the interns."

Diana opened her mouth to say more but Jen shook her head.

"Breathe," she repeated. "Is this the first time you two have gotten away from the kids since Melanie was born?"

"For more than a few hours, yes," Diana conceded. "One or the other of us have always been with the kids, except for a few hours at a time. Work and the Disruptions."

Jen shuddered. "You're worried about the Disruptions even on the Mountain?"

"Taking the kids near Disruption sites when we're working," Diana clarified. "But I don't feel safe leaving them behind unless Will's there. We can't guarantee their safety otherwise."

"I thought you had Security."

"Not enough to split three ways between me, Will, and the kids. Especially since Brenda is just coming back to work after Angela's birth. And when Will caught the last nanny trying to hand them over to Francis Stewart—" Diana shivered. Fortunately, Will hadn't resorted to the LT 9572 to handle that particular incursion. Though she was sure he'd been tempted. "So when you offered, it was a godsend."

It wasn't like they hadn't talked about getting away.

There had been enough times in the past six months where either

Diana or Will would look across the office, or at each other in the field, and say to the other, *we need some time off.*

But there was always something interfering. She wasn't sure which one of them had finally insisted they find a means to go somewhere alone, without Drew and Mel, that wasn't work-related. Adult time.

They had been chasing the Disruption Machine for three years, without a break. And if they weren't chasing the Machine, they were building up their Do It Right bioremediation/biotech business. When Jen had responded to Diana's tentative question about watching the kids for two nights over Valentine's Day with a firm invitation, it had been a relief.

There wasn't another option for childcare, at least not one they both trusted.

Will's parents were both dead, and Sarah didn't do kids except for short visits of no more than a couple of hours. Diana had family in Neahcom, the Oregon Coast town where they would be staying in the Stephens beach house, but she didn't know them well enough to trust them with Drew and Mel. Her mother's commentaries about the Neahcom kin were enough to warn her.

That meant her only option for family-based childcare was what remained of her father's family, Jen and Rita at the old Andrews Ranch, now administered as a tribal protected heritage site. The location was as safe, if not safer, than their Mountain headquarters.

Will was working on a tribal contract to set up a protective barrier around the extended Tribal Protectorate, a prototype of future protections against the unknown machine causing the Disruptions. Right now, he and the tribal interns responsible for sensor and beacon maintenance were setting up the trial barrier around the Ranch, as a test for the future extension over the entire reserve. It was the same protective barrier technology they had devised for DIR's headquarters, but Will was concerned about the strength of the signal over the larger and more rugged territory of the Ranch.

Still, if it works here, then it should work for the rest of the Tribal Protectorate. And then, perhaps, we can start selling this technology.

Diana was already fending off tentative feelers about commercial availability of the barrier, which Will called the No-Fence. She wasn't certain how the information about it had gotten out, but—if they could pull off developing it, then the No-Fence would cement DIR's reputation as a tech company as well as a bioremediation company. Ease them into a transition where they focused on the tech that facilitated bioremediation.

Will thought the tech focus *might* be a better option in the long run. Competition in bioremediation work was getting crowded, and while Do It Right still held a stellar reputation in the field, bigger conglomerates were moving in. They needed a more specific focus—and security tech coupled with bioremediation provided an outlet for some of the security-related technical designs that his late father's company, Landreth Technologies, had been doing.

"You and Will work way too hard," Jen continued. "While I understand the reasons why you have the kids at your worksite, you need some down time when you're not working or being parents. You're as bad as your father was when it comes to working constantly!"

At least Jen didn't compare her to her mother, like most people would have.

"It's a question of security, Jen. Francis is targeting the kids."

More than that, her mother felt guilty because she still didn't understand quite why her former lover Francis Stewart had turned against her and was attacking her grandchildren. Discovering that spending time with them made them a target had the effect of driving Sarah further away from regular contact with Drew and Mel—and Diana saw the effects on Drew, who dearly loved his grandmother.

Mom and her damned guilt.

Sarah Stephens didn't do well with acknowledging guilt in any form.

"I understand. But come on. Have a cup of coffee and settle for a minute." Jen led Diana through the living room to the big dining room that looked out on the mountains. "Will went out with the team before it was light. I've made bread. Want some?"

Diana's mouth watered at the thought of Jen's bread. "Oh yes."

She followed Jen into the kitchen and reached for a mug to pour herself some coffee while Jen sliced the fresh, sweet-smelling loaf. She *should* be working, checking on the latest reports from Rio Bravo, and inspecting what the transponders for the Ranch's bioremediation bots were saying.

But for once, Diana felt like stepping aside and catching her breath. This was supposed to be a break. Their first real break in years. If she took the time to relax, then perhaps Will would too, once he came in from the field.

It's not a race, she reminded herself.

Still, when it came to the Disruption Machine, and Francis's potential connection to it—them—whatever it was, it sure seemed like they were racing against the clock.

INTERRUPTION

"This is going to be *all right*," Diana said firmly as she settled behind the skimmer's controls. Will slumped in the passenger seat, staring at his tablet, waiting for them to lift off before activating the protective beacons. "Isn't it?"

"I don't know," Will sighed, echoing her uneasiness. He jabbed at the screen as Diana ran through pre-flight checks, then activated the skimmer's drive. It lifted straight up until the ranch was toy-size beneath them. "Hold here for a moment, would you?"

"Okay." Her hands tightened on the steering yoke as Will activated the beacons. She forced herself not to look as the barrier shimmered into being.

What happens if it doesn't work?

She wouldn't want to leave the kids again, nor would Will.

Don't think about that.

Instead, she acknowledged the text from their Security escort, and set their link so that any changes she made in-flight would automatically transmit over. Normally they would chat with the secured com open, but for this trip, she wanted as much privacy as they could squeeze out of Brenda.

Getting away from the constant Security reminders was as much a vacation as taking a break from the kids.

"Well, now, that looks right pretty."

The relief in Will's voice encouraged Diana to glance down. She saw the lovely green shimmer of the protective field. Will tapped a text message, frowning in concentration. Then his face lightened.

"No interference with messaging Jen through the barrier. Everything's working just like planned, for once." He grinned. "Di, let's go, before we have too many more second thoughts!"

"We're going." Diana pushed the throttle into regular mode, turning the skimmer toward Portland, where they planned to have dinner before traveling on to Neahcom. Once clear of the Protectorate, she set the autopilot, unstrapping her shoulder restraint while keeping her lap belt on.

Will continued to pore over his tablet.

"Gonna work all the way to Portland?" she asked.

Will looked up, a smile slowly spreading across his face as he secured his tablet and undid his shoulder restraint.

"Now I'm not." He reached for her hand. "Don't want to get *too* busy while we're in flight, but I can think of a few other things to do." He raised her hand to his lips and kissed her fingers.

Diana giggled as the contact sent prickles up her arm and down her spine. Will turned her hand, his lips caressing her palm before moving to her wrist.

"Mmm."

Will dropped her hand and cupped one of his hands around the back of her head as his lips touched hers. Diana abandoned herself to everything but the kiss, her heart pounding as she got a deep whiff of the faint musk that meant Will, always had meant Will and no one else. She leaned over the console as his free hand fumbled with the snaps over the chest of her protective stealthsuit.

"BEEP BEEP BEEP BEEP!"

The blare of a proximity alert jerked them apart. Diana jolted back to the yoke, grabbing it and switching off the autopilot. Will yanked his tablet free from its clasp.

"What the hell?" he growled. "Is someone after us?"

"Switching to secure stealth mode!" Diana's heart still pounded, but for a different reason than it had just seconds ago.

She punched the stealth control to activate it, then pulled back on the yoke, sending the skimmer as close to straight up as it would go, slamming the throttle forward to accelerate to the skimmer's top tolerance. The blare switched off and she leveled the skimmer, still keeping it at highest speed.

"What was that?" Brenda's voice broke radio silence.

"You didn't see what the proximity was?"

"No. Something fast."

"Disruption Machine signature," Will said grimly.

"Get that, Brenda?"

"I heard. Heading?"

"Loading now. Looks like it's targeting Seattle," Will said.

Diana nodded sharply. She banked the skimmer and set a course for the heading Will had just sent. "Can we catch up?"

"*We* can't," Will said. "But the 9572—"

"Can it catch the machine?" She remembered the last time they'd gotten a lead on the Disruption Machine. It had disappeared before they could deploy the LT 9572.

"We'll see." Will unstrapped his lap belt and crawled back into the skimmer's main compartment. "Don't go auto until I bring the box up. Keep the skimmer at speed as best as you can until then."

"Understood." Diana bit her lip, gripping the yoke and the throttle as if sheer force would lend more speed to the pursuit.

Last time they had encountered the Machine, it had already attacked Fairbanks, dumping a load of radiological and chemical weaponry. But it had been a transient blip on their sensors, and it had disappeared before they could deploy the 9572. They'd never encountered the Machine between or before attacks until now.

Always after an attack.

The damned thing evaded conventional tracking mechanisms, and it had some means of stealthing and shielding that even Will, in cooperation with other top international weapons experts, couldn't detect and counter. Running across the Machine en route to a target like this *just didn't happen.*

Luck, or a trap?

Damnably frustrating that it had to happen *now.*

Will clambered back into his seat, the black box marked with the now-defunct sun logo of Landreth Technologies in his hands.

"Tell me when to switch to auto." Diana stared straight ahead.

She hated these sessions when she was Number Two to Will in controlling the last of the Landreth war machines. There was something malevolent about the LT 9572's voice that she *heard* via the external neural nets, even if she was only helping Will direct it on a deep-sea mission, or recovering satellites for repair.

The malignant tone never seemed to affect Will, or else it wasn't projected to him. But she felt a thrumming, sinister, sullen presence every time she joined Will while guiding the machine, a surliness that reeked of resentment at being used for something other than war. It reminded Diana of Parker, Will's father, and how he'd hated her.

It's just a machine. And you're bloodbonded to it, so not only does it have to obey you, it can't attack you.

"Your net."

Will carefully held the secondary control net out to her on his fingertips. Diana switched on the autopilot. Then she eased the delicate wire framework over her scalp, pressing the edges to contact skin at temples and the base of her neck, gathering her shoulder-length brown hair into a loose fall at the back of her head to avoid tangling.

"Activate Diana Landreth 1," she murmured.

The dry whispery presence of the 9572 filled her awareness. She switched off the autopilot to take back control, cranking the throttle for as much speed as she dared coax from the skimmer. The 9572 linked into the skimmer control systems, providing a swift backup to Diana's reflexes. She moved to fingertip touches on the yoke, because reaction speed was now faster.

Will came on line, a sunny warmth permeating the dry whispers of the 9572.

"Target programmed," he said.

<Release in five,> the 9572 hummed in a half-humanoid, half-mechanical voice. None of the growly grumpiness was in its tone now. <Capture or kill?>

"Capture if you can," Will said. "Kill—"

The 9572's emergency override grabbed the yoke, nearly twisting it out of her hands. The skimmer shook from a blast as it banked steeper and harder than Diana would normally risk. Control released back to Diana as the skimmer tried to shake into a stall.

She shook her head and bit back a curse, plying yoke and throttle to steady their craft. The 9572's link to flight controls through her net had saved them before, but it didn't always pay attention to human tolerances. Especially when it was still on board.

"You two all right?" Brenda yelled.

"The Machine shot at us!" Will answered. "And I've lost track of it."

<Send me,> the 9572 purred, a note of yearning chiming deep and steady in its projected voice. *<Send me.>*

As they had worked with the war machine, it gained more sentience.

"Not without a visual," Will said to the 9572. "Too many unknown targets."

<ID Lock,> the 9572 responded. It projected a screen on a visual overlay, showing the target. *<Contact confirmed.>*

"Send it," Diana rasped. "We've a chance to stop that damned machine now."

For once she agreed with the 9572.

Get that thing down as fast as we can!

If they could deter even one Disruption....

Will glanced sharply at Diana, then nodded. "Bring it down. Inactivate if possible but don't destroy. We need to study it. Go!"

<Go,> Diana breathed mentally.

For once, she felt a sharp, solid approval from the 9572.

The skimmer quivered as the 9572 launched from its special compartment.

<EMP lock!> the 9572 sent to Diana. *<Prepare for resistance from target acquisition!>*

She braked and switched to full secured manual mode, signaling Brenda to do the same in the Security skimmer behind them.

"Why did you do that?" Will asked.

Diana's hands tightened on the yoke. Orange blossomed in front of them. The blast buffeted the skimmer and bounced them around. She wrestled with the controls, pressing her lips tightly together.

"Stabilizer hit!" she growled as the warning light flared. "I need to take us down! Brenda, you copy?"

Static answered her.

"Damn, damn, damn!"

"Working on it," Will bent forward and tapped the control panel open in front of him. "Just get us down fast, Di. Good thing it's you and not me flying!"

Diana nodded, still struggling with the yoke. Normally, skimmers handled with the lightest of touches, but once stabilizers and other controllers failed, they handled worse than the old farm truck she used to drive during hay season on the Ranch.

Her early remote bioremediation work had required the ability to handle clunky, half-functional skimmers if needed. As part of her initial training, Sarah insisted that Diana learn to handle skimmers under the worst conditions possible. Sarah's lover Francis Stewart had the best private instruction setup—except for Landreth Technologies, and there was no way Sarah would submit Diana to LT—so she asked Francis for help. Diana was grateful, but—

God damn you Francis, why did you betray her—betray us?

The skimmer bucked and bounced, but at least this design had a decent glide ratio. Diana looked for a landing site. They were still over the high desert. Somewhere in here, they would encounter the deep canyons of the Columbia scablands. She hoped to find a flat spot. No time to check her locator. Besides, she couldn't trust it after that localized EMP.

The land underneath them was uncultivated.

Not in the wheat fields, then.

Ridge to her right.

She wrenched the yoke so that they glided parallel to the ridge and up a wide draw, easing the throttle back to slow them as she looked ahead. No windmills, no power lines, no fences that she could see. Uneasiness crept up her. Only one place in the high desert where she could come across this type of emptiness, these days.

No, no, this isn't Northstar.

This wasn't the abandoned weapons manufacturing site. Couldn't be. She was just in a big pasture somewhere. Diana saw a clear space—some sort of bare road—and pointed the skimmer at it. She activated the rarely used landing gear.

"Brace!" she yelled at Will.

Their landing was bumpy and they bounced several times, but Diana finally got them down and stopped. She shut down the skimmer and leaned back in the seat, breathing hard. To her surprise, the 9572 link still functioned.

"Now *this* was not exactly what I had in mind." Will rose from crash position. "But we have results!"

"Results?" Diana shakily undid her lap belt.

"The 9572 caught the Machine," Will said. "Now we just need to find where they went down. Blowback from the capture battle knocked out the stabilizer."

"That simple?"

"Well, no. But we're farther along than we've been before—and hey, it didn't make it to Seattle!"

"At least there's that," Diana conceded.

Did Brenda make it down?

Static crackled. Brenda's voice came in on a local channel. "Fine place you picked to crash, Di. Right in the middle of Northstar."

"I couldn't help it—"

"It's probably the best choice of any in this location. But just letting you know."

"The 9572's caught the Machine," Diana said.

Brenda's breath audibly caught. "Northstar. Of all places to catch the Machine. If only it had happened before the Stephens contract expired."

"At least it didn't make it to Seattle. And I can work with Chen. Would have been simpler if Mom still had the contract, but at least Chen and I can talk."

Chen Tiěrén was the bioremediation manager for Mei-lein Enterprises, the new reclamation contractor at Northstar. He had been her official connection with the Chinese contractor in Vietnam during her tenure as onsite assistant manager for a Stephens Reclamation project.

Diana and Chen had butted heads a time or two, but for the most part Chen was a reasonable man.

However, she didn't know what Chen would think about the appearance of both a Landreth war machine and the Disruption Machine in the middle of one of the most complex and political reclamation projects on the current market.

Especially since Diana was also on site. DIR was independent of her mother's Stephens Reclamation, but not everyone accepted that reality. Stephens had defused the radiological issues at Northstar, but there was much more to Northstar than radiological contamination.

And then there's what might have been released when the 9572 brought the Disruption Machine down.

Diana nervously refastened her protective stealthsuit's seals. Radiologicals, biologicals, chemicals…who knew what witches' brew that damned machine could have released to deter capture?

Brenda came back on line. "You got a strategy?"

"Working on it now," Will said, poring over his tablet. "We can't just go barging in. God knows what kind of payload that damn Disruption Machine is carrying."

"Setting up perimeter. We'll signal when it's clear. If you hadn't gone to manual and ordered me to do the same when you did, Di, we'd have been in a world of hurt," Brenda said.

"That was good timing," Will said. "How did you know to go to manual?"

"The 9572 warned me," Diana said.

Will raised his brows. "Huh," was all he said.

SCARY DISCLOSURE

Fifteen minutes later, Diana followed Will up the draw, Brenda's team fanning out to the sides with weapons locked and loaded. They wore helmets, but hadn't gone to full filters yet. Will concentrated on his tablet's tracking device while Diana and Brenda handled the comealongs for both the 9572 and the Disruption Machine.

Diana tried to send a personal message to Chen, but the EMP had taken down the Mei-lein networks in this section of Northstar. Instead, she settled for voice texts through official links, and hoped that Chen picked up the careful nuances. Warn him, without spreading the news too widely that the Disruption Machine was in custody.

Someone from Mei-lein will be out to check soon.

For safety's sake, they needed to reach the 9572 before anyone else. The war machine still carried netspiders, and despite Will's best efforts to teach it otherwise, its programming often reverted to defensive elements when deployed in *capture and retrieve* mode. Their contracts for the 9572's use explicitly stated that either Will or Diana needed to be on the retrieval team.

But this wasn't a contracted retrieval job. This was close to the 9572's original design purpose. Who knew what reverting to those tasks did to its processing?

Then there was Chen. Former military. How likely was it that he would be thrown back into a defensive mentality?

If there was one thing that Diana knew about how Chen Tiĕrén thought, he wouldn't overlook the sudden disruption of a local network. Especially if he had picked up a Disruption Machine trace. Nor would he let the presence of a Landreth war machine stop him from claiming the prize that the Disruption Machine represented. Besides the six-figure financial award for capture, there was the information that this device must be carrying.

She wanted that information for Do It Right. Not give it away to Iron Man Chen.

"Halt," Will said as his tablet pinged loudly. "It's up there." He pointed to the top of the twenty-foot cliff they stood under.

Brenda signed to the Security team. They moved in. "We can climb this cliff."

"No." Will scowled. "We need to take a slow approach. The 9572 got damaged in the capture. I don't trust it not to attack anyone but me and Diana. We don't dare pop up abruptly over the cliff edge. We have to backtrack and come at it on the level."

"We can do that," Brenda said.

One of the local networks taken out by the EMP quivered back into life. Diana ignored Will and Brenda's further conversation as she traced the connection. Local skimmer pinging the connection, resetting links using protected short-term codes and batteries that would keep the network live, until someone could go through on the ground and replace the active nodes.

Damn, Chen's going to be pissed about this.

The highly shielded temp nodes weren't cheap, nor was replacing the regular network. She blinked as she noted the local skimmer's ID. Chen himself.

Did the Third Force tell him we'd picked up a Disruption trace, or was that his own tracker?

Normally network replacement wouldn't be something a manager at Chen's level would do. Something else must have caught his attention.

Trackers? Her mother hadn't been running Disruption Machine trackers at Northstar during the Stephens contract.

But that had been a different era, and two contracts ago.

"Got to do it fast." She interrupted Will. "Chen himself is investigating. We weren't the only one who IDed that Disruption Machine trace."

"Okay. Let's go. Diana, can you do direct comms with Chen yet?"

She shook her head. "Not down here."

"Take point," Brenda told Red Morley. "Will, Di, you're in the middle."

"You'll need us in front as we get close."

"Not sticking you out there until then," Brenda said flatly. "Who knows what Northstar is bringing out?"

Will nodded. Red wheeled, Brenda at his side. Diana and Will fell in behind Brenda and they headed back down the draw at a jog trot, Security tight around them.

"We have a problem," Will said to Diana on their private comm. "The 9572's stats are veering toward rogue. That EMP stripped out my recent programming."

"How much have we lost?" God, she hoped it hadn't reverted completely to the old Landreth structures. Will had backups, but were they on his tablet?

"Won't know until I get my hands on it." He switched comms. "Brenda. Let's go up here." He waved at the steep hillside.

Diana looked at it and groaned inside as Brenda and Red smoothly swung around to angle up the slope.

Hope I can keep up, with my bum knee.

Fortunately, Brenda slowed the pace, and Diana didn't twist her leg too badly as they climbed.

"It's further from the cliff edge than I thought," Will muttered.

Her comm buzzed as they reached the top. Diana paused, raising her hand to signal Will and Brenda, then checked her messages. One from her mother, another from Chen. "I have a message from Chen."

Advice taken. Will follow your direction and wait for further explanations.

Good. He still remembered her discreet codes from Vietnam. She had referred back to the incident with failed Landreth chips which turned bioremediation bots into netspiders.

But that message had come from too close a location for her

comfort. They would still have to deal with Chen, and that might require favors or fees they could ill afford.

"Anyone else?" Will asked.

"My mother." Diana opened that message.

Need help?

Diana laughed. "Mom saw the alert. I'm texting her back. Wouldn't hurt to have her on reserve if necessary."

Sarah could help pay for access fees. In return, Diana would gladly share information with her.

"Could be," Will said. "Do it before we get closer."

"Got it. How far out do you think we are? Chen's closer than I like."

"Five minutes at a brisk jog."

"Texting now."

Got our location? Machine's down. Touchy situation. May need backup, Diana sent.

Transmit location pinned in GPS. Best spot in Northstar. Will be there. Fifteen minutes.

"Mom's fifteen minutes out."

"Okay," Will said. "We're in the lead. Max your suit repulsers and filters. If the Disruption Machine has anything left, it'll be biologicals and chemicals. Di, monitor channels and handle comms. More as we get there."

Diana flipped her face filters to highest levels before Will finished speaking. She switched on the air filter systems and nodded at Will. He set off at a brisk jog. She matched his stride, her longer legs giving her the advantage, half-focusing on notifications while watching out for her footing so she didn't wrench her knee, and keeping one eye on Will.

Singed brush was the first sign that they were near the downed machines. Will slowed to a walk. Diana looked ahead, seeing the faint shimmer of the 9572's restraining field glowing over an object she couldn't clearly see.

"Stage arrivals over there, Brenda." Will pointed to a flatter area behind them. "We need to go alone from here."

Diana nodded at Will. His lips tightened and he turned back

toward the restraining field.

"Overlay comms from here on out," he said. "No more glasses comms."

Diana deactivated her glasses and whispered the overlay codes. Both comm and 9572 codes flickered into life, projected on her helmet's face screen.

They walked together, step by cautious step. As they drew closer to the machines, a layer of pale pink foam thinly coated the desert soil and burned brush. The ID tag that came up on Diana's overlay marked it as DIR bacterial suppression foam, one of the mixtures they had loaded into the 9572 for Disruption Machine post-attack containments.

So the 9572 did deploy protective measures on its own, despite that damned machine.

She clucked a query about the nature of the release, although the pale pink color already told her it was a nasty mix.

Aerosolized quick-acting hemorrhagic measles, she interpreted from the readout, her gut chilling with worry. *95% containment.*

What twisted imagination created *that*?

Diana flashed a warning to Brenda. She knelt to shake out a couple of feeder biobots into the foam, a protective bioremediation reinforcement that she always kept tucked into a sleeve pocket whenever she went out into the field. They weren't specific, but would boost any existing treatments.

The foam around her first turned bright blue, then faded to a paler pink, the colors spreading out from her and Will in slow circles.

99% containment.

She minimized the bot stats in her overlay as Will commed an ID to the 9572. Diana tensed. Older code. Would it be one that acknowledged her control as well, or would it only accept Will?

<*Diana Landreth confirm.*> Relief washed over her. The status stats indicated a version from three months ago.

"Good," Will whispered. "The update's holding."

"Is that the newest Disruption Machine programming?"

"Not the latest. But it's the fallback if the Machine pulled what it did. Otherwise, that EMP lock would have taken the 9572 back to original settings. It's a trick I picked up from the PAZ." Will growled deep in his throat. "Some of that experience finally pays off. Learned to run sacrifice screens."

They slowed as they approached the 9572 and its prey. Diana winced back two steps as she spotted the netspiders, until she saw that the containment web holding the Machine was attached to them—a new skill Will had programmed into the devices. She wasn't certain if the netspiders were projecting an energy field, or if there was an actual, tangible restraint on the Disruption Machine.

Both, she decided.

It was hard to get a clear impression of the Machine's design, because the energy field projected by the net distorted what she saw. The Disruption Machine seemed to be a copper-colored sphere covered with blunt conical spikes. The spherical shape wasn't entirely perfectly round. It looked like one side was slightly caved in. Or was that impression an artifact of the energy field distortion?

"Approach the 9572 first," Will said. "I don't want to deal with the Disruption Machine except in a Level 4 containment. With remotes. In a suit."

"Do we need to renew the bloodbonding to strengthen the 9572?" Diana braced herself for that prospect, though she wasn't eager to breach her suit's protections this close to the Disruption Machine's witches' brew.

The last Disruption had involved aerosolized Ebola, measles, diphtheria, Sarin, and VX mixtures as well as radioactive cobalt dust. Now it contained this hemorrhagic measles mix. The last Third Force Council meeting she'd attended as a consultant had considered the possibility that the Machine might be carrying small tactical nukes as well.

Where is it getting its supplies?

"Not this time," Will said absently, his focus on the 9572. "Fortunately. That little release is a nasty piece of shit. I don't think the Disruption Machine identified the 9572 as a mechanical device, so it released a bioweapon as well as an EMP, assuming it was dealing with a biological entity."

"You'd think it would have learned."

Will shrugged, his suit making the gesture appear more massive than usual. "We've never been able to directly deploy the 9572 against the Disruption Machine before, so it interpreted it as a living thing. The Machine is either damaged, or else it needs a prior encounter to apply what it's learned from contact. Let's not give it a chance to learn more about the 9572, if we can help it."

He rested his right hand on the 9572's skin and tapped out a code. Then he set his tablet on the war machine. Linking codes popped up on Diana's 9572 overlay as she faintly heard the whisper of a skimmer.

Chen's here, Brenda texted.

Hold him there until we give the all clear, and make sure he has a protective suit. We're not at 100% containment for that little nasty's release, Diana whispered to text. *Tell him it contains hemorrhagic measles.*

Confirm.

She turned her attention to the 9572 overlays as it finished uploading Will's backups. Light flashed over the containment net, and a bluish tinge obscured the Disruption Machine further. The netspiders skittered closer to the Machine centimeter by cautious centimeter, closing down the restraint field to a smaller, denser, more form-fitting confinement with a reinforced comm block.

"I don't want to unwrap this little darling until we're in a controlled environment," Will said. "But no one's going to get it out of here unless they use a floater."

A brief regret at the loss of their weekend escape flowed through Diana, warring with relief at the reality that they had finally, *finally,* caught this damnable machine.

"Take it to the Mountain?" she asked.

Will snorted. "If Chen and your mother will let us. We'll have to fight for custody. I'm also not certain I want to dig into that machine right away. There's a lot we can learn from remote scanning." His gloved hand caressed the 9572's metallic skin and it rippled underneath his touch like a playful cat, a tiny talon batting at his hand before the skin settled back into its usual shape. "But having the 9572 containment gives us an edge toward keeping it."

"What else did you put into that programming, Will?" Her voice seemed far away as she asked. Sometimes he pushed the Third Force restrictions on what he was allowed to program.

"They can try to take it away from us," he said. "I wouldn't recommend it. I don't think any of the other companies out there have a containment field to match the 9572."

She didn't say more, as two more skimmers arrived.

Will's evasiveness worried her. He hung onto secrets from his Landreth days as a weapons designer. While he couldn't share some things due to national security constraints, occasionally he decided she didn't need to know details for her own deniability. She understood why he made that choice, but—if those skimmers hadn't been so close, she would have pressed harder for more information in this circumstance.

Those skimmers. Her mother and her Security, or her mother and someone else?

Francis?

Had Will and the 9572 been able to block comms from the Disruption Machine before it crashed? Would Francis try to rescue the device?

Just what were his ties to the Machine?

Your mother and an unidentified skimmer, Brenda texted. *Highest alert. Sent warnings to Chen and your mother.*

The 9572 bristled with a soft clatter of metal, external skin changing from pliable to stiff, shifting to restraint-plus-external defense mode. Weapons turrets opened around its pointed tip as it rose to vertical instead of lying on its side. A side panel opened, revealing blasters. Will grabbed one and tossed the other to Diana. She swallowed hard as she caught it.

9572 IDs that incoming as hostile, she texted Brenda, with a copy to her mother. Will had told her that if the 9572 ever offered a weapon, she was to take it without question. That hadn't happened often, but when it did—

"Any idea who that is?" she asked Will, forcing the words out through a suddenly dry throat as she checked and armed her blaster.

"The signal's obscured," he said slowly. "But it looks like it might be Francis."

Targeting overlays overrode her others. They focused on the obscured signal.

"Lock in," Will whispered. "Disarm and restrain."

With a soft cough, the 9572 launched a projectile. It flared brightly around the incoming skimmer, releasing bright nanofilaments forming into a super-strong net. For a moment it looked like the restraints would hold—and then they fell. But the skimmer delicately touched down.

Disabled? I sure hope so.

"That's Francis all right. Damn it, I'd hoped he wasn't able to upgrade from the last tools I gave him before he went rogue!" Will growled.

"Can't the 9572 try a stronger restraint on his skimmer?"

"The Machine's maxed the 9572's ceilings. I don't dare increase the control factors because we'll lose the Machine otherwise. I think I've bought us a few minutes. If he has self-repair circuits, he can be on his way soon enough at half-power. At least I made him land."

"But if we don't stop Francis—"

"I know, Di, *I know!*" Will spun back to the 9572, tracing codes onto the machine's skin. "I've one more option." He took her weapon and slammed it down on the skin. "This gives you a chance to capture Francis even without a direct hit, if you can get him into the open. A new trick. But he can't be inside that skimmer for it to work, and I need to stay here to run overrides so we don't lose that Disruption Machine. What the—? No. Oh no." He shook his head.

"Got it—Will, what's wrong?"

Will yanked her blaster off of the 9572. He pointed to a bright green button. "That's ID-locked to Francis. Be careful when you aim it, because if he's amped up his defenses more than I think he has, it could backlash. Hit him the minute he gets out of that skimmer. Oh. What's wrong? I just learned *that damned Disruption Machine had changed its target from Seattle to the Ranch.*"

CONFRONTATION

Time stopped as Diana stared at Will.

He nodded. "Transmission from Francis's skimmer to the Disruption Machine, just before the 9572 took it down." His voice was hard, matching her mood.

"He'll pay," she said roughly. "If not from you, then me. *He'll pay.*" Cold fury pulsed through Diana as she took the blaster from Will. She headed for Brenda, running as hard as she dared.

"*That's Francis,*" she broadbanded as she ran. "Get him out of that skimmer!"

Brenda sent an acknowledgement code before she continued, speaking aloud. "Unidentified skimmer, you are encroaching on a protected and contaminated site. Surrender."

Her mother emerged from her skimmer, wearing her own stealth-suit, blaster in hand, two of her Security at her shoulder.

"That's Francis."

"Get him out of the skimmer and give me a clear shot," Diana growled. "Let me handle it."

She hoped she didn't have to be too explicit. Diana wasn't certain how secure her mother's comms were, given Francis's presence.

She waved her hands to catch her mother's attention. Sarah's gaze met hers. Diana jerked a thumb back toward the Disruption Machine, pointed in the direction of the Ranch, then to Francis's skimmer.

Her mother's eyes widened and she scowled. "Got it," Sarah acknowledged. "I'll take care of that fucking coward." She signed to her Security, handing off her blaster, and marched toward the hostile skimmer by herself.

"Mother, *no,*" Diana whispered.

Sarah might have a hidden weapon, in fact knowing how her mother thought, she probably *did* have a hidden weapon. But would it be effective against her ex-lover, who had designed the foundations of her systems? Diana broke into a run, as hard as she could manage with the stiff stealthsuit.

"Diana, *stop.*" Francis's voice crackled in her com. "One more step and I'll kill your mother."

"Bullshit," Sarah drawled in her most annoying, authoritative voice as Diana skidded to a halt. Still, Sarah also stopped and held her hands wide. "You wouldn't dare kill me like this."

"I wouldn't recommend touching *either* Diana or Sarah," Will added.

"You don't have the guts to face me directly," Sarah continued in a tight angry voice. "Go ahead and try to shoot me. To my face. When I'm unarmed. Coward."

Francis laughed, a hysteric note in his voice. "With you begging for it? With your daughter and weapons designer son-in-law behind you? You think I'm that much of a fool? I don't believe you're unarmed, and your daughter and son-in-law sure aren't."

The 9572 remote display stirred into life.

Backup targeting if he won't leave his skimmer, Will texted. *But his defenses are strong enough that I don't think we can override them easily, not with the limited capacity due to trying to keep the Disruption Machine under control.*

Got it. Even with subvocal texting Diana's throat was dry. *What's Mom carrying?*

Nothing that the 9572 can detect. She may be telling the truth about being unarmed.

Hell of a time for Sarah to start telling the truth.

"I'm unarmed." Sarah's voice cracked. "I'll take off the suit to prove it."

"Mother, *no*," Diana broke in. "The Machine dumped a hemor-rhagic mix—"

Her mother held up her hand. "Enough, Diana." She slowly began to work apart her suit glove seals. "I'll start with bare hands. If I have to strip down naked to prove to Francis that I'm unarmed, then I will."

Diana couldn't interpret Sarah's tone.

What's her game? Bluffing Francis? Delaying to give us more time?

For once she wished she had easier secure comm links to her mother. The 9572 comm structures kept Diana's private comms locked within internal DIR links—which meant Will and Brenda only.

"What do you want, Francis?" Diana asked, hoping to draw attention away from her mother, if Sarah was actually carrying a weapon in her gloves.

She could be. God, she hoped her mother carried a weapon.

"The Machine."

"No!" Will and Sarah said together.

"Then you'll die," Francis said. "Starting with Diana and Sarah." One of his skimmer gun turrets began to whine open.

"You ever think about who and what restrains me from doing my worst?" Will's voice went dead and cold.

"You dance to the Third Force's tune." The skimmer gun turret door stopped, half-open. "You got rid of your father's weaponry. You're still under indictment because they don't trust you. You're a fool."

Was that a trace of uncertainty she heard in Francis's voice?

"For a good fucking reason." Will's icy tones sent chills down Diana's spine and made the back of her neck prickle. "And if you think it's the Third Force that's tamed me, that kept me from turning into my father, *you're wrong*. There are three reasons I submit. Diana, Andrew, and Melanie. *And you've just threatened all of them.*" Light flared behind them, tracing over their heads, arcing toward Francis's skimmer.

The skimmer exploded faint moments before the light completed its arc. Light flashed back to the Machine. Diana whirled and raced toward Will and the 9572. A second, smaller blast detonated over the Machine, overloading her sensors after the previous explosion so that the world briefly went black. This one was close enough to shake through her body.

But the 9572 links held. So it still existed.

Will?

The 9572 would protect him, wouldn't it? Her filters cleared and she could see again. Will slumped against the 9572.

Alive?

"Text links dead," Will rasped, his voice still carrying that chill. "Brenda, tear that skimmer wreckage apart for any traces of a body. Diana—" She heard the familiar faint thread of pain in his voice. "I—" he gasped.

Will pushed himself upright as she joined him, one hand locked around a grip the 9572 had made. Diana groaned as she saw the crack in his face shield, a gash in the suit. Blood trickled from both nostrils.

"The 9572's shielding me as long as I hold this grip," Will said, his voice cold and distant, the tone she recognized as Will keeping a hard lock on his body's weaknesses in the face of a life-threatening situation. The skill that had kept him alive during weeks of torture in the Petroleum Autonomous Zone.

She opened a thigh pocket. "I can do quick repair, that'll keep you safe for a while, long enough to take care—"

"No, not the first thing." Will pointed toward the Disruption Machine with his free hand. A bright orange ball of what looked like plasma bounced against the shielding. "You need to catch that before you do anything with me."

"What is it?" She broadened her query to include both Will and the 9572, slamming a hand down on the 9572 for an improved com link.

<Francis Stewart positive ID in that plasma cloud,> the 9572 answered.

How? she wondered. "What do you recommend?" she asked Will and the 9572.

Will continued to stare stonily at the Disruption Machine, unresponsive.

Dear God, he's shut himself down to stay focused and safe while he's keeping the restraint field up manually. It's up to me to take it further.

<Over here,> the 9572 answered, a light blinking on its opposite side. It sounded like Will talking through the Machine. *<That cloud has*

Stewart's consciousness in it, and it's trying to breach the containment. The Disruption Machine is aiding it from inside. Don't dare break away. Love.>

God, it *was* Will talking through the 9572.

Diana kept her fingertips on the 9572 as she circled toward the flashing light, wondering just what on earth it was talking about. A sentient cloud or ball of plasma? That wasn't possible; that couldn't be possible.

<Hurry,> the 9572—or Will?—nagged.

The flashing light was over one of the 9572's netspider compartments. Diana tapped it open. A netspider with thinner legs than usual and long, knife-like, talons clambered onto her hand. Diana restrained a shudder at the light pressure of talons through her suit as the netspider scuttled onto her forearm.

<What do I do now?> she asked.

<Wait for my cues.> the 9572 answered.

The netspider rose high on its slender legs and sent forth a spinneret of nanofiber, followed by heavier threads that shimmered with fine strands of reinforced steel. The filaments joined to form a translucent web. Diana sharpened her overlay's focus to identify tiny nanobots scrambling along the fibers.

<Launch it like you would a falcon.>

She obeyed the 9572's direction, flicking the netspider free. It closed its legs upon itself as it floated toward the roiling orange plasma ball, swinging freely back and forth like a child's toy suspended from a balloon.

<Fire at the plasma cloud.>

Diana raised her blaster and shot. The plasma veered away from bashing itself against the Disruption Machine's restraint field and headed toward her. She fired again.

<Enough.>

Diana almost disregarded the command as the plasma ball drew closer, bypassing the netspider. She stared as the ball approached her, its surface churning.

The netspider ceased swaying aimlessly under its net and turned toward its prey. It cast the fine fibrous net toward the plasma ball with two talons while the other six clutched the webbing. The lattice-like web wrapped around the ball. The netspider reeled in the netting, the orange glow fading as the nanofibers grew together to form a silvery coating and she could no longer see the plasma.

The netspider coiled itself around the silvery ball. It imploded, a white light flaring before snuffing out, ball and netspider disappearing.

The Disruption Machine *roared*. It strained against its bindings.

Will screamed and clutched at the 9572 with both hands. Diana instinctively yanked Will as tight to her as she could, one arm around his waist while slamming her hand on the 9572. Pain jolted through her, hot prickly needlepoints of sharp agony, the Disruption Machine striking through the linking restraint interfaces to try and shake them free.

She drew in deep, sobbing breaths, resting her head on Will's back.

Can't yield. We can't yield. Can't yield.

If there was some way to feed more strength to Will…dimly, she realized she clutched at a handhold like the two Will now grasped.

Hold steady hold steady hold steady, she told herself.

Francis was part of that mix with the Disruption Machine that raged through the 9572's links. Diana had no idea how she recognized his persona, or even how it had become part of that machine, but she knew it was Francis, damn it, quixotic, puzzling Francis without any of his deliciously wry humor and joy.

All that was gone, replaced by a dark version of the man she'd known. Whatever this sinister, howling, *evil* thing was that would have killed her kids and poisoned the Ranch, it wasn't the Francis Stewart she'd known as her mother's lover.

This Francis was angry, twisted, and full of hate.

How did this happen?

Arms wrapped around Diana, holding her upright and steady, much as she now did for Will. Arms she recognized as belonging to her mother, though Sarah didn't reach for the 9572.

"Chen. This wasn't the contingency I expected when I left those bots I told you about," Sarah said. "But Stephens had prepared one of those old double shell tanks with two extra liners just in case we ever got our hands on this machine. I know we left that setup intact."

"Want—study," Diana croaked.

"Not now. Not until everything's secured. Chen, get those damn transports out here now!"

"She's—right," Will gasped. "Containment—most important."

Was his voice fading? Diana held him tighter. "Keep talking."

"Sarah." Will coughed. "When you. Challenged Francis. Unarmed?"

"What do you think?" Her mother clenched Diana in a stronger grip.

"Not—scannable."

"It wasn't supposed to be. Transports here now." Sarah didn't release her hold on Diana. "Hang on, you two."

Diana lost track of the discussion. Finally, the transports loaded them up; Disruption Machine, 9572, Will, Diana, and Sarah as one.

Relief finally came as the transports carried them underground. Will sagged against her, still holding tight to the 9572 as the Machine was shoved into containment.

"You have to let the 9572 go with the Disruption Machine," Sarah said.

"We can't," Diana said. "Not—"

Will coughed. "We have to. No way I'm going to be able to sort out the programming, and it's just not safe."

She winced at the agony in his voice. "We could try."

"Not as twisted as it is." His voice was harsh and hard. Still, she noticed that he gently patted the 9572's skin with one hand while still clutching the grip with the other. "Slide the 9572 in. I'll release at the door. Diana, we have to shed the nets then. Can't trust them either."

All your work gone, she wanted to object. But she couldn't argue with the issue of trust. Not with tech as intimate as the neural nets that drove the 9572.

Will maintained his grip until the very last moment. He stroked the skin of the 9572, then stood back as the doors slid almost closed, leaving the tiniest slit. Together, he and Diana popped off their helmets. She detached the net from her head, fingers heavy—*last time!*—and tossed her net through the opening.

Will slowly copied her actions.

The door closed.

Will collapsed, coughing, Diana following him down. She resisted as medical staff tried to separate them. At last, Medical gave in and transported them together.

Diana refused to leave Will until Medical had treated him and settled him in a bed at Northstar Main, her mother fussing over both of them. Then she let Medical check her out while Sarah stood watch over Will. Finally, Diana crawled into Will's hospital bed, despite Sarah's attempts to persuade her to sleep separately.

Memories of *that look on his face* when he had locked down hard kept wheeling through her brain, alternating with the realization that Francis had ordered the Machine to attack the kids. The Ranch.

She had almost lost her family.

While she desperately wanted to see her children, she also wanted to keep Will safe. Holding him. Burying her head in his shoulder while he slept off the meds. That was the most Diana was capable of doing at that moment, while she gave in to the fear.

She had almost lost everything dear to her.

VALENTINE ESCAPE

T HE RHYTHMIC ROAR OF WAVES ON THE BEACHES OF N EAHCOM B AY weren't as soothing as usual, jangled as Diana's nerves still were from yesterday's events.

Diana and Will leaned against each other as they stood on the balcony of the old Stephens house overlooking Neahcom Bay, watching the sun shimmer below the horizon. A whisper of wind made the Valentine's banner at the balcony's corner flicker.

She shivered. Despite warm coats and a big deck heater, Diana still felt cold.

Psychological?

Most likely.

"Well, a few hours of escape are better than nothing," Will murmured into Diana's ear.

"Considering the alternative."

Jen, Rita and the kids were in the neighboring, smaller house. Sarah had her own suite within the big house, and they hadn't seen her emerge since they came to Neahcom from Northstar this morning.

Will's grip tightened on Diana's waist. "Yeah." He still seemed sad and wistful.

"Will, I'm sorry about the 9572," she blurted.

He heaved a big sigh. "It's about time I let that side of me go. I can design a civilian equivalent, no weaponry. It'll be better for what we need."

She played with a long lock of his hair. "It was one of your best designs."

And your first love.

He had poured his heart into that damned machine and its modifications after they took control of it. Much as Diana had hated the 9572, she recognized it as a source of his strength.

"Designs can be improved. And it ultimately did the best war machine task ever. It brought down the Disruption Machine. Once things have calmed down a bit, I'll study what happened with both those machines."

"After Chen and everyone else," she protested. "That's not fair."

Will raised a brow at her. "Nothing says they're getting everything. I have hidden files."

A commotion arose from inside the house. Diana turned, preparing to deal with an escaped child, and froze. Guided by Jen and Rita, Melanie and Andrew solemnly carried small heart-shaped chocolate cakes to the glass-topped picnic table.

"Happy Valentine's Day, Mama and Daddy!" Andrew burst out. "We brought chocolate and fizzy drinks!"

She looked at Will. He grinned. They sat on the bench facing away from the bay and the kids climbed into their laps, Drew in Will's and Mel in Diana's. Jen poured champagne for the adults and sparkling cider for the kids. Diana cut the small cakes into enough pieces to share out. Then she looked up and saw her mother gazing wistfully at them from the neighboring balcony.

She waved at Sarah. "Come join us." There was more than enough cake for all.

Her mother shook her head. "I'm not in the mood for celebrations today."

"Grandmama, please join us," Drew said.

"It's for family," Will added. "Not just romance. After what happened—"

"Come join us," Jen added.

Sarah grimaced, but she joined them after a few minutes, sitting next to Will. Drew abandoned Will's lap for Sarah's. Will chuckled and slid closer to Diana and Melanie, throwing his arm around Diana's shoulder. Rita got Sarah a glass and a plate.

Not quite the romantic getaway I'd envisioned.

Diana pressed her lips to the top of Melanie's head to dispel the dread that throbbed through her. Considering the close call they just had, she'd take the lack of time away from family over no family at all.

When she sat back up, Will kissed her. Their lips lingered before they separated. Diana looked over to see wetness in her mother's eyes.

"We're a family, and we're all here together," she said softly to Sarah. "Sometimes that has to be enough."

"Sometimes," her mother said. "And sometimes that isn't enough. Right, Jen?"

"All too true. But there are days when you take what you can get. Even if it isn't enough." She poured the last of the champagne into Sarah's glass and handed it to her. "A toast to getting what you can."

Sarah's mouth quirked. "A toast." They tapped their glasses together.

Finished with cake, Melanie squirmed out of Diana's lap. "Play ball now." She headed down the balcony steps toward the basketball court between the two houses, where a small basketball standard had been set up, Rita following close behind her.

"Maybe we should join your sister?" Sarah asked Drew.

He scowled. "Melly always beats me."

"I'll show you a trick or two," Sarah promised. She looked over at Jen. "Coming? Let's leave these two alone for a while."

Jen chuckled. "Be right there." She gathered up the dirty dishes and glasses, except for Will and Diana's half-filled champagne flutes, and took them inside before joining Sarah and the kids.

"Let's watch the ocean," Diana suggested.

They rose, hands still entwined. Will led Diana to a lounge chair with a folded blanket at its foot. He carefully lowered himself into it, then slid over to make room for her. She pulled the throw over them and they snuggled in silence, Will gently stroking Diana's cheek.

"You did great yesterday. I couldn't have done it without you," he said. "But God, Diana. We came so damn close to losing it all. Too damn close."

"I don't know if I'll be able to leave the kids again without worrying."

"I don't think the worry ever goes away."

"Perhaps not. But after this—and oh God, Will, when I saw you there, your suit breached—" She gulped and shivered, tears coming into her eyes.

I could have lost you.

"I know. All I could think about was the kids, and Francis threatening you. I couldn't let it happen. Even if it meant I had to sacrifice myself."

"Don't do that."

"Believe me, it's not my first choice. But for you and the kids?"

"I was thinking the same thing."

"I know." He kissed her. "Let's hope we never have to make that choice. I want to grow old with you, and see our kids grow up."

"God, Will." She tried to blink away the tears.

He brushed them away and kissed her. "The worst didn't happen. It was a minor disruption to our plans. But what could have happened —didn't. Let's hold on to that."

"Yes. Let's." She leaned into him and closed her eyes, listening to him breathe. His arms tightened even more around her.

I am awfully damned lucky.

The memory of her mother's desolate look chilled her. True, Francis had been gone from Sarah's life for several years now—but for it to be this final?

Diana hoped she wouldn't have to face this reality with Will, for a good long time.

At least the Disruptions are over. Now we can get back to a normal life.

If they even *knew* what normal looked like, anymore.

MAY, 2058

KIDNAPPED!

KATHY MILLER SCOWLED AT THE RESULTS OF THE LATEST NEURAL NET implant interface test, then slumped back in her chair, pulled off her comm glasses and rubbed her eyes. She *had* hoped to clean up this programming mess before Melanie and Andrew Landreth arrived for their lessons. She shook her head, pushed a strand of graying brunette hair behind her left ear, and slid her glasses back on.

At least she could salvage this test run by assigning it to the Landreth teens to review. Fixing this jumble would be good training for both kids.

Sure was a lot easier to chase illegal biohackers than work as a legit biohack herself, even if it was just as a glorified nanny. But there was that little matter of telling National Security to take a flying leap five years ago, after Dale's death and the collapse of the Third Force government.

Finding a position with Will and Diana Landreth at Do It Right had been a godsend, facilitated by Kathy's niece Ness Ryan, who already worked for Do It Right. After the Landreths had captured the machine causing the worldwide Disruptions ten years ago, their reputation as providers of security programs and biodevices had soared. Will Landreth already had a ton of credentials because of his experience designing war machines and programming for his late father's now-dissolved company. Diana Landreth had earned respect for her bioremediation biobot design skills, which had been Do It Right's original focus.

But combine the two, and—well, Do It Right had a need for someone like Kathy Miller who could take over biotech teaching responsibilities for the Landreth kids, along with fine-tuning DIR security products. Especially since the paranoid Landreth parents were becoming more estranged from Diana's mother, Sarah Stephens, now a leader in the new American Federation.

Which was yet another reason why Kathy jumped at this position. Even if it meant she spent most of her time teaching the Landreth kids about biohacks. Both showed talent, especially young Melanie.

Sooner or later, Sarah Stephens would make a mistake. And when she did—

Meanwhile, working for the Landreths provided Kathy with protection from Stephens. And her evil son, Peter.

The hologlobe chimed a warning. Time for the kids' tutorial session. Kathy prepped the results for them to review. One thing led to another, and she ran the sim once again, shaking her head at the end.

So damn promising, and yet it's useless! Oh well, let's see what the kids make of it. Mel shows programming promise, and Drew can do something with it if he exerts himself.

Ten minutes later, a reminder chime caught her attention. Mel and Drew should be here. Not right.

Kathy started to type a text to Diana. Before she pressed *send*, the hologlobe pulsed red.

Urgent message, from Diana.

"Miller here," Kathy said.

Diana stared at her, face blank, hard and pale. "Kathy. The kids—"

"Not here yet."

"The kids," Diana shook her head. "I've just gotten a video—oh God, Kathy, I didn't expect something like this to happen here on the Mountain." She dropped her face into her hands. "Will's down with chemo, and not able to go after them."

"Diana, what is it?"

Diana raised her head. "They've been kidnapped. I was hoping it was just a hoax, Security says there's been no breach, but—there's a video that's been uploaded to my private account—if it's real—Will's running checks on it now."

"I'll be right over," Kathy said. "Don't go anywhere, don't do anything."

The video played on a continuous loop when Kathy entered Diana and Will's quarters.

"Thank you for coming so quickly. It's just…." Diana's voice trailed off limply as she threw her hands up, pacing the room. "I don't know what to think, Kathy. Something's weird about this. *I* had to tell *Security*, and they didn't believe me until they ran it!"

"Does Security have *anything?* Those protective nanos in Melanie and Drew should have triggered *something.*"

"Nothing but the video. One small blip from the nanos. Kathy, I didn't think they could be overridden!"

"They shouldn't have been, not without raising a fuss." Kathy tightened her lips. "Wild biohacks can't pull off this level of smoothness. Any ideas?"

The left corner of Diana's mouth twitched in a brief, sardonic grin. "The kidnappers name Stephens Reclamation as their go-between."

Oh, this is going to be a fucking mess.

"What do the Corporate Courts say?"

"What you would expect," Will muttered, from his position reclining on the couch, as was typical for a chemo day. "Totally legit." He waved a far-too-bony hand in the air. "Totally coincidental. Has nothing to do with the dispute with Stephens over our current research into the neural interface for wireless biobot command implants."

Kathy snorted. "What good are the Courts if Stephens owns them like this?"

Silence.

But Kathy expected that. The Landreths were *quite* closed-mouth about their disputes with Sarah and Peter Stephens.

Sometimes family can be the worst.

"As long as the Courts keep Giz—the *device*—under wraps, I can't argue with them," Diana said finally.

Kathy shuddered at the oblique mention of the Gizmo. Had it only been ten years since it last ran wild?

One feature of the new international order after the Great War following the capture of the Disruption device—now known as the Gizmo—had been the establishment of the Corporate Courts, an international, corporate body tasked with custody and control of the Gizmo.

The Courts set up a separate, international governing body regulating big corporations as part of that custody and control. No national governments involved; the argument had been that these multinational corporations were more stable than governments and abler to collaborate across national barriers. Access to the Gizmo provided the participants with unbelievable jumps in technological developments. National governments were demoted to just that—governance of individual nations, with international disputes taken to the Courts.

But Corporate Courts connections also included corporate leaders serving in political positions. Like Sarah Stephens, advisor to American Federation President Anne Whitman—and rumored to be more than that to Whitman.

That also meant Stephens Reclamation, with Sarah Stephens and her son Peter as principals, was absurdly powerful, in both Corporate Courts and the American Federation.

"I don't know how much of this is a Corporate matter," Diana said finally, after exchanging significant glances with Will. "I've been getting backchannel info about Stephens-related neural research, in combination with Troubadour Shipping. Their neural net results aren't as good as ours."

Kathy scowled at her. "*How* backchannel?"

Diana tightened her lips. "The new guy working with Ness."

"Shit." Kathy knew just who that was. Marty Fielding. Young, bright, just out of college. Scholarship paid by Stephens Rec—or was it Troubadour? How he had managed to end up in Do It Right was something Kathy hadn't been told. "Damn it, Diana, what do you expect when you go raiding their people?"

"Hey, I didn't raid him! *He* came to *me!*"

"Are they making any demands yet?" Perhaps it wasn't what she thought, and the involvement of Stephens Reclamation was just a coincidence.

Sarah Stephens *did* have a decent reputation as a hostage negotiator, after all. And despite their other differences, Diana and Sarah were apparently in agreement about Gizmo-related issues. Stephens could easily have planted Fielding as a disinformation agent or as her own spy.

"No demands," Will muttered. "Kathy, you're former NatSecure. What do you think they'll want?"

"They'll want a trade of some sort. Let's look at that video."

Diana toggled the start button, and turned off the sound.

The loop began with a tight focus on Melanie and Andrew's faces. Melanie looked defiant, her brunette hair disarrayed from its usual neat styling. Her hazel eyes glared at the camera—clear, not dull.

Good.

Kathy froze the picture, zooming in on Melanie's left cheek. Yes. A bruise was forming.

"I didn't see that," Diana muttered next to her. "They'll pay."

"Maybe that means a struggle, and maybe that means something else. Those security nanos implanted in the kids carry Quickheal and drug antidotes. Bruises *shouldn't* happen."

Unless someone else's nanos were in Melanie's system. But damn, those security nanos were close to prototype, and Kathy had made Ness swear they were stable before she put them into the kids. Other nanos shouldn't have a serious effect.

Maybe her niece was wrong.

Kathy changed the zoom focus, concentrating now on Melanie's pupils, rewinding the scene back to the start, then running it in slow motion. The light beam crossed Melanie's eyes. Kathy ran it again, timing the pupil reactivity.

She didn't like what she saw. Whatever was in Melanie's system was warring with her nanos—thankfully enough to trigger her ADHD instead of suppressing it. Melanie was *angry*, and Kathy wouldn't mess with *this* thirteen-year-old when anger came into the equation.

Kathy switched focus to Andrew. He was in worse shape than Melanie, struggling to hold his head upright. His eyes were dull and reactive.

"Damn," she breathed. Drew's nanos were an older generation than Melanie's, and should be more stable.

The video cut away from Melanie and Drew. A bearded man's face filled the screen.

Bold asshat to dare show me his face without screening.

Kathy frowned. Something was familiar about this man's features. She opened a second globe within the first and tapped out a series of commands to bring up a file picture.

"I don't believe it," she breathed, comparing pictures, then adding years and a beard to it. "I just don't believe it."

It was her fiancé Dale's killer. Alan Adam Jones.

resolved, she'd put Security through a full-bore NatSecure-style audit.

If I'd only taken the time to do it before now....

Too bad Brenda Garcia and Tony Hernandez were no longer part of Do It Right Security due to Tony's health issues. Maybe she could bring them back as consultants.

Kathy forwarded copies of the video to Ness. If she could figure out what was wrong with Melanie and Drew's nanos, then replacements would be ready when the kids were released.

If they were released.

Kathy switched on her own private security circuit, measures that Do It Right Security couldn't break. She fiddled with her copy of the video, adding the old picture of the kidnapper and the simulation update. Then she dialed a private number, tapping her fingers on the desk, hoping it still worked.

The craggy face of the current head of NatSecure, Nick Parton, popped up. "Who the hell? Oh, hi, Kathy. I didn't realize you had my priority number!"

"Still up to my old tricks." Kathy grinned at her old boss. "Have something interesting to show you. Off the record." She forwarded the first part of the video to Nick. He watched it quietly, running it back and forth several times, just like she had.

"So," he said finally. "We haven't received a report of this yet."

"Not likely, not until the Landreths are convinced it's necessary to disclose it. But here's more food for thought." She forwarded the remainder of the video, along with her additions. "Tell me what you think."

She watched Nick's expression change. He ran it back, zoomed it, his frown deepening. At last, he looked up.

"I thought the days of your blindsiding me were over."

"The case is still open, isn't it?"

Nick sighed and rubbed the bridge of his nose. "I can't touch him. You know that."

"Nick, he killed Dale! And God only knows what will happen to these kids!"

"Kathy, I don't have the power to help you this time. Jones is protected."

"You wouldn't let me go after Jones last time. What's so special about him?"

"Nothing has changed about Jones," Nick sighed. "I'm sorry, Kathy. It's not Jones, it's who he works for. And that's *all* I can tell you. Don't ask anything more of me!" He switched off the screen.

Kathy tried the number again. This time her call was blocked. "Damn it!" She slammed her fist on her desk, then broke into a litany of soft curses. She dropped her head into her hands. What to do, what to do?

She went back to Diana and Will's quarters.

Diana screamed at someone. Kathy could hear her through what was supposed to be a soundproof door. She used her personal override to let herself in.

Her gut tightened as she saw the silver-haired woman in Diana's hologlobe. Diana acknowledged Kathy's presence with a brief nod.

"Who's that?" Sarah Stephens demanded.

"Kathy Miller," Diana snapped.

Stephens's eyebrows shot up. "Kathy Miller. I wondered where you'd disappeared to after leaving NatSecure."

Why does she know who I am?

Kathy spoke quickly, before Diana could. "What role do you have in your grandchildren's disappearance?" She reached for a couple of chairs, guided Diana to one, then sat in the other.

A wry smile touched Stephens's lips, then faded. "Right to the point. I regret my daughter hired you before I could, Kathy—may I call you Kathy?"

"No. Ms. Miller or Miller is preferable."

"Ms. Miller, then. With your reputation, my programs would be further along than with the pathetic excuses I can barely hold onto around here."

"What role do you have in your grandchildren's disappearance?" Kathy repeated, tightening her lips to keep from snapping at Stephens.

Dale's comments from the last time he and his partner had interrogated Stephens came to mind.

She ducks questions by flooding you with compliments or trying to piss you off.

"And why would you think I know anything about this?"

"Ms. Stephens, let's stop playing games. The kidnappers named you as a go-between in negotiations. I assume that's why you and Diana are communicating right now. I want to know what role you played in their disappearance."

Stephens shrugged. "Why should I be involved in their disappearance? Can't I have an interest in their safety, as their grandmother?"

"It'd be more believable if you had ever spent time with these children in the past. Have you even met them?"

"*That,*" Stephens said emphatically, "is a question best put to my daughter."

"I'm not asking her. I'm asking you. How did you get involved with this?"

"*Some* people respect my interests."

"You're saying that we're in competition for these children? I assume you will fully cooperate with us?"

"I intend to protect them," Sarah Stephens said firmly. "There is no reason these children should be in this situation."

"You know, I thoroughly agree with you."

Stephens raised one brow. "Interesting you should say that."

"Yes. There's no reason why any children, not just these two, should ever be part of a corporate power game. But they are. What's your price to negotiate terms?"

Stephens leaned back in her chair, steepleing her fingers and pressing the fingertips to her lips. "Let's see. One of Stephens Rec's scholarship interns went to work for Do It Right upon graduation, instead of us."

"Of his own initiative," Diana snapped.

"Whatever. I've lost his input into a crucial piece of our neural research. As part of my role in this negotiation, I think I'm owed compensation for losing him."

"What would you want?"

Stephens pursed her lips thoughtfully. "Let's see." She tapped her chin, then grinned. "What's the value of a schematic of your current neural interface?"

"I think that's worth more than two teenagers and your negotiation fee." Kathy met Stephens eye-for-eye.

It's a piece of shit, anyway. We aren't losing anything.

Diana's lips tightened but she didn't react—probably because she agreed.

Stephens shrugged. "That's the level of compensation needed. They aren't easy people to deal with."

"The neural net interface schematic is worth more than the kids and your fee," Kathy repeated. "Besides the safe return of both kids, I want one of the kidnappers."

Both of Stephens's brows shot up. "*Real—ly.* And which one would that be?"

"The gentleman on the video. I don't care what kind of shape he's in when you deliver him to me."

"Hmm. That *is* interesting." Stephens's comm glasses flashed. "Ah. I see. He appears to have had some connection to the death of your fiancé, doesn't he? You left NatSecure after his murder remained unsolved."

"Correct." She met Stephens's cool gray eyes without flinching.

"You know, if you'd come to me then, I might have been able to help you."

"I think you can still help me now."

"Could be. Could be. But is that kidnapper worth what you're asking?"

Kathy forced herself to relax and be casual under Stephens's scrutiny. "Don't know how much good he's going to be to his partners after this. After all, he's the most visible on this action. They might be willing to give him up."

"He does seem to be a liability," Stephens agreed. "Somewhat lacking in subtlety, wouldn't you say?"

Kathy raised a hand, wobbled it back and forth. "So—so. I'd think his bosses would be getting tired of the liability caused by his lack of technique. What he did to Dale *was* rather crude. There were other things he could have done."

I can't believe I said that.

Stephens chuckled. "Ms. Miller, I'm growing fonder of you by the moment. I hope my daughter fully appreciates what she has in you."

"I do," Diana said tersely.

"So," Kathy said. "Is it a deal?"

"I'll let you know within a couple of hours." The hologlobe went dark, and Kathy slowly expelled a deep breath.

"Damn," she said. "I'd hate to have grown up with that."

Diana snorted. "She's gotten much better at scheming over the years. She got the interface out of you. What were you thinking?"

"It's a piece of junk. Seriously. I was going to turn it over to the kids as a test run because it wasn't working. Let her people fight with it."

And I have a hunch that Fielding's tip plus whatever's in those kids will show us the way. Damn, I hope she gets them to us before it wears off!

"What if she wants to test it first?"

"She asked for it, didn't she? She must think we have something worthwhile. She's wrong, at least with our current interface. *I want* what she has in the kids. Something that can overcome our systems like that is something we need to study."

Diana shook her head. "Kathy, just be careful when you're playing with her. You can't trust her. And what was that last bit? That's for real?"

Kathy sighed and stretched. "The kidnapper killed Dale."

"What are you going to do?"

Kathy gave Diana a toothy grin. "Nick Parton of NatSecure says he's untouchable. If Sarah Stephens turns him over to me, then I guess that means he's not untouchable any more, doesn't it?"

"There's turning over and then there's screwing over," Diana said. "She'll screw you on this. Mark my words."

"I expect her to do that."

"What are you going to do?"

"Well, I guess it depends on what shape he's in when she turns him over to me now."

"What good's a dead body?"

"I don't expect her to kill him or mindwipe him. I expect she's going to turn him loose to kill me." Kathy let herself bare her teeth in a feral grin. "That's the mistake Dale made five years ago. I'm better at this stuff than Dale was. He should have ditched his regular partner and taken me along."

"Kathy, be careful."

"I will. And I'll get the kids back, too." She stood up. "I don't expect to hear from her until two hours is up, and then things'll move pretty fast. I'd better get ready."

And that includes a session of weapons practice. Plus a little chat with Marty Fielding to find out what he knows about Stephens Reclamation's neural net systems.

DOUBLE CROSS

Kathy took several steps to prepare for the transfer of the kids and Jones.

First, she and Will Landreth created an isolated download link for the neural net interface. Will set up the firewalls—he never trusted anyone else to touch those systems—so the download couldn't be piggybacked into an attack on Do It Right.

Then she handpicked the Security that would take custody of the kids.

Finally, she prepared an emergency message to Nick Parton and several of her NatSecure friends, including her partner after Dale, to be triggered when she transferred the schematic. Once she knew the transfer site, she planned to send an anonymous message to Nick which would have him nearby, but not so close that he'd interfere.

Now there was nothing left to do but wait in Diana and Will's quarters for Sarah Stephens to call back with the transfer location. Diana paced while Will glowered.

The hologlobe chimed. Diana answered.

"You there, Miller?" Stephens looked past Diana at Kathy.

"Affirmative." Kathy chose not to rise, but stared at Stephens from her chair.

"Neahcom River North Jetty parking lot. Thirty minutes. You. No one else."

"I want Security in the skimmer, to take care of the kids. I promise they won't come out."

"Better not be any interference."

"Same for you."

"Jones will bring the kids. You'll give him the schematic."

"No. I have a remote link on a tablet, prepared for upload. He gives me the kids; I trigger it to upload to the address you give him. You confirm its arrival, I send the kids to my skimmer and take care of Jones."

"Thirty minutes." The hologlobe switched off.

"And that," Kathy said quietly, "is that."

"Good luck," Diana said. "Be careful with the kids, Kathy. Please."

"You'll get your kids back. Don't worry."

Kathy rose and headed out the door, impatience and fretfulness now replaced by the unearthly calmness she had grown to expect when facing an immediate situation.

SHE SHOULD HAVE KNOWN IT WOULD COME TO THIS. THE NEAHCOM RIVER jetty was as stormy as it had been five years ago, when Kathy had visited the place where Dale died. The parking lot was empty in the growing dusk. Dark clouds threatened imminent rain.

One way in, one way out. She was two minutes early. Kathy climbed onto the rocks but chose not to walk out very far—just enough to see an incoming vehicle. The oncoming storm drove the waves over the furthest reach of the jetty. Eventually, they would sweep over the entire jetty, and possibly the parking lot at high tide.

So how are they coming? I see all skimmer approach routes from here.

The rhythmic beat of a helicopter answered her.

She checked her wrist sheaths. Knife in one, blaster in the other. Same for both ankles. One blaster in the holster in her back. Hideaway in her armpit. Another in her coat lining.

If Kathy wasn't ready to take Jones on now, she would never be.

The helicopter landed. Jones and the kids climbed out. Once they were clear, the helicopter lifted, circling once, then heading back up the coast. Jones whirled, waving frantically, not expecting this, cursing and pulling out a weapon.

Kathy damped the sudden sweet thrill which raced through her. Jones being abandoned still didn't make this process any less fraught.

Jones shoved the kids ahead of him. Both Melanie and Andrew looked better than they had on the video. On the other hand, that could mean problems for tracking whatever had gone into their systems.

Nicely calculated.

"Here they are," Jones growled. "The key." He held out a hand.

"Not so fast. The kids go to the skimmer."

Jones held his blaster to Andrew's head. "The schematic, or this one eats it!"

Melanie held back, looking frantically back and forth between Kathy and Jones.

Kathy jerked her head toward the skimmer. "Start walking."

She waited until Melanie was safely ten steps away, then pulled out the small tablet that held the link.

Eyes gleaming, a greedy smirk on his lips, Jones lowered the blaster from Andrew's head and grabbed the tablet from her hand. Followed the instructions to tap in the link, staring eagerly at the screen. Kathy took advantage of his distraction to push Andrew toward the skimmer, and placed herself between the kids and Jones.

"Yes!" Jones chortled. She raised her blaster as he did his.

This is it.

Before she could brush the trigger of her blaster, the side of his head exploded.

"What the hell?" Kathy wiped the blood off of her face.

"Here he is," Sarah Stephens's voice came out of the tablet's speaker. "I take pleasure in delivering him in a manner I find useful. Thank you for providing opportunity to do so. I find your package very satisfactory, and hope you have the same pleasure in yours. Remember, if you ever tire of my daughter's service, I'm always willing to talk. At Stephens Reclamation, we exist to serve."

"Damn!" Kathy whirled and ran for the car.

If she did this to him, what did she do to the kids?

FIVE DAYS LATER FOUND KATHY BACK ON THE JETTY, AT DUSK, WITH another storm blowing in. She carried a bouquet of red roses. Dale had delighted in giving her red roses on the slightest occasion—especially precious because of how rare they were anymore.

She found a rock to sit on, high above the waves. Slowly, petal by petal, she tossed the roses into the water.

That book is closed. Now what?

Kathy shook her head. Even the paranoid Landreths didn't believe that Sarah Stephens was behind the kidnapping, but no one else had come forward.

She wouldn't kidnap her own grandchildren, Diana kept saying.

But her troubled expression and the degree to which she wrung her hands when she said it made Kathy think otherwise. Especially after the way Jones died.

Dale's killer is dead, at the hands of the person I believed ordered Dale's murder. What did I accomplish?

She sighed. Got up to walk back to her skimmer. Noticed another one waiting.

Kathy palmed her blaster. This had been a reckless thing to do, especially without a Security cover. But she'd had a hunch...which was now paying off.

As she approached the skimmer a small, slender silver-haired woman got out. Chills ran down Kathy's spine as she realized who it was.

Sarah Stephens strolled over to Kathy's skimmer and leaned against it.

"I just wanted to thank you for giving me a reason to get rid of bad trash," she said as Kathy came close. "And to deliver a message to my darling daughter." Then she raised an odd-looking weapon and shot Kathy.

Oh. My. God.

It took a couple of moments for Kathy to realize she'd been hit with a restraint field, not a killing shot. She tried to struggle against it as Stephens bent over her.

"I suspect you'd be quite resourceful in doing me harm after what I have to say to you. Don't fight it," she added as Kathy struggled harder to make her frozen limbs move. "That will only make things worse."

Kathy tried to grunt *why are you doing this?*

Stephens smirked. "Here's what you're to tell Diana. Thank you for the research help. I'm certain you have appreciated my contributions after analyzing those nanos in the kids' blood. Now we're equal." Her face hardened. "However. Melanie is hers to keep. Drew will be mine. She can't stop it. If she tries, she'll find more problems. My programming's still better. You understand?"

Kathy was able to nod her head enough to respond.

"Oh. One last bit for you. I gave you Jones, but you should know this." A feral grin crossed Stephens's lips. "Jones isn't your fiancé's killer." Her voice dropped to a whisper. "I killed your fiancé. In return for your life."

Kathy tried to protest.

"He loved you too much to kill you when your investigation got too close to me. I calculated that his death would remove you as a threat, and it has." She pressed an injector behind Kathy's left ear. "Don't forget about this. You can't remove it. My guarantee of your cooperation in the matter of Andrew."

Darkness swept over Kathy.

When she woke, she was alone, lying on the gravel lot next to her skimmer. Kathy sat up and felt her head. A small lump rose where Stephens had injected her.

Now that she thought about it, Dale had one like it for the last six months of his life, in about the same spot. Had told her he'd had a doctor look at it, that it was okay and not malignant.

He was wrong. Boy, was he wrong.

She shivered and wrapped her arms around herself. Maybe Fielding knew what this was—chemical? Nano? Listening device? The tool by which Stephens had killed Dale and Jones? All of the above?

I really screwed up.

Was this what Dale had felt?

She watched the waves crash over the jetty.

Briefly considered letting the waves take her.

Then Kathy shook her head. That wasn't the answer.

Slowly, she rose to her feet and got into the skimmer. For a moment she leaned her head against the steering yoke, briefly weary. She hadn't solved a damned thing.

Then she raised her head and her lips tightened.

On the other hand, Sarah Stephens had finally made a miscalculation. Nothing could keep Kathy from hunting her down; not NatSecure, not Dale, Diana, Melanie, or Do It Right.

You're mine, Stephens. You don't know it yet, but you're mine. You can't win at this game. I don't have anything left to lose.

She'd bring this nightmare to an end, even if it took the rest of her life to do it.

9 / INCONVENIENT TRUTHS

OCTOBER, 2058

FUNERAL PROBLEMS

What a freaking mess.

Diana squinted into the rays of the weak January sun slanting across the bier that held the coffin of the late American Federation President, Anne Whitman. The ceremony was already running an hour late, and functionaries had made Diana switch seats twice. Each move made the sun glare worse.

Why isn't this funeral better organized?

That the sun was shining instead of the typical rainy Oregon coast weather in Neahcom was a miracle of its own. But who had decided to place the podium so that the sun would be directly behind it? Diana's mother Sarah, in her new role as Federation President? Or someone else?

The fact of Sarah's Presidency was unexpected weirdness. There should have been at least two people between Sarah and the Presidency. Diana spotted one of them, Marjie Montgomery, the Chamber Speaker, in a front-row seat.

Furthermore, none of the reports about Anne's death Diana had heard made sense. Someone—reports differed as to *who*—had attacked Anne in her personal quarters. But whether Anne had died there, or in the hospital later, was still unanswered. The cause of her death—unexplained.

"Sure taking Sarah a while to get up there." Diana's closest advisor,

Dr. Kathy Miller, leaned over and whispered in her ear. "You sure she's okay?"

Diana eyed the crowd instead of responding right away. Ever since her mother had announced that Anne Whitman's deathbed executive order named her as Anne's successor instead of Vice President Needham or Speaker Montgomery, Diana had been pondering Sarah's state of mind. She scowled at the cordon of Security surrounding the attendees. They wore black helmets and black stealthsuits, with a silver insignia she couldn't make out.

"Leadership transition stuff is what I'm thinking," Diana said, after failing to see her mother anywhere amongst the blacksuits. Sarah's personal skimmer was parked amongst others when they arrived at the cemetery.

She didn't want to admit that something felt wrong about her mother's behavior.

But much had changed about Sarah in the ten years since the Third Force faded and the Federation had risen in its place.

What's really going on?

Kathy hadn't found any directives or Assassination Contracts sworn out on Anne when she had searched the Corporate Court records this morning.

Then again, if Needham really had given those assassins access to Anne's quarters—

"There she is." Was that relief in Kathy's voice? "I was worried. This is an exposed location. One President being assassinated is enough."

"My mother has enough Security to keep herself safe," Diana countered. She shaded her eyes from the sun as another phalanx of black-helmeted Security in black protective stealthsuits and carrying unsheathed blasters marched up to the podium. The Security cordon was so tight that Diana couldn't see her mother except as the occasional flash of white amongst the black stealthsuits. The hovercams buzzed even closer to Sarah and her Security.

Why is she wearing white? Diana bit her lower lip. *Perhaps it's a tribute to Anne. Anne always wore white for the suffragettes.*

Four of Sarah's guard stood at the stage corners, facing the crowd with blasters held to their side and facing down. Four more lined up next to the podium, two on each side. As her mother stepped up to the podium, flanked by two blacksuits at each shoulder, Diana noted the black lapels and edging on her jacket.

White as a tribute to Anne, then.

Nonetheless, Diana's uneasiness rose while Sarah looked over the crowd, waiting for—what? Diana's Dialogue wireless implant's visual overlays flickered into light, pale gray text flitting across them.

Not Federation uniform, Kathy texted in subvocal shorthand. *What do those uniforms represent? Corporate Courts? Stephens Reclamation?*

Diana's throat was dry as she blinked to activate her own Dialogue text function and carefully subvocaled a response.

Not Stephens. Not Courts.

She was still getting used to these overlay projections that were directly in her line of sight and not on comm glasses.

Sarah cleared her throat. "I apologize for the delay in the beginning of these services. It is always a tragedy when we have to bury a leader because of violence, especially one as visionary as Anne was." Her voice sharpened. "In the past few hours, I have become aware of a significant threat. I have needed to take extreme measures to manage the situation we now face, and I apologize for the delay that taking these actions has caused in this ceremony." She paused.

Her mother defiantly glared right at Diana. Then Sarah gestured. In one single, coordinated movement, her Security raised their blasters and fired at the hovercams. Six members of the Security cordon marched into the media section, blasters pointed at the reporters.

"Up!" one ordered. Slowly, the reporters stood. As they rose, individual blacksuits roughly grabbed their arms and marched them out.

"What?" Diana started to rise in objection but Kathy pulled her down.

"Don't move," she hissed.

More blacksuits behind us. Waiting, she texted.

What the hell? Diana subvocaled a text back, but Kathy shook her head.

A single silver hovercam floated into sight from below the stage.

"Unfortunately, we have reason to believe that indiscretions on the part of the media contributed to President Whitman's death, which is why they have been ejected." Sarah gestured toward the single hover-cam. "We will release the recording of this event after the ceremony has been concluded."

Diana raised a brow at Kathy.

Kathy shrugged.

"Now that this business is dealt with, let me read the full statement issued by our beloved leader Anne Whitman an hour before her death." Sarah cleared her throat. "Anne dictated this to me." Her voice caught.

Diana scowled. Real or staged? Emotion rarely choked her mother when speaking publicly.

Sarah coughed again and took a deep breath. She reached into her pocket and pulled out a tablet as well as half-frame reading glasses. An image of Anne lying on her hospital bed, head bandaged, lines attached to her body, appeared on an invisible screen behind Sarah. Diana squinted as Anne's eyes opened and her lips moved. She blinked a command to her Dialogue to record it.

"The voice recording did not come through," Sarah continued. "But I did my best to transcribe her final words. Here is what Anne had to say to me." She closed her eyes, then opened them. "At 4 am this morning, a force led by Vice President Ben Needham broke into my bedroom, overpowered my Security, and attacked me."

Anne shuddered on screen and Diana frowned. Something didn't fit.

Sarah paused. "I fought back and killed Vice President Needham, turning his own knife on him, but not before he had stabbed me in the body and face. He identified himself as a member of the Freedom Army. I nominate my Secretary of State, Sarah Stephens, as my successor until such time as I can resume command."

Diana eyed Marjie Montgomery. She only saw Montgomery's face in profile, but her lips were pursed in disapproval.

Why had Anne chosen to bypass Marjie?

Interesting, Kathy texted as Anne's eyes closed and the image faded away.

How so? Diana asked.

Some words don't match.

Sarah putting words into Anne's mouth?

Kathy shook her head. *Can't tell.*

Sarah tucked her glasses back into her jacket pocket.

"National Security has been investigating this attack and had not reached a conclusion until just now. Here are their results. Vice President Ben Needham, using a strike force from the Freedom Army, launched an attempted coup on the leadership of the North American Federation. This attempt included an attack on me, as well as assassinating President Anne Whitman. Per President Whitman's request, I have succeeded to the Presidency. Due to unfortunate circumstances caused by schisms within the Federation, I have taken a vote of confidence from a majority of the Assembly to dissolve the Federation and replace it with a new Confederation, the Confederation of American States. This is the official announcement of that decision."

The murmuring around Diana rose. She checked Montgomery's reaction once again, but couldn't see Marjie's face because of the blacksuits standing next to Marjie.

"At this time, the Confederation is under martial law, and will remain so, until this emergency is resolved. It was a difficult choice to make, but it had to be done." Sarah's eyes met Diana's again, cold and hard, challenging. "Confederation National Security is currently securing all potential dangers, political and corporate alike."

Kathy moaned softly next to Diana as Sarah continued speaking.

What's wrong? Diana subvocaled.

Before Kathy could answer, a faint red spot pulsed in the upper right-hand corner of Diana's vision. The ID code embedded in the red spot marked it as an urgent notice from her daughter Melanie. Diana blinked acknowledgement and opened it.

Ness Ryan and Marty Fielding in custody. Outfit claims to be Confederation National Security.

Icy shards stabbed through Diana's gut. Ness and Marty were two of the top Do It Right researchers. Melanie had been working with them on perfecting the use of Dialogue to control bioremediation nanobots.

More than that. Ness was Kathy's niece.

She cleared her throat to subvocal again. A nudge on her shoulder interrupted her. Diana looked up. One of the blacksuits had moved from standing behind them to take up a position next to her, and another next to Kathy.

"Now that we've dispensed with politics, let me speak about our heroic late President," Sarah continued. As she spoke, Diana tuned out. They knew she was texting. How?

How much does Sarah know about Dialogue?

If Sarah's people had taken Ness and Marty into custody, then Dialogue was compromised.

Diana blinked her Dialogue into quiet and faced straight ahead, staring at her mother, emulating Kathy.

FUNERAL COMPLICATIONS

Diana half-expected the blacksuits to grab her once the funeral ceremony was complete. When they didn't, she tried to make her way to Marjie Montgomery. The blacksuits herded Diana away from Marjie. Diana veered away from the reception line, heading for her own Security and her skimmer, urgency driving her since she obviously wasn't going to be allowed to talk to Montgomery.

Need to get to Hoodland and figure out what's going on with Ness and Marty.

She wanted more information before she confronted her mother.

Sergio, her Security chief, nodded sharply at the blacksuits, and escorted Diana and Kathy into the skimmer. As they settled into the seats, she noted that instead of the usual combination of Sergio and Paul in her skimmer and the remainder of her Security contingent in the follow-along skimmer, four members of her Security crowded into the main skimmer with them.

"What's going on, Serg?" she asked as Paul piloted them away. "Why did we have that blacksuit escort, and who are they?"

Sergio sighed. "They're the new Confederation National Security force. Not a one of them was anyone I knew."

"Melanie reported that Ness and Marty have been taken into custody. What the hell is going on?"

"We don't know yet," Sergio said. "They picked up Marty and Ness at the shuttleport on their way back from Rio."

"We must know something."

Sergio looked uncomfortable. "It—needs to wait for a more secure location." He glanced at Kathy.

"Oh don't beat around the bush," Kathy said irritably. "What Sergio isn't saying is that I'm compromised. I just found out how much so."

"*What?*" Diana stared at her friend. "How?"

"Remember when Melanie and Andrew were abducted in their teens, and Sarah got her hands on them?"

Diana nodded, a chill coming over her at the memory of the kidnapping of her daughter and son. Even though it had been ten years ago, she still had nightmares about that time.

"She claimed the kidnappers would only work with her. But she got them back."

Kathy snorted. "She got them back because she hired the kidnappers in the first place." She swallowed hard, paling. "I can't say much more. She inserted a blocking chip. Give me a tablet, please."

Diana reached into the side pocket of her seat and handed the tablet tucked in there to Kathy. Kathy typed, biting her lip, occasionally moaning softly. Sweat beaded on her brow.

"Are you all right?" Diana asked.

Kathy shook her head. At last, she finished and handed the tablet to Diana, then slumped back against her seat.

Diana gestured for Sergio to lean over. She angled the tablet so they could both read what Kathy wrote.

Alan Adam Jones, the kidnapper of the kids, has always worked for Sarah. He killed my fiancé, Dale. I left NatSecure after Dale's death, and I was targeted—but it wasn't until the kids were kidnapped that I found out why. Sarah had co-opted Dale to cover up some things her company did—had something on him until he resisted. When I recovered the kids and recognized Jones, I confronted Sarah. She gave me Jones as part of the deal—then killed him, and chipped me. I can't stay around you now. I thought our research would allow me to block her chip influence, and it has—until now. Activation during the funeral. I'm sorry. I thought I could beat it.

"Why didn't you tell me?" Diana asked.

"Couldn't," Kathy gasped. She swallowed hard. "Fighting—influence—now. Push—much—harder and it kills me. Best I can do is block auditory transmission from other speakers. Not reliable."

"I don't feel comfortable taking her to Hoodland." Sergio said.

"He's right," Kathy said. "Sorry."

Sergio and Diana exchanged glances.

Kathy's apartment in Portland compound? she texted.

Works, Sergio texted. Aloud, he continued. "I was informed by Sarah's staff that Confederation Security wants us to turn Kathy over to them. There was enough desire to avoid a scene at the funeral for us to get away without them pushing it. We won't be able to dodge them in Hoodland."

"Just—buy me some time," Kathy said through gritted teeth.

Sergio nodded. "We'll drop you at your Portland apartment."

"Thank you." Kathy shuddered. "Sorry, Di. Ness was working on a solution."

"You didn't tell me!" Diana let her outrage fill her voice.

"I couldn't." Kathy winced. "Ness—safe. You—not. I tried to tell you. Day of headache when I collapsed, remember?"

"Yes."

"That's what would happen if I tried to tell anyone." A brief, grim smile crossed Kathy's lips. "At least I was able to feed Sarah disinformation."

Diana shook her head and buried it in her hands. Then she sat back up in her seat, staring straight ahead, ignoring Kathy even though she wanted to say something, anything to break through the sense of betrayal pulsing through her.

Why couldn't you have found a way to tell me about this before now?

She suspected the blocking chip wouldn't let Kathy tell her.

At least she hoped that was it. Damn it. She needed to talk to Will. But he was in Nagano, and they needed a safe line.

That is, if any comms were safe now.

REVELATIONS

After they dropped Kathy off at her apartment, they hurried to the Do It Right headquarters in Hoodland. Melanie met them at the landing pad, leaning heavily on the crutches she needed to use after her third knee surgery, flanked by her Security leads, Nik and Angela.

"Where's Kathy?" she asked.

"Compromised," Diana said bluntly. "Sarah apparently chipped her ten years ago. Ness had been helping her hide it. You know anything about that?"

Melanie shook her head. "Haven't had much to do with Kathy, and I talk to Marty more than Ness." She pivoted and hobbled along slowly, moving along the covered walkway toward the family quarters, not the offices.

Diana frowned. Melanie's knee still wasn't healing right after that skimmer crash in Nagano earlier that year. "What happened with Ness and Marty?"

"Grabbed at Spaceport California shuttleport. Andrew helped, but it was led by Confederation National Security. *Which* I didn't understand until Sarah's announcement went live. I've been trying to get them back. No answer from National Security yet. What the hell is going on there?"

"All I know is what Sarah said at the funeral," Diana said. "She and Anne were attacked, only your grandmother survived and Anne didn't. The attack on Anne was led by Ben Needham. Anne killed Needham but was injured too badly to survive."

"That doesn't fit," Nik Morley said. "Not the part with Anne. She was competent, but for Needham to have done the actual killing? Doesn't match what I've seen of the man at Corporate Courts. Never came to the gym. Never trained."

The sense of foreboding that had been pulling at Diana grew stronger. "Could he have just not practiced at the Courts?"

"Possibly," Morley said. "But unlikely. He didn't move right. No, there's more to the story. Drugging? Someone else who actually did it?"

"You saw Sarah's recounting of Anne's statement," Diana said.

Morley shook his head as they entered the large shared family common space. Melanie and Diana had separate suites off of the living room area, with a third guest suite that had been used by Sarah in the past, when family relationships had been better.

Melanie sank into a recliner and raised the footrest to support her injured leg, sliding a pillow underneath her knee. "We've seen no visual of that announcement, Mom. It's all been in writing."

"Sarah projected a recording—no sound, just visual—at the funeral."

"Well, that's not what she's releasing," Melanie grumbled. "I'd like to see that footage."

"I recorded it," Diana said.

"So did others," Sergio said. "But every Security person I've talked to said their copies were blocked or jammed."

"I'll try to upload mine."

"Did you use Dialogue?" Melanie asked.

"Yes."

"Then your recording might work. Ness and Marty put in some good workarounds—damn it, now their work is compromised."

"Perhaps that's best done abroad, not in North America," Diana said carefully. "Your father."

"Yes. Isolate your vid, in case the block is coming from an external source," Melanie said. She handed Diana a hologlobe cube. "Secured globe. See if you can bring up your version in it."

Diana opened the globe and set the command cube on the coffee table that sat in the middle of the arrangement of couch and recliners. The globe expanded to half-size. Diana sent the recording into the globe. It stuttered and was static-y.

"Doesn't look like this one works either," she said.

Melanie leaned forward, frowning more intently. "Don't write it off yet. Give me some time with it—wish Dad were here and not in Nagano. He could help."

Diana blinked a time check. "He'd be in bed right now." *At least he'd better be.* This last round of chemo was hard on Will.

"S'okay." Melanie stared at the globe. "I'll see what I can do." With a snap of her fingers, she called the globe closer to her, until it hovered over her lap, a single silver thread keeping it connected to the globe generator. "Might be a few hours. Make yourself comfortable."

"I'll work in my quarters. Need to figure out what's compromised."

Melanie nodded, her focus already intent on the globe.

Have something. Melanie's text startled Diana out of her review of Do It Right company resources in North America. She had been making a list of who and what might need to be relocated. Melanie knew more about what programs Ness and Marty might compromise at Hoodland, but only Diana knew the extent to which Will had created protective systems to keep Do It Right safe in circumstances like this.

Be right there, she texted back to Melanie.

Diana shivered and pulled on a sweater. The weather had changed from sunny to a cold, driving rain that threatened to become sleet.

I never expected to have to worry about my own mother taking over the country.

Melanie scowled at the globe as Diana joined her in the common room. "First, I heard back from Confederated National Security. Ness and Marty have been conscripted for their labs. No word on when they'll be released—if ever."

"Damn it." Diana sat down, tapping her fingers tensely on her chair's arm. "What about the video?"

"Let's save details for Nik and Sergio so I can do it all at once," Melanie said.

"I've been sorting resources," Diana said. "Haven't activated the button for the hidden nukes yet."

"You'd better activate that dead man's switch," Melanie said coldly. "Now."

"That bad?"

"Worst case scenario."

"But Mother and Anne were lovers for many years."

"It didn't protect Anne," Melanie said in that harsh, bitter voice. "Activate it as soon as you can."

Diana nodded and pulled up a smaller globe. She tapped her way through the process that activated the network of hidden, shielded suitcase nukes Will had installed around the various seats of the American Federation government ten years ago.

Never thought we would need to use them.

Diana had indulged Will's paranoia, figuring his past history as a weapons designer drove that caution. Now she wondered what he had seen in the political currents that had driven his choices ten years ago.

When it came to the final authorization, Diana hesitated. Normally these weapons were keyed to her.

Make Melanie part of it. Just in case.

Two hands on the trigger were better than one, and Will was certainly in no shape to be her backup. A gut instinct made her designate Melanie as the primary on the dead man's switch.

Nik, Paul, Sergio, and Angela entered and took seats around the globe.

Melanie inhaled deeply before speaking. "We're in deep trouble. Sarah's story about what happened is pure bullshit."

I knew it.

"How bad?"

"I wasn't able to get full sound. Just what Sarah said." Melanie snapped her fingers and the recording appeared. "But I was able to run a lipreading program we put together as part of the Dialogue subvocal training process—not something available to everyone else." She scooted up in her chair. "Ready? It'll come up as subtitles. There was also a masking layer over that vid Sarah ran. I stripped that off—and, well, you'll see for yourself."

"Run it." Diana's gaze was fixed on Anne's prone body in the bed. The upper end of the bed rose, and Anne's eyes popped open, glazed, signaling death's approach.

I want you to read this, the captioning read.

Diana recognized the ring on the fourth finger of the hand that thrust the tablet in front of Anne. A silver rose with a ruby set into it. Her mother had worn it from Diana's earliest memory.

Anne shook her head.

Read it. Sarah came into sight now, giving Anne a shake.

Anne's eyes widened. *Help me,* her lips moved. *Poison.*

"What?" Nik Morley leaned closer to the vid.

No one will help you now. Read it, and we'll finish you quickly. Otherwise, it will hurt.

What are you doing, Sarah? Why? Anne shuddered. Diana recognized that motion from the vid she'd seen at the funeral.

Read it and you'll stop hurting. Repeat this after me. I killed Needham after he attacked me. He identified himself as part of the Freedom Army. I nominate Sarah Stephens, my Secretary of State, to serve in my place until I have recovered sufficiently to reassume command.

Anne's body spasmed. Her eyes focused on something beyond Sarah.

All right. I'll say it. I killed Needham after he attacked me. He identified himself as leading a coup in the name of the Freedom Army. I nominate Sarah Stephens, my Secretary of State, to serve in my place until I have recovered sufficiently to reassume command.

The video stopped there. Diana sat back in her chair, shaken. "Are you sure this is correct?"

"I've run several test checks to make sure the program wasn't adding things. The overlay masks Sarah's presence and adds the head bandages. The lipreading on the overlay matches what Sarah reported Anne as saying. Strip off that overlay—this is what you get."

"But how did she think she'd get away with it?" Diana began to pace. "I—Melanie, we have to be sure. If we could dig this out, then others could as well."

"Not unless they have our Dialogue prototypes, and that's only been available within Do It Right," Melanie said. "With Ness and Marty in National Security's clutches, no telling how long Dialogue will remain proprietary."

"I see. But when she realizes we know what she's done, she'll come after us."

Oh Mother.

Diana wanted to scream. Cry. But now was not the time.

"Maybe." Melanie tapped her fingers on the arm of her chair, chewing her lower lip thoughtfully. "And maybe not. Remember, as far as Grandmother is concerned, I'm just a ski bum dilettante. *Do* you want to confront her? If so, say that you routed your recording to Dad in Nagano, and had him work his magic on it. Leave Do It Right North America out of it entirely."

"I'm not going to confront her with this unless I have to." Diana stared out the window at the icy sleet pounding against the glass, the clatter still quieter than the pounding of her heart in her ears. "Unless." She turned to face Melanie. "I'll go back to Nagano. She can't touch me there. I'll tell her that if something happens to you, I'll trigger your father's nukes. I'll leave you in charge of Do It Right North America, and draw attention to me. Your hand is on the dead man's switch."

"Will that be enough?" Melanie struggled to get out of her chair. "You'd better get moving if that's the case. Once you say something—"

Diana sighed. "First, I need to sign and file the transfer authorization papers. Then I'll go back to the Portland compound tonight, and leave on the first shuttle to Japan tomorrow. I won't say anything to her until the morning—that will make having your father break the code sound more plausible."

"Makes sense."

Diana hugged her daughter. "Stay safe, Mel. I'm sorry to leave you here, but—you could designate someone to stay behind, and go with me."

Melanie shook her head. "And drop our research here? Leave everything you and Dad built in Hoodland? No. I'll be all right."

"You sure?"

Melanie, Nik, and Angela looked at each other. "Positive," Melanie said. "We've set up and run our evacuation protocols." She grimaced and gestured at her knee. "It'll be better when this is healed. But if I have to…" Her voice trailed off.

"Be careful." Diana hugged her daughter again, bending over to compensate for the difference in their height, burying her nose deep in her daughter's neck like she hadn't done since Melanie was little.

Memorizing her scent.

That brought back a faint memory of Sarah picking her up as a small child, and burying her nose in the exact same place. After that hug, Diana hadn't remembered seeing her mother for a long time, not until she was older. Her arms tightened around Melanie.

Then she straightened up. "I'd better go now."

"Tell Dad to stay strong," Melanie said. "And you stay safe."

"I will to both." Now that she had decided on her course, Diana was impatient to get moving.

It's been a while since I've played for these stakes.

With any luck, she would have the night to rehearse before talking to Sarah.

Nonetheless, as she went through the process of filing papers transferring her authority in Do It Right North America to Melanie, Diana reviewed what she would say to Sarah. At this point she wasn't about to share her true feelings with her mother.

No sooner had they settled into Diana's apartment in the Do It Right Portland building than an intrusion alarm jangled, joined by the lobby pager.

Sergio switched off the alarm and answered the pager. "Hernandez. Landreth Security." He listened. "One moment." He looked at Diana. "It's Sarah with her Security—Confederation National Security, that is."

Diana sighed and got up from her dinner. She strapped on the blaster that she had put down on the table, just in case. "Then let her in the rest of the way."

Sergio pointed at her blaster. "Get rid of that. It will give that Confederation Security bunch the excuse they need to take you into custody. If not kill you outright."

"I'm licensed. Accredited. Given the official story of Anne's death, I have reason to believe I'm a Freedom Army target. Plus—" and now Diana grinned at Sergio. "I just messaged her people about our dead man's switch. Sarah should know about that already—she agreed to it when Will placed them. Announce to her Security that I'm armed because we fear an attack."

"All right," Sergio said.

"Keep your weapons out and visible. Anne didn't believe in being armed. That was her mistake." Diana took a deep breath. "I won't make that one."

She faced the door, tense, as Sergio relayed her message, wishing she could hear the full conversation.

"We're ready," Sergio said into the pager. He and Paul took up positions on either side of Diana, blasters drawn.

Four blacksuits marched into the room, pointing weapons at Diana's Security, who aimed theirs back.

"Oh, good grief," Sarah grumbled as she entered the apartment. "I'm not going to kill you, Diana. We're just trying to find Kathy Miller. Do you know where she is?"

Diana rested her hand on the butt of her blaster. "I haven't the faintest idea. She asked us to leave her while we went to Hoodland. Isn't she in her apartment?"

"Funny thing, that." Sarah walked over to a chair and sat down. "She isn't there. So, are we going to put our weapons away and sit like civilized people, or do we need to continue this farce?"

"What farce?"

"Your Security knew I wanted Kathy Miller. She's not here. Where is she?"

"The last I saw of Kathy, she was headed for her apartment." Diana remained standing. "I have no idea where she is."

"So you don't know anything about why she packed up her things and left." Sarah rose and started pacing. "Bullshit. I know better. What did she tell you?"

"Nothing of significance."

"When are you going to stop lying?" Sarah stopped sharply and faced Diana. "How much did she disclose to you? Did she say anything about Jones? Did she tell you she reported to me about everything you were doing?"

Pain welled up within Diana at the thought that Kathy might have betrayed her.

No. Trust Kathy. She said she fed Sarah disinformation.

"You're accusing *me* of lying?" she countered.

"Are you calling me a liar?"

"Are you calling me one?" Diana parried.

They glared at each other.

"I *am* your President as well as your mother," Sarah snarled. "How much did Kathy tell you?"

"Enough to let me know you didn't learn anything important!"

A moment, then Sarah barked a short, biting, laugh. "She had outlived her usefulness to me. I've not gotten anything important out of her for the past year or so."

"If that's all you wanted from me, then perhaps I can go back to eating dinner," Diana said. "Unfortunately, I'd just as soon not invite you to join me."

"I'm disappointed. I *was* hoping to offer you a position in the new government."

Diana shook her head. "I have a company to run. I don't have the time."

"I'm surprised you're here and not at Hoodland," Sarah said, her voice going poisonously soft. "One would think Melanie would appreciate seeing her mother."

"Melanie's busy with her own *affairs*." Diana made a face. *Lay the foundation.* "I'm a little old for that level of partying."

Sarah snorted. "Always the ski bum, huh?"

"There is that element around her, yes."

Sarah walked toward Diana. "I will require you to swear loyalty to me before you leave North America."

Diana shook her head, unable to speak.

Murderer. You caused Anne's death.

Could she say that and still escape? No, for Melanie's sake, she had to hide any hint of her suspicions.

"Why?"

"I—I don't support the martial law declaration." Diana looked directly into her mother's eyes—the eyes of a murderer. Multiple times. "And I'm still unsure about what really happened to Anne."

"Oh really?" Sarah came closer, took Diana's chin in her hand. Sergio tightened up, preparing to attack, and Diana rested her right hand on his arm, fingertapping the code not to react. "What don't you believe?"

Dissemble. Dissemble.

"I don't understand why Ben Needham went with the Freedom

Army." Diana steadily met Sarah's glare. "That doesn't make sense. I don't support the martial law declaration, much less the dissolution of the Federation."

Sarah shook Diana's chin before releasing it. "Then I will confiscate Do It Right in North America."

"No." Diana kept her voice firm. "I had already made the decision to leave. I've turned over all North American responsibility to Melanie. She'll swear to you, I'm sure. Go ahead and check—the documents are filed with the Corporate Courts."

Sarah stepped back and pulled out her tablet. She tapped on it, frowning. Diana schooled herself to remain calm while Sarah scowled at the tablet.

"You'd trust your business to that ski bum daughter of yours?" Sarah growled.

"I don't have much of a choice." Diana shrugged, forcing a calmness she didn't feel. "Are we good now? I'd like to return to my dinner."

"You're lucky that you're my daughter, and that this transfer to Melanie gives me no reason to force you to stay. I'll give you until 9 AM to get the hell out of my country," Sarah said. "And if you ever return, well—I won't answer for the consequences."

She signaled to her Security and marched out of the apartment.

Diana returned to the table and sank her head into her hands. Then she reached for her food and forced herself to take a bite.

Survive. That's the first rule.

And after that—find a way to reveal the inconvenient truths.

She cynically wondered if it wasn't already too late to do so.

10 / SOME WORDS

FEBRUARY, 2075

SOME WORDS

Some words can't be unsaid or reasoned out of existence.

Words like "Sarah. This is your terminal diagnosis. The cancer has metastasized to your lungs and liver. We can't do anything more."

"Didn't you promise me that these nanos would stop the cancer from metastasizing?"

"You've pushed your luck, Sarah. Too many years of doing them for beauty. Your system doesn't respond as effectively to nanomanipulation anymore."

God, Dr. Martino can be harsh. Maybe there's some things better done with a little sugar-coating.

Well, all her long life she'd disdained having things sugar-coated. Why would anyone expect she'd want anything else at this point?

Maybe Diana's company has something up their sleeves. But damn. That means talking to my granddaughter because she's the one who has the nanotech down solid, not her mother. I can break through to Di, always have.

Melanie, not so much. Do I really want to make myself that vulnerable to Melanie?

She still couldn't figure out how much of her granddaughter's dilettante ski bum behavior was a façade. Too much about Melanie suggested the likelihood that her ski bum habits served as a cover for a deadly serious manager.

Gizmo doesn't like Melanie, never has liked Melanie.

Surely the enigmatic war machine the Gizmo Protectorate guarded wouldn't react to Melanie's presence like it did if she wasn't more than she seemed, would it?

But then there's her ADHD. That's enough to make anyone nervous, especially when she gets wired up.

Sarah shook her head to dismiss that distraction. "You're the one who recommended anti-aging nanos," she retorted.

Martino waved his right hand dismissively. "They weren't the wrong choice until they turned on you. Which we knew would happen sooner or later. We've just been lucky with you and nanos over the years. You tolerate them well."

"How long do I have?" she asked.

God. My programs. Everything that I'm going to leave half-finished. If I can get some time free to wrap things up, then all will be well.

"Days to three weeks," Martino said bluntly. "I'm measuring too damned much memory loss as well. I've not seen a metastasis to the brain. Yet. Not likely now. It'll be a race to see if nano-caused dementia or cancer kills you first."

"You sure about that? I've always had memory problems when I get stressed. Doesn't mean dementia."

"It's dementia," Martino snapped. "Peter has been in contact with me over the past week. He's worried about some of the things you're doing and saying. I have examples that he's given me, if you want to check them."

Is it Peter who worries, or is it Gizmo driving him because I won't give in to it?

God, Gizmo. The projects around that.

Don't dare tell anyone how much Gizmo's pushing on me at night.

"I don't need to see those examples. True or not, I won't trust them. I need you to be straight with me, Martino. Tell me the parameters I'll encounter," she said hoarsely. "What will it look like?"

Martino gave her a sideways look. "Unlike some of my other patients, at least I can count on you for pragmatism. So. Here's what you can expect."

Sarah half-listened to Martino as she started making the mental checklist of what she needed to do before it was too late.

Like twisting the screws down tighter on Ness Ryan's project. This news made it more important than ever.

I'm not going to leave Gizmo unsupervised. If Francis could make the jump to virtual life through Gizmo when he died, I can do my best to activate my alternate route to block him.

As long as her granddaughter didn't find a way to interfere before Sarah's systems were in place.

Sarah's mouth quirked. Making sure that Melanie didn't interfere would also involve Ness Ryan.

She just had to get the timing right.

And if she planned it correctly, her son Peter might just end up contributing to her plans, after all.

The old fox still had a few tricks left to pull. Peter didn't know as much as he thought he did.

Whereas I can always count on Melanie to surprise me. Okay, girl. Surprise me yet again. Show me you're worthy of your legacy.

In the long run, that was truly what mattered.

FEBRUARY, 2075

WALKING AWAY

DAMN SNOW.

Kathy Miller methodically packed her survival backpack, emptying her data hidies, glancing up occasionally to check the intrusion scanner. Nothing human moving near her backwoods cabin—not yet, anyway. Unless they could block her sensors.

They could, possibly, in this snow.

Damn snow. Any other season of the year she could pull off a clean getaway on foot; cross the meadow and drop into the draws leading to the deep inland river canyons. Between the rugged contours of the land and her all-weather stealthsuit, she could disappear from all but the skilled eyes of the Indians who had reclaimed this isolated part of their original homeland.

But not in snow. Crusted snow with a firm ice coating, maybe. Not in the soft powdery stuff that had fallen last night. Damn snow.

Kathy allowed herself a couple of minutes for a quick breakfast, idly rubbing the sore spot behind her ear where Sarah Stephens had injected a behavioral/monitoring implant seventeen years ago. The implant was the reason for her urgent departure. Sarah had left her alone since she activated the implant seven years ago, not tried to issue compulsions or activate the monitoring devices.

Until early this morning, when Kathy's protective nanos blocked the first compulsion attempt, and woke her.

This was it; the time she'd both hoped for and dreaded was now.

Kathy looked around her cabin one last time. It had been a nice hidey-hole, while she waited for Sarah to take action. But now its usefulness was over.

One last thing to pack. She picked up the picture taken many years ago of her fiancé, Dale, killed by Sarah. She smiled wistfully at it.

Then Kathy tucked the picture into her backpack, sealed her stealthsuit and pulled the backpack on. She left the cabin without looking back, triggering one of the thermal cartridges hidden in the doorway as she stepped into her snowshoes.

The cabin was in flames by the time she reached the meadow's edge. She followed the canyon rim around to its steepest pitch, stripped off her snowshoes and fastened them to her pack, then used her rope to lower her pack, then belay herself, a process she would repeat three times to reach the bottom of Grouse Creek.

Just like she had practiced over the past seven years. And, had it not been so snowy, it would have been more effective.

Damn snow.

GHOSTS

Damn snow, the ghosts in her mind whispered to Sarah Stephens as she paced through the knee-deep stuff while waiting on the blacksuits searching through the remains of Kathy Miller's cabin. Others might attribute the whispers to failing sanity or a glitch in nanolink programming.

Sarah knew better. These ghosts were real, and one day they would bring her down. The thought made her mouth twitch. She'd kept them at bay for forty years now. No reason why she couldn't continue to do so.

Except for that impending dementia that Dr. Martino warned you about.

She let the wind push her along Kathy's path to the rimrock edging the canyon. She stared across the narrow, ponderosa pine thickets to the rim on the other side, then down the steep canyon carved into the earth below her. Rimrocks, steep slopes, caves, null spots where no detector worked. Kathy was down there somewhere, unless she'd fallen and her broken body lay quietly among the trees and snow.

No. If Kathy were dead, her voice would have joined the others inside Sarah's head. Her implant guaranteed that.

So she was still alive—but where? Where was she going? And how had she known when to run?

The whomp-whomp-whomp of an approaching helicopter caught Sarah's attention. She trudged back to the staging area, doubled over against the rising wind, only now noticing how steeply the meadow dropped toward the canyon edge. The effort made her wheeze.

Another reminder of the limits she faced.

Rob Meacham climbed out of the helicopter.

"Why isn't Miller's implant working?" Sarah demanded.

"I don't know! Ness Ryan screwed up all the data!" Meacham whimpered. "I haven't been able to find one complete backup—still trying to recover files."

Sarah clenched her hands into fists. "It was your job to make sure this didn't happen!" she snapped. "You knew she was operating under duress."

She started to raise one hand to slap him, then dropped it. No time for this. Ness Ryan had fooled them all, even Sarah. She had thought Ryan was settling down. After all, Sarah offered twice the power which her daughter Diana's company could give Ryan; twice the influence. Twice the money.

"President Stephens," the blacksuit commander said nervously.

"Yes." She turned away from Meacham.

"We've lost Miller's trail." He swallowed hard but didn't flinch under her steady glare. "My people have discovered a cache of half-destroyed security equipment in the cabin. I think she has equipment to match ours. If not better."

Damn it, Diana, you lied to me!

Sarah clenched her fists again. Her daughter had sworn up and down that her company's nano and neural net research had no security implications; that her Security research was nothing more than what a savvy company had to do in order to get along. She had believed Diana.

Mistake.

"Run a full Inquiry on Do It Right," she ordered the blacksuit. "Miller has connections with them, and probably kept it up in spite of blackout orders. I want you to issue a Notice of Takeover from Stephens Rec—put Peter on it."

"What about Miller?"

"Can we catch her?" Sarah asked.

"Harder than we thought. The snow drops off pretty light as you go down into the canyon. Harder to find her tracks. Hard enough to track down someone who *wants* to be found in this country. Add the crap the natives have put up, and it's damn near impossible."

"Find her. I don't care how you do it, just find her. Put Meacham to work; he knows what her implant can do."

"Yes, ma'am." The commander saluted her, then turned away, Meacham tagging along behind like a whipped puppy.

Sarah sighed.

If they would all just listen to her and get along, everything would go just fine. If only Anne had listened to her. If only Diana would. Why did they all have to argue with her? Why wouldn't they listen? Would they all have to die?

At last. Kathy reached the old mine shaft deep in the main canyon. She fiddled with the confusion screen controls and waited for them to stabilize, revealing the obscured opening. After she went inside, she restored the confusion screen, then slipped off her back-pack. Before she went further, however, she checked the intrusion sensors, running down the registry of all who had accessed this place since her last visit.

Nothing untoward.

Good.

Kathy activated a space heater, dug in the stores for food, and set up a pallet to rest on. After she ate, she lay down, but her mind kept racing.

What to do now? Dare she try to contact anyone, or should she wait until she was safe in the native longhouses? No one messed with the tribe these days, not since they activated Joseph's Ghost, the floating electromagnetic pulse generators, and other varieties of protective electronics seeded throughout these deep canyons.

Curiosity got the best of her. Kathy rolled off the pallet and went to work at the comconsole.

She checked individual contacts first. Nothing.

Corporate contacts. Nothing.

But there was a transmission, low-band, on the emergency DIR network.

Diaspora Preparation. Diaspora Preparation. Diaspora Preparation. Pause, then repeated.

Oh shit.

Something had happened, bad enough for Melanie to send Do It Right staff fleeing. Kathy tapped over to the subband that carried coded traffic.

It yielded only the briefest report. The internal labs of the Confederated States reported that Vanessa Ryan, formerly employed by Do It Right, Inc until her services had been conscripted by the Confeds, had perished under unknown circumstances.

Shit!

Now Kathy knew what had gone wrong. Her niece Ness had decided to sabotage the Confed labs and gotten killed in the process. Which meant that the Confeds were too damn close to Do It Right's research.

Wearily, she signed off the comm. Now what to do?

Revenge is a dish best served cold.

She had waited for years to avenge Dale's death. This was the perfect time; the perfect place. It would also be the perfect distraction from Ness's death.

But how to do it?

The glimmerings of a plan began to emerge. Kathy pulled out a tablet and started to organize her thoughts.

She would only get one chance.

But if it worked…oh, it would be so sweet.

Revenge is a dish best served cold. And, oh, Sarah Stephens, this dish has gotten very, very cold.

PAST SHADOWS

As she sat in the blacksuit mobile headquarters, staring out at the blizzard which had started up again, Sarah felt old. Ancient.

There was something about this country which reminded her that she was, after all, in her nineties. Somehow, it counteracted the nanos that kept her body stabilized.

Of course, the nanos were failing. An effect of those defensive systems she had heard about but—so far—not seen in action?

What's in those native floaties? That Joseph's Ghost and the others?

She carefully glanced at her hand, the marker of the antigeriatic nano effectiveness.

No change.

Sarah relaxed.

A mental illusion then, simply tension. Just old memories from when she'd wandered this country in her youth. Back before she had earned acknowledgment as the Stephens family heir, when she could afford to be idealistic. She vaguely remembered camping here, of exploring the cliffs below, examining old mining shafts—*old mining shafts*.

Damn. How many of those old mine shafts were on a map or database somewhere? A lot of them were situated so that their openings could be easily obscured by a shielding device.

Sarah clicked her comm. "Meacham. I have something for you to check."

EVASION TECHNIQUES

SHE WOULD BARELY HAVE ENOUGH TIME TO GET IT ALL DONE BEFORE needing to leave.

Kathy popped a stimtab and pulled up the EMP generator monitors. The increased activity caused by Sarah's blacksuits had several of them drifting toward the Grouse Creek drainage and the deeper canyons.

Would they get here in time?

She tweaked the command codes for a hurry up. Then she set about tracking the big one, Joseph's Ghost, the EMP-plus generator.

Joseph's Ghost was her own creation; one of the reasons she had taken up residence on Grouse Creek. The tribal scientists were pretty damn good, but they weren't about to reject any help from outside, especially from Do It Right. The canyon country near the Bucket Mountains was a prime testing site for the bioremediation security gadgets DIR had been devising, both in Nagano and in Hoodland. Bioremediation bots with real teeth to protect the sites they were reconstructing; stuff to disable those devices who would interfere with the reclamation process.

Joseph's Ghost went beyond disabling individual devices. Joseph's Ghost could kill. It had the ability to trace back the wireless links of any device it encountered and hack its source by reprogramming the network to self-destruct, bringing down anything networked into its target. Commlinks, nanodrivers, the computers monitoring the devices, any individual chips linked into the target device, perhaps even the medical nanos of those connected to the target.

Kathy wasn't entirely certain how far the Ghost would go. It had started as a Ness Ryan project which Kathy had taken over, because the tribal scientists had asked for bioremediation enforcement help with teeth. There'd been a lot of tweaking done to the Ghost by the natives since she'd last played with it. While she roughly knew the Ghost's parameters, for all Kathy knew, the Ghost could bring down all North American networks.

If not world networks.

The Ghost could kill Sarah's control over the North American Confederated States. Question was, how far did Kathy dare to go?

As far as it takes.

She pulled up the Ghost's programming and got to work.

"This is the best map I can find," Meacham said. "The damn thing's one hundred years out of date. It doesn't show any shafts, just mining sites. No information on what's a shaft, gravel site, you name it."

Sarah scowled at the screen. "I *know* there's better maps than this available."

"There probably are. Buried in paper records God only knows where. Maybe in Salem, maybe back in D.C. This is what we've been able to unearth online. The natives destroyed a lot of our local records when they hacked into the system ten years ago. We've never been able to restore them."

"What about mineral surveys? We might be able to cross-link them."

Meacham shook his head. "Tribal proprietary info. They locked it up. I have bots spidering through what records we can get into, but it's going to take time."

Sarah sighed.

Damn, damn, and damn!

Years of unrest caused by the Gizmo and—other sources—had undermined a lot of systems. Too many of the country's leaders had handed power over to those who would trash an effective, centralized bureaucracy.

And you were one of them, she wryly reminded herself.

It hadn't been just dissidents seeking protection from powerful centralized governments, but corporations seeking fewer restrictions on their activities.

Did it to myself.

Oh well. Memory was fleeting and transient, but it was all she had right now. Sarah pulled up the Grouse Creek area and scanned the sites. Too bad this wasn't one of the places she'd haunted in the old days.

"Let's check out these sites," she said finally, pointing out five claims. "If Miller's gone to ground somewhere it has to be close. She's on foot. She can't get too far away."

Unless she has help.

For all she knew, Miller could be miles away by now.

Easy enough to do in this country. And damn it, time was running out.

KATHY POPPED ANOTHER STIMTAB AND BEGAN PROGRAMMING THE destruction cascade sequence for this control center. She needed to leave a trail, something to get the blacksuits within range of the Ghost, now drifting up the canyon.

She left most of her things behind as she left the mine shaft. It was time to travel light and fast; maybe the natives would reach her in time once she was done, and maybe they wouldn't.

That didn't matter. Taking Sarah out did.

The comms in the mine shaft signaled her just before the control center died.

"That's it, then." Kathy dropped her shielding. "Stephens!" she yelled into the canyon. "You want me? You come get me! *Yourself!*"

ACTION

"We've got her!" Meacham yelled. He cranked up the volume on the monitor implant, in time for everyone in the control center to hear Miller's defiant scream. Then the signal started moving. Fast.

"How the *hell* is she doing that?" Sarah demanded. "She get a ride?"

The blacksuit captain ran a scan. "Augmented stealthsuit," he reported. "Gives her a boost. But it's an energy drain. She can't keep that pace up for long."

Sarah nodded. "She alone?"

"That's what the scanners say."

"Pull together a crew and let's go. Get me a suit. I'm not taking any chances."

"It could be a trap," the blacksuit captain said.

"It probably is. But she's more valuable to me alive. If I'm out there myself, then any mistakes are mine."

"I don't like it," Meacham said.

"You're not paid to like it." Sarah grabbed the suit the blacksuit captain handed her and pulled it on. "If anything happens to me, this is what you do."

She gave Meacham detailed instructions.

With any luck, this won't be necessary.

Just to be safe, she performed one last memory upload as the helicopter lifted. Her own little secret; her personal gamble on immortality.

They can kill me but they can't get rid of me.

Unless Ness Ryan had screwed this one up, too.

But that would hurt Ness as well, wouldn't it?

Sarah stifled a sudden impulse to giggle. She broke off the link and triple-secured it. If something happened—well, these memories would make it into the record.

And if it didn't, she'd have time for another update. No sense in taking a risk on losing everything.

Sarah had heard too many rumors about the capacity of some of those tribal devices.

And she knew too damn much about the capabilities of her son-in-law.

Now her granddaughter's abilities—well, she would have to gamble on those, wouldn't she?

WAITING

Running, running, running. Kathy's breath came in deep, hurting sobs, but she didn't dare stop yet. The Ghost was still too far away. There was almost enough time for the hunters to find her before she would be ready.

Get up here, you piece of electronic shit!

She kept listening for the pinging signal which would tell her that the Ghost was within range.

There! Gotcha!

Kathy slowed to a stop and bent over, breathing hard. She dropped to the ground, gasping for air as the Ghost drifted nearer.

Was this place going to work? She looked around. There was a flat spot on the bench just above her, big enough for a medium-sized helicopter to land.

Perfect.

Could she find a credible flight path down the hillside which would still keep her within launcher range? The Ghost would take out the computers, but she would still have to deal with the people. Unless she crashed the helicopter in mid-air—no, she wanted time to ensure that the Ghost had done its work.

Yes. Perfect.

This was the place Sarah would die. Kathy pulled out her tablet and programmed the last touches into the Ghost.

Then she armed her launcher, hid it, and waited.

AN ENDING—OR A BEGINNING?

"Got her," the blacksuit captain reported. He pointed out a small, black-suited figure bent over double on the trail. "She might be able to run a bit further, but my guys can get her. We can set down close by."

"*Alive*," Sarah said. "She's no good to me dead. Don't chase her over a cliff!"

"We won't."

Sarah sat back, her eyes fixed firmly on Miller. As the helicopter circled above her, Miller rose. She shook a defiant fist at them, then slid down the side of the canyon toward a cliff.

"Hurry *up*, she's getting away! I don't trust her not to jump!"

It took too long before the helicopter was on the ground. The blacksuits leapt downhill after Miller, depending on their suits for controlled landing.

Sarah cursed softly as Miller raced toward the cliff.

Then the helicopter motor stopped. Electronic chatter silenced. The blacksuits crumpled and two of them crashed, rolling downhill in an uncontrolled slide. Sarah gulped for breath, suddenly light-headed and unable to control her trembling limbs.

"*EMP!*" the blacksuit captain screamed.

Shit, shit, shit!

It would all be for nothing if she didn't do *something*, now!

By pure force of will Sarah dragged herself back toward the helicopter, feeling all of her ninety years. There was one last chance to upload these final memories, one last chance to trigger the save feature.

She barely reached the helicopter and pressed the button for shielded manual upload.

Something whistled overhead. The world exploded around her.

Joke's on you— was all she had time to think, before everything went black.

COLD DISH

"Pretty damn spectacular," Joaquin Ridge said to Kathy. "Weren't sure we could get to you before their folks did."

"How far did the cybercrash go?"

Ridge laughed. "It's a mess. Didn't bring down all the North American networks, but close enough. You set things back quite a bit."

"That's what the Ghost was supposed to do."

"Yep. Our networks are shielded, so we're the powers that be here for a while."

"Good." Kathy leaned back. "Any word from Do It Right?"

He shook his head. "Took their network down with everything else. Someone had linked it into the main stuff—I thought they hadn't done that."

"Probably got done to them, before Diaspora."

"Yeah. Probably." He paused. "Be a mess for a while. Could use a good hand to fix things up and network with your folks. Think you could help?"

"Don't see why not. Give me a couple of days to rest first."

"Oh, you'll have that. No problem at all." He got up and left Kathy alone in the longhouse portion assigned to her.

Kathy sighed with relief. She rubbed the skin over her implant. Her nanos reported it as dead. She wasn't sure how she'd managed to save them while killing the implant, but damn, it was worth it to know Sarah's shadow no longer hung over her.

Or did it?

Something nagged at her. She shouldn't have been able to hear that last thought in Sarah's voice.

Joke's on you—

She wondered what the hell that was all about.

Nothing I need to worry about.

And still—she thought she could hear Sarah laughing.

Don't stop looking over your shoulder.

Meanwhile, she was going to savor her vengeance. Not just for Ness, but for Dale, and for all those other lives that Sarah Stephens had disrupted and destroyed.

My only regret is that it took me this long to make it happen.

12 / TO WALK TOWARD
YOUR DOOM

FEBRUARY, 2075

"NO CHOICE THEN," WILL SAID, RESIGNED.

Diana looked up from the light bag she was packing. "If there were any other way—"

Her voice trailed off as she gaze across their bed at Will, stooped over his cane. Today was a bad day. He had not slept well after Melanie's call advising them of Ness Ryan's death. Dark circles blackened the skin under his eyes, and they glowed with a Burnout haze.

He's pushing himself too hard.

What if he dies while I'm gone?

No. She couldn't, she *wouldn't*, think of that. Will would be there when she came back. She would send Melanie here, keep both of her loved ones safe.

"I know." Will sank down on the bed, left hand resting on the top of the cane. "But I still don't like this."

"I wish I knew what Peter's game was."

And Andrew's.

She didn't know her son any more, not since her mother and brother had taken charge of him. Diana frowned at the small pile of clothing in her bag. She'd have more at DIR HQ on the Mountain.

I don't have a good feeling for what's been going on with Gizmo. Zoë's always been able to keep Mother steered straight when it comes to that, but—

something in virtual just doesn't feel right. Really not right. And with Ness Ryan dead—what was she doing at the end?

Marty will be at DIR when I get there. He can tell us what Ness was doing. I hope.

"You need to assume the worst." Will's right hand joined the left on his cane and he rested his forehead on them. "I have some new toys that will keep you safe."

Diana stopped packing. She walked around the bed to join Will. "Is that why you didn't sleep last night? Riding the dragon to keep me safe?"

Will turned his head to grin mischievously. "Do I ever really need an excuse to ride the dragon?" His smile faded. "Anything to protect you, my dear. I took the data Melanie sent us and tweaked it. At the least, we'll be able to defuse that Shadow she mentioned." He sat up. "I've been working on several miniaturized hidey weapons. They don't have much of a battery—keep them charged all the time—but you'll be able to get a shot off faster than Peter."

Diana leaned her forehead on Will's shoulder.

"Oh Will. Thank you. But you should have rested. At least not taken any more Burnout." She wanted to hug Will, but he was so thin and frail that she was afraid of bruising him.

Will reached out and pulled her close with a surprising strength. "The cost of taking the Burnout was worth it. I want to make sure you come safely back to me." He kissed her forehead, his lips hotter than she'd otherwise anticipate them to be.

"I want *you* to still have the strength to be here when I come back."

"I'll try, dearest. But I will rest better knowing you have the best weapons I can give you."

"Oh my love. Just—try to hang on?"

"I will do what I can," Will promised. "But you. Don't—if it comes to a choice between survival or stopping your brother—*stop him*." His voice grew fiercer. "He's too close to the gadget. He's dangerous and he's ambitious. With him replacing your mother—"

"And he has Drew," Diana said. "If I can—I want to save our son, too. I didn't do enough when he was younger. Paying for that now."

"It's a risk," Will said. "Di, he made his choice. What more can you do?

"Nonetheless, I'm going to try to save both our kids. I will get Melanie out of there. I'll do what I can for the New Feds. I'll try to find out what's going on with Gizmo."

"And, after that, you'll do your best to stay alive."

"And get Andrew away from Peter. Meanwhile—" Diana took Will's head gently in her hands. She kissed his forehead. "You—" she kissed his right eye— "work on—" she kissed his left eye— "keeping your strength up—" she kissed the tip of his nose— "and staying alive. For me."

Her lips brushed his lightly. Will's lips pressed more firmly back against hers. His hands reached for her again and they held each other.

Then he broke away as coughing wracked his body. Will clung to his cane with both hands as he hacked. Diana sat back, helpless.

He's going to die before I get back.

That's why he was working on her weapons last night. A final gift. She told herself that she was not going to cry, *absolutely* not going to cry, and leave Will with that last memory of her in tears.

At last he stopped and fumbled in his robe for a tissue, hands trembling with the effort. She took the tissue from his fingers and delicately wiped his nose and mouth.

"Thank you," Will croaked as she dropped the tissue into the recycling.

Diana got him a glass of water. Will took it with a shaky hand and she helped him steady it. When he was finished, he handed her the glass, then used the cane to lever himself up.

"So," he said. "Are you ready to see your new toys?" He grinned at her, looking almost like a death's head skeleton.

A chill at how boney he looked tempered the glow she felt at his clear happiness at being able to prepare her to go into danger one last time.

"But of course, my love." She offered Will her arm. "I'm assuming you want to go to the lab?"

"Where else?" His grin deepened.

It made Diana even happier to see how much younger he looked, even if it was for just that moment. She suddenly remembered her athletic young husband, capable of spending days without sleep to run a promising lab test. That same light still glimmered in his eyes, even under the glaze of too much Burnout, making his eyes bloodshot.

"Lead on, dearest," she said, even as her heart was breaking at how frail and light he felt on her arm.

His grip tightened on hers. "Di," he said softly. "I mean it. Do what you need to do. Don't be worrying about what happens to me."

"I just—I'll feel awful if I'm not here at the end."

"Oh love." He stopped and again, she felt that surprisingly strong grip. "Don't agonize if I die before you get back. Promise?"

"Only if you promise to do your best to stay with us."

"I'm not leaving any sooner than I have to," Will continued. "I'm going to fight it as much as I can. No regrets. Okay?"

"No regrets. And if something happens to me?"

"*No regrets,*" Will repeated. "We're doing what we have to. What we've spent a lifetime preparing to face. And—dearest. We've had a good long run. If we don't get more time together—just know this. I wouldn't change what we've done. I love you."

"And I you." She bent in for another kiss.

This time, coughing didn't interrupt. Will finally pulled away from her, his eyes feverishly bright. "Now it's time to go see those little tricks that are going to keep you alive."

If anything, he looked happier and brighter than he had even a few minutes ago. But as he pulled ahead of her in his impatience, moisture briefly flooded Diana's eyes, now that it was safe and Will couldn't see.

I won't see you alive again.

Deep in her gut, she knew one of them was going to fall this time, and, given the odds, it could be either one of them. Or both. Away from each other.

Diana stopped, dashed the tears from her eyes, then hurried to catch up with Will. She'd do her best to make the most of the few moments they had left together.

To give both their sacrifices some meaning.

Like what you've read? Want to follow Joyce either through her monthly newsletter or through an email feed of her irregular blog posts?

Sign up for Joyce's newsletter here:

https://tinyletter.com/JoyceReynolds-Ward

Or follow Joyce's irregular blog posts on her Substack, here:

https://joycereynoldsward.substack.com/

BOOKS AND PUBLICATIONS

The Martiniere Legacy

First Meetings: A Martiniere Legacy Short Story
Inheritance: The Martiniere Legacy Book One
Ascendant: The Martiniere Legacy Book Two
Realization: The Martiniere Legacy Book Three
A Belated Christmas Honeymoon: A Martiniere Legacy Short Story
The Enduring Legacy: The Martiniere Legacy Book Four

People of the Martiniere Legacy

The Heritage of Michael Martiniere: A Martiniere Legacy Novel
Broken Angel: The Lost Years of Gabriel Martiniere: A Martiniere Legacy Novel
Justine Fixes Everything: Reflections on Mortality

The Martiniere Multiverse

A Different Life: What If?
A Different Life: Now. Always. Forever.

Goddess's Honor titles currently available (chronological order):

The Goddess's Choice: A Goddess's Honor Short Story
Beyond Honor: A Goddess's Honor Novella
Exile's Honor: A Goddess's Honor Novelette

Birth of Sorrow: A Goddess's Honor Short Story
Pledges of Honor: Goddess's Honor Book One
Return to Wickmasa: A Goddess's Honor Short Story
Crown Anniversary: A Goddess's Honor Short Story
Challenges of Honor: Goddess's Honor Book Two
Cleaning House: A Goddess's Honor Outtake Story
Unexpected Alliances: A Goddess's Honor Rough Draft Outtake Story
Choices of Honor: Goddess's Honor Book Three
Judgment of Honor: Goddess's Honor Book Four

Netwalk Sequence Author Preferred 2022 Editions
Life in the Shadows: Book One
Netwalk: Book Two
Netwalker Uprising: Book Three
Netwalk's Children: Book Four
Learning in Space: Book Five
Netwalking Space: Book Six

Non-Series Titles currently available:
Alien Savvy: A Western SF Novella
Klone's Stronghold
Beating the Apocalypse
Bearing Witness
Becoming Solo

Vella Titles:
Falcon of the Martinieres (part of *Justine Fixes Everything*)
Bearing Witness
Beating the Apocalypse
A Different Life—What If? An Alternative Martiniere Legacy Novel
Becoming Solo
A Different Life—Linda's Story: An Alternative Martiniere Legacy Novel
Federation Cowboy

Audiobooks Available:
Alien Savvy: A Western SF Novella

Released from other publishers:

"Queen of the Snows," in *Once Upon A Winter: A Folk and Fairy Tale Anthology*, edited by H. L. Macfarlane

"My Man Left Me, My Dog Hates Me, and There Goes My Truck," in *Black-Eyed Peas on New Year's Day: An Anthology of Hope*, edited by Shannon Page

"Lost Loves," in *All Worlds Wayfarer*

"The Wisdom of Robins," in *Whimsical Beasts: A Campcon Anthology*, edited by Joyce Reynolds-Ward

"The Cow at the End of the World," in *Well…It's Your Cow*, edited by Frog Jones

"To Plant or Pull Up Stakes," in *Pulling Up Stakes: A Campcon Anthology*, edited by Joyce Reynolds-Ward

"The Notice," in *Children of a Different Sky*, edited by Alma Alexander

ABOUT THE AUTHOR

Joyce Reynolds-Ward is a speculative fiction writer who splits her time between Enterprise and Portland, Oregon. Her short stories include appearances in *Once Upon A Winter: A Folk and Fairy Tale Anthology, Well…It's Your Cow, Children of a Different Sky, Allegory, River*, and *Fantasy Scroll Magazine*, as well as in her Substack about the Martiniere Legacy, *Martiniere Stories*. Besides the Martiniere Legacy series, her books include *Shadow Harvest, Alien Savvy, Pledges of Honor* (2018 Self Published Fantasy BlogOff Semifinalist), *Challenges of Honor, Choices of Honor*, and *Klone's Stronghold*. Joyce has edited two anthologies, *Pulling Up Stakes* (2018), and *Whimsical Beasts* (2019). Besides writing, Joyce enjoys reading, quilting, horses, skiing, and outdoor activities, and is a member of Soroptimist International, Northwest Independent Writers Association, and the Science Fiction and Fantasy Writers Association.

Inquiries about graphic novel or game development are encouraged and should be directed to Joyce through her website.

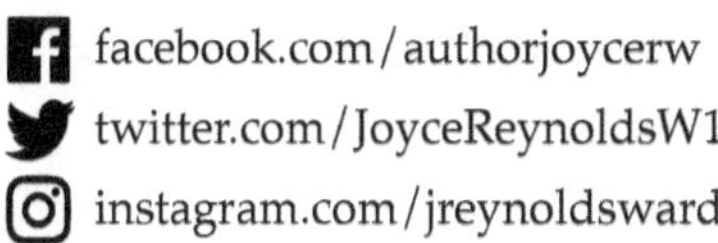

facebook.com/authorjoycerw
twitter.com/JoyceReynoldsW1
instagram.com/jreynoldsward